T0023681

SAMANTHA

ALSO BY ANDREA KANE

HISTORICAL ROMANCES:

MY HEART'S DESIRE
DREAM CASTLE
MASQUE OF BETRAYAL
ECHOES IN THE MIST
SAMANTHA
THE LAST DUKE
EMERALD GARDEN
WISHES IN THE WIND
LEGACY OF THE DIAMOND
THE BLACK DIAMOND
THE MUSIC BOX
THE THEFT
THE GOLD COIN
THE SILVER COIN

FORENSIC INSTINCTS NOVELS:

THE GIRL WHO DISAPPEARED TWICE
THE LINE BETWEEN HERE AND GONE
THE STRANGER YOU KNOW
THE SILENCE THAT SPEAKS
THE MURDER THAT NEVER WAS

OTHER SUSPENSE THRILLERS:

RUN FOR YOUR LIFE
NO WAY OUT
SCENT OF DANGER
I'LL BE WATCHING YOU
WRONG PLACE, WRONG TIME
DARK ROOM
TWISTED
DRAWN IN BLOOD

SAMANTHA

ANDREA KANE

ISBN-13: 978-1-68232-005-1

SAMANTHA

Copyright © 2016, 1994 by Rainbow Connection Enterprises, Inc.

All right reserved. Except for use in any review, the reproduction or utilization of this work in whole or in part in any form by any electronic, mechanical or other means, now known or hereafter invented, including xerography, photocopying and recording, or in any information storage or retrieval system, is prohibited without prior written permission of the publisher, Bonnie Meadow Publishing LLC, 16 Mount Bethel Road #777, Warren, NJ 07059, USA.

This is a work of fiction. Names, characters, places and incidents are either the product of the author's imagination or are used fictitiously, and any resemblance to actual persons, living or dead, business establishements, events or locales is entirely coincidental.

For questions and comments about the quality of this book, please contact us at CustomerService@bonniemeadowpublishing.com.

www.BonnieMeadowPublishing.com

Printed in USA

Publisher's Cataloging-in-Publication

Kane, Andrea, author.
    Samantha / Andrea Kane.
    Originally published: New York : Pocket Books, ©1994.
    LCCN 2016947258
    ISBN 978-1-68232-005-1 (trade pbk.)

    1. Man-woman relationships--England--London--19th century--Fiction. 2. Nobility--England--London--19th century--Fiction. 3. London (England)--Social life and customs--19th century--Fiction. 4. Romance fiction. 5. Historical fiction.   I. Title.

PS3561.A463S26 2016   813'.54
                QBI16-900028

Samantha is lovingly dedicated to all my wonderful readers who asked for Sammy's story, then waited patiently while she told it to me.

AUTHOR'S PREFACE

When I was writing *My Heart's Desire*, I knew by mid-book that Samantha Barrett would someday have a book of her own. Sammy was one of the most compelling secondary characters I've ever written, with a personality that came to life long before her story was ready to be told.

Although I understood (and shared) my readers' impatient requests for Sammy's book, I knew it wasn't time. She needed to grow up and I needed to creatively grow with her. I thought about her often, marinated her character in my mind, and choreographed in my head her transition from girl to woman. It took loving concentration and a lot of research (not to mention creating and developing Remington Worth, the precise man to be Sammy's hero), but somehow I knew it would be worth the wait.

Four years later magic time arrived. Sammy had successfully evolved from an innocent fifteen-year-old with a loving heart and a core of inner strength, to an eighteen-year-old who was wise beyond her years, who was exposed to so much and yet to so little, and who viewed the world with a wonder that was genuine and untainted. She was hovering on the brink of womanhood and ready for her first London Season.

That Season—along with glorious new ball gowns, scores of parties, and titled suitors vying for a dance and so much more—might have been a dream-come-true for some, but it wasn't for Sammy. Her dream was to find and marry a hero—*her* hero.

"In walked the man of her dreams."

Perhaps the best opening line of a romance I've ever written, and perfect for *Samantha*. The sentiment was just so Sammy, listening to the dictates of her heart, and ignoring the glaring obstacles and insurmountable differences between her and Remington. To Sammy, he was everything she'd imagined him to be, and, in her mind, their forever-after was a fête accompli.

Rem had a different agenda—one that was diametrically opposed to Sammy's—but you'll soon see how that plays out.

Samantha is the ultimate fairytale, with threads of reality woven throughout it. As in all classic love stories, the two lovers draw close together only to push apart, and then move back together again as they learn to navigate the perfection and imperfection of their relationship.

Rem feels doubts, denial, guilt. Sammy feels only joy and awe.

And so it begins.

As much as I adored taking Sammy from the role of a secondary character to the role of a heroine in her own right, I also loved bringing Alex and Drake back from the pages of *My Heart's Desire* and giving them their rightful places in Sammy's book. The protective big brother, once a dark hero himself, now fiercely guarding his innocent little sister as she leaves the safety of her home to carve her own path in life. And the loving sister-in-law, who's always been more like a real sister to Sammy, now taking on a maternal role in her life—while also serving as a peacemaker between Drake and Rem, who each see Sammy in entirely different lights. Big brother vs. lover? Drake vs. Rem? Not a pretty picture. And a battle that only Alex could mediate.

Writing *Samantha* was this author's dream. Bringing her to life on the pages seemed to happen on its own. The words flew from my mind to my fingers to the computer screen. It was the fastest and smoothest book I've ever written. It required little to no editing and was overwhelmingly well-received. FYI, I hope to experience this phenomenon again, but twenty-something books and over 2 million words later, I'm still waiting.

Readers often ask me where my characters come from—are they modeled after real people or are they totally fictitious? I never have a clear-cut answer to give. The best I can do is to say that my characters are indeed fictitious but they contain characteristics of real people—sometimes those I know and sometimes those I've seen. In this case, I have to admit, I saw facets of myself in Sammy. As a teenager, I was a total romantic and a book-aholic, and I had dreams of true love and happily-ever-after.

And later, of course, there was Rascal.

My husband, daughter and I had gotten a new Maltese puppy, who we named Rascal, just before I began writing *Samantha*. He was just as his name depicted—a little troublemaker who wreaked havoc throughout the house, who turned our lives upside-down, and who we loved with all our hearts.

Gifting Sammy with that same little Rascal felt completely natural. He was the cutest of brats and she was the perfect ray of rule-breaking sunshine to match wits with him and his antics. Her very best traits came out when she was with him—her joy, her laughter, and her nurturing heart. There was no better way for me to immortalize my little guy.

In the world of today women have difficult choices to make, challenges to face, and goals to achieve.

When we think of highborn women in Regency England, we think of quite the opposite—women whose choices were made for them, who abided by a stringent set of rules that were devised for them, and who had no goals to strive for other than those that were ascribed to them, the chief one being to marry and produce a proper heir to carry on the family name.

I never seem to write those kind of women. Even with their privileged lives, their unlimited budgets, and their non-stop social whirl, my heroines are smart, independent, and intent on following their own path. Sammy is no exception. I wouldn't have been either. From childhood on, I always got in trouble for breaking the rules (in school that was for talking out of turn and too much, as my teachers would attest), and, outside the classroom, for speaking my mind and following the dictates of my exuberance and my imagination.

I never rode in a Regency carriage. But I rode my bicycle voraciously, dreaming the same kinds of dreams as Sammy did. It was my vehicle for traveling to places in my mind and for letting my imagination soar as I created story after story. If I could have fit Sammy's book collection in my bike basket, I would have!

On the topic of carriages, I'm absolutely in love with this new book cover. It's exquisite, and to me the carriage symbolizes the magic of fairytales, of love, and of the beautiful story Sammy and Rem create between the pages of their book.

I hope you live (or relive) the wonder as you read.

ONE

London, England
March 1815

IN WALKED THE MAN OF HER DREAMS.

Samantha stared, transfixed, as the vision stepped directly from the pages of her latest Gothic romance into the noisy, smoke-filled tavern.

He had arrived … her long-awaited hero.

It mattered not that he was a total stranger to her, nor that he patronized so seedy an establishment as this, nor that he pointedly displayed an ominous-looking knife handle from the top of one muddied Hessian boot. All that mattered was his towering height, his thick black hair, his uncompromising jaw, his piercing gray eyes. And that dimple … it was just where she'd always known it would be; in his left cheek. It flashed briefly as he nodded a greeting to someone, then vanished into the taut lines of his face.

Yes, it was irrefutably he—the hero of all her fantasies.

Breathless and eager, Samantha watched as he carelessly swung off his greatcoat, shaking rivulets of rain from it with swift, purposeful strokes. Simultaneously, he surveyed the room, his cool gaze taking in the shoddy furnishings and seedy occupants in one enveloping glance.

He moved forward, commanding and sure, coming closer to where Sammy sat—close enough so she could see the drops of water glistening in his hair, causing the ends to curl a bit at the nape. He seemed to be looking for someone.

Instead, he found her.

His dark brows rose, not with instantaneous, adoring surrender, but with decided, disapproving surprise.

Without hesitating, Sammy flashed him a smile, drinking in his splendid, chiseled features and exciting, leashed power. He was just as she had imagined him—no, better.

Her heart tightened in her chest as he approached her.

"What despicable cad deserted you here, little one?"

"Pardon me?" Sammy blinked in confusion.

With apparent disgust, her hero scanned the room. "You needn't feel ashamed. Just tell me what unscrupulous blackguard accompanied you to such a place, then abandoned you."

"Oh, nothing like that, sir." Sammy assured him brightly. "Actually, it was I who spotted this establishment from my carriage window and chose to stop here. Given the circumstances, it seemed the best place …"

"The best place … to what?" He looked censuring now, his gray eyes chilling, stormier than the skies that heralded tonight's downpour. "Is this your idea of an evening adventure? If so, you've either lost your way or your mind! Tell me, have you looked about you? I seriously doubt that you have, else you would have bolted. And, thankfully, it seems that these low-lifes have yet to spot you as prey. Had they done so, I assure you that your elegant gown would have long since been tossed up over your foolish, beautiful head!"

Sammy sucked in her breath. This wasn't at all the way she'd envisioned their first meeting.

Following her hero's icy, pointed gaze, she surveyed the dimly lit tavern, trying to see what was upsetting him so. True, the tables were a bit shabby, even broken in spots, and the pungent smell of gin—mixed with some other, unrecognizable foul odor—permeated the room. And, she had to admit, the occupants of the tavern did need to shave … as well as to bathe. Still, they'd shown no signs of harming or even approaching her; so why was her hero hinting at violence?

"I don't know what you mean, sir," she confessed, bewildered. "Despite their rather coarse attire and unpolished manners, the gentlemen here have made no improper advances toward me. They are merely enjoying their spirits and each other's company."

The stranger gaped in utter disbelief. "Gentlemen?" he managed. Leaning forward, he lowered his voice to a muffled hiss. "Sheltered innocent, what you see are pickpockets, highwaymen, and drunks … and an occasional murderer or two." He straightened, emphatic and fierce. "This is Boydry's—as unsavory a pub as they come—not the bloody Clarendon Hotel!"

"Really?" Samantha was finding it very difficult to share the intensity of his tirade. She was too busy drowning in the hypnotic spell of his towering presence. And, after all, he was only trying to protect her—the foremost duty of a true hero.

"If such is the case, then why are *you* here?" she asked, half tempted to stroke the hard, uncompromising line of his jaw. "You don't appear unsavory to me."

His dimple flickered in response. "Don't I? That is only because you don't know me."

"No … but I'd like to."

He blinked. "You'd like to"

"Oh yes. Don't you see?" Sammy leaned forward, making an animated sweep with her hands. "It's as if Mrs. Radcliffe had penned it; a young woman alone … darkness … danger." A pause. "Of course I would have preferred a castle turret to a tavern"—she gave a philosophical shrug—"nevertheless, you've arrived … and you're exactly as I pictured you."

"You *have* lost your mind," he muttered.

"My lady, it's no use."

A portly gentleman with a stricken expression interrupted them. Hastening over, he mopped sheets of rain from his saturated face with a neatly folded, if soggy, handkerchief.

"I've tried to hail a half-dozen carriages. None of their drivers can even see me through this downpour. We shall have to wait until the rain relents. Our only other choice is for me to make my way farther into Town to seek help, and I refuse to leave you alone in"—he scanned the rear of the tavern and shuddered—"this place." Abruptly, he tensed, evidently becoming aware that they were not alone. With great dignity he turned to cast a disparaging look at the man standing beside Samantha, a look that transformed into reserved politeness as recognition dawned on his weathered face. "Well … good evening, my lord."

The stranger inclined his head in surprise. "Smithers! What on earth are you doing at Boydry's? In fact, why have you even ventured from Allonshire on a night like tonight?"

"We are on our way to the Barrett's London Town house," the older man replied tersely. "It was barely drizzling when we departed from Allonshire. A quarter hour later, the heavens opened up. As bad luck would have it, one of our carriage wheels broke. We had no choice but to seek shelter—and assistance—at the nearest sanctuary; which, unfortunately, happened to be here."

"We?" The handsome stranger glanced expectantly toward the doorway. "Is the duke with you, then?"

"No, my lord. His Grace is at home with the duchess. The birth of their second child is imminent … hardly a time to travel. He has entrusted Lady Samantha into my care."

"Lady Samantha." Startled gray eyes darted back to Sammy, a warm golden light melting the chill from their frosty depths. "*This* is little Samantha? What happened to the tot with chocolate on her chin?"

Samantha blushed. "She grew up," she returned quickly, shifting in her seat. Taken aback by this unexpected turn of events, Sammy forced herself to regain control. "Smitty..." She turned to her uneasy companion. "I'm ready for a proper introduction."

"Lady Samantha, permit me to introduce the Earl of Gresham." Smitty's tone clearly indicated that introducing the earl to Samantha was about as desirable as emptying a chamber pot. "You were little more than a babe when last you met—far too young to recall your casual acquaintance."

The Earl of Gresham.

Samantha might not recall their acquaintance, but she knew that name well. It appeared repeatedly in the newspapers, and had for years, both in the socials and the headlines.

Remington Worth—the Earl of Gresham—initially a promising protégé to the legendary Admiral Nelson, eventually the Royal Navy's youngest, most brilliant captain; hero of the Battle of Trafalgar, ingenious commander of the War of 1812. Renowned by sea as an undefeated, unyielding naval leader.

By land as London's most notorious rake and womanizer.

Sammy had no trouble understanding the latter. Remington Worth was dangerously exciting, dashing and forbidden—every bit a hero.

He was magnificent.

"Lord Gresham." Sammy gave him her hand, willing it to stop trembling as the earl brushed it with his lips. Ignoring Smitty's glowering disapproval, Sammy lifted questioning eyes to Gresham's. "You asked if the duke were with us. Are you a friend of Drake's?"

"Your brother's path and mine have crossed many times over the years, in business and socially," the earl answered smoothly. "I have nothing but the greatest respect for the duke ... and his trusted valet," he added, with a courteous nod in Smitty's direction.

Smitty's only response was a rather haughty sniff.

Apparently unbothered, Gresham released Sammy's hand and
bowed. "Forgive my earlier rudeness, my lady. I had no idea who you
were or why you were at Boydry's."

"As I said, we are on our way to the family Town house," Smitty
supplied, his tone crisp. "This is to be Lady Samantha's first London
Season."

"Is it?" Gresham's teeth gleamed—the smile, not of a besotted
lover, but of an amused and indulgent uncle. "Well, we cannot have
Lady Samantha miss one dazzling moment of her first Season." He
turned to Smitty. "Let me have a look at your carriage. Perhaps I can
be of some help."

Smitty appeared to be on the verge of refusing when, with a
resigned sigh, he relented. "Fine. Thank you very much, my lord."

"Not at all." Gresham turned his hypnotic silvery gaze on Sammy again. "I'm afraid I must ask you to accompany us. I realize the
weather is dreadful, but I cannot allow you to remain alone with
these"—his lips twitched—"gentlemen."

Samantha was on her feet instantly. "Of course not, Lord Gresham. I would feel much safer with you."

Loudly, Smitty cleared his throat. "The carriage is out by the
road, my lord."

Leaving his drenched greatcoat behind, the earl made his way
back out of the tavern. Kneeling beside the deserted Barrett carriage,
he noted that the left rear wheel was shattered beyond repair, leaving
the regal coach tilted precariously along the flooded roadside.

"I had the footmen and driver ride the horses on ahead to seek
help," Smitty informed the earl. Squinting through the ceaseless
downpour, he shoved a shock of drenched white hair off his forehead. "That was nearly an hour ago. There's been no sign of them
since."

"That doesn't surprise me," Gresham replied, frowning at the
irreparable slivers of wood. He rose, his fine lawn shirt nearly trans-

parent from the soaking it had already received. "Your carriage is going nowhere tonight," he announced. "The wheel cannot be fixed, even temporarily. I had hoped I could patch it well enough to take you the short distance to London, but 'tis impossible. I'm sorry."

Smitty shook his head in distress, turning to Lady Samantha to offer her comfort.

Vaguely, Sammy wondered why Smitty was regarding her with such regret. But the majority of her concentration was on her hero.

Never had she seen shoulders so broad, so incredibly muscled. Because the rain had molded his clothing to his body, she could make out his corded biceps, the strong tendons in his forearms.

The rippling columns of his thighs.

Despite the storm's chill, a fine sheen of perspiration broke out on Sammy's skin. What would it be like to touch him? she wondered. To kiss him? To be crushed in those powerful arms?

"Take mine."

Samantha blinked. "P-Pardon me?"

Gresham assessed her with paternal concern, tucking a wet strand of hair behind her ear. "You and Smithers take my carriage and go on to your Town house."

Sammy's tremble had naught to do with the cold and everything to do with the warmth of his fingers.

The earl frowned. "You're shivering. You'll take ill if you don't get out of this storm. We cannot have that—you'll miss your first ball at Almack's." Turning, he strode back into the tavern, returning instantly with his coat, which he draped about Samantha's shoulders.

Dazedly, Sammy wondered if he noticed that his touch worsened her trembling threefold.

Evidently not. "There." Gresham peered through the rain, his expression intense. "Smithers, my driver has instructions to await me on that side street over there." He pointed. "Go and direct him to bring the carriage around. Tell him those are my orders. In the meantime, I'll collect whatever essentials you have in your coach, so that we can transfer them immediately and you can be on your way."

"My lord, I cannot ask that you—" Smitty protested.

"You didn't ask. I offered."

"Surely you did not intend to *stay* at this"—Smitty shuddered anew—"place."

One corner of Gresham's mouth lifted. "I'll have no trouble arranging for a ride home, I assure you. Tomorrow, I'll come by to collect my carriage ... and to deliver yours." He waved Smitty off. "Now do as I say."

"But—"

"Yes, Smitty," Sammy interrupted. She had no intention of allowing her guardian's suffocating sense of protocol to undermine this rare opportunity to be alone with her hero. "Let's do as Lord Gresham says," she added pointedly.

Smitty grunted, but obeyed without further question. However, he paused once or twice to glower over his shoulder before walking off.

Knowing she hadn't a precious moment to waste, Sammy turned to gaze up at her hero. "Thank you for your coat," she whispered, hoping she'd inserted just the right sultry note in her voice.

"You're quite welcome. Keep it. Your gown is thin and offers little in the way of protection from the rain." Purposefully, he yanked open the carriage door. "Let's take only what you'll need—"

Before Gresham could finish his sentence, a small white ball of fur shot through the air and crashed into the hard wall of the earl's chest. Toppling to the ground, the tiny puppy began to whimper, trying to see through the wet strands of hair that hung in his eyes.

"Oh, Rascal, I'm sorry." Sammy bent to scoop up the wriggling pup, gathering his damp, shivering body inside the thick folds of Gresham's coat. "You must have been terrified alone in there. Forgive me."

"Is that a dog or a rodent of some kind?" Gresham inquired.

"A dog, of course!" Sammy replied, indignant. "He's a Maltese—bred for royalty, I'll have you know. Certainly not a rodent of any kind!"

Gresham cocked a brow. "Again, I beg your forgiveness, my lady. I did not mean to offend your pet."

Glancing at Rascal, Sammy's lips curved upward. "He does look a bit like a mouse," she admitted. "He's only three months old and still very tiny. But he'll grow to be hale and hardy."

"A veritable tiger, I'm certain." The earl's smile was infectious.

"I've read of you, my lord," Sammy blurted out.

"Have you? And what did your sources tell you?"

"That you're a hero; a brilliant leader—fearless and undefeated. You're also a terrible rogue, breaking hearts throughout England, leaving ruined women in your wake."

Gresham threw back his head and laughed. "So I'm both saint and sinner, am I?"

"So I've read."

"Tell me, imp," he touched his forefinger to the tip of her nose, "do you believe everything you read?"

"Only those things that are true." Her gaze fell on his strong, tanned finger. "And those things I will to be true."

"You're quite the romantic, are you not?"

"Quite." She licked raindrops from her lips.

Gresham watched the motion, his expression unreadable. Abruptly, he seized her arm, guiding her into the carriage. "We might as well amass things in here where it's dry. What else must go with you tonight?" He paused, staring amazedly at the stacks of books piled on the carriage seat. "What on earth …?"

"My books." Sammy scooted past him, holding Rascal against her with one hand and gathering the novels with the other. "I must take them with me."

"Do you plan to read them all tonight?"

"No, but I don't know which ones I *will* read. So I cannot leave any behind. We can forfeit my clothing and other personal items. I'll make due with whatever Aunt Gertrude has at the Town house. But I must have my books."

Gresham shook his head. "You are astonishing. All right, imp. The books go with you." He began to gather them. "Who is Aunt Gertrude?"

"She's actually my great-aunt on my father's side," Sammy told him, stroking a volume of her newest Gothic romance. "Aunt Gertie is quite old, entirely deaf, and, if you ask me, a bit eccentric. However, given that Alexandria is very much with child, Aunt Gertrude will be my official chaperon this Season."

"Alexandria. Yes, I've met your brother's wife at several house parties. She's a beautiful woman."

"She's wonderful," Sammy answered fervently. "She's the best thing that ever happened to Drake. But then, love always is."

"*Quite* the romantic." Gresham regarded Samantha soberly, an odd light in his eyes. "I envy you, imp. For you, the world is still a resplendent place, beckoning you forward to experience all its wonder." A fleeting sadness grazed his handsome features, vanishing as quickly as it had come. "Revel in it, little innocent … but be cautious. Disenchantment is inevitable, and ofttimes painful."

"You'll protect me." The words were out before Sammy could censor them, and a bright flush stained her cheeks as the earl reacted with a start.

"I?" He looked astounded, his heart stopping gaze sweeping over her. His smile, though faint, clearly revealed that he'd missed none of her untutored reaction. Leaning forward, he brushed his knuckles across her hot cheek. "That's the loveliest compliment I've ever received. But I'm hardly the one to ensure your safety. As you yourself pointed out, I'm less than reputable when it comes to women."

"Will you be staying in London for the Season?"

"Now and again, yes."

"Good." Relief flowed through her in a rush. "Then I—and Aunt Gertrude, of course—can expect to see you at an occasional ball?"

He chuckled. "You can. You can also expect to see me tomorrow when I come to collect my carriage and to return yours."

"Our Town house is number Fifteen Abingdon Street," Sammy replied swiftly. "I'll be home settling in most of the day. Sometime after lunch I hope to convince Aunt Gertie to accompany me to Hatchard's so that I might purchase a few new titles."

Gresham gestured at the piles of books surrounding them. "These aren't enough?"

"Oh, no, I'll have read and reread these in a fortnight. Besides, I've heard glowing praise for *Mansfield Park* and I must have it."

"Of course." The earl leaned back, folding his arms across his broad chest. "Very well, my persistent lady. I'll make certain to arrive prior to four o'clock. How would that be?"

"That would be perfect." Sammy's eyes sparkled.

"Good. Now that we've settled on a time, do you think we might collect your treasures so that you, Smithers, and your regal pet can be on your way?"

Sammy nodded, silently berating herself for sounding too eager. She had to learn to be coy, sophisticated. After all, Remington Worth was a worldly man, one who had known countless women.

Lowering her eyes, Samantha carefully gathered a pile of books together, rearranged her wriggling pup within Gresham's thick coat, and slid gracefully over to the carriage door just as a magnificent coach and four rounded the corner and pulled alongside them.

"Excellent timing," Gresham proclaimed with great satisfaction, signaling his approval to the waiting driver. Seemingly unaware of Sammy's newly enacted savoir faire, he helped her alight, assisting her into his own elegantly appointed vehicle. "My coach awaits you, my lady."

"Thank you so much." Samantha snuggled into the plush seat, wrapping Gresham's greatcoat more tightly about herself and Rascal. She felt very adult and thoroughly buoyant, tucked away in a dashing hero's carriage, ready to begin her great adventure in the exhilarating rainstorm.

It took mere minutes for the earl and Smitty to transfer the majority of Sammy's belongings from the Barrett's carriage to the earl's. That task completed, Smitty hoisted himself into the seat across from Sammy and turned to address Gresham through the open window.

"I cannot thank you enough, my lord."

"No thanks are necessary," Gresham assured the elderly valet, then gave Samantha a conspiratorial wink. "Number Fifteen Abingdon Street. Between two and four o'clock. I'll be by with your mended coach."

"I'll be waiting."

If Gresham saw Smitty's disapproving scowl, he gave no notice. "Have a safe trip. It was a pleasure to see you again Smithers. And to meet the lovely young lady you've become, Samantha."

The chill in Sammy's bones instantly melted. "I'm delighted to have met you as well … Remington."

His eyes twinkled. "Until tomorrow." Backing away from the carriage, he signaled his driver to be off.

Sammy watched until Remington disappeared from view. Then she sighed, leaning her head dreamily against the seat, running her fingers over the luxuriously appointed material.

"Lady Samantha," Smitty began, "I really don't think—"

"Oh, Smitty," she murmured, interrupting whatever he had been about to say. "Isn't he dashing?"

"His Grace would never approve—"

"Drake. Yes." Her smile was jubilant. "I wonder what my brother will say when I tell him that I'm going to become the Countess of Gresham."

TWO

"Hello, Boyd."

The stocky tavern keeper looked up and grinned, putting down the mug he'd been filling. "Rem ... I thought I saw you come in. But then you disappeared."

"I was temporarily waylaid."

"Yes, well, I don't blame you. I spied the little chit who waylaid you. Quite a beauty. Well-bred, too. What the hell was she doing in here?"

"Her carriage broke down. She needed assistance."

Boyd's dark eyes gleamed. "And I'll just bet you gave it to her." He shook his shaggy head, sighing with mock dismay. "Ah, why did I choose that particular time to check my supplies? I'd have been delighted to offer her my help ... or anything else she wanted."

Unreasonable annoyance struck Rem, hard. "She's half your age, Boyd—not yet out of her teens." A pause. "She's also Drake Barrett's little sister."

A low whistle escaped Boyd's lips. "No wonder she looked so bloody regal. Well, that changes things. If I were you, I'd stay the hell away from her. You've got enough women nipping at your heels without involving yourself with—"

"I'm not getting involved with her," Rem snapped. "I just loaned her my carriage and offered to have hers repaired. I'll return it tomorrow. After that, I'll probably never see her again. Besides," he lowered his voice, "I didn't come in to discuss Samantha Barrett."

Boyd's eyes narrowed slightly—his only overt reaction to Rem's uncustomary loss of composure. "Are you here to see me, or are you meeting Briggs?"

"Meeting Briggs. I take it he's not yet arrived?"

"No. But that shouldn't surprise you. This storm could delay him for hours. Here," Boyd handed him a glass of beer, "have a drink while you wait. Where have you been? I haven't seen you in weeks."

Rem relaxed into a roguish grin. "I've been busy."

"Busy, huh? Which one is it this time?"

"Never one, Boyd." Rem took a deep, appreciative swallow. "In my situation, that's far too risky. Several. Always several."

"The Season's under way. Will you be staying in London or heading back to Gresham?"

"That depends."

"On?"

"On what Briggs needs to see me about."

The two men's gazes met in silent understanding.

"Take the table in the far left corner," Boyd suggested without altering his expression. "The riffraff back there are too deep in their cups to hear or see anything. That way you'll be assured privacy."

"Fine."

"Do you want me to join you?"

"No." Rem shook his head. "Not this time. Briggs specified that he wished to speak with me alone. Let me hear what the Admiralty has to say. Once I understand the nature of the dilemma, I'll give the appearance of leaving, then wait for you behind the tavern. We'll discuss our strategy then."

"Good enough." Boyd reached over to take Rem's glass, his eyes darting to the door as it clicked shut. "Briggs just arrived." Casually, he continued clearing the counter. "Good luck."

Rem waited a full minute, then, without glancing behind him, swung around and headed toward the designated table.

Shortly thereafter, a tall, distinguished-looking man with gray hair and a grim expression walked over.

"Hello, Remington."

Leaning casually back in his chair, Rem acknowledged Sir Edmund Briggs with a professional nod. "Edmund. Have a seat."

Briggs complied, folding his hands on the table's rotted wooden surface. "I appreciate your coming out on a night like tonight."

"Your note made it seem rather urgent."

"It is." Briggs cleared his throat. "Before I begin, let me reiterate that you are free to elicit assistance from your usual sources." He inclined his head meaningfully toward the front of the tavern, and Boyd.

"I understand."

"Good. Then I'll get right to the point. Over the past six months a dozen British merchant ships have mysteriously disappeared, together with their cargoes and crews. Each of them was last seen in British waters."

"Mysteriously?" Rem jumped on Briggs's choice of words at once. "Does that mean your investigations have ruled out the obvious?"

"Evidently, yes. My men were extraordinarily thorough. All nations unfriendly to England have been scrutinized … and eliminated."

"Specifically?"

"We began, of course, with Napoleon, despite the fact that, as you know firsthand, his navy was virtually annihilated during the Battle of Trafalgar. We then investigated, not only France, but Spain, Portugal—Napoleon's entire European empire. We posted our men throughout the Strait of Gibraltar and in various points along the length of the Mediterranean and the Baltic." Briggs shook his head in frustration. "Nothing. Lastly, we considered the possibility of the Americans, although with the Treaty of Ghent scarcely signed, I am certain they have as little desire as we to initiate another war."

"And?"

"And it seems that not a single foreign vessel has been spied encroaching on British waters, nor have any of our missing ships appeared in enemy territory after their disappearance. Hence, if the British ships are falling prey to a hostile nation, that country is covering its tracks most brilliantly."

"Indeed." Rem lit a cheroot.

"We've also ruled out foul weather," Briggs added, anticipating Rem's next query. "In more than half the cases, the voyages were accompanied by fair skies and moderate winds ... posing no threat to the safety of the ships or their crews."

Rem exhaled, wafts of smoke drifting into the already murky room. "What about the ships themselves? Were they built to specification? By whom?"

"Another impasse. The vessels were built, not by one, but by several different companies, all of them renowned and reliable."

"So," Rem mused thoughtfully, "if it wasn't our enemies, the elements, or inferior construction, then what—or who—caused the ships' disappearances?"

"Precisely the question. Of course, as we both know, the seas are swarming with smugglers. Perhaps—"

"Smugglers take booty; they don't seize vessels."

"I agree."

"Which leaves us with the ugly probability that our culprit is right here in England." Rem regarded his glowing ash with unruffled detachment. "Do you suspect anyone in particular?"

Briggs sighed. "To be frank, Remington, we are at our wits' end. Fear is growing, not only at the Admiralty, but throughout Parliament, to the Crown itself. With each lost vessel, the intelligence reports reaching Lloyd's grow more ominous, forcing our merchants and shipping companies to pay higher and higher insurance rates for their cargoes and the vessels that transport them.

"Should this atrocity continue, many merchants will be unable to meet the escalated insurance costs. Even those who can will find their goods too expensive for foreign buyers. In any case, the delicate balance of British trade will be threatened; trade that is the very backbone of the British Empire. We cannot afford that risk—I needn't tell you that." With a quick, furtive look around, Briggs withdrew folded papers from the lining of his coat. "This is a list of the ships that have vanished, the companies who built them, their captains, cargo, and crew, and the dates and locations they were discovered missing. There's also a detailed accounting of the Admiralty's findings thus far."

Gravely, Briggs slid the documents over to Rem. "The Crown would like you to undertake your own investigation. The Admiralty will, of course, continue to employ conventional methods." Briggs gripped the table and leaned forward, his message clear, his urgency palpable. "We are counting on you to explore *unconventional* avenues. It is vital we locate the anonymous foe who is destroying our merchant fleet, and rid our country of this growing menace as soon as possible."

Rem brought his cheroot to his lips, inhaling for one long, thoughtful moment. Then he drew the papers toward him, perusing them quickly and efficiently. "Any limitations, land or sea?"

"None."

"My methods, my men."

"Agreed."

"I assume the Admiralty will disavow any knowledge of my actions?"

"As always."

With a chilling scrape, Rem's chair slid back and he stood, tucking the documents into the waistband of his breeches. "I'll contact you when I have information to pass along." He ground the cheroot beneath the heel of his Hessian boot. "You know how to reach me."

Briggs nodded, arising as well. "The Crown is grateful—"

"The Crown can be grateful when I've done my job," Rem replied in a low, terse tone. Purposefully, he stretched, deftly dispelling the coiled intensity that until now had permeated his powerful body.

In a heartbeat he was the Earl of Gresham again.

"I'd best be getting home, Briggs. The storm is subsiding."

"Yes, as should I," Sir Edmund echoed, all traces of his earlier gravity having vanished. "Although I fear the remainder of my evening will be dull compared to yours. Whoever she is *this* time, don't keep her waiting."

"Fear not," Rem returned, cocking a brow at Briggs's ironic taunt. A woman? At the onset of a mission? Briggs knew better. "My partner will be savoring my company within the hour."

"May you enjoy a fruitful evening." Briggs donned his hat. "Good night, Gresham." Without a backward glance, he was gone.

At the loud mention of Rem's name, one of the seedy derelicts loudly swilling gin in the opposite corner of the room lifted his head. " 'Ey, Gresham, did y' just get 'ere? 'Ave a drink with us!"

A corner of Rem's mouth lifted. After all his years at sea and, more recently, his countless hours surreptitiously visiting unsavory docks and taverns such as this one, fitting in with the dregs of London came as naturally to him as attending an Almack's ball.

"Why not, Sullivan?" he answered easily, heading toward the intimidating mob of unkempt patrons. "I certainly didn't ride all this way in a bloody downpour to eat Boyd's miserable excuse for food."

Shouts of appreciative laughter greeted his pronouncement. "Did ye 'ear that, Boyd?" another voice called. "Bring th'man some gin! That way 'e can wash away th'taste of yer food!"

With a good-natured grin, Boyd crossed the room and handed Rem a bottle. "Need a glass?"

"No. I'll do just fine without one." Straddling a chair, Rem took a deep swallow of the cheap liquor.

"Where've ye been, Gresham?" Sullivan demanded, wiping his sleeve across his mouth. "What do earls do when they're not drinkin'?"

Lowering his bottle to the table, Rem chuckled, unbothered by the rowdy, pointed referral to his title. He was well aware that every low-life in that room knew he was anything but a pampered nobleman. They also knew he could single-handedly take on the whole lot of them—and win. If the former weren't impressive enough to earn their respect, the latter most definitively was.

"Well Gresham?" Sullivan persisted. "What *do* titled navy captains do when they're not at sea?"

Rem deliberately tossed off another gulp of gin before replying. "The same things you do." A pregnant pause. "I've been occupied."

Hoots and howls accompanied Rem's implication.

"Was she any good, Gresham?" a grimy fellow with two missing teeth piped up.

Coming to his feet, Rem shrugged, a mischievous light in his eyes. "You know better than to ask me that, Parker. How many times have I told you I never discuss a lady's attributes—at least not publicly?" Rem glanced out the front window, his gaze lingering for the briefest moment on Boyd. "Speaking of which, I'd best be on my way."

"I heard ye say y'were meetin' someone. She waitin' for ye?"

"Yes, indeed. This moment, as a matter of fact."

More raucous laughter. "Be off with ye, Gresham. Before she finds someone better—like a duke!"

"A distinct possibility." Rem headed for the door, depositing the empty bottle on the counter without breaking stride. "I'll do my best to prevent it. Good night men, Boyd." Nodding in the tavern keeper's direction, he slipped out into the night.

Boyd polished two glasses until they gleamed.

The men returned to their drinking.

Boyd unloaded three more cases of gin.

The men drank on.

Boyd eased his way through the storage room door at the rear of the tavern, confident that his now thoroughly inebriated patrons wouldn't have noticed if Wellington's troops had defeated Napoleon before their very eyes.

"Is it safe?"

Boyd closed the door behind him, giving Rem a tight-lipped smile. "I'm down to one quart of gin, but yes, it's safe." His smile faded. "What did Briggs say?"

In a lightning-quick motion as natural as breathing itself, Rem swerved his head from side to side, scanning the empty storeroom, assuring himself that they were indeed alone. Temporarily convinced, he nevertheless remained attuned to every sound lest the situation change.

Leaning against the stockroom wall, he regarded Boyd through penetrating gray eyes. "British ships are vanishing. Foreign enemies have been investigated … and all but ruled out. The same applies to privateers and foul weather."

Rem's terse explanation was more than sufficient for Boyd, who had served by the earl's side for a dozen years, primarily by sea, ultimately by land. "Napoleon?"

"Impossible." Not a flicker of emotion registered on Rem's face. "All our information has been dispatched to Wellington. Napoleon's demise will be a reality by Season's end."

Boyd inclined his head. "America?"

"No."

"You believe the culprit is right here in England," Boyd concluded, unsurprised. Through experience, both he and Rem had learned that when it came to the issue of financial gain, most men would abandon both principles and allegiance for the overpowering allure of securing great wealth. "Briggs is turning the problem over to you."

"Yes."

"Who do you need?"

"Give me a day or two on my own. I'll head for London imme-diately."

Boyd nodded. "I guess this determines where you'll be spending this Season."

"Evidently. I'll go directly to my Town house and get a few hours' sleep. At daybreak I'll visit the docks—gather whatever facts I can. Then I'll contact you … and Bow Street. By then I'll know exactly who I'll require, and for what."

"Good."

Rem straightened, all heightened energy and staunch resolve. "I'll find you tomorrow."

"Before or after you deliver the Barrett carriage?"

The pointed taunt struck Rem full force. "Dammit! I forgot all about that."

"I'll take care of it. What's the address?"

"No." The word was out before Rem could recall it, much less understand it. Seeing Boyd's stunned expression, he added, "Saman-tha Barrett may be young, but she's not stupid. Let's not feed her curi-osity or incite her questions by sending you in my stead. I told her I'd deliver the carriage—she's expecting me to arrive between two and four o'clock. That still gives me all morning to poke around the river-front. I can cover the West India and London docks in that amount of time. Meet me in front of Covent Garden Theater at half past one. By then I'll be able to tell you which Bow Street men to notify. In the interim, I need you to make arrangements for the Barrett carriage to be repaired. Can you manage it?"

"Undoubtedly."

"Good. Bring it with you tomorrow." Rem frowned for a mo-ment. "As my own carriage is currently on loan, I'll need to borrow your horse to take me to London."

"Help yourself." Boyd gestured toward the rear door. "I'll see to my tasks and meet you as planned."

Rem nodded, regarding Boyd with unspoken warmth and respect; a bond that had been forged over long, trying years and dangerous, adverse conditions. "Get some sleep, Boyd."

"I'll do my best."

Forty minutes later the Earl of Gresham poured himself a brandy and tried to relax in the sitting room of his Town house. The chill of the rain was still in his bones, but he ignored it, for it was a condition the brandy would soon extinguish. Besides, the storm's lingering effects were nearly eclipsed by the fiery thrill of the chase, which had already begun pumping through his veins, heightening his senses, honing his instincts. It was like this with each assignment, a mental metamorphosis that seized him, pervaded him, and ultimately prepared him for the grueling, disciplined weeks that lay ahead.

The danger, the challenge, unraveling the ugliest of lies to find the core of truth buried within—Rem relished it all. For it satisfied not only his relentless craving for adventure, but his equally compelling need to see justice served.

There was a time when things were different, when nothing but the sea could fill that restless void inside him. How he'd reveled in the danger of guiding England's incomparable fleet into the dangers of war, armed with skill, cunning … and youth's foolish conviction that mortality was an impalpable entity that need not be faced.

How drastically all that had changed.

The zealous dedication of his youth had eroded into bewilderment, then outrage, as he'd quickly learned that war's price was death—a price paid not only by evil men, but by decent ones as well. His idealism had disintegrated further with each battle; first Copenhagen, then the Mediterranean, the Atlantic, and culminating with the most heinous injustice of all.

Trafalgar.

With an anguished shudder, Rem fought the hated ghosts, wondering if he would ever be able to erase the image of his revered friend and mentor, the unrivaled Admiral Lord Nelson, lying amid a pool of his own blood on the deck of the *Victory*. Rem could still picture the admiral struggling for breath, being carried below to the surgeon's cockpit before the horrified gazes of his crew. Nelson died during what should have been his most triumphant victory—the utter annihilation of Napoleon's naval fleet.

Never had Rem felt so powerless, so hollow.

So unpatriotically bitter.

He had planned to resign from the Royal Navy. His resignation was never submitted. Instead, fate chose that moment to intercede in the form of the First Lord of the Admiralty himself. Based on the meticulous notes of Lord Nelson, which exuded praise for his young captain's keen instincts and intricate mind, and the glowing recommendations not only of Admiral Nelson, but of three rear admirals and two commodores and commanders-in-chief, the First Lord respectfully requested that Rem consider working for the Admiralty— as a covert agent of the British Crown.

Rem had accepted, recognizing it as his opportunity to ensure that life's equity would be in his hands, rather than in fate's. He had been undeterred by the escalated dangers his forthcoming missions would pose, for after years of naval service amid death's hovering presence, the thought of dying did not frighten him.

What had truly frightened him was the void in his soul, the loss of purpose he'd needed to regain.

Tossing off his drink, Rem rolled the empty glass between his palms as he contemplated the outcome of his unconventional career. He'd successfully ferreted out countless French and American spies, eliminated an equal number of English-born traitors to the Crown, apprehended elusive, highly effective privateers, undermined American naval strategy during the War of 1812, and, most recently, transmitted urgent, confidential missives to the Duke of Wellington— missives that would soon result in Napoleon's downfall.

Rem's methods were not always orthodox, but his results were infinitely satisfactory. His identity had never been discovered, and he and his men could triumphantly boast not merely success, but success employing Rem's cardinal rule: to expose and punish the guilty while sparing the innocent. About this Rem was adamant, determined to ensure that while warfare was undiscriminating about the lives it claimed, his men would not be. And they had yet to disappoint him.

Yes, he'd achieved all he'd sought a decade ago.

The clock in the hallway struck two, interrupting Rem's musings, reminding him of the lateness of the hour and the multitude of tasks that lay ahead.

He deposited his glass on the side table and rested his chin on his chest. Slowly, he inhaled, then exhaled, beginning a practiced breathing method he knew would swiftly relax his body and free his mind for all it needed to plan during the remaining hours of night.

He would depart for the docks at daybreak.

"Samantha, my little lamb! You're drenched!"

"We were caught in that dreadful storm, Aunt Gertie," Samantha replied, stifling a smile. If anyone resembled a lamb, she thought, hugging her elderly aunt, it was Gertrude, with her spindly legs, imploring brown eyes, and wiry white hair. Why, she could almost hear her aunt bleat.

"You brought … what?" Gertie cocked her head to one side in an attempt to make out Sammy's words.

"Not *brought*, Aunt," Sammy replied patiently, and loudly. "*Caught*. We were caught in the storm."

Gertrude gave a grand shrug. "Fine, dear. I'll have the servants fetch it." She glanced expectantly around the quiet hallway, then jabbed a wrinkled finger in Smitty's direction. "You, young man, kindly put down that mangy rat and bring in my great-niece's belongings."

"Aunt Gertie, that's Smithers." Were it not for the terribly offended look on Smitty's face, Samantha would have exploded into laughter. Instead she hastily transferred her wriggling pup from Smitty's arms to her own. "And this is my dog—Rascal. I assure you, he is very friendly and bears absolutely no resemblance to a rat when he is dry."

"Rascal?" Gertrude scowled. "A rather odd name for a footman."

"No, Aunt." Sammy was practically bellowing. "Rascal is my *dog*. Although your error is understandable. You're the second person tonight to mistake Rascal for a rodent."

"Your *dog?* Then who is this man? I'm sure he wasn't here before you arrived, so if he isn't one of Allonshire's footmen, what on earth is he doing here?"

Sammy leaned forward and seized her aunt's hands. "Smithers is Drake's valet; you've met him. And remember? Drake wrote and told you that Smithers would be accompanying me to London because—"

"Oh yes, yes, yes," the old woman interrupted with an apologetic shake of her head. "The birth of my next great-great-nephew or niece is impending. I apologize, Smithers … I don't know how I could have forgotten."

"That's quite all right, my lady."

"Although why Drake would send his valet along as Samantha's chaperon is beyond my comprehension. No offense intended, Smithers."

"None taken, Madame."

"But after all, a valet for a young woman's—"

"Smitty is much more than Drake's valet, Aunt Gertie," Samantha interceded at a shout. "He's been with our family for years and years, and I regard him as an uncle, not a servant. Drake has the utmost trust in him, as do I."

"Oh … I see. My apologies once again, Smithers. I do recall now that Drake wrote something of the kind in his letter."

"I understand, my lady," Smitty managed in clipped tones.

Gertrude sighed. "I seem to be becoming terribly absent-minded these days."

"Fatigue, I'm certain." Sammy cast a please-be-tolerant glance in Smitty's direction. "I hope your visit here with us this Season won't tire you out."

"Oh, definitely not! I'm savoring the thought of introducing you to London society. Let me have a look at you." Gertrude stepped back, scrutinizing Sammy with a satisfied lift of her creased lips. "Why, you've become a true beauty, Samantha! Drake never mentioned *that* in his letter!"

"I was quite gawky and shapeless until this past year. Drake probably hasn't noticed the change, and continues to view me as his homely little sister."

"Impossible!" Gertrude smoothed Sammy's damp ebony tresses from her face, smiling into eyes the color of a velvet-green meadow. "Why, the gentlemen at Almack's will be tripping each other in order to be the first to claim a dance with you."

A mischievous smile touched Sammy's lips. "Then I'll be in luck. If all the gentlemen are sprawled in an undignified heap, they can never discover how graceless a dancer I am."

"You don't care for dancing?"

"Oh, I adore dancing … but it doesn't return my affection. My last instructor told me that my movements much resemble those of a newborn colt."

Gertrude gasped. "A boring dolt? Why, the audacity of that scoundrel. I assume your brother discharged him at once!"

From behind Sammy, Smitty gave a discreet cough, which sounded suspiciously like a stifled chuckle. "Pardon me, my lady," he offered in as loud a voice as he could muster. "But I do believe Lady Samantha will catch a chill if she remains in her wet gown …?"

"But of course!" Gertrude snapped to action at once. "I'll send for Millie—she'll be attending you during the Season, my dear. I brought her with me from Hampshire—a delightful young girl. The two of you will get on famously. I'll advise the footmen—wherever they are—to bring a tub of hot water to your room. Oh, your room." She looked about in bewilderment, then turned befuddled eyes to the second floor landing. "Do you remember where it is?"

"Yes, Aunt Gertrude; I remember. I spent last Season here with Alex and Drake."

"Did you? Then why on earth didn't your brother bring you out?"

"Drake thought seventeen was too young." Sammy jumped quickly to her revered brother's defense, despite the numerous arguments they'd had on this very subject. "Since Father's death, Drake has taken on a rather paternal role with me … and, well, he tends to be a bit protective. But only because he loves me."

"I see."

Sammy wasn't certain whether Gertrude saw or not, because her vapid look clearly indicated that her aunt hadn't heard a word of her explanation.

"I'll go to my chambers and await my bath," Samantha said.

"Since you know which room is yours, why don't you go up and await your bath?" Gertrude replied brightly.

"Good idea." Ducking her head so Gertrude wouldn't see her uncontainable grin, Sammy hastened up the stairway.

The room was as she remembered it; a deep rose with white frilly bedding and rich mahogany furniture. And the bath, which arrived shortly, did indeed feel wonderful.

"Ah, Rascal, this is going to be a splendid Season," Sammy informed the white ball of fur, who was now curled lazily before the roaring fire, absorbed in the process of drying himself.

Smiling, Sammy sank into the tub, closing her eyes and leaning back against the smooth copper surface. "And I *am* looking forward to all the balls and parties and excitement. But I can't help feeling a bit guilty about allowing Aunt Gertie to go to such trouble. After all, she's quite old, deaf, and a bit feebleminded. Acting the part of my chaperon is bound to be an enormous drain on her. And it's really quite unnecessary, given the circumstances. After all, my future is already decided for me."

Dreamily, Sammy wrapped her arms around herself, ripples of water lapping up about her slender shoulders. "The Earl of Gresham," she whispered reverently. "Remington Worth. It's a glorious name, don't you think Rascal?" She didn't wait for a reply. "Did you see his eyes—that incredible piercing gray? Did you feel his power—that authoritative strength he emanates?" She wet her lips with the tip of her tongue. "He'll be here tomorrow, Rascal. Here. I wonder if he'll ask to call again the next day. No. He's too polished, too experienced to act in so boorish a manner. He'll most likely wait several days ... then ask permission to call. Perhaps he'll be my first partner at my first ball. Perhaps he'll be my *only* partner at my first ball! Is that permitted? Or must he alternate with other gentlemen? Oh, how I wish Alexandria were here! Aunt Gertrude is hardly the one to consult on romantic matters ... my books promise to be more informative than she." The bright gleam of anticipation burned within Sammy's eyes once again. "Ah, well. I suppose I'll have to discover all there is to know about love on my own." She grinned impishly. "Well ... not entirely on my own. I'll have the finest of instructors. Remington."

THREE

The sun had not shown itself, and a lingering fog hung over the muddy banks of the Thames, nearly concealing London Dock from view. The burly man hoisted his pants higher about his waist, shifting from one foot to the other and rubbing the back of his neck impatiently.

"The *River Run* won't sail by here for … I'd say twenty minutes. You must be losing your touch, Johnson."

The startled man whirled about, paling beneath his dirt-smeared face, his terrified eyes searching the murky bank for his detector.

A small orange glow caught his gaze, the burning cheroot a mere ten feet from where he stood. How could he not have heard its holder approach?

There was only one man deft enough to catch him so totally off guard.

"Gresham?" The question was a hopeful croak.

Rem dropped his cheroot to the mud and ground it under his heel. "As I said, the *River Run* won't be arriving for"—he squinted thoughtfully downriver—"about a quarter hour. Last night's storm will have delayed her at least that long."

Johnson licked his lips. "Wha' makes ye think I'm waitin' fer—"

"The shipment of liquor and tobacco you intend to pilfer is even larger than anticipated. The question is, will you have time to take your greedy fill before you're spotted? You see, I happen to know that the night watchman has unexpectedly decided to diverge from his customary route tonight. He should be strolling by this section of the river in about three-quarters of an hour, and I would hate to see him catch you in the act of piracy." Rem shrugged carelessly, folding his arms across his chest. "Of course, the fog is heavy and the watchman's vision is poor; he probably won't even see you—unless, of course, someone ensures that he does."

"What d'ye want, Gresham?"

"Your other choice, of course, is to abandon the idea of confiscating the *River Run's* cargo and flee. Unfortunately, that wouldn't help if the watchman were to know about that weasely little Tower Street fence you're on your way to see … and why you need to see him. Why, a decent watchman would then be forced to search you, only to discover the"—Rem's omniscient gaze swept Johnson's bulky frame—"ten odd pieces of jewelry stashed in your shirt and pants."

"Ye're a bloody bastard, ye know that, Gresham?"

"I've been called worse." A corner of Rem's mouth lifted slightly. "Your decision?"

Johnson's broad shoulders sagged. "As I said, what d'ye want?"

"A very small favor, actually."

"Yer favors are never small, Gresham."

"Neither are your crimes, Johnson."

Silence.

"I need you to gather a few of your cronies—the more intelligent, observant, malleable ones—and keep a little vigil for me."

"Wha' kind of vigil?"

"The kind you're best at—scrutinizing ships. Check for anything out of the ordinary: unusually light cargo, shipments or seamen that look odd or out-of-place … whatever your instincts warn you might be amiss. As for the men you select"—Rem stroked his chin thoughtfully—"I recommend that you start with Jarvers; an excellent choice. He's got a sharp eye and an equally strong incentive. Should the magistrate learn of the opium shipment he smuggled off the *Traveler* last week, he'd be on his way to Newgate—and a hanging. Yes, I'd definitely call on Jarvers if I were you."

"Nothin' escapes ye, does it, Gresham? Ye know everthin'."

"If that were the case, I wouldn't need your help." Rem turned to go. "Cover the entire Thames. Quickly. Get your men and get busy. Boyd will be in touch at week's end to hear of your findings."

"What about the watchman?" Johnson called out fearfully.

"He'll be diverted." Rem never glanced back. "Oh, and Johnson, forget the *River Run*—the people of London need that cargo, and I hear Newgate is really a most unpleasant place to take up residence."

Johnson cursed explicitly, spitting after Rem's retreating figure.

He was particularly careful to make certain the earl was too far off to witness his actions.

"The carriage is as good as new."

Boyd gestured toward the Barrett's vehicle, scratching his unruly head of sandy hair.

"I owe you one, Boyd." The refined nobleman in the tight black breeches, cutaway coat, and snow-white cravat bore little resemblance to the threatening rogue who'd returned from the Thames's unsavory banks mere hours ago.

"The only thing you owe me is some information." Boyd's terse response contrasted directly and purposefully with his casual stance, a stance that was as deliberate as was their meeting. It ensured that anyone strolling through the crowded streets of Covent Gardens would see only a pair of close, if slightly mismatched, friends enjoying an amiable chat.

Their friendship was hardly a secret.

Their conversation was hardly a chat.

"I got Johnson." Idly, Rem smoothed the collar of his coat. "He'll serve us well. He's contacting Jarvers and a few others. The docks will be covered."

"I'll make sure of it."

Rem nodded. "I let him know you'd be checking on him at week's end."

"Fine."

No more needed to be said. Excluding predawn hours when concealment was assured, the docks were Boyd's undisputed turf. Heavily muscled, intentionally unkempt, a seaman turned tavern keeper, Boyd blended easily into the wharf's riffraff. Rem was different—a respected naval captain, a feared adversary, a welcome drinking and gambling partner. But still, an earl.

"Who do you want from Bow Street?" Boyd asked quietly.

"Templar and Harris. Assure them they'll be well-compensated."

"When and where do we meet?"

"Tonight. One A.M. In Shadwell."

"Annie's place?"

"It's the most prudent choice."

"And the safest," Boyd grinned. "Besides, it'll be added incentive to our men."

"Undoubtedly," Rem agreed dryly. "Just make sure they know that it's business first, pleasure later."

"I will. And you?"

"What about me?"

"Should I ask Annie to arrange for someone special?"

"For yourself, certainly. I'll find my own."

"You always do. And if not, they find you."

Unconsciously, Rem glanced past Boyd to the gleaming Barrett coach. "I'd best take care of my errand."

"Yes … the inadvertent hero. Well, you certainly look the part. A nobleman, right down to your polished Hessians. That should please Lady Samantha tremendously."

"Very amusing." Rem stubbornly refused to meet the speculative gleam in Boyd's eye. "Now take your cocky grin off to Bow Street. I'll see you at one."

"Oh, Millie, this one is as dreadful as the last."

Samantha cast the mauve silk gown to the bed. "They all make me look like a child on her way to a birthday party. All that's missing is a gaily wrapped parcel. Can't we find something that makes me look ... older?"

The frail young lady's maid wrung her hands worriedly. "But they all look beautiful on you, m'lady. I don't know what you have in mind."

The quiver in Millie's voice struck Sammy hard, melting her tender heart. Swiftly she turned, giving the stunned servant an impulsive hug. "I apologize, Millie. I know I'm being terribly difficult. It's just that ..." She paused. "Can you keep a secret?"

"Yes, ma'am."

"The gentleman who is returning our carriage ... he's not just *any* man."

"No, ma'am?"

"No." Sammy shook her head adamantly. "He is soon to be my betrothed."

"Oh!" Millie's jaw dropped. "But I thought ... that is, Lady Gertrude ... what I mean is—"

"My aunt knows nothing about this," Sammy cautioned at once. She frowned, biting her lower lip. "Unfortunately, neither does the gentleman in question. But he will—soon."

"I don't understand."

"I'll explain it all to you later. For now, let's just find me a suitable gown. I want Remington to see how sophisticated and worldly I am."

"Sophisticated and worldly, m'lady?"

"Yes." Sammy swept across the room and seized one of the books from a towering pile that teetered precariously at the edge of her nightstand. "Just look at this heroine," she demanded, flipping through to a page and pointing. "She's self-assured, charming ... yet enticingly aloof in the presence of all her adoring admirers." She lay the book reverently on the bed. "All heroines possess those traits."

"I see."

"What about this gown?" Tearing through her wardrobe, Sammy spotted a flowing morning dress in a rich, burnished amber color. She yanked it out, holding it up against her before the looking glass. The neckline wasn't adorned with three tiers of lace such as the one worn by her current heroine in Chapter Three. Still, it would have to do.

"It's lovely."

"Good. Then that's settled." As Sammy spoke, her clock chimed two. "We'll have to hurry. Tell me, Millie, how are you at dressing hair?"

"I've never tried," the maid confessed.

"Well, I'm abysmal. So whatever you do will be an improvement. Would you be willing to try?" Sammy swept her hair off her face and looked questioningly at Millie, whose pale skin turned one shade lighter.

"Are you certain, m'lady? I wouldn't want to spoil your beautiful hair, especially given how important this caller of yours is."

"Nonsense. Just use your judgment." Sammy sank down at her dressing table. "Only use it quickly. Remington will be here any moment."

"Well, if you're certain …"

"I'm certain. Between the two of us, how horrid can the results be?"

Thirty minutes later Samantha wanted to eat her words, and her mortified lady's maid was in hysterical tears.

"Forgive me, m'lady, I've ruined everything!" Millie wailed into her handkerchief. "Now you'll lose your suitor and I'll lose my job. What will I tell my family?"

Torn between sympathy and dismayed disbelief, Samantha eyed her own tangled disarray, wondering how Millie had managed to transform her from a reasonably attractive young woman into an untrimmed garden vine in so short a time. A garden vine that was now being watered by the maid's melodramatic tears.

"It's all right, Millie. Stop crying," Sammy heard herself soothe. "You're not going to lose your job. Nor do I plan to lose my suitor." Rapidly, she began to pull out the pins that Millie had haphazardly jabbed into her hair. "Under the circumstances, we'll have to settle for simplicity."

"But I thought you said you had to be sophisticated?" Millie sniffled.

"I did. But even Remington will prefer unadorned tresses to an unchecked weed." Vigorously, Sammy began to brush out her hair. "Would you help me, Millie?"

"I obviously can't." A new round of sobs.

"Yes, you can. Now dry your eyes and locate a ribbon that matches this gown."

"Yes, ma'am." Blowing her nose loudly, Millie proceeded to scurry about the room, at last producing a pale amber ribbon. "Will this do?"

"Perfect! See how efficient you are? Now let's tie my hair back."

In between their task and Millie's hiccups, the sound of an approaching carriage reached their ears.

Sammy rushed to the window. "He's here!" she announced, recognizing the Barrett family crest from far down the street. Leaning against the sill, she watched the vehicle draw to a stop, her heart accelerating to a frantic rate as Remington alit.

With customary impulsiveness, Sammy spun on her heel, gathered her skirts and sprinted toward the door.

"Where are you going, m'lady?" Millie sounded horrified.

In a burst of insight, Sammy suddenly understood why.

Abruptly, she halted.

You are no longer a reckless child, Samantha, she silently berated herself. *For heaven's sake, act like a lady, not a hoyden.*

Counting slowly to ten, she released her breath, smoothed down her gown and gave Millie a beatific smile. "What would you say is a respectable period of time to wait before greeting a gentleman caller?"

Millie blinked. "Why, I don't know, m'lady. A quarter hour perhaps?"

"I'd never last. Five minutes." Sammy turned decisively, her gaze fixed on the clock. Four minutes and a flurry of pacing later, she headed back toward the door, this time maintaining the proper pace and gentility. "Wish me luck, Millie."

"I do, m'lady."

As Sammy descended the stairway, she could make out Remington's rich baritone as he introduced himself to Hatterly, the Barrett's Town house butler.

"It's an honor, my lord," Hatterly responded with his customary starched dignity. "Lady Gertrude will be very grateful for your kindness. I'm certain she wishes to thank you herself, but unfortunately, she is currently indisposed."

"There is no need to disturb Lady Gertrude," came Rem's gallant reply. "I merely wanted to return the carriage and make certain that Lady Samantha and Smithers arrived safely despite last night's storm."

"We did, thanks to you, Lord Gresham." Sammy advanced toward the doorway, mentally cautioning herself not to bound at Rem like a welcoming, exuberant puppy. "Without your assistance, I shudder to think what the evening's outcome would have been. You acted quite the hero."

Rem's chin came up, an indulgent light warming his eyes as they met Sammy's. Fleetingly, almost involuntarily, his gaze flickered over her body, the action so swift that Sammy thought she might have imagined it. She prayed she hadn't.

Leaning forward, Rem captured her hand and brushed it with his lips. "Hello, imp," he murmured against her knuckles. "I'm pleased to see you looking so well." He raised his head, gifting her with a slow, dazzling smile. "Have you read your cumbersome stack of books yet?"

"No." Sammy could still feel the warmth of his breath on her hand. "We arrived quite late last night. I barely had time to bathe before falling asleep. But this morning I reread *Mysteries of Udolpho*, the Gothic I described last night."

"I see. Then perhaps you'd prefer I take my leave so you can—"

"No!" Her protest erupted with a will all its own. "That is … you did come specifically to return our carriage."

"True." Another melting smile. "It is repaired, and as promised, brought here between two and four o'clock."

"You're prompt as well as kind, my lord. The very least I can do is invite you in."

"I believe the earl is already in, my lady." Smitty's disapproving voice descended from the second floor landing like a bucket of ice water.

Sammy winced. "Lord Gresham has returned our mended coach, Smitty. I'm certain Aunt Gertie would want to properly thank him. Since she is abed, I believe the responsibility to do so falls upon us."

"We appreciate your generosity, Lord Gresham," Smitty said stiffly, coming to stand beside Samantha. "You have our gratitude. I'm certain the Duke of Allonshire will contact you personally once I've advised him of your kind rescue; Lady Samantha means the world to him." A meaningful silence. "On behalf of His Grace, I must apologize for putting you to so much trouble. It won't happen again. Your greatcoat is restored and has already been placed in your carriage. And now, as I'm certain you have pressing matters that await you, we shan't take up any more of your time."

"'Twas no trouble and no thanks are necessary, from His Grace or yourself," Rem assured Smitty with more than a twinge of amusement. "As for taking up my time—"

"We can at least offer you some refreshment before you go," Sammy broke in.

Rem's penetrating gaze returned to her face and he made a formal bow. "Refreshment sounds delightful, my lady." The teasing tone in his voice indicated that he was still vastly amused.

Amusement was not the emotion Sammy sought.

She blurted out the first thing she could think of to alter that. "I was just about to adjourn to the sitting room for a glass of brandy when you arrived. Please join me."

"*Brandy?*" Smitty nearly choked on the word.

"Yes, *brandy.*" Samantha shot him a withering look. "Of course, the earl and I will understand if you haven't the time to join us, Smitty."

Without awaiting a reply, Sammy marched into the sitting room and seized the decanter of brandy from the sideboard. How much of the spirit did one pour into a glass, anyway? she wondered. It appeared innocuous enough. A gentleman would require a hefty portion in order to satisfy his thirst. As for a lady ... Sammy reminded herself again that Remington was used to women of great sophistication.

She filled two goblets to the brim.

"Your brandy, Lord Gresham." Sammy extended a glass to Rem, whose expression had, at last, gone from amusement to incredulity. So, she'd finally made an impression! Well, she'd only just begun.

With a thoroughly adult smile, Sammy raised her glass. "In honor of your kind assistance, I toast you, my lord." Lifting the glass to her lips, Sammy swallowed liberally ... once, twice.

Her first thought was that her throat was on fire.

Coughing violently, Sammy sagged against the sideboard, struggling to suck in a breath. Vaguely, she was aware that Remington was at her side, removing the drink from her hand and pressing a glass of water to her lips.

She gulped it gratefully.

"Are you all right?" he demanded, hooking his forefinger beneath her chin.

Mutely, she nodded.

"Imp, brandy is meant to be sipped, not guzzled." Rem caressed her flushed cheek with his thumb. "Perhaps tea would be more appropriate—just this once?"

"Perhaps what Lady Samantha needs is rest rather than food," Smitty suggested pointedly from the doorway.

What Lady Samantha needs, she thought, utterly mortified, *is for the floor to swallow her whole.* Valiantly, she fought the tears of embarrassment that burned more painfully than her throat.

"I have a better alternative, if you'll allow me, Smithers," Rem returned. His tone was gentle, his expression unreadable. "Lady Samantha mentioned that she wished to select some new reading material at Hatchard's today. As it happens, I'm heading to Piccadilly myself. Since Samantha's aunt is obviously unable to accompany her at this time, perhaps I can serve as a substitute ... with a proper chaperon, of course."

"That would be wonderful; I'd love to go," Sammy answered before Smitty could utter a word.

"Good." Rem inclined his head in Smitty's direction. "Would that be acceptable, Smithers?"

Smitty was in the process of shaking his head when he caught the pleading look in Sammy's eyes—his perpetual undoing. "Well, I suppose ..." he faltered.

"Oh, thank you, Smitty!" Forgetting her earlier resolution to act demurely, Sammy flew across the room and hugged the valet. "I'll alert Millie at once and we can be off!"

Rem watched her rapid departure with a rich chuckle, until he caught the disapproval on Smitty's face. "Smithers," he began tactfully, "I'm aware of your concern, and I respect it—though, I assure you, it is entirely unnecessary. Despite my reputation, I'm not in the habit of seducing innocents. Especially well-bred innocents who are barely out of the schoolroom. So, stop worrying. My intentions toward your charge are completely honorable. I shall bring her home happy, submerged in new reading material and thoroughly intact."

"Thank you for your assurances, my lord."

Smitty sounded as encouraged as a fly who'd just been told to make himself at home in a spider's web—by the spider himself.

Moments later, studying Samantha's shining head in the Piccadilly-bound carriage, Rem wondered at his own curious reaction to the lovely, hopelessly romantic young woman beside him. It wasn't her artless infatuation that touched him, for he was wise enough to know how swiftly those tenuous feelings would fade once she was introduced to an army of adoring men. No, it was a deeper quality—an unconditional, untainted faith she seemed to possess.

Still, she thought him a hero; a moral, gallant gentleman.

He was anything but.

It was time to quickly dispel her misguided notion.

"Samantha ..." he began quietly, hoping the rattle of the carriage would keep Millie from overhearing.

"Yes?" Sammy turned, tilting her chin back to gaze up at him.

Her eyes were as green as rare chips of jade; subtle, yet compelling, and so wrenchingly vulnerable.

Maybe there was still a bit of the hero in him after all.

"I suggest you avoid drinking brandy," he said solemnly. "It doesn't appear to agree with you."

"I've never tasted it before today. What I did was stupid. I apologize."

With uncustomary tenderness, Rem tucked a lock of ebony hair behind Sammy's ear. "It wasn't stupid and there's no need to apologize. Imp, are you always so very honest?" At her questioning look, he continued, "Sweetheart, let me give you some advice. You're about to embark on your first Season. Dozens of men will be attempting to win your hand ... and anything else they can acquire in the process. I would suggest you temper your sincerity just a bit."

"Why?"

He started. "Why? Because if you bare your heart before the entire *ton,* you'll have no protection from the unscrupulous black-guards of the world."

"As I said yesterday, you'll protect me." Sammy lay her hand on his. "So I feel quite safe."

She turned to gaze out the window.

Strangely moved, Rem stared down at the small hand covering his. Her faith was staggering; as astounding as it was misplaced. What the hell was he going to do with her?

"Oh look, Remington! There's Hatchard's!" Sammy was out of the carriage almost before it stopped, leaving a bewildered footman staring after her.

Rem helped Millie alight with a sympathetic chuckle. The poor lady's maid looked positively stricken, as if she had no idea what to do next. Not that Rem could blame her. Acting as Samantha's chaperon was a bit like standing in the path of an oncoming tidal wave.

"Why don't you have a seat, Millie?" he suggested, gesturing toward the row of benches outside Hatchard's, where a line of patient servants awaited their employers. "I'm certain we shan't be long."

"Oh, thank you, m'lord." Millie curtsied, then darted to the bench like a relieved prisoner whose life had just been spared.

Still grinning, Rem entered the bookstore, scanning the busy room for Samantha. He met three colleagues with whom he gambled at White's before he spotted her, submerged in a copy of *Mansfield Park.*

"Enjoying yourself, imp?"

Sammy raised glowing eyes to his. "Yes … immensely. I've already spied four or five new Gothics I have yet to read, and, of course"—she caressed the book lovingly—"this."

"Don't let me disturb you. I'll select the volumes I need for my library. You'll find me by the fire reading the dailies."

"Mmm … I'll just be a minute." Sammy was already reimmersed in her book.

An hour later Rem was still settled by Hatchard's fireplace. He picked up a copy of the *London Times* and began scanning the pages containing news. Abruptly, the words: BRITISH SHIPS CONTINUE TO VANISH MYSTERIOUSLY sprang out at him.

"Bloody hell," he muttered, poring over the article.

It was as bad as he feared. Despite the sketchy details provided, there was enough information to cause alarm among the business community. Concern was escalating proportionately with the number of missing ships. A few more articles such as this, and England's trading partners would balk, her insurance rates soar—and havoc would be wreaked on the English economy. He *had* to unearth the culprit, and soon.

"Have you finished your business?" Sammy asked from beside his elbow.

"No. That is, yes, I'm finished here." Rem slapped down the paper.

Sammy frowned at his brusqueness. "Did I tarry too long?"

"No, of course not." He rose. "I was just engrossed in an article."

Reflexively, Samantha glanced down at the page Rem had been reading. "So many ships lost," she murmured, shaking her head in obvious distress. "It seems that British waters are no longer safe."

He tensed like a bowstring. "Why do you say that?"

"Because, as you've obviously just read, quite a few ships have gone down these past months. One of the lost schooners was built by Barrett Shipping. Drake is very concerned and very angry." At the speculative lift of Rem's brows, she explained, "If you know my brother, you know that he is an extremely proud and volatile man. Even the vaguest suggestion that his family's company would produce an inferior quality vessel sends him into a tirade."

"Has someone actually accused—"

"No, of course not. Anyone who's had business dealings with Drake knows he's the most honorable, trustworthy—"

"I agree," Rem interrupted. Nonchalantly, he refolded the newspaper. "Has your brother any clue as to what might have caused his ship to go down?"

"None." Sammy shook her head. "But all of our colleagues are becoming increasingly alarmed. Barrett Shipping has been lucky—we've lost only one ship. Some of our competitors have suffered more severe losses. Why, I overheard Lord Hartley, an old and dear friend of Father's, telling Drake that three vessels manufactured by his shipbuilding company have been lost in as many months."

"A significant number," Rem agreed, vividly recalling the detailed list Briggs had given him at Boydry's. Yes, three of the missing ships had been Hartley's, while only one had been built by Barrett Shipping. Samantha's information was indeed accurate—remarkably so.

An unwanted idea materialized in Rem's brain.

"You're acquainted with many people in the shipbuilding industry, are you not?" he asked casually.

"I suppose so … Why?"

Rem fought a raging battle with his conscience, and won. A link was a link and had to be taken. "I'm impressed, that's all. I hadn't realized you were so involved in your brother's business."

"*You* hadn't realized I had grown past the age of six."

Her quip broke through the rapid-fire pace of his thoughts, and he smiled—a bone-melting smile. "But you have grown, haven't you, Samantha?" he murmured huskily.

"Indeed I have," Sammy replied, lifting her chin a notch. "Quite a bit, actually."

"It seems I have a lot to discover about Lady Samantha Barrett."

"Then I suggest you begin at once."

Years of discipline silenced pangs of guilt. "I intend to, imp. I intend to."

FOUR

A nearby clock chimed one.

Rem swung open the door to Annie's, pausing while his eyes adjusted to the sudden burst of gaslight and bustle of activity. As one of Shadwell's few clean, uninfested brothels, Annie's boasted a wealth of decent liquor, continuous music and dancing, and a host of attractive, accommodating women—all of which resulted in a thriving clientele.

Automatically, Rem peered beyond the sailors whirling their enthusiastic partners about the floor, and the rows of gin-swilling couples occupying the benches on either side of the long room. It never occurred to him to search among the raucous merriment for his men—they knew better than to partake in pleasure before business was concluded.

Sure enough, he caught a glimpse of Boyd seated at a far corner table mere seconds before Annie sauntered up to him. "Hello, Rem," she greeted him above the drunken din. "It's good to see you."

Turning his attention to the buxom, flaxen-haired woman he knew to be as sharp in business as any man, Rem grinned. "Annie, my love." Gallantly, he kissed her hand. "You're looking more beautiful than I remembered. It's been far too long."

Amused awareness twinkled in Annie's shrewd blue eyes. "If I didn't know you so well, I'd believe you, Gresham. But I *do* know you, ever since you first took to the sea. Flattery passes through your lips more naturally than gin. There's not a woman alive who stands a chance of resisting you. And you bloody well know it."

Rem chuckled. "I've been properly chastised."

"Besides, what you're looking for at the moment isn't a willing lady." Hands on ample hips, Annie inclined her head toward Boyd. "They're waiting for you."

"Thanks, love."

"Rem." She stayed him with her hand. "As far as later—do you want me to make arrangements? Katrina is free."

"Katrina is many things, Annie, but never free."

Annie gave a throaty laugh. "True. But she's beautiful, young, and firmly refusing to entertain any other customers since the last time you were here. Apparently, you made quite an impression; one that's costing me considerable income."

"Now who's stooping to false flattery?" Rem's tone was dry. "Lest you've forgotten, my sexual prowess is not the cause of Katrina's recent selectiveness. *That* you can attribute to the ample compensation I provided her—and you—in order to enable her to be more discerning. If I estimated correctly, my payment exceeded what Katrina normally earns in a month."

"That helped, of course. Without it I'd never be allowing her to remain so particular." Annie gave a frank shrug. "Be that as it may, she wants only you."

"Then I *am* flattered. But as you yourself said, my mind is currently cluttered with pressing business matters. I wouldn't be very good company."

"That's debatable. But assuming such is the case, what about when those business matters have been resolved?"

"Let's explore that possibility later, shall we? In the interim"— Rem flashed her one of his dazzling smiles—"I promise you won't go hungry. Between the bottles of gin the lot of us will consume and the temptation your lovely ladies provide to my men, the evening promises to be most lucrative."

"I'm certain it will be. Believe me, Gresham, much as I adore your devastatingly handsome face, I wouldn't allow you to hoard precious space in my establishment for your mystery meetings if I didn't expect the visits to be profitable. Business *is* business." Annie tossed him a saucy grin.

Rem threw back his head and laughed. "You're incomparable, Annie—a constant source of wonder."

"In more ways than one." She leaned into Rem, her deeply cut bodice tantalizingly exposed. "My long time offer still stands, you know. I never mingle with my customers, but with you ... I'd make an exception." With a wink, she sauntered off.

Chuckling, Rem weaved his way through the crowd.

"Rem." Boyd nodded a greeting, handing Rem a mug.

"Thanks." All traces of amusement gone, Rem slid into an empty chair, his eyes on the two men seated across the table. "Templar. Harris."

"Hello, Gresham." Templar, a slight, scattered, nervous-looking man was, in truth, the complete antithesis of what his appearance implied. Actually, the wiry fellow possessed nerves of steel and an aptitude for details rivaled by none. "What's this case about?"

Rem lit a cheroot, then took a liberal swallow of gin. "What has Boyd told you?"

"The same thing he always tells us before we meet with you. Nothing." Harris, tall and sallow, was nondescript enough to blend into any crowd, and dull enough, once there, to be overlooked. These traits worked beautifully in his favor, for his lightning-quick mind missed nothing, his flawless memory retained it all, and his gut instincts knew just when to act on it.

As always, Rem had chosen well.

"Here's the situation. I'm sure it's no secret to you that an unusual number of British ships have inexplicably disappeared. Our job is to find out why."

"What you really mean, is who," Harris qualified.

"Exactly. It could be privateers, foreign ships … or culprits right here in England."

"Which one do you want us to look into first?"

Rem regarded the glowing tip of his cheroot thoughtfully. "Let's suppose, for a moment, that the criminal—or criminals—are English. What could they hope to gain?"

"Money," Templar chimed in at once.

"From the booty they take, you mean?"

"Or the insurance," Harris added quietly.

"Precisely." Rem gave Harris a mock salute. "So, while Boyd and I are investigating the possibilities of privateers or enemy activity, you will be exploring more local avenues—a delicate task indeed."

"How so?"

"Think about it, Templar. If insurance money is the motivating factor, then who serves to collect?"

"Whoever has cargo on the lost ship."

"Or the ship's owner," Harris added.

"Right. And in the case of the latter, you'll be dealing with wealthy businessmen. Men who would take grave exception to being accused of committing a felony."

"How are we supposed to get information from these ship owners?"

"Ask them for it," Rem returned calmly.

"We can't do that, Gresham." Harris came to his feet. "No matter how discreet we are. We'd need to see their records in order to learn anything. What reason would we give for barging in and demanding to do so?"

"You wouldn't need a reason."

"What the hell does that mean? Even *your* name is not powerful enough to gain us access—"

"My name is not to be used." Rem's voice cut through Harris's tirade like a lethal sword. "Ever. Under *any* circumstances." He leaned forward, all coiled fury and suppressed strength. "Just as it never has been ... and as it never will be. Right, Harris?"

Harris sank back into his seat. "Of course, Gresham. I was merely making a point."

"Your point is justified." Rem eased back, tossing off his gin. "But as I said, you won't need to fabricate a reason. The magistrate will provide you with a legitimate one."

"What?" Both Harris and Templar gaped.

"I'll see to it that the Bow Street Magistrate happens upon a situation that will require his runners to investigate various companies ... these companies, specifically." Rem took a folded sheet of paper from his coat pocket.

"How?"

"You leave that to me." Smoothing out the page, Rem continued. "Take this list. Once I provide you with the magistrate's order, I want you to call on all these establishments in an official capacity— quickly, before they can be alerted to your forthcoming visit. Some of the names here are of merchants, others are of powerful shipping magnates. I want their records fully examined, with any unusual expenses or income duly noted. Should you discover anything out of the ordinary, report it to me at once.

"Over and above these scheduled visits, your services will be required to assist Boyd at the docks. I've already hired men to scrutinize the Thames, but I need trained officials to question any unorthodox-looking sailors, sea captains, or dock workers. Use whatever means of persuasion you deem necessary ... and if that fails, let me know. Skeletons lurk in everyone's closet, and I'm quite adept at finding them." Rem flicked his ash carelessly. "So is Boyd. It's amazing how the casual mention of an indiscretion encourages a man to talk freely, isn't it?"

"Indeed it is." Boyd refilled his mug.

"As always," Rem added, "the docks are Boyd's turf; he is completely in charge. Follow his orders unconditionally. Is that clear?"

Harris and Templar nodded.

"Did I omit anything?"

It wasn't the Bow Street men Rem was consulting, but Boyd.

"I see no problems."

"Good." Rem turned back to the other men. "Any questions?"

"Only one." Uncomfortably, Templar scuffed the tip of his boot along the wooden floor. "About payment …"

"Ah, yes, I almost forgot," Rem interrupted. "This is a complicated dilemma that must be resolved swiftly and cleanly with a minimum of public knowledge. If—I should say *when*—you've accomplished that goal, you'll receive twice your normal amount."

"*Twice?*"

"Yes. Does that suit you?"

Templar raised his mug in satisfied tribute. "You're a generous man, Gresham."

"And a determined one." Rem pushed his own drink away. "I'll be in touch."

"You're leaving?" Known for his ability to remain unruffled at all costs, Boyd now looked positively startled.

"We're finished for tonight."

"But …"

Rem grinned. "Enjoy yourselves men." He turned to go.

"Rem?" Boyd caught his arm, speaking in low tones so as not to be overheard. "Are you all right?"

"Of course. Why?"

"You know damned well why. It's not like you to decline a night with a beautiful woman. Do you have other plans?" He shot Rem a look that no one but Boyd could get away with. "With Lady Saman-tha Barrett, for example?"

Rem stiffened. "What the hell does that mean?"

"Did you return her carriage?"

"Yes."

"And …?"

"And nothing. I told you—she's a bloody child, for God's sake!"

"A child who seems to have the most unusual effect on you. Are you sure you did no more than drop off her carriage?"

"Yes. Why? Did you think I tumbled her in her brother's Town house?"

"Testy, aren't we?"

"Don't push me, Boyd."

"Don't get in over your head, Rem."

"I have my reasons."

"You always do."

"Not *those* kind of reasons." Rem shook his arm free. "Look, if you want to hear my motives, I'm on my way home. You're welcome to join me. If you'd prefer to indulge in Annie's entertainment, I understand. But I won't discuss Samantha with you while standing in a brothel. So which is it?"

"I'll get my coat."

"Do you want another drink?"

"Thanks, no … I've had my fill." Boyd folded his arms behind his head and settled himself on a straight-backed chair in Rem's study.

Rem poured himself a brandy.

"Evidently, *you* haven't," Boyd noted dryly.

"Haven't what?"

"Had your fill. Is the brandy for pleasure or courage?"

"I'm not enjoying your barbs tonight, Boyd." Perching on the edge of his desk, Rem raised the glass to his lips. A sudden image flashed through his mind, of Samantha's mortified face when she'd downed half a goblet of brandy in two gulps. Her charming, transparent attempt at sophistication had blown up in her beautiful, disappointed face.

He'd actually felt her unwarranted shame, and his response had been instant and fierce—he had to restore her smile and resurrect her spirit. Hatchard's had been the ideal solution; seeing her lost in her joyous world of books had given him more satisfaction than—

"Rem?"

Boyd's questioning voice yanked Rem from his musings. "What?"

"Where are you tonight? You're staring at that brandy as if there were somebody in it."

"Sorry." Rem sipped his drink, then placed it on his desk. "Templar and Harris will do quite well, don't you think?"

"You know they will. We're not here to talk about Templar and Harris. In fact, we're not here to discuss business at all. We're here to talk about Samantha Barrett."

"I beg to disagree with you, Boyd. Samantha Barrett *is* business."

Boyd frowned. "You've lost me."

Rem extracted his copy of Briggs's list. "Did you read the names of the shipping companies on this list?"

"Of course."

"Did you notice that one of them was Barrett Shipping?"

"You knew Samantha was Drake Barrett's sister. What's the great revelation?"

"When I was scanning the *Times* at Hatchard's this afternoon, Samantha noticed—"

"You took Samantha to Hatchard's?" Boyd's shaggy brows shot up. "I thought you only returned her carriage?"

"I did. Then I offered to escort her to Hatchard's so that she might purchase some books. It was hardly a romantic liaison."

"I see."

Clearing his throat, Rem ignored the pointed disbelief in Boyd's tone. "As I was saying, Samantha noted that I was reading an article concerning the missing British ships. We chatted about the situation. I discovered that she is highly knowledgeable ... much more so than I expected."

"Rem ..." Boyd leaned forward. "You're telling me that the girl you keep referring to as 'a child' knows something about who's guilty of—"

"No. Rather, if she does know something, she isn't consciously aware of that fact. But she's obviously privy to detailed conversations between her brother and his colleagues ... conversations that could prove highly useful to us." Rem gripped his knees. "Boyd, if I spend time in her company, encourage her to talk, it's possible she could provide me with motives or information that would otherwise take me weeks to learn."

"And if she suspects what you're doing?"

A small smile touched Rem's lips. "Samantha is the most guileless, trusting young woman I've ever met. It would never occur to her to suspect anything other than genuine friendship."

"Friendship? Rem, what if the innocent, young Lady Samantha, like every other breathing female in the world, develops feelings for you?"

Rem's smile faded and his jaw tightened reflexively. "Feelings won't be an issue."

"I could argue that point, but you'd be too stubborn to listen. So, let's discuss physical involvement instead. Exactly how far are you willing to carry this scheme?"

"I won't ruin her, if that's what you're asking."

"Only use her, then discard her."

"Dammit, Boyd!" Rem slammed down his fist. "Since when have you become so bloody noble?"

"Nobility has nothing to do with it—pragmatism does. Drake Barrett is a powerful, influential, hotheaded man. By toying with his sister, you're inviting trouble."

"Trouble? Hell, Boyd, we've got a crisis on our hands!"

"And are you going to explain that crisis—along with all our other *secret* missions—to the Duke of Allonshire when he calls you out?"

"Allonshire needn't know anything. Not if I'm discreet. His valet, Smithers, tells me the duke is preoccupied with the forthcoming birth of his second heir. It's doubtful he'll even make an appearance this Season."

"Berkshire is a mere hour's drive. Gossip travels faster than coach."

"Enough!" Rem exploded. "That's a chance I'll just have to take, then. What the hell's gotten into you, Boyd? Our only concern is to eliminate the threat to England."

"Yes, our sole duty ... to see that justice is done." Boyd's gaze was filled with sorrowful understanding of the forces driving his friend. "Very well, Rem. Have it your way."

Rem averted his eyes, staring intently at a single spot on the carpet. "Let's not argue further over Samantha Barrett. She is but one thread in this web of discovery. The Season is commencing with its first official ball at Almack's the night after next. Imagine the information I can glean there."

"As always," Boyd agreed.

The fashionable world was Rem's undisputed domain, mingling within it one of his most fruitful methods of garnering incriminating details.

Ignorant of Rem's connection to the Admiralty, the *ton* never questioned that Lord Gresham was exactly what he appeared—a dashing earl, returned from sea to drown in life's wanton pleasures. And Rem used that impression to his advantage; attending one ball after the next, charming men and women alike until they lowered their guards, revealing tidbits that often alerted Rem to possible suspects.

Too often, traitors and thieves were actually respected members of the peerage who had fallen out of favor with the Crown or foolishly squandered away their wealth. If Rem happened to hear of a notoriously destitute nobleman who was suddenly and inexplicably brandishing large sums of money, or an ousted member of the House of Lords who was receiving mysterious visits from powerful foreign figures, his warning bells would immediately sound. Nine times out of ten his instincts were right, the culprits were apprehended, and no one was any the wiser.

"The *ton* will, once again, be caught unaware as you strip them of their secrets," Boyd murmured with perpetual amazement. "More's the pity, for they will never know how truly brilliant you are."

"Not brilliant, Boyd, just resourceful. As for the naiveté of the *beau monde,* it is essential to our cause that they remain so. Let them see only that side of me I choose to reveal—it harms no one but those who deserve to be harmed."

"Remember that in your dealings with Samantha Barrett," Boyd added quietly, and with far greater insight than Rem could yet perceive.

"You've made your point … quite clearly." Rem frowned, more bothered by Boyd's words than he cared to admit, even to himself. "I'll do my best to see that Samantha—and her feelings—remain intact."

Boyd cleared his throat. "So, you escorted Samantha to Hatchard's. …I take it she enjoys reading?"

"I don't think the term 'enjoy' is powerful enough to describe the relationship Samantha has with her books." Rem grinned, remembering the look on the harried footman's face when he'd seen the towering pile of reading matter Sammy had purchased in one hour's time. "The stack we carried to the carriage was taller than Samantha herself. She assures me, however, that she will have read the whole lot of them in a fortnight."

"Then you'll have to take her back for new ones, won't you?" Boyd asked carefully, studying his friend's face.

"Yes. I suppose I will."

A flicker of awareness registered in Boyd's eyes, then vanished. "I'd best get some rest. The next few days promise to be taxing ones."

He rose. "How do you want to handle the situation with the Bow Street Magistrate? Do you want me to contact Briggs?"

Rem nodded in obvious relief. "I had planned to pen him a note—in code, of course—and have one of my servants deliver it, but since you're here rather than at Annie's ..." Leaning over his desk, Rem extracted a plain sheet of paper and a quill. "It would be safer for you to handle the situation. Briggs must receive the message before dawn, so that the Admiralty can arrange things immediately ... by midday, hopefully."

"It's as good as done." Boyd glanced out the window at the pitch-black skies. "I'll go to Briggs's residence directly from here, while it's still dark. Then I'll snatch a few hours' sleep and make my way to the docks." A corner of his mouth lifted. "I'll arrive just in time to have breakfast with our assistants on the wharf."

"Excellent." Rem completed his cryptic note with a flourish, folded it and handed it to Boyd. "Can you be back here by mid-afternoon? I should have news from the Admiralty by then."

"I'll be here. Your food is better than mine, anyway."

Rem didn't smile. "We've both grown spoiled, my friend. Do you remember what we used to eat at sea?"

A shadow crossed Boyd's tired face. "I have the same memories you do, Rem. But those days are behind us now."

"Are they?"

"They must be."

"I still have nightmares ... vivid ones." Rem inclined his head, meeting Boyd's eyes with a penetrating stare. "Do you?"

"Sometimes."

"Don't you find yourself questioning the fates?"

"No." Boyd brushed a lock of shaggy hair from his face. "Nor should you. Because it's futile to do so. All the answers we ever hope to attain, we already possess." He held up one finger. "I joined the navy to escape my mother's interfering domination and managing a dull textile business. You had a relentless dream to leave your mark on this world and a spirit that refused to be tamed."

Counting off his second finger, Boyd continued. "I left the navy because I no longer wanted to run. I felt I had something meaningful to do—you provided me with that opportunity. You left because the innocent bloodshed sickened you and your dream was transformed into an obsession for justice. As for everything else—the death, the futility—there are no answers to those things, Rem. Stop looking for them. All you're succeeding in doing is torturing yourself. You're accomplishing all you intended—righting the inequities within your control. The rest is up to fate. When are you going to accept that?"

"Perhaps never."

"Never is a long time, my friend." Boyd lay his hand on Rem's shoulder. "Isn't it time you made peace with yourself?"

"I don't know if that's possible. Not in a world as ugly and unjust as ours."

"There's beauty, too. Seek it out."

"I'd rather not. Beauty elicits emotion, and I have no desire to grapple with feelings of any kind, other than conviction and passion. I find solace in my conviction and distraction in the arms of willing women."

"You're still searching," Boyd assessed quietly.

"You're wrong. The dream you alluded to died long ago, along with the boy who envisioned it. Now there is only reality."

Boyd held Rem's gaze. "That's no longer enough. Not for me … and I don't think for you. Your thirtieth birthday came and went last year, and mine two years before that. Surely life must hold more for us than rushing from one mission to the next?"

Rem's brows rose. "I had no idea you were unhappy."

"Not unhappy, Rem. Just lonely. Even jaded seamen can want something tangible to turn to in their old age, can't they? Something that is truly theirs?"

Abruptly, Rem turned away. "I don't know, Boyd. I honestly don't know."

"No ... you don't," Boyd said sadly, scooping up his coat. "I pray that changes, for your sake. Good night, Rem."

FIVE

"Almack's," Sammy breathed. "AT last."

She scarcely heard her own name or Aunt Gertrude's being announced, so intent was she on drinking in the graceful arches that defined Almack's famous ballroom, the rainbow of colors filling the assembly walls as the *beau monde's* most noted ladies twirled by in gowns of the latest fashion and hue.

Almack's. How many nights had she watched Alexandria ready herself for balls such as these, always wishing, dreaming, that she could accompany her beautiful sister-in-law? How many arguments had she and Drake had over this issue, ending always with his firm refusal to bring her out one single day before her eighteenth birthday?

At long last, she was here.

"Aunt Gertie, I'm so happy," Sammy breathed fervently.

"Oh dear." Gertrude pressed her fingers to her throat in distress. "I *am* becoming absentminded. I forgot to warn you, didn't I?" She leaned closer to Sammy's ear. "The food they serve here is atrocious," she confided, speaking in what she presumed to be a whisper. Two of Almack's patronesses turned around to scowl. "If you were hungry, you should have eaten before we came."

"I said *happy*, not *hungry*, Aunt Gertie," Samantha explained over the strains of violin music, simultaneously gifting the notorious Lady Jersey with an apologetic smile.

The influential matron wavered for a moment, then relented beneath Sammy's innocent charm. With a curt nod of acceptance, she moved off.

"I'm glad, dear." Gertrude absently patted Sammy's arm. "For it appears you shan't have time to eat, anyway." Pointedly, she rolled her eyes in the direction of the dance floor, where three eager gentlemen were crossing toward them, their delighted gazes glued to Samantha. "Your first ball promises to be a great success!"

"If I can remember how to dance," Sammy muttered under her breath.

Evidently, she did, because the next few hours were spent breathlessly whirling about the room, her attention vied for by the affluent Marquess of Katerly, the persuasive Earl of Tadum, and the charmingly handsome Viscount Anders. It seemed she only just returned to her aunt's side after each dance when she was claimed for yet another.

Samantha's first ball was an unequivocal and overwhelming success.

Samantha, on the other hand, was thoroughly miserable.

Where was he? she wondered, anxiously peering over Lord Anders's shoulder. Why hadn't he arrived?

Anders winced as Sammy trod upon his foot.

"I'm dreadfully sorry, my lord," she apologized instantly. "I'm afraid the minuet is the dance at which I'm the clumsiest."

"Nonsense." The viscount's smile was gently reassuring. "You're a splendid dancer. You merely missed a step, 'tis all."

"You're very kind, sir."

"And you're very beautiful, if I might be so bold as to say."

Samantha lowered her lashes, wondering how to respond to such overt flattery.

"Now it's my turn to apologize," Anders murmured over the delicate strains of the strings. "I fear I've embarrassed you. That was not my intent. But you are extraordinarily lovely. Tell me, when was your presentation at court? I don't recall hearing any news of it ... or of the ball that followed in your honor."

"That's because there was no ball. As for my court presentation, it was far less dramatic than originally planned, due to the timing." Seeing Anders's questioning look, Sammy smiled. "My brother's wife is on the verge of making a presentation of her own. She is about to gift Drake with the birth of their second child. Hence, neither she nor Drake are in London this Season, and therefore could not host the lavish party they'd initially intended in honor of my coming out. Instead, Drake brought me to St. James's Palace for a private audience, then placed me in Aunt Gertrude's capable hands for the Season's festivities."

"Then tonight is your first official ball?" Anders asked delightedly.

"Indeed it is."

"How fortunate! Then I've not missed any previous opportunities to dance with you."

"No, my lord, you haven't. Although, considering the damage I've just done to your foot, I shouldn't think you'd want—" Sammy's breath lodged in her throat, cutting off the remainder of her reply. Mesmerized, she stared, her gaze riveted on the ballroom entranceway ... and its occupant.

She recognized him long before the attendant announced his name.

Clad in elegant dark evening clothes, his crisp white cravat impeccably tied, Remington assessed Almack's with the same bold appraisal as he had Boydry's.

Sammy began to tremble.

"Are you fatigued, my lady?" Anders asked, concern knitting his brows.

"What? Oh, yes, I suppose I am. I'm unused to so much excitement. It is my first ball." Sammy wondered if she were babbling.

"Of course. I'll return you to your aunt at once."

"Thank you, yes. I mean … that would be best. That is … perhaps if I rested a bit …" Now she *knew* she was babbling.

Safely restored to Aunt Gertie's side, Sammy berated herself for acting such a ninny. She'd expected Remington to attend … prayed he would do so. Now he was here and she was behaving like a lovesick schoolgirl.

Samantha helped herself to a glass of punch from a passing tray. *That's because I* am *a lovesick schoolgirl,* she mourned, gulping down her drink. Steeling herself, she placed the empty glass on another tray. *Remember: act sophisticated. Adult. Worldly.*

"Hello, imp."

His husky voice shattered her reserve, her nerves, and her heart, simultaneously. Pulses racing, she turned to face him. "Good evening, my lord."

Penetrating gray eyes roamed leisurely over her face and figure, blatantly appraising every inch of her from the pearl-woven crown of her tresses to the full skirt of her deep green satin gown. When Rem's eyes again met hers, Sammy flushed at the flagrant admiration he made no attempt to hide.

"You look breathtaking, Lady Samantha," he murmured, kissing her gloved hand. "Almack's should be honored to have you join its coveted ranks."

"You're mocking me."

"Never." He shook his head, thus catching sight of the elderly woman who stood beside Samantha. "You must be Lady Gertrude—'tis a pleasure to make your acquaintance. Your great-niece has spoken highly of you." With an engaging smile, Rem bowed.

"Aunt Gertie, this is the Earl of Gresham," Sammy explained. "He's the kind gentleman I spoke of … do you recall? The one who rescued Smitty and me from the storm and made arrangements for my carriage."

Gertrude blanched. "Really, Samantha, that's preposterous! Despite your youth, you must realize that it's not up to a gentleman—

kind or not—to arrange a lady's marriage. That's what your brother has entrusted me to do!"

Sammy felt her cheeks flame.

"The duke has chosen wisely, Lady Gertrude," Rem answered smoothly, his smile never wavering. "For I'm certain he could not have entrusted his sister to a more discerning guardian."

"Why … no, he couldn't have; thank you, Lord Gresham." Gertie stood a tad taller, preening her thin wisps of white hair.

The musicians struck up a waltz.

"May I have your permission to dance with Lady Samantha?" Rem requested, the essence of proper decorum.

"Of course, Lord Gresham." Gertie tucked Sammy's hand through Rem's arm. "I only wish every gentleman were as well-bred as you."

Her hopes shattering along with her pride, Sammy lowered her lashes, accompanying Rem to the dance floor in distraught silence. For the first time, he'd actually been viewing her as she willed him to—not as an amusing child, but as a woman. Now Aunt Gertie had ruined everything with her appalling announcement. Not only did it make her sound like a mindless dolt who relied upon others to unearth her proper mate, but it made her feel like a piece of sought-after chattel.

She wanted to die.

"You *can* look at me, you know," Rem murmured as he led her into a waltz.

"No … I can't." Sammy stared at the buttons of his waistcoat.

"Why not?"

"I'm certain you know the answer to that, my lord. You were present during that disaster of an exchange."

Rem chuckled. "Hardly a disaster, imp. You yourself told me your aunt was deaf; consequently, I was prepared." He paused, tightening his grip around Sammy's fingers. "What I wasn't prepared for was you."

Embarrassment cast aside, Sammy's chin came up, her eyes meeting his. "I?"

"Ah … you *can* raise your head above my waistcoat. Tell me, am I really so dreadful to look at?"

Her lips curved. "You know you're sinfully handsome, my lord."

"And you're exquisitely beautiful, my lady."

Which scorched her more deeply? Samantha wondered, pleasure shooting through her in lightning streaks. Was it the heat of his gaze, his words, or his touch, which burned right through her glove?

The combination was lethal.

Hope was reborn.

"Are you warm?"

"Hmmm?"

Rem's thumb brushed her cheek. "You're flushed. I was wondering if you were warm."

"I don't know."

He smiled. "Would you like some punch?"

"I've had some, thank you."

"Shall I return you to your aunt for further instruction?"

"No. Nor should you continue to tease me. It makes me feel flustered."

"I see." He swept her around the far corner of the ballroom. "You aren't thirsty, you don't wish to join your aunt, and you won't allow me to tease you. Then, as we have no reading material to divert you, the only other remedy I can suggest is a few minutes respite in less frenzied surroundings. Would you care to stroll through Almack's with me?"

"Yes," Sammy answered without hesitating.

"I'll just tell your aunt—"

"No." Glancing over, Sammy saw that her aunt was talking with the elderly Dowager Duchess of Arvel. "Aunt Gertie won't object. In fact, she'll probably never notice."

Chuckling, Rem led her into the hall. After a quick perusal of the nearby chambers, he guided her into a small, dimly lit anteroom. "How's this?"

"Perfect." Sammy could scarcely see, especially after Rem shut the door behind him. Still, she'd managed to determine the most important thing—they were alone. She turned to face him.

"Are you enjoying your first ball, Lady Samantha?" Rem's voice was deep and husky as it echoed through the empty room.

Sammy's heart slammed against her ribs. "Very much."

"I'm glad." He wrapped a tendril of her hair around his finger. "And is the uncrowded room helping to cool you?"

"No." She stepped closer, wishing she knew what to do next, unaware that she was already doing it. "I don't think a change of scene is what I require."

Something smoky and intangible flashed in his eyes. "Really?" His fingers left her hair, trailed across her cheek and down the side of her neck. "What is it you require then?"

She trembled. "I …"

"Is it this, Samantha?" He framed her face between his hands. "Is this what you want?"

Her eyes slid shut as she unconsciously leaned into him, awaiting his kiss. *Will it be all I imagined?* she wondered in the dizzying second before their lips touched.

The reality exceeded the dream.

Rem's mouth brushed hers softly, gently, circling slowly around to repeat the caress. Butterfly light and infinitely controlled, he continued the motion, a chaste prelude to sensation, a maiden's first kiss.

For Samantha, it was not nearly enough.

Reflexively, her hands clutched his coat, urging him nearer as she rose on tiptoe to reach his mouth. She felt him start, then draw back, catching her hands in his.

"Don't, imp," he cautioned, an uneven whisper against her lips.

"I want to," she breathed back, unable to think beyond the wondrous new awakening.

He hesitated, and Sammy could actually feel his indecision.

"I do want to," she repeated softly, freeing her hands to glide up the front of his shirt. "Please."

Rem's muscles tightened, with surprise or pleasure, she wasn't certain. Then he lowered his head, catching her arms to bring her closer, taking her mouth wholly under his.

Sammy dug her fingers into his shirt as he worked his magic, kissing her in a way that made her knees buckle.

"Better?" he murmured.

"Yes, better … but not enough."

Again she felt him start. "What am I going to do with you, imp?" He lifted a handful of her hair, sifted it slowly through his fingers. "Your honesty constantly astounds me. But tell me, my trusting Samantha, whose undoing will it be, yours … or mine?"

"There is more, isn't there? There must be."

"Must there?" He nibbled at her lower lip. "Don't you think you've had enough of a lesson for one night?"

He was going to pull away. Sammy knew it. And she couldn't allow it—not yet. "Please, Remington …" She pressed closer, twining her arms about his neck and lifting her gaze to his. Her eyes were candid, appealing, wide with discovery, misty with pleasure. "Please … kiss me."

Was it her entreaty that did it? She never knew. Nor did she care. All she knew was that he swallowed her plea with his mouth, crushing her against him, taking her lips in a series of long, drugging kisses that made tension coil inside her like a drawn bowstring. A never-before envisioned yearning ignited inside her, a need like none she had ever imagined. Whatever this wildness was, only her hero could assuage it.

"Remington …"

She parted her lips to ask him to do more, and by her very action, received what she sought.

Rem's tongue slid into her mouth, touching every sensitized nerve ending, gliding over each tingling surface until it mated with her own.

Sammy whimpered, bright lights exploding inside her head. She relented without thought or hesitation, opening to him, yes, but so much more than that ... eagerly joining in the wondrous caresses. Her tongue intertwined with his, mimicked his every motion, then gracefully eased into his mouth to intensify the heady sensations and share the euphoria.

A hard shudder wracked Rem's powerful frame. With a muffled curse, he drew her tongue deeper, more completely, into his mouth, kissing her with a naked urgency that seemed to stun him even more than it did her.

For one endless, exquisite moment Sammy teetered, suspended on the fringes of a tantalizing, unknown inferno.

Abruptly, Rem pulled back.

"Dammit!" Dragging air into his lungs, he released her, his gaze filled with shock and condemnation. "I don't believe this!"

Sammy crashed back to earth. Trembling violently, she regained her balance, uncertain what she should say or do. He was furious about what had just happened, that was obvious. Evidently, he blamed her for initiating the kiss. Initiating it? She'd practically forced him to kiss her! "I'm sorry," she whispered. "I didn't mean—"

Rem's head jerked around. "*You're* sorry?" His tone softened. "You have nothing to be sorry for, imp. I do. That loss of control was inexcusable. I don't know what got into me." He took her gloved hands in his. "Forgive me."

"F-Forgive you?" Sammy shook her head, dazed. "No."

"No?"

"No. Because I wanted you to kiss me. I've dreamed of little else since we met … in truth, *before* we met." She raised glowing eyes to his. "And it was even more glorious than I expected."

Cloaked in shadows, Rem's expression was indistinguishable. "I'm delighted that I didn't disappoint you, little romantic." The sound of laughing voices drifted in from the hallway, and Rem brought his head up like a wolf scenting danger. "We'd best get you back to the ball. You'll be missed. And I'm the last person the gossips should discover you with."

"Ah, yes. Your wicked reputation." Sammy smoothed her hair back into place, fervently wishing she could read Rem's thoughts. Was it pleasure she heard in his tone, or was it simply amusement?

Easing open the door, she paused, striving to prolong the moment. "Do you know, my lord, for a notorious rake, you really do make the most wonderful hero."

Silence.

A narrow shaft of light from the hallway illuminated Rem's face, and, with a sinking heart, Sammy got her answer. There was no doubt of what Lord Gresham was feeling. It was not the pleasure she'd prayed for, not even the amusement she'd feared. It was guilt … guilt and regret.

"Remington—"

"Go back to the ball, imp." Crossing over, Rem glanced surreptitiously through the open doorway. Assured that no one was about, he propelled Sammy gently into the hall. "I'll follow shortly. Tell your aunt you felt light-headed and went out for some air. Alone."

She hesitated another second before she complied. Then, bewildered and hurt—and desperately trying to conceal both—she did as he asked.

* * *

Her attempts at concealment failed miserably.

Alone in the anteroom, Rem could visualize naught but Samantha's anguished expression, and his guilt magnified by the minute. Because, no matter how sound were his motives, the reality didn't change. He was using her.

Or was he?

Swearing softly, Rem stared down at his tightly clenched fists. How long had it been since he'd so totally lost control; behaving like an inexperienced schoolboy in the arms of his first woman ... and from a mere kiss?

Dammit.

He hadn't counted on this. He had a job to do. Samantha was a possible link to the discovery of a criminal, an undeniable entry to the circle he needed to infiltrate. His plan had been simple, and formulated to cause Samantha the least amount of distress: He would fuel her infatuation with a bit of harmless flirtation, a few chaste kisses, and, hopefully, long hours of carefully maneuvered conversation that would provide him with the information he sought. Tonight had been the perfect opportunity to begin ... Samantha's first ball.

She'd looked so beautiful in her forest-green gown, the elegant satin lending the very air of sophistication she so desperately sought. Rem's only reminder of the fanciful young woman he'd met at Boydry's was the transparent play of emotions mirrored on her face: pleasure when she first saw him, nervousness when they spoke, humiliation at her aunt's bumbling remark.

When he'd witnessed her untainted spirit crushed, Rem's immediate reaction had been a rush of protectiveness much like the one he'd experienced when she scalded her throat gulping brandy. It was atypical of him, to say the least, but not alarming. Given the extent of Samantha's innocence and faith, he was convinced that the need to shelter her would be as natural to a man as breathing.

But that didn't explain the queer surge in his chest when they danced ... nor the magnitude of his response when they kissed.

Prowling restlessly about the room, Rem attempted to examine the situation with his customary objectivity. Passion was something he'd discovered at a young age, closely followed by proficiency. Physical pleasure was a wondrous balm for the body, a needed escape for the mind. And, since he'd begun his covert activities with the Crown, an incomparable method of finding out what he needed to know.

His magnetism had served him well, as had his resulting reputation as a womanizer. The widespread knowledge that the Earl of Gresham never restricted himself to the same lady twice allowed Rem to come and go as he pleased, arousing no one's suspicions, jeopardizing no one's well-being. His missions and his peace of mind remained unthreatened.

Until now.

Tonight, when he'd held Samantha in his arms, tasted the sweetness of her mouth, something inside him had snapped, given way to a deluge of sensations to which he was immune.

Or so he'd thought.

Slowly, Rem unclenched his fists, gazing fixedly at them. Sometime during the past half hour, control had shifted from these expert, insusceptible hands into those of an enchanting, vibrant young woman with the heart of a dreamer and the sincerity of a child.

It wouldn't happen again.

Samantha Barrett was an obstacle that had been thrown in his path. He was accustomed to subverting obstacles. All he needed was a clear, methodical plan. Inhaling sharply, he formulated one.

Regardless of Samantha's unexpected effect on him, as well as her blatant infatuation, he could not simply dismiss her. Not when she could very well supply him with an important inside view of Barrett Shipping and its competitors. On the other hand, to fuel these disconcerting emotions would be unfair to Samantha and dangerous to him.

A week. He would give himself a week.

Seven days of concentrated time with Lady Samantha Barrett. More than enough to learn what she knew, far too brief to render any permanent damage.

Certainly fleeting enough for him to master any odd twinges of emotion he might experience.

A purposeful gleam in his eye, Rem left the anteroom and returned to the ball ... and his evening's work.

* * *

"It only goes to show that reputation is often rumor," Aunt Gertrude proclaimed loudly.

Sammy winced.

"Why, the Dowager Duchess of Arvel was spouting all sorts of nonsense about Lord Gresham being a libertine of the worst order. According to her, the whole *ton* is buzzing with stories of his indiscretions. She had the sheer audacity to chastise me for allowing you to dance with him. Well!" Gertrude sniffed. "I told her in no uncertain terms that the earl was a total gentleman ... with me as well as with you."

Nodding woodenly, Sammy wondered how much more she could bear.

"Speaking of Lord Gresham, I haven't seen him in some time"— Gertrude craned her neck to survey the room—"since you danced with him, as a matter of fact. Did he take his leave?"

"I don't know, Aunt Gertrude."

"Lady Samantha, are you all right?" The Viscount Anders, his expression taut with concern, hastened up to them.

"Why ... yes, my lord. Why wouldn't I be?" Sammy fingered the satin folds of her gown.

"During our last dance, you looked pale and distressed. I wanted to assure myself that you'd recovered. I've been searching the entire ballroom for you. ...I was becoming alarmed."

"Oh." Sammy stared at the intricately stitched leaf pattern above her hem. "That was very kind of you, my lord. Actually, I left for a brief time ... to get some air. I feel much better now."

He looked relieved. "I'm glad. That being the case, may I have the honor of another dance with you?"

"There's the earl, dear!" Aunt Gertrude suddenly exclaimed, pointing. "In the entranceway. Why, he, too, must have gone out for some air."

In response to Gertrude's announcement, Anders pivoted toward the doorway. When he saw the person to whom she referred, he glanced at Samantha, a question in his eyes.

Sammy's cheeks flamed. Certain that guilt was written all over her face, she avoided the viscount's gaze.

An instant of silence followed—an eternity to Samantha.

Finally, Anders cleared his throat. "The strings have begun, my lady. About the dance ...?"

"Certainly, my lord." Somehow Sammy found the ability to go through the motions, allowing Anders to guide her onto the dance floor. She forced herself not to look about, although she sensed Rem's eyes on her, assessing her ... probably with pity and remorse. Pity for the self-loathing she was undoubtedly feeling in light of her scandalous behavior, remorse for his contribution to rendering her a fallen woman.

How would he react if he knew she longed to run back into his arms, to relive that first exquisite kiss? Would his gray eyes turn chilling with censure, as they had in the tavern, or indulgent with humor, as they had when she'd guzzled her brandy?

Either way, she didn't want to know.

"The next time you need air, I'd be delighted to escort you," Anders was saying. "You shouldn't stroll about Almack's on your own."

"Thank you. I'll remember that." Where was Rem now? Sammy couldn't see him anywhere.

"Did you lose your way?"

"Pardon me?" She blinked.

"Did you lose your way?" Anders repeated. "You were gone from the ball for quite some time."

Sammy lifted her gaze, dreading the condemnation she expected to see. But the viscount's expression was solicitous, not reproving. Perhaps he really didn't know. "No, my lord," she answered, determined to be as honest as she could without damning herself. "I found a small anteroom and renewed myself."

"I see. An unoccupied anteroom?"

He most definitely knew. "Yes, the room was empty ... when I arrived." She wanted to kick herself for the hesitation.

"Not everyone at Almack's is honorable, my lady." Anders held her eyes. "I would feel much better if you would call on me the next time you leave the party."

"Very well, my lord." Sammy fell silent again.

Despite her best resolution to the contrary, she found herself scanning the room for Remington.

She found him ... and wished she hadn't.

Leaning against the far wall, he was immersed in intimate conversation with one of the most exotically stunning women Sammy had ever seen.

How much more could she withstand?

"You're far lovelier, you know."

"Pardon me?" Sammy blinked.

Anders followed Sammy's gaze. "Lady Sheltane—she cannot compare to you in beauty."

Sammy almost laughed aloud. "You must need spectacles, my lord."

"I assure you, I do not."

His stiff tone alerted Sammy to the brusqueness of her reply. "I apologize. That was dreadfully rude of me. Tis only that I feel so inadequate beside these accomplished ladies."

"Believe me, Samantha, their accomplishments are nothing you should envy."

She looked startled. "Why? What are they?"

"Things that are unsuitable for a lady's ear."

"Oh." Sammy blushed.

"You're especially charming when you blush." Anders's teeth gleamed.

"My lord—"

"Stephen."

"Stephen." Sammy wondered where all this was leading. She could tell by the envious glances being cast her way that most women would swoon with pleasure over the attention she was receiving from the handsome viscount. Unfortunately, he left her cold. But then, he wasn't her hero.

The sound of tinkling laughter caught Sammy's ear, and she glanced over in time to see Rem touch Lady Sheltane's arm in an obviously intimate gesture. She had an excellent notion where *that* was leading.

"Who is Lady Sheltane, my lor—Stephen," Sammy corrected herself. "Her name sounds familiar."

"It must. Do you recall last Season when the elderly Marquis of Sheltane's magnificent thoroughbred stunned the entire *ton* by sweeping Newmarket?"

"Oh!" Sammy's eyes widened. "Is Lady Sheltane related to the marquis? His granddaughter … no, then her title would be …"

"His wife."

"His *wife?*" Sammy's head jerked around, and she stared openly at the beautiful flaxen-haired woman of whom they spoke. "Why, she can't be older than five and twenty!"

"True. And Lord Sheltane is nearing sixty—and exceedingly rich."

"I don't doubt it. Where is the marquis?"

"Home … ailing."

"And she—" Sammy's mouth snapped shut.

"Yes." Anders whirled Samantha about the room. "You are refreshingly naive, my dear. A rarity, to say the least."

Sweetheart, let me give you some advice ... Sammy could hear Rem's voice as clearly as if he were speaking the words aloud. *You're about to embark on your first Season. Dozens of men will be attempting to win your hand ... and anything else they can acquire in the process. I would suggest you temper your sincerity just a bit. If you bare your heart before the entire ton, you'll have no protection from the unscrupulous blackguards of the world.*

"I suppose I am, Stephen," she replied, unwilling to explain that, in this case, naiveté had nothing to do with it. She'd witnessed more than her share of infidelity in her lifetime ... but her hero?

The strings fell silent, and Sammy stepped away from Anders. "Will you excuse me, please?"

"Of course." He bowed.

Sammy gathered her skirts and made her way through the crowd, uncertain precisely where she was going, only knowing that she needed to get away.

She collided head-on with the instigator of her flight.

"Samantha?" Rem caught her elbows to steady her. "Why are you fleeing through Almack's like a bandit?"

"I—That is ..." It was too much. Despite her best efforts to regain control, Samantha felt tears well up in her eyes.

"Are you all right?"

Miserably, Sammy shook her head. "I apologize for walking into you. ...I'm not feeling well. If you'll allow me to go ..." She made one futile attempt to pass.

Rem didn't release her. "Has someone said something; done something?"

"No!" she snapped. "Fear not—my honor is intact, Lord Gresham. I just wish to leave."

"I'll take you home."

"And interrupt your intimate evening? I wouldn't hear of it!" Were those biting words really coming from her?

Rem's dimple flashed. "My intimate evening?"

"There you are, Rem." Lady Sheltane breezed over, gifting him with a tantalizing smile. Simultaneously, her frosty blue eyes appraised Samantha. "I don't believe I've met your little friend."

"Clarissa, may I present Lady Samantha Barrett. Samantha … the Marchioness of Sheltane."

"Lady Sheltane." Samantha wanted to slap her mocking face.

"Samantha, of course. I'd heard you were coming out this Season." The marchioness patted Sammy's hand in a patronizing gesture. "And what a coincidence. We were just discussing your brother."

"You were?" Sammy's tears vanished. "Why?"

"Because my dear husband has commissioned Barrett Shipping to build a personal yacht for my use. It will be called the *Clarissa*."

"How lovely. Your husband must be thoroughly devoted to you." Was it her imagination, Sammy wondered, or did Rem's lips twitch?

"He is. Actually, he considered several companies before selecting your brother's. He was determined to attain the finest quality for the *Clarissa*, considering the number of English ships that have been lost these past months. Henry says poor workmanship is the reason they vanished, no doubt to the bottom of the sea."

"The quality at Barrett Shipping is impeccable, I assure you, Lady Sheltane. The marquis will not be disappointed. Now, if you'll excuse me, I really must find my aunt."

She didn't wait to see if Lady Sheltane excused her or not. She bolted.

Sprinting down the hall, Sammy found the anteroom she'd frequented earlier and slipped inside. Burying her face in her hands, she gave in to the weeping she'd suppressed.

"Samantha?"

She froze.

"Why are you crying?"

"For no reason you would understand, Lord Gresham. Now please … leave me alone."

He came up behind her. "Did Anders make any improper—"

"No. The only one who was improper tonight was me."

Gently, he turned her to face him. "It's your first ball, imp. Don't cry."

She gazed up at him from beneath wet, spiky lashes, her eyes emanating confusion, hurt and pain. "It's just that I … when we … I don't understand, why did you—"

With a rough sound, Rem dragged her into his arms, burying his face in her bright hair. "Samantha …" He tipped her chin up, brushing his lips through the tracks of tears on her cheeks. "I want to see you smile."

"Then kiss me," she heard herself say. "But this time don't pull away, and don't apologize." She stood on tiptoe, twining her arms about his neck.

"Sweetheart, you don't know what you're asking …"

"Yes, I do." She tugged him down to her. "Please …"

Capitulation was inevitable.

Rem bent to capture her mouth with his, relenting before either of them could think. Their lips met, fused, parted … then melded in a searing, blazing, devouring kiss that burned with a life of its own.

Pressing closer, Sammy's last coherent thought was that heaven itself would bow before these sensations. She felt Rem's hands rove restlessly over her back and shoulders, pulling her harder against him. She arched her neck as his lips scorched a searing path down her throat to her collarbone, then back to her mouth again.

"Samantha …" This time her name was an endearment, and Sammy reveled in the sound. She met the rhythmic strokes of his tongue, felt the hammering of his heart against hers. But when she slid her hands inside his coat, eager to feel the warmth of his skin through only the thin barrier of his shirt, he stayed her, catching her fingers in his. "Stop, sweetheart. Stop now."

"Why?"

"Why?" He jerked his head up. "Dammit, Samantha, you can't be *that* naive." Live embers smoldered in his eyes. "Surely you have some idea where this can lead."

"Where it was leading with Lady Sheltane?"

"Is that what this is all about—Clarissa?"

"Yes … and no." Sammy wet her lips. "I hate the thought of you and … *her* together. But I also adore being in your arms."

There was that dimple again. "How do I combat such enchanting honesty?"

"She's married, Remington."

The dimple vanished. "Samantha … there are some things you don't understand …"

"Oh, I understand better than you think," Sammy returned, holding Rem's gaze. "My mother was as faithless as your Clarissa. From what I eventually learned from Drake, she enjoyed countless lovers—and my poor father never discovered her duplicity. And Drake, well, married women have pursued him since as far back as I can recall. Many still do, despite the fact that no one exists for him but Alex." Sammy gripped Rem's arms. "A dishonest liaison is beneath you, Remington."

Some intangible emotion crossed his face. "Hell, imp, you don't even know me," he muttered, a muscle working in his jaw. "I'm *not* the fictional hero you imagine me to be."

"Yes," Sammy breathed, "you are. If you weren't, you'd be with her right now. Instead, you're with me." She brought his fingers to her lips.

A muffled oath rumbled from Rem's chest. Involuntarily, he tugged Sammy against him, ravaging her mouth in another series of deep, probing kisses. He shifted restlessly, taut with some imperceptible need—a struggle between mind and heart.

"I don't want you to stop," Sammy whispered.

"And God help me, I don't want to stop," he returned in a strangled tone.

"Samantha? Where are you, dear?"

Sammy's fingers dug into Rem's coat. "Aunt Gertie."

"It's all right." Instantly taking control, Rem murmured soothing words as he quickly rearranged Sammy's disheveled tresses. "Go. I'll stand behind the door until you and your aunt are no longer in the hallway. She'll assume you were alone."

"Again?" Sammy couldn't help but smile.

"The alternative is to tell her you were in my arms. And, given that she is almost entirely deaf, you'd have to shout the truth throughout Almack's." Rem grinned. "Is that preferable?"

"Good night, my lord." Sammy scurried for the door.

He chuckled. "Good night, imp."

One hand on the latch, Sammy hesitated, inclining her head in Rem's direction.

"Tomorrow, my transparent dreamer," he promised, "I'll take you and your skittish maid for a ride in Hyde Park. How would that be?"

"Perfect." Sammy's eyes glowed. "Well … almost perfect. Perfect is what just happened here."

She was treated to a fleeting glimpse of that incomparable dimple before closing the door behind her.

"Here I am, Aunt Gertie." Sammy tried, in vain, to keep her exultation from showing. "Are you ready to go home?"

"There you are, Samantha! I'm ready to go home," Gertrude declared brightly. "By the way, the Viscount Anders has been insistently searching for you. You seem to have made quite an impression."

"I'll locate him and say good night." This time Sammy pronounced her intentions loudly.

"Fine, dear. I'll wait here."

Sammy didn't have far to go.

Just outside the ballroom, his back to her, was the Viscount Anders. He was deep in troubled conversation with Lord Keefe, the prominent banker who managed the majority of the ton's funds, including her family's.

"It wasn't just his ship, Anders," Keefe was saying. "Nor even the cargo, although evidently Goddfrey lost a fortune in goods. The heinous part is the loss of his crew—quite a substantial one, from what I hear—and his finest captain."

"A tragedy," Anders agreed somberly. "I myself have lost two ships in much the same manner. Something *must* be done."

"Chaos is beginning to set in—and not only among the businessmen whose ships and cargo are being destroyed. The docks are buzzing with rumors and fear. Crewmen are already demanding higher wages. Some are even refusing to sail at all, preferring the loss of gainful employment to death."

Sammy's hand flew to her mouth and she gasped aloud.

Both men turned.

"Samantha! How long have you been standing there?" Anders went to her side.

"Drake still captains *La Belle Alexandria*," she whispered. "I never realized—"

"I'm terribly sorry you overheard that, my dear," Keefe said, utterly mortified.

Anders took Sammy's hands in his. "Your brother spends most of his time at Allonshire and very little of it at sea," he reminded her. "Since your father's death—certainly since wedding Alexandria and siring a son—Drake's involvement with Barrett Shipping has been primarily on land."

"Still ..." Fear gripped Sammy's heart.

"I don't want you to concern yourself about this." Gently but purposefully, Anders led her aside, mollifying her as one would a small child. "Both the Admiralty and Lloyd's are conducting investigations into the cause of these disasters. By the time Drake sets sail again, the problem will most assuredly be resolved."

Mutely, Sammy nodded.

"May I call on you, my lady?"

Lost in the turmoil of her thoughts, Sammy gave Anders a quiz-zical look. "Pardon me?"

He smiled. "I'm requesting the right to vie for your affections, Samantha. Will you grant me the honor of doing so?"

"Oh." Sammy blinked. "I … that is … well, my lord …"

"Stephen."

"Stephen."

"I am as charming as most and more scrupulous than some—if given a chance." There was no missing his meaning. "Please, Saman-tha, give me that chance."

What could she say? Especially in the hallway of Almack's be-fore a milling crowd of gossips, all craning their necks to hear her reply. Moreover, her head ached from the worry of what she had just learned. She needed to think.

"All right … yes, Stephen, you may call on me."

"Tomorrow?"

"No." She blurted out the refusal, softening it immediately. "I need a day to recover. Perhaps Friday?"

"Friday it is. I look forward to it with great anticipation." Anders kissed her gloved hand. "You won't regret your decision, my lady. You have my word on it."

Samantha didn't even hear him. Her mind was consumed with the possibility that Drake could be in danger. How could she subvert it? Talking to her brother would be useless; he was as stubborn as a mule. The only person who had any influence on him was Alex, and with a new babe due any day now, Sammy refused to burden her. No, Sammy knew she was on her own.

Abruptly, she halted, realizing she'd just stumbled upon her answer.

It was as clear as her future with Remington.

She'd found her Gothic hero.

It was time she became a heroine.

SIX

Considering it was two in the morning before Sammy dismissed Millie and settled under her quilt, dawn should have arrived with a great deal more expedience.

Instead, it dawdled endlessly, leaving Sammy frustrated and impatient. Abandoning her warm bed, she paced about her chambers, wondering if the sun were ever going to rise enough to shed some light on the darkened streets.

Not an abundance of light, merely enough for her to see her way along the north bank of the Thames until she reached London Dock. There, she would implement her plan.

A faint glint from the horizon prodded Sammy into scooping up the disheveled bundle of clothing she'd confiscated an hour ago from the washroom in the servants' quarters. The breeches and shirt, left hung to dry, were still a bit damp. But they were also small—obviously belonging to a slight man—and were therefore the only garments that came close to fitting her. So, damp or not, they would have to suffice.

Donning them rapidly, she went in search of the darkest pair of slippers she could find. To wear men's shoes would be absurd; she had miles to walk and refused to be hindered by ill-fitting footwear.

There. Done.

Last, she twisted her hair into a tight knot atop her head and yanked the cap she'd found—a gardener's cap, complete with mud and grass stains—over it, tugging the brim down almost to her eyes. She grinned at her reflection in the glass. All she needed was a shovel and shears and she could comfortably prune the hedges at Allonshire.

Sneaking out was infinitely easier than anticipated. But of course Aunt Gertie was deaf, the servants were sleeping, and Drake's perpetually protective eye was absent.

Drake.

Just the thought of her beloved brother being injured, or worse, made a lump form in her throat. No. She had to prevent it.

Purposefully, Sammy hastened down Abingdon Street and made her way to the Thames. She'd venture her two-mile journey to London's East End along the riverbank, safely away from the streets surrounding St. James … and the curious eyes of any last minute partygoers on their carriage rides home.

There was scarcely enough light to see, but she knew the route along the Thames almost as well as she knew the grounds of Allonshire. As a child, she'd spent countless hours following Drake to his ship, watching him depart, fervently wishing he wouldn't leave her behind.

Always he promised her he would return. And he kept his word—only to become restless and traverse the seas once more. Sammy hurt, not only for her own loneliness, but for the emptiness that drove Drake away, always searching, never finding.

Then, three years ago, everything changed. This time when Drake returned home he brought with him the most precious gift he'd ever given her, and himself. Alexandria.

Magically, Drake's restlessness vanished, replaced by an overwhelming joy and contentment that permeated Allonshire and made Drake whole.

Sammy intended to ensure he remained that way.

The West End of London was predictably quiet, as the *haut ton* slept on, at least until noon. The faint sounds and smells of Covent Gardens drifted to her senses, strangely comforting, as they reminded her that others were up and about. Relief was short-lived, for the soothing sounds of the new day faded as Sammy hurried along the very dark, very deserted strand that led to London Bridge.

There, she rested, leaning her head against a wooden pier, wondering why her plan no longer seemed quite so brilliant as it had on the carriage ride home from Almack's. After all, if the Admiralty itself hadn't determined the cause of the ships' demises, what made her believe she could?

It was too late to turn back now. Just beyond that curve was London Dock. Perhaps the fates would smile down on her.

She approached the wharf, slowing her step as she cautiously inched through the rows of warehouses, peeking around to watch the docks come to life.

Activity abounded, cargo being readied for boarding, cranes hoisting wooden crates onto waiting ships, workers calling out to each other as they scanned the skies to assess the day's sailing conditions. A normal daybreak at London Dock.

How precisely did one perceive an unusual occurrence? Sammy wondered, chewing her lip. Her heroines all seemed to possess innate instincts for sizing up danger. Why didn't she?

Evidently, she had to plunge right into the heart of things.

"Outta th'way, boy!" A craggy-faced sailor nearly knocked Sammy over, stifling her determined approach to the wharf. Giving her a thoroughly irritated look, he continued hauling his load to the pier's end. "If ye ain't workin', clear out! Ye're in th'way."

"Sorry," Sammy muttered in as deep a voice as she could muster. Pulling the cap lower on her face, she scampered off to find a more discreet spot to begin her covert observations. The warehouses afforded no access; the pier afforded no privacy.

Blend in. That's what she had to do.

Stooping over, Sammy retrieved an empty bottle of ale and a dried scrap of bread from the ground. Moving unsteadily about, she kept her full attention riveted on the bottle, periodically raising it to her lips for a fictitious swallow. Better, much better, she congratulated herself.

A scraggly dog slithered up to her and yanked her breeches with his teeth.

"No!" she hissed under her breath. She shook her leg free.

The dog sniffed her and barked.

Sammy was certain all eyes were upon her.

"Please," she whispered fiercely. "Go away."

The dog nipped at her foot and howled.

By now everyone on the dock must have figured out her disguise. Including this odorous mongrel.

Slowly, she raised her eyes.

Not one person had even glanced her way.

Sammy sagged with relief. "What do you want?" she demanded through clenched teeth.

The dog sat and wagged his tail, his eyes glued to her hand.

The bread. She had completely forgotten about the bread. "Here." She thrust the bit of crusty food at him. "Take it."

Eyes gleaming, the mongrel snatched the bread and bolted.

Sammy rolled her eyes skyward. How could she solve a critical mystery when she couldn't even deduce that a half-starved dog would be lured by a stale piece of bread?

"How much ye drink last night, Grady?"

The voice made her jump. Whirling about, she spied two staggering workmen en route to the wharf.

"Not as much as ye did!" The other man laughed heartily. "But we'd better be sober enough t' make sure all that cargo gets on the right ship ... and that th'ship checks out okay."

"What d'ye mean?"

"This one's Allonshire's, and his foreman says if anything goes wrong, our jobs might go with it. 'E's even sendin' another carpenter around to check out the ship before she sails."

The first man looked startled. "What's up?"

"They're all gettin' nervous, what with th'ships goin' down one after th'other. I'll tell ye, I wouldn't want t'be sailin' on one of these … rather be loadin'. 'Tis safer."

"Yer right about that. Did ye 'ear about Goddfrey? 'E's disappeared since 'is last ship went down."

"Disappeared?"

"Mm-hum. They say 'e couldn't take it—all the questions, and the guilt. Lost a full crew, 'e did. And 'is best cap'n."

"So 'e took off?"

"That's right." The workman leaned closer to his friend. "Although I don't think it was only 'is conscience what made him bolt. Between ye and me …"

Sammy strained her ears, inclining her head as far in the men's direction as she could without toppling over.

"… rumor 'as it that until 'e gets some insurance money, 'e's in trouble. And I've seen 'is wife—she's one who likes 'er men plump in the pocket."

"Goddfrey's been 'it bad," his companion agreed. " 'Is customers are all lookin' elsewhere to ship their cargo." He snickered. "Maybe 'is wife's arrangin' for 'is ships to go down as an excuse to get rid of 'im."

Howling with laughter, the workmen made their way to the dock.

An interesting thought, Sammy speculated, sidestepping a crane preparing to load. Could one person actually be the target for all these disasters, with the other disappearances merely diversions employed to cast aspersion elsewhere?

It was a high price to pay for profit, but perhaps profit alone was not the motive. Perhaps it was vengeance. Or jealousy. Or power. Not to mention the measures a criminal might take to avoid discovery.

Sammy's eyes sparkled. Yes. It made sense. She would find this Goddfrey and interrogate him. His name sounded vaguely familiar, which could only mean she'd heard it from Drake. And, since Drake was at Allonshire, she'd have to question his right hand, trusted friend, first mate and valet.

She could hardly wait to get back to the Town house and grill Smitty.

All caution cast to the wind, Sammy took off at a dead run, dodging crewmen and equipment alike, darting toward the warehouses.

The drone of voices accosted her an instant before she saw the two gentlemen conversing alongside the warehouse wall. Normally, their appearance wouldn't have troubled her at all. Given the view she had of the gray-haired gentleman facing her, it did.

"Lord Hartley," she muttered under her breath. Now what was she going to do? There wasn't a doubt that, if the marquis saw her face, he'd recognize her. As one of her father's oldest friends, he'd known her since birth.

Sammy cursed her timing. Lord Hartley owned a shipbuilding company, yes, but why did he have to pick this morning to visit the docks? And how on earth could she explain her ridiculous garb?

Desperately, Sammy tugged the brim of her cap lower, ducking into the receding shadows of dawn. The other gentleman glanced up, and for a fleeting instant before the shadows concealed her, Sammy felt his quizzical gaze on her. Poised against the warehouse wall, she held her breath, aware that Lord Hartley had stopped speaking.

"Summerson?" she heard him ask questioningly. "What is it?"

"Nothing. Just an odd-looking lad. Probably prowling about looking for food. Now, what were you saying?"

The rest of the conversation was lost to Sammy. Weak with relief, she sagged against the brick wall. The marquis hadn't spied her. As for the man called Summerson, she'd never seen him before in her life, so it mattered not that he'd spotted her nor that he thought her odd-looking.

Gratefully, she inched her way around the warehouse and headed away from the dock.

The *ton* was still deep in slumber when Sammy trudged down Abingdon Street an hour later. In truth, she envied them their repose. Her feet ached, her head throbbed, and her breeches were sliding down her hips. The thought of sleep sounded distinctly appealing.

Smitty was nowhere to be found—a further incentive for her to take to her bed. Even Millie hadn't ventured into her room, evidently having been told that her mistress would be sleeping late after her first Almack's ball.

Sammy placed her pilfered clothing in the hallway. A chambermaid was bound to come by and assume the clothes had been erroneously delivered to Lady Samantha's chambers, at which point she would promptly return them to the servants' quarters.

The bed felt wonderful—better than wonderful, Sammy thought, snuggling into the pillows. There would be plenty of time for heroism later ...

Rem closed the file he'd been reading and leaned back in his chair. He'd memorized the damned thing anyway. And, thus far, it had provided him with no new insights.

He came to his feet in a rush. Who was he kidding? He'd stayed up all night, but it wasn't the lost ships that had dominated his thoughts.

It was Samantha.

Why the hell did she affect him the way she did? It was bad enough she elicited protective urges he'd never known he possessed—urges to shelter her, not only from physical harm, but from emotional harm, as well. But the rush of passion she invoked in him, the downright trembling need to absorb her into himself—it was unthinkable, unacceptable, untenable.

Undeniable.

If he doubted it the first time they kissed, his doubts were put to rest the second time she was in his arms. Not to mention the overwhelming desire to beat Anders senseless when the viscount turned his skillfully polished charm on Samantha. That bloody bastard would only use her, then cast her aside.

Rem inhaled sharply. And what was *he* doing? Wasn't he also using Samantha, planning to discard her when he'd acquired the information he sought?

Damn. Damn. Damn.

He'd never before had trouble concentrating on his work, never felt guilty for the means he'd used to gather his information.

He could still see the crestfallen pain and accusation on Samantha's face when she'd spotted him with Clarissa, making him feel like a reprehensible bastard. The irony of the situation was comical. For the first time in eons, his motives for charming a beautiful woman had nothing to do with the thrill of conquest. Oh, he'd been delighted to see the lovely marchioness. But not for the reasons Samantha suspected.

Who better to probe for tidbits of confidential data than a woman who spent most of her time in various noblemen's beds; the place where men's defenses were at their lowest, and secrets, normally hoarded, were often divulged? The marchioness's paramours consisted of at least four major shipping magnates, making her a potential wealth of information.

But from Samantha's perspective, he'd been cavorting with a married woman.

And what if he was?

Lord knew, it wouldn't be the first time. Why the hell did he care *what* Samantha Barrett thought of his behavior? She was a romantic, innocent child.

A child who so thoroughly ravaged his control that he'd almost made love to her on the floor of the bloody anteroom at Almack's.

She'd tasted her first kiss in his arms. He wanted more … her first touch, her first sigh … her first time.

Rem raked his fingers through his hair, more off balance than he could remember being since he left the navy.

Was he mad?

Emotions had no place in his life. They were dangerous to his missions, a threat to his sanity.

Yet, he'd gone to Almack's for a purpose, accomplished absolutely nothing of value, and come home mentally besieged by thoughts of an unquestionably unattainable young woman.

Seven days was far too long.

Four days would have to suffice. Yes, he'd allow himself four days to grill Samantha. Then, for both their sakes, he'd walk away.

"Pardon me, my lord."

Rem glanced wearily at his butler. "Yes, Peldon?"

"Mr. Hayword to see you, sir."

"Send Boyd in. And Peldon, bring some coffee into the study. I need it."

"Yes, my lord."

Boyd and the coffee arrived simultaneously. Once Peldon had taken his leave, Boyd looked closely at Rem and whistled. "You look like hell."

"Thanks. That's much the way I feel. Sit down." Rem gulped down some coffee, then began prowling restlessly about the room.

"Who do you suspect?"

"What?" Rem halted.

"The only time you pace like that is when you're on the verge of some unpleasant discovery. So what is it?"

Rem gave a hollow laugh. "You couldn't be more right … and more wrong." Seeing Boyd's questioning look, he continued. "I've made an unpleasant discovery, all right, but it has nothing to do with our case. As far as that goes, I didn't learn a damned thing. Not that I didn't have opportunity; I did. Clarissa was at Almack's. I managed to steer the conversation in the right direction—not a difficult feat, considering Henry apparently commissioned Barrett Shipping to build his precious bride a yacht—but various intrusions interfered and I never got to the heart of the matter."

"I see." Boyd stared intently into his coffee. "Do these intrusions have anything to do with your unpleasant discovery?"

Rem grunted an affirmation.

"And does this unpleasant discovery relate in any way to Samantha Barrett?"

Rem shot Boyd a look. "I don't want to discuss it."

"You're drawn to her."

"She's a child."

"You spoke with her."

"Not about what I should have."

"She's refreshing and beautiful."

"She's Drake Barrett's sister."

"You want her."

"She's a virgin, for Christ's sake."

"But you still want her."

"Yes … I want her."

"And that's it?" Boyd prodded.

"No, God dammit, that's not it!" Rem exploded. "She arouses me like hell, all right? I wanted her so much last night, I forgot all the reasons I'd gone to Almack's. I was shaking like a bloody schoolboy and I wanted her under me more than I wanted to breathe! Are you satisfied now?"

"Evidently, you're not." Boyd's lips twitched.

"That's not even faintly amusing."

"Aren't you overreacting a bit, Rem? Is it so terrible to be reminded you're not just a machine? That you *do* have feelings?"

"Since when does passion require feelings?"

"We're not talking solely about passion, and you know it. You've had an army of women over the years. Not one of them has affected you this way."

"Then perhaps I should continue in that vein."

Boyd made a wide sweep with his hand. "Go ahead. You can have virtually any woman you want. What's stopping you?"

"Shut up, Boyd."

"No, I don't think another woman would be your solution," Boyd continued, unbothered by Rem's warning scowl. "Not any longer. I think it's this particular woman you want … and I think you want her in more than just your bed."

"This conversation is pointless." Brusquely, Rem cut Boyd off, his expression fierce. "Whether or not I want Samantha Barrett—in bed or out—is irrelevant. It's not going to happen. She has her fanciful dreams, and I have a job to do."

"But what if—"

"Enough, Boyd! I mean it." Rem rubbed his temples. "Did the Bow Street Magistrate come through?"

"I just left Harris. The magistrate will have the order prepared by morning. Harris and Templar will begin visiting the shipping companies on their lists tomorrow."

"Fine. Unless something happens sooner, let's meet with them on Monday night at Annie's."

Boyd nodded. "I stopped by the docks. No news yet. But it's still early."

Early. The word clicked in Rem's head, bringing to mind the data he'd acquired from one of his informants just prior to last night's ball. He should have taken care of it first thing this morning, but he'd been so bloody preoccupied with thoughts of Samantha. "What time is it?" he demanded.

"A little after ten. Why?"

"I've got to change clothes. I'm off to see Goddfrey; I want to surprise him by noon."

"Goddfrey … I thought he fled after that last ship of his went down?"

"He did. I've tracked him down in Bedfordshire. I have some questions for him before he bolts for parts unknown."

"Such as?"

"Evidently, Goddfrey's business reverses are severe, and have been steadily worsening for some time. Coincidentally, more than a few of his ships have been among those lost—enough to collect a substantial amount in insurance."

"A possible motive," Boyd commented.

"Indeed. And his sudden attack of conscience makes me want to chat with him before he vanishes into thin air."

"Understood. But why by noon?"

"Because I need to be back in London by late afternoon," Rem replied offhandedly. "I'm taking Samantha for a ride in Hyde Park at five."

"I see."

"Wipe that smug look off your face, Boyd. I arranged the outing to discover exactly what Samantha knows about Barrett Shipping."

"I don't doubt it." Boyd came to his feet. "I'm certain you can unearth numerous truths from Lady Samantha—and possibly from yourself in the process." He grinned, placing his empty cup on the desk. "You know, Rem, it is a bit chilly during the fashionable hour. Might I suggest you abandon your phaeton in favor of your coach? It affords a good deal more warmth … and privacy."

"You're treading dangerously, Boyd, very dangerously."

Unconcerned, Boyd chuckled. "You'll have to fill me in later; on Goddfrey … and on your fruitful outing in the park."

"Oh! I beg your pardon."

The Viscount Goddfrey recovered his balance in the inn entranceway, glancing up quickly to see if the person with whom he'd just collided was unhurt. "Gresham?" He paled.

"Goddfrey, whatever are you doing here?" Rem smoothed his coat, his brows lifting in apparent surprise.

"I'm … that is …" Goddfrey swallowed audibly. "I'm meeting someone."

"As am I. Quite a coincidence." Impatiently, Rem glared up and down the quiet street. "However, my colleague is late." He frowned. "And yours?"

"Late as well."

Rem's eyes widened as if a brilliant notion had just occurred to him. "Being that both our associates have evidently been detained, can I interest you in joining me for a glass of claret?"

"C-Certainly."

Seated in the inn's coffee room, Rem casually crossed one leg over the other and savored his drink. "I'm pleased to see you looking so well, Goddfrey. I was terribly sorry to hear about your recent misfortune."

Goddfrey started. "Pardon me?"

"Your ship. A terrible loss."

"Oh, yes … my ship." Goddfrey seemed to relax. "Well, 'twas far from the first that's gone down."

"True, but I gather that you've been particularly hard hit. Isn't this the fourth ship you've lost?"

"Yes."

"Thank goodness there is insurance to cover such devastating mishaps. Have you collected already?"

"No, Gresham, I haven't." Goddfrey gulped down his drink and ordered another, polishing it off in record time. He signaled for a third glass of claret. "Who did you say you were meeting?"

"An old navy chum, actually. We haven't seen each other in years. It doesn't surprise me that he's yet to arrive—Broderick is notoriously late." Abruptly, Rem leaned forward. "Forgive my presumptuousness, Goddfrey, but if a small loan would help make things easier until the insurance is paid, I'd be happy to—"

"No!" Goddfrey leapt to his feet. "I'm not taking another cent!" Sweat dotted his forehead. "Who sent you, Gresham? Why are you offering me money?"

Rem blinked. "What do you mean? I'm only proposing—"

"Are you working with Knollwood? Did he pay you to track me down? Is that what this chance meeting is all about?"

"Sit down Goddfrey," Rem said quietly. "No one sent me. But perhaps it's fortunate we did run into each other. Your drink has arrived. Finish it. Then tell me who Knollwood is and why he so desperately wants to find you."

Goddfrey sank back down, shaking. "How do I know I can trust you?"

"I don't recall cheating you in the past." Rem grinned. "Not even at whist; and you are perhaps the worst card player I've ever met. I think you also know me to be extremely discreet—with my reputation, I have to be." Rem's grin faded. "Besides, it appears to me that you have to trust someone."

The viscount didn't smile, but he did toss off his drink. "He's a parasite, Gresham. A filthy bastard who makes his living off pathetic souls like me. I owe him a bloody fortune … and I can't pay it."

"How much do you owe him?"

"Two hundred thousand pounds. I kept praying for a miracle. …None occurred."

Silently, Rem studied Goddfrey's bent head. "Certainly your insurance pays enough—"

"Not in time. Knollwood wants his money now." Goddfrey laughed bitterly. "The ironic thing is, I dispatched that last ship posthaste because the merchant whose cargo it carried was willing to pay me an exorbitant sum of money to do so. It held three English-built carriages, and evidently, the American importer for whom they were destined had a very urgent, very rich customer awaiting their arrival." Goddfrey buried his head in his hands. "I should have checked the ship more thoroughly … had a carpenter go through it, especially in light of all the sea disasters. But I didn't. I needed that money so badly, I silenced my own conscience. Dozens of men are dead now because of my greed, and I've lost the finest captain I ever had."

"Who is this merchant?"

"Hayes."

A dead end. Rem knew Hayes well. He was as decent a man as they came. A sudden possibility gnawed at the edges of Rem's mind. "This Knollwood—did he know you hadn't the time to check your ship?"

"I assume so … why?"

Because, Rem thought, *perhaps the bloodsucker's crimes are far more sinister than extortion.* "I was just wondering if he expected you to bolt—the combination of guilt and pressure would be too much for many men to handle."

"I cannot go back, Gresham." Tears filled Goddfrey's eyes. "I have nothing to offer him in terms of payment … nothing."

"What about your family? Surely they're worried sick over your whereabouts?"

"My wife has no knowledge of our dire straits. She would cheerfully hand me over to Knollwood if she did."

"Running will solve nothing."

"Staying will solve less."

Rem inhaled sharply, weighing his options. Instinct told him that Goddfrey's guilt extended only as far as carelessness, greed, and weakness of character. It also told him that the viscount was at the end of his rope. The question was, how could he assist Goddfrey without revealing too much?

"I beg of you, Gresham. Don't tell anyone you saw me. By nightfall I'll be gone. If Knollwood should learn of my previous whereabouts, he'll come after me."

"I'll make a deal with you, Goddfrey," Rem replied. "I'll tell no one of our meeting … under one condition."

"Which is?"

"Tell me all you know about this low-life Knollwood."

"Why?" Suspicion flashed in Goddfrey's eyes.

"Because I want to anonymously alert the authorities that he should be investigated. I won't mention your name or my own. But wouldn't it ease your guilt to know you've spared others the agony you're now experiencing?"

A brief silence, then a nod. "I know very little about him. I don't find him—he finds me."

"Where?"

"At the Tower. Always at one A.M. He sends a message to my office."

"How does he know when you need money?"

Goddfrey shrugged. "He just does. He also decides when to demand repayment. And the price he exacts is excruciatingly high."

"What does he look like?"

"Short. Plump. Pale blue eyes. Unkempt gray hair. Of middle years. That's really all I can tell you."

"It's enough. I'll take it from here." Rem slid his chair back.

"Gresham!" Goddfrey bolted to his feet. "Remember, you swore not to tell anyone."

"And I won't." Rem rose, gazing at Goddfrey with a somber, pitying expression. "However, I will need to know your destination." He held up his hand to ward off Goddfrey's immediate protest. "I give you my word I'll share the information with no one."

"Why do you need to know where I'll be?"

"Because if Knollwood is apprehended, I'll be able to advise you."

"I'm not sure it matters anymore … at least not to me. My life is beyond redemption."

"Well, it matters to me. Have you forgotten that you owe me fifty pounds from our last evening at White's? I intend to make certain you return to London this Season so that I might collect."

Goddfrey smiled faintly. "Thank you, Gresham." Furtively, he looked about the coffee room. "I'm staying with a distant cousin in Edinburgh. I'll write down his address for you."

Rem took the slip of paper and rose. "Good. Now I'm off to meet my friend. Stay well, Goddfrey. And don't lose heart."

Samantha was waiting at the door when Rem arrived. "Hello, my lord."

Rem couldn't help but smile, despite his pensive mood. "You're supposed to keep me fashionably waiting, imp. You also have servants to answer the door."

"I know. I'm terribly impulsive. But I couldn't wait."

"You look lovely." Rem drank in her elegant white muslin carriage dress, more than a hint of pleasure in his gaze. Her innocent beauty was a wondrous balm after the ugly events of the day.

"And you look dashing." Boldly, she studied his dark trousers, Wellington boots, and striped waistcoat. "A splendid escort."

He chuckled. "Shall we?"

"I suppose we must wait for Millie." Sammy glanced impatiently toward the stairs. "She should be down in a moment."

"I'm ready, my lady." Millie scurried down and curtsied. "Good afternoon, my lord."

"Good afternoon, Millie." Rem turned back to Sammy. "Our chariot awaits."

"Oh, you didn't bring a phaeton!" Sammy sounded ecstatic, for much the reason Boyd had, Rem suspected. In truth, he didn't know why he'd brought the enclosed coach. He'd told himself it was because he would acquire more information from Lady Samantha if there were fewer distractions. Now, feeling the inexorable pull between them, he wondered if he'd been lying to himself.

"It's a lovely evening, Millie. Enjoy the fresh air," Sammy called gaily, gesturing toward the coach's rear outer seat.

"But …" Millie looked flabbergasted. She had no opportunity to elaborate, because Sammy had already climbed into the chariot.

Rem handed Millie up to her designated seat beside the coachmen, before climbing in beside Sammy and ordering his driver to proceed.

He then promptly burst out laughing.

"You are incorrigible; do you know that, imp? Have you any idea how tattered your reputation will be if anyone should realize we are alone in this carriage?"

"I don't care." Sammy leaned forward. "I wish to be alone with you."

"And I wish to be alone with you." The words were out before Rem could evaluate them, but he knew immediately that his pleasure had little to do with his mission. Whatever he hoped to learn from Samantha could wait a few minutes. For now he just wanted to immerse himself in her exuberance. "So, did you enjoy your first ball at Almack's?"

"You know I did."

"Any lingering fatigue from your ceaseless night of dancing?"

"None."

"Did any of the gentlemen that comprised your multitude of admirers make an impression on you?" Now why the hell was he asking that?

Sammy shrugged. "A few of them asked to call on me."

"Like Anders?"

Her brows arched in surprise. "Yes, the Viscount Anders did ask if he might call."

"The man is a master at seduction—a noted blackguard with the morals of a snake, and a reputation to equal it."

"Like you, my lord?" Sammy's eyes twinkled.

Rem sucked in his breath. "No … yes. Dammit, Samantha, I just don't want to see you get hurt."

"I won't get hurt, Remington," she replied softly. "I told you—you'll protect me."

Gazing into those trusting eyes, green as a summer meadow, Rem felt his chest constrict. Without thinking, he drew her against him, tunneling his fingers through her thick sable tresses. "What am I going to do with you, imp?"

"I believe you asked me that question, as well. And I answered it."

His eyes gleamed. "So you did. And is the answer still the same?"

"It is."

"Very well … kiss me, my beautiful romantic." He caressed the sides of her neck with his thumbs, guided by a need that unfolded with a life of its own. "I can imagine nothing more magnificent than tasting your soft, sweet mouth."

Sammy needed no encouragement. "Last night," she whispered, stroking Rem's jaw, "when you kissed me … it was heaven. I dreamed about it all night."

"Then let me give you something else to dream about," he murmured, covering her lips with his. "Let me …"

What was it that happened when he held this woman? he wondered dazedly. It was as if nothing existed outside the magic they made when she was in his arms. All he wanted was more: to hold her closer, to taste her more fully, to possess her more completely.

Reason be damned.

Beginning as pure fire, the kiss exploded into streamers of white-hot sensation. Rem pressed Samantha back onto the carriage seat, following her down, his lips already leaving hers to caress her throat, her neck, her shoulders. Sammy arched, breathing his name, and Rem's fingers dug into the sleeves of her gown, dragging them down her arms to give him access to the upper swell of her breasts. He could feel the pounding of her heart, the harsh little sounds of pleasure she made.

"You're so bloody beautiful," he rasped, his hands gliding around to cup her breasts through the fine material of her gown. "So impossibly, irresistibly beautiful."

Sammy whimpered, her breasts swelling at his touch. His thumbs brushed ever so lightly across her nipples, feeling them harden instantly at the fleeting caress. The urge to see, touch, taste her exquisitely responsive flesh, was almost more than he could bear. But he couldn't, not in a carriage with the entire *ton* frolicking about them.

He settled for a far less satisfying substitute. Lowering his head, he nuzzled her through her gown, tugging lightly at her nipples with his teeth.

Sammy's reaction nearly undid him. She cried out in undisguised pleasure, drawing his head closer, more intimately, against her.

"Christ, Samantha, stop." Rem was barely able to breathe, let alone think. "If you don't, I'm going to lose all control."

"And what would happen then?" Sammy asked breathlessly, gazing up at him with wide, questioning eyes.

"I'd do something we'd both regret."

"Would we?"

"You, imp, are playing with fire." Rem pressed his lips to the pulse at her throat.

"I'm not playing at all."

"We're in the middle of Hyde Park, sweetheart." He kissed her again, deeply. "It's not the time."

"When will it be the time?"

Their gazes locked.

"Samantha ... you're a beautiful, enchanting young woman."

"But I'm not proficient enough for you." Sadly, Sammy drew herself upright, adjusting her bodice and smoothing her hair.

"Proficiency isn't the issue. The fact is, a quick tumble in my carriage is beneath you. You deserve everything a woman dreams of: flowers ... wine ... firelight ... music ... long hours of preparation ..." His mouth snapped shut as he realized how his own words were affecting him.

"It sounds like heaven," Sammy whispered, her face flushed with the picture Rem had conjured up. "When can it be?"

God, he wanted to take her to bed. "On your wedding night, imp. With a man you have yet to meet—the man who will be your husband." Seeing Sammy's anguished expression, feeling the insistent throbbing in his loins, Rem decided that he was a saint. "Samantha, love ..." He cupped her face. "You deserve it all—commitment, a husband, a family."

"A hero?" She tilted her head back, studying him with those mesmerizing jade-green eyes.

"Yes ... a hero."

"I've found him."

Why the hell did he want to be all that she believed he was?

It didn't matter. He wasn't.

"No, sweetheart. I'm not a hero."

"Are you deterred by my inexperience?"

He sucked in his breath. "To some extent ... yes."

"Fine." Her small chin set, Sammy folded her hands purposefully in her lap. "That obstacle is easily remedied. I'll make certain to gain some experience at once. The Viscount Anders is calling on me tomorrow; I'll begin with him. In no time at all, I'll be able—"

"Over my dead body!" Rem couldn't believe the vehemence of his reply, or the cold fury that rose in his chest at the thought of her in another man's arms—least of all a charming viper like Anders.

Sammy seemed sincerely startled. "Why ever not? You just said—"

"I said you should save your innocence for your husband. Not hand it over to an unworthy cad who'll toss you aside the moment he's had his way with you."

"But I *want* to be tossed aside. I have no aspirations to wed Stephen."

"*Stephen?*" Again, that surprising surge of jealousy. "If he lays a hand on you, I'll kill him."

A dazzling smile illuminated Sammy's face. "Yet another rescue. How can you deny your heroism?"

"Tell me about Barrett Shipping." Hearing himself blurt out the question, Rem was horrified. When had he *ever* approached a covert subject with so little finesse?

"Barrett Shipping?" Sammy blinked. "I assume you feel, the need to change the subject, Remington."

Without meaning to, Samantha had provided him with a logical motive for his sloppy tactics. "I think a change in subject is definitely in order, imp."

"What is it you wish to discuss?"

"Is your brother abandoning his trips to sea until the cause of the disappearances have been determined?"

Sammy averted her head, staring out the window. "I don't know."

"You're worried about him."

"Of course I am. If anything ever happened to Drake, I'd die."

Rem took her hand in his. "I didn't mean to upset you, Samantha."

"It's not just Drake. It's the whole situation. So many needless deaths. So few avenues to explore. Perhaps the Viscount Goddfrey could explain—" Abruptly, she stopped.

"What did you say?"

"Only that so many men have died." Sammy twisted her fingers nervously in the fabric of her gown.

"What made you mention Goddfrey?"

"I—I heard that he'd lost a large crew with his last ship."

What the hell wasn't she saying? Rem needed to know.

"Samantha ..."

"I'd like to go home now, my lord."

She was as transparent as glass. "All right," Rem replied, wisely electing to bide his time. "May I take you to the opera tomorrow?"

Sammy chewed her lip in distressed indecision. "I promised Stephen ..."

"Get rid of him." Rem lightly stroked her palm with his thumb. "Let him call on you in the afternoon. Then come to Covent Garden Theater with me in the evening."

"All right."

"And Samantha—I meant what I said. If Anders touches you—"

"Like this?" she murmured. Without warning, she slid closer, leaned up and kissed him.

"No," Rem replied huskily. "Like this." He crushed her against him, buried his lips in hers and kissed her until they were both breathless.

Long minutes later Rem tore himself away. "I'd better take you home now, my lovely lady. Else I'll forget every good intention I ever possessed."

"I look forward to that day, my lord." Sammy smiled. "In fact, I can hardly wait."

SEVEN

Finding Smitty was infinitely easier than Sammy expected.

He was standing in the front hallway, glowering like an angry lion, when she entered the Town house at twilight.

"Oh, Smitty! I'm glad you're here. I looked for you at noontime, but you weren't—"

"My lady, we need to talk," he interrupted.

Sammy's eyes widened in surprise. It was rare that Smitty spoke to her in so harsh a tone. "Of course. What is it?"

"I think we should adjourn to the library," he replied stiffly.

"Very well." She proceeded him down the hall, wondering what on earth this was about. Once inside the library, she turned. "You seem upset."

"I am."

A sudden chill ran down Sammy's spine. "It isn't Alex … or the baby …?"

"No, my lady." Smitty shook his head at once. "I received a message from His Grace today. All is well; the doctor and midwife agree that the new babe should be making an appearance by next week's end."

"Thank goodness." Visibly, she relaxed. "Then what is it?"

Smitty cleared his throat with rough unease. "This is extremely difficult for me, Lady Samantha. I've known you since you came into this world, and care for you as if you were my own."

A fond smile touched Sammy's lips. "I feel the same way about you, Smitty—you're a member of our family."

"Thank you. And I apologize in advance for my impertinence."

"You are never impertinent, Smitty." Sammy grinned.

Her grin was not returned. "When His Grace realized he couldn't be in London this Season, he entrusted you into my care …" Smitty met Sammy's gaze. "I take that responsibility very seriously."

"I know you do,"

"Then I must interfere in a way I customarily would not."

"Very well."

"To be blunt, I understand you went riding with the Earl of Gresham this evening."

"My goodness, news travels quickly!" Sammy laughed. "I only just arrived home. But yes, I rode through Hyde Park with Remington."

"I don't think the earl is proper company for you, my lady."

"Why not?"

An uncomfortable pause. "You're very young, Lady Samantha, and very naive about … certain things. The earl has a reputation that is—in polite terms—scandalous, making it ill-advised for a well-bred woman such as yourself to keep company with him. I don't expect you to fully understand what I am saying, however—"

"Oh, I understand," Sammy assured him brightly. "Remington spends a good portion of his time charming women, and the rest of his time bedding those he has charmed. Isn't that right?"

Smitty's mouth dropped open.

"I'm touched by your concern, truly I am." Sammy squeezed Smitty's arm. "But your request that I stop seeing Remington would be quite impossible for me to honor."

"And why is that?" Smitty's voice sounded strangled.

"Because, as I told you, I plan to wed him." She watched in dismay as Smitty sagged against the wall. "Of course, first I'll reform his rakish ways. Please don't worry, Smitty. Remington has exercised"—

she frowned, perplexed by the truth of her own revelation—"inordinate self-restraint with me."

Taking pity on Smitty's ashen expression, Sammy curbed her own speculations and attempted to soften the blow. "In the interim, Viscount Anders will be calling tomorrow. So I'm acquainting myself with many eligible gentlemen … at least until Remington comes to his senses and proposes. All right?"

She didn't wait for a reply. "I was wondering if you recall a gentleman named Goddfrey who does business with Drake?"

"Pardon me?" The abrupt change in subject was too much for Smitty to absorb. He still hadn't recovered from the shock of Samantha's proclamation.

"Goddfrey. Does that name sound familiar?"

"Uh … yes, my lady." Smitty shook his head to clear it. "The Viscount Goddfrey owns a fairly substantial shipping company in London. He's purchased quite a few ships from your brother over the past years. Why do you ask?"

Sammy tried to look casual. "Oh, because last night at Almack's I overheard some gentlemen discussing the fact that several of the viscount's vessels had been lost. …I was hoping Barrett Shipping hadn't constructed them."

"I don't believe so, my lady."

"The gentlemen also mentioned that Viscount Goddfrey had bolted."

"Idle gossip, I'm certain." Smitty sounded equally as uncomfortable with this subject as he had with the previous one. "If I were you, I shouldn't waste my time on business matters, Lady Samantha. Nor on the Earl of Gresham," he repeated emphatically, bringing the conversation back to its original topic. "Your great aunt will undoubtedly introduce you to many suitable escorts during the Season."

"Actually, Aunt Gertie was quite taken with Remington," Sammy replied, a twinkle in her eye.

"Perhaps she hasn't heard of his reputation."

"That's very likely. Aunt Gertie hasn't *heard* anything for years now." Sammy laughed and leaned up to kiss Smitty's weathered cheek. "Stop fretting. I'll be fine." She gave him a warm hug. "I'm going to my bedchamber to continue reading *Mansfield Park*. I'll be down for dinner."

Hearing her footsteps fade away, Smitty mopped his damp brow with a handkerchief. Facing an armed naval brigade was beginning to look infinitely more appealing to him than chaperoning Lady Samantha through her first London Season.

And being taken prisoner would pale in comparison to facing the duke.

Rem tore Boyd's message into shreds and tossed the remains into the fire. Good. The groundwork had been laid. Rumors were already circulating that Rem had just lost a sizable fortune on an ill-fated business venture, and that he was in grave financial straits. Icily, he wondered how long it would take the news to reach Knollwood. Goddfrey had implied that the bloodsucker acquired his information posthaste. That remained to be seen. But in the meantime, all Rem could do was wait.

Goddfrey.

The viscount's name triggered the same unanswered question that had nagged at Rem since yesterday's ride in Hyde Park. What did Samantha know of Goddfrey's predicament? How had she linked Goddfrey's name with the vanishing ships? Where the hell did she get her facts?

The logical answer was from her brother. Drake Barrett must have a private source of information; Rem knew he had to learn what, or who, that was. Tonight. He'd gently pry the facts from Samantha tonight, without further encouraging her romantic fantasy.

Which was turning into his sexual preoccupation.

It had to stop. Now.

Only hurt could result from fueling the passion that blazed between him and Drake Barrett's sister. Rem refused to succumb to
it—not when the result would mean Samantha's ruin. There was no
other plausible alternative. A lasting relationship was inconceivable
in his type of life. His future consisted of but two things, both of
which thoroughly conflicted with Samantha's dreams of marriage
and family: freedom to satisfy his missions, and variety to satisfy his
passions.

Variety. An amusing concept, he reflected with a self-deprecating smile. In truth, he hadn't sought out one damned woman since
the night he'd met Samantha … nor had he any desire to do so.

Well, he'd have to change all that. Immediately.

Jaw set with purpose, Rem headed upstairs to dress for the opera.

His final thought was that he'd kill Anders if the bastard so much
as touched Samantha.

"Millie, for heaven's sake, stop crying! I know you didn't mean
to tear the gown—let's just choose another." Sammy was beginning
to lose patience with her wailing maid.

"It's no use, my lady." Millie wrung her hands, staring mourn-
fully at the rended bodice of Samantha's evening gown. "I'm just no
good at being a lady's maid."

With an exasperated sigh, Sammy turned. "You're perfectly capable. It's only—"

"I hate it."

"Pardon me?" Samantha dropped her arms to her sides.

"Forgive me, Lady Samantha, but I just hate doin' this!" A fresh
wave of tears. "I'm not suited to it!"

For the first time Sammy realized that Millie wasn't just inept,
she was unhappy. "There, there, Millie, don't cry." Tossing the ruined
dress to the bed, Sammy handed Millie a handkerchief and patted
her shaking shoulders. "Every problem has a solution. Tell me, what
do you do at my aunt's home in Hampshire?"

"Oh, my lady, I never cry there!" Instantly, Millie brightened. "I help in the kitchen—the cook is *my* aunt, you see. I also tidy up the lower level, and sometimes I even gather fresh flowers for the morning room."

"I see." Thoughtfully, Sammy tapped her chin.

"Please don't be angry, my lady. 'Tisn't you, I swear it. You've been as kind and patient as a saint—"

"You needn't explain, I understand. Tell me, Millie, would you be happy if I could arrange for you to return to Hampshire?" When the maid hesitated, Sammy pressed, "The truth now, Millie."

"Yes, ma'am. I would."

"Very well. Give me a day or two. I have to think of a way to bring this up to Aunt Gertie without upsetting her. I personally would have no objections to forfeiting a maid altogether, but I don't think my aunt would approve. So let me think of a worthy substitute for you, all right?"

"Oh, thank you! Thank you, my lady! Thank you!" Impulsively, Millie flung her arms about Sammy's neck, then backed off, red-faced.

"It's quite all right." Samantha grinned. "But until your replacement is found, do you think we might make the best of things and *try* to get me dressed for the opera so I don't have to greet Remington in a chemise?"

"Yes, ma'am. Of course, ma'am." Millie scurried over to the wardrobe with new determination. "Which gown would you like, my lady?"

"I thought perhaps the crimson velvet. What do you think?"

"I think it would be perfect."

"Wonderful! Then let's make an attempt to get it on without mishap."

"Yes, ma'am." Clumsily, Millie helped Sammy into the rich layers of fabric, sighing with relief when, at last, she finished buttoning up the back. "The viscount is terribly handsome, my lady."

"Hmm?" Sammy was already lost in thought, imagining what new ground she would break with Remington tonight.

"The gentleman who called on you this afternoon. Viscount Anders, wasn't it?"

"Oh, Stephen. Yes, he is handsome." Sammy gathered up her tresses. "I believe I'll wear my hair up tonight—it makes me look older, more experienced, wouldn't you say?"

"I suppose so, my lady. Will the viscount be escorting you tonight, as well?"

"Oh, no." In truth, Sammy could scarcely remember the quarter hour she'd spent in Stephen's company. He'd been delightful, respectful, and charming … and all she'd thought about was Remington. "The Earl of Gresham will be my escort this evening."

"Oh! Isn't that the gentleman you consider … special?"

"It is indeed." Sammy sat down at the dressing table and proceeded to toy with her hair. "Let's do our best to make me as desirable as possible, shall we, Millie?"

Millie blushed. "Yes, ma'am."

Thirty minutes later Sammy whirled about before the looking glass, slipping her final hairpin into the coronet of roses upon her head. "Well, have we succeeded, Millie?" she demanded with a grin. "Do I look so enticing that no man could resist me?"

"Oh, yes, my lady," Millie breathed, her eyes wide with admiration. "You look beautiful."

"Thank you. I only hope that Remington agrees."

Remington agreed.

He, who, over the years, had beheld countless ravishing women in every possible state of dress and undress, required a full minute to recover himself when Samantha first made her appearance.

"Will I do, my lord?"

She was going to be the death of him yet. "You'll more than do, my lady." Rem swallowed, audibly. "I don't believe a single gentleman in Covent Garden Theater will be able to concentrate on tonight's opera."

"Will you?" She tipped her head back, gazing up at him with innocent provocation.

Again, that damned guileless candor. Rem clenched his fists against his sides. He wasn't going to yield to it again. He couldn't.

His loins throbbed their disagreement.

"I'll do my best," he replied carefully.

"In that case, I hope the coach ride is endless."

Rem's lips twitched as he guided her from the Town house. "It won't be. We're only a short distance from the theater. And tonight I did bring my phaeton."

Sammy stopped short, crestfallen. "Oh."

"I thought you were going to control that dangerous honesty of yours," Rem reminded her gently when they were on their way.

"I tried. I cannot. It seems to be an unshakable part of me."

"I see. Was it conspicuous with Viscount Anders this afternoon?" Rem realized he sounded exactly the way he felt: possessive.

"I don't know," Sammy replied in uncertain bewilderment.

"What does that mean?"

"It means, I don't recall much of Stephen's visit." She bit her tongue to keep from blurting out that all she'd been able to think about was Rem. "I was preoccupied."

"With what we discussed yesterday?"

"Pardon me?"

"Barrett Shipping."

"Oh … that. I suppose so." It was better for Remington to believe she was pondering the family business than the truth: that she was trying to think of ways to make him fall in love with her. "I'm c-concerned about our ships." Oh, why did she have to be such a wretched liar?

Rem was thinking much the same thing. He knew what he had to do, and felt guilty as hell for doing it. With substantial effort, he pushed his conscience aside. "You mentioned a man named Goddfrey. Is he a friend of your family's?"

"A business associate." She prayed Rem would attribute the trembling in her voice to the swaying of the carriage. "Why?"

"Just curious." Rem's tone was nonchalant, his gaze fixed on the road.

"Are *you* acquainted with Viscount Goddfrey?" Sammy knew her own attempt at nonchalance was an abysmal failure.

"Somewhat. We've run into each other at White's from time to time."

"Was he gambling or abstaining?"

"Now, that's a curious question." Rem feigned surprised. "Why would you inquire about something like that?"

Sammy averted her eyes. "I'd heard he's endured recent business losses."

Rem shrugged. "Idle gossip, most likely. You know how rumors pass from one wagging tongue to the next."

"You sound just like Smitty," Sammy muttered, half to herself. "He mollified me with almost those exact words."

So she'd been questioning Smithers about Goddfrey, Rem thought. Interesting. And evidently, Allonshire's trusted valet had told her nothing.

Did he know more?

The silence in the carriage stretched, as Rem cautiously chose his next approach.

"Remington?" Sammy lay a gloved hand over his.

"What?" Perhaps Samantha herself would provide him with the appropriate avenue.

"Before we arrive ..." She hesitated, chewing worriedly at her lower lip.

"Go on."

"Would you kiss me? Just once?"

Whatever Rem had been expecting, it hadn't been this. "Would I ...?"

"We shan't be alone all evening," she rushed on. "And I've never experienced sensations like the ones I feel when I'm in your arms. It's as if tiny bubbles are bursting inside my chest, growing larger, popping faster, while at the same time my stomach is sliding down a long hill to my feet. My head swims until I'm so dizzy, I can't think." Tentatively, Sammy stroked the fine material of Rem's sleeve. "The feelings are truly miraculous. At least for me. I simply hoped—"

That did it.

With a muffled curse, Rem veered the phaeton sharply to the roadside and brought it to an abrupt halt. Before Samantha could regain her balance, he took it away again, dragging her into his arms with shaking hands.

"It's no use. Dammit, it's no use," he growled, burying his lips in hers. With the reckless intensity of a summer storm, he gave reign to the fierce emotions she spawned inside him. His tongue invaded her mouth, stroking hungrily, giving her what she wanted, taking for himself what he craved.

For the endless moments they kissed, all else was forgotten. Resolutions were cast to the wind, unanswered questions were gladly relinquished, the past was laid to rest.

And Samantha was his.

"Christ, you intoxicate me," he muttered. "I can't let this happen ... yet I can't keep my hands off you."

"You didn't initiate this, Remington," she whispered back, caressing his smooth-shaven jaw, reveling in the joy of being in his arms once more. "I did."

"That doesn't excuse my lack of control." He circled his lips sensuously against hers, making no move to release her.

"Must we go to the opera?"

"Yes."

"Why?"

"Because if we don't, I'll take you to bed."

"That doesn't frighten me." She kissed his chin.

"It should." Instinctively, his arms tightened about her. "The problem is, you're just too damned innocent to know what it means."

Sammy leaned back—only enough to meet his gaze. "I know that people make love in bed. I know they take off their clothes and join their bodies in some manner that is wonderful for both of them. I know that new lives are created this way."

A warm, tender light flickered in Rem's eyes, kindled in his heart. "You're almost beautiful enough to make me believe again."

"Believe what? What is it you don't believe?"

Rem eased away from her. "That, imp, would take hours to discuss. And, as the opera begins in ten minutes—"

"Was it a woman?"

"No." Shutters descended over his eyes. "That would be far easier from which to recover."

"Then …"

"Now is not the time, Samantha." He lifted the reins.

"Remington." Sammy stayed him with her hand. "It's never the time; not for us to talk, nor to be in each other's arms. You tell me I'm a dreamer. Perhaps I am. But, in truth, I think it is you who seeks to escape, not I."

For a long moment Rem was silent, motionless. Then he brought Sammy's fingers to his lips.

"Perhaps you're right, imp. Perhaps you're right."

With a snap of his wrist, they were on their way.

The opera had scarcely ended when a stout, purposeful messenger scurried down the aisle, halting beside Rem's seat.

"Lord Gresham?"

"Yes?"

"I have an urgent message for you, my lord."

"Thank you." Rem took the slip of paper, pressing several shillings into the grateful man's palm.

"Thank *you,* sir." He waited while Rem scanned the contents of the note. "Will there be any reply, my lord?"

"Hmm?" Rem looked up, his thoughts already far away. "No, no reply will be necessary."

"Very good, sir. And thank you again, sir. Good night." The messenger bowed and took his leave.

"Remington? What is it?" Sammy peered around to see what the note said.

Hastily, Rem crumpled the message and jammed it into his pocket. "I have to meet someone. Immediately."

"Oh. I see. Is anything amiss?"

"No, only a business matter. But a crucial one." He raised his voice a bit. "One that could result in my recovering a great deal of money."

Sammy looked startled. "Are you in need of funds?"

"Unfortunately … yes, at the moment I am." He frowned. "Samantha, would you be terribly upset if I arranged for someone else to see you home?"

"Disappointed, yes, but not upset—especially if it's a matter of such grave importance." Sammy scrutinized the room. "I see at least a dozen people I know, Remington. Any one of them can escort me home. Please don't be concerned."

A smile touched his lips. "I fear I'm destined to be perpetually concerned over your well-being, imp. I don't seem to be able to help it."

"That's because you're a—"

"I know. A hero." He touched the tip of her nose. "We'll argue that point another time. In the interim—"

"There's Aunt Gertie's dear friend, the Dowager Duchess of Arvel," Sammy interrupted. "I'll seek a ride with her."

"Fine. Let's go speak with her."

"You needn't—"

"Samantha, I'm not leaving until I know you're provided for."

"Very well."

The wistful note in her voice gave him pause. "I'm sorry our evening is ending like this, imp. I promise to make it up to you."

"When?"

He gave a rich chuckle. "Monday evening? Vauxhall will be admitting guests. We can stroll through the gardens."

"It's still chilly. Very few people will be about." Sammy's lips curved upward. "It sounds heavenly."

"Come." He seized her elbow. "I'll arrange for your safe transport home."

The arrangements quickly and efficiently made, Rem expressed his gratitude to the elderly dowager and, with a quick, discreet wink at Samantha, wove his way through the crowd and out the theater door.

Where could he be going? Sammy wondered, staring after his retreating back. Who on earth could he be meeting at this hour of night? The circumstances must be dire, else it could certainly wait until day.

The thought made Sammy's tender heart melt, and her active brain buzz. What could she do to help?

Drake. Sammy's eyes lit up as the idea struck her. Her brother had more than enough money to offer Remington a loan. Oh, to be sure, Drake would require more details before he'd agree to do so—details that the indulgent Earl of Gresham was highly unlikely to divulge, at least to her.

She'd obtain them herself.

Impulsively, wholeheartedly, Sammy made her decision. How many times now had Remington proven himself to be her hero? Didn't she owe it to him to be his heroine as well?

Indeed she did. Thus, she was going to rescue him … with or without his permission.

"Are you ready, Samantha?" The elderly dowager peered down her long nose at Sammy.

"Actually ... no." Sammy glanced quickly at the door. Remington couldn't have gotten far, yet, but she had no time to waste.

"Pardon me?"

"I mean ... thank you, Your Grace, but I won't be needing your kind assistance, after all. Smitty evidently sent a carriage for me—I recognize our driver gesturing to me from the doorway."

Smoothing the ostrich plume in her turban, the dowager scowled over the milling crowd. "Where? I don't see him."

"He's there—trust me." Sammy was already moving away. "I don't want to miss him. Thank you ever so much, Your Grace. I'll be sure to send your regards to Aunt Gertie."

Sammy was still babbling when she exploded onto the sidewalk a half minute later. Inhaling sharply, she searched the street.

Luck was with her. Remington's phaeton was just being brought around front.

She tarried as long as she dared, then inched forward a fraction at a time, praying Remington wouldn't pivot about and spy her.

An eternity passed in the space of a moment.

At last. He was seated, his back turned toward her.

Her breath held in abeyance, Sammy took the final steps swiftly, fervently hoping the crowd was too thick, the patrons too preoccupied, to notice her. She tucked her skirts beneath her and slid into the groom's seat at the rear of the carriage. Ducking down, she curled into what she hoped was an invisible ball.

Shrouded in darkness, the phaeton sped off through the night.

EIGHT

Samantha had the feeling she wasn't in fashionable London anymore.

Conversely, she had absolutely *no* feeling in her arms and legs, and if the carriage hit one more bump, she was going to be violently ill on the groom's seat.

Where were they?

It seemed they'd ridden for hours, leaving the opera and the *ton* far behind. In Sammy's contorted position she was unable to see much of her surroundings, but she could make out a few broken-down houses and an occasional unkempt, dirty vagrant in the street.

What sort of business meeting could take place here?

Certainly, anyone who lived in such a shabby section of town couldn't afford to loan Remington money. Perhaps something sinister was planned, something that would place Remington in grave danger.

It was a good thing she'd come.

The phaeton slowed, then halted, shifting a bit as Remington alighted.

"I'll be less than an hour," Sammy heard Rem mutter to someone.

"I'll watch the phaeton fer ye, sir," a gruff voice replied.

"Fine." Remington's heels echoed on the pavement, and a moment later a door opened, then closed.

Sammy could have argued with how "fine" it was. How in the world was she going to alight with a sentry posted beside the carriage?

Her luck held.

" 'Ello, Jack."

"Chelsea! I didn't know ye were workin' tonight."

"I wasn't s'posed to … but I 'eard from Annie ye were comin'."

Evidently, Remington's helper had met a lady with whom he was acquainted. Now was Sammy's only chance.

Gingerly, she eased herself onto her haunches, nearly crying aloud as shards of pain shot through her cramped limbs. She bit back the cry, maneuvering herself to the side of the phaeton farthest from the chatting couple. She paused.

"I've missed ye, Chels. It's not the same without ye."

A throaty chuckle. "And just 'ow many women 'ave you told that line to?"

An answering chuckle, one that told Sammy the man called Jack was still very much engrossed in his lady friend.

Sammy sprang lightly to the street, ducking beside the carriage and waiting.

"I'm not busy with anyone else tonight, Jack. Are ye interested?"

"Ye know I am."

Peeking over the top of the phaeton, Sammy blinked. Working? Busy with anyone else? What sort of establishment was this shoddy place anyway?

She intended to find out.

"Annie." Rem tipped his hat.

"Well, hello, Rem, don't you look dashing tonight?"

Glancing down at his formal attire, Rem grinned. "I came directly from my evening engagement."

"Then she must not have been as good as my girls. You're wearing far too much clothing."

A corner of Rem's mouth lifted. "I do emerge from the bedroom occasionally, you know."

"Occasionally." Annie's tone was dry. Seeing Rem scan the room, she added, "Boyd's in his usual spot. Go on. I'll send some drinks back."

"Thanks, love." Rem kissed her hand and headed to the back of the room.

"That one's special, Cynthia," Annie murmured to the dark-eyed young woman who walked over just then. "He has a way of making a whore feel like a lady." Wistfully, Annie touched her hand where Rem had kissed it.

"There are very few of those," Cynthia replied. "Very few."

Annie glanced up at the cynicism in her new girl's tone. It wasn't the first time she'd heard that note of disdain for men—not only from Cynthia, but from many of her girls. She understood it well. She also understood, however, that its manifestation had no place in their line of work. Therefore, all her girls had strict instructions to leave their personal grievances outside the paying customer's door. And Cynthia was no exception.

In every other way, however, she was.

Cynthia had been in Annie's employ just shy of a week, but it had taken less than a day for the men to start clamoring for the creamy-skinned beauty, and less time still for Annie to realize that Cynthia was far too refined to be a prostitute.

Adhering to her usual policy, Annie asked no questions, not even when the brothel was quiet and she could hear Cynthia's muffled sobs echo from behind her tightly closed door. No, whatever ailed the new girl was none of her concern, Annie told herself. Cynthia commanded a good price, and her past—along with any heartache it contained—was her own business.

And speaking of business ... "Wouldn't hurt you to stroll back there," Annie suggested shrewdly, gesturing toward Rem and Boyd. "Rem is rich as hell and handsome as sin. He's an earl."

Cynthia's slender brows rose. "A member of the peerage, is he?"

"Yes, why? Do noblemen entice you?"

A bitter laugh was her reply. "Hardly, Annie. I assure you, in bed, all men are alike. And there's nothing noble about them."

"He pays well … and he's good. Just ask Katrina. She swears he spends more time satisfying her than—"

"I understand," Cynthia interrupted. "I'll make it my business to stop by the earl's table and see if I appeal to him."

Annie surveyed Cynthia's warm, wheat-colored hair, the startling contrast of her jet-black eyes and thick, sooty lashes, the regal features and delicate curves that belonged more to a lady than a whore. "Honey, you appeal to everyone."

Cynthia didn't smile. "Thanks." She walked off to do her job.

"Rem. Good. You're here." Boyd leaned forward eagerly to greet his friend.

"I came as soon as I got your message. I take it we heard from Knollwood." Briefly, Rem glanced over his shoulder, scanning the room through narrowed eyes. After a minute he turned back to Boyd.

"We sure did." Boyd was unfolding a sheet of paper, his tone laced with sarcasm. "He got word that you're in need of money, and he'd like to help."

"Let me see." Rem took the scrawled message. "That was certainly fast."

"Parasites have many ears," Boyd replied dryly. "And I have many sources. I used them all."

"How did you handle my proviso—demanding that Knollwood contact me solely through you?"

"Simple. I specified that you're desperately trying to salvage the remains of your reputation … a futile effort, should anyone link your name with his."

"He voiced no objections?" Rem pored over the note.

"None—as you can see for yourself." Boyd took an angry swallow of gin. "Evidently, Mr. Knollwood is a most reasonable man, until he owns your very soul. Then, he becomes the miserable gutter rat he really is."

"Ummm … we're to meet in the alley at the west end of Wentworth Street near Petticoat Lane."

"A charming neighborhood." Boyd scowled. "Watch your pockets, Rem—and your back."

"Three A.M.," Rem continued. "Tonight."

"That's why I sent a messenger to drag you out of the theater. We have very little time to plan our tactics." Boyd paused. "How was the opera, by the way?"

"Fine."

"And Samantha?"

"Driving me crazy."

Boyd chuckled. "You're fighting a losing battle, I fear."

"Let's stick to the subject at hand, shall we?"

A twinkle. "All right." Boyd set down his mug. "Do you want me to back you up? In case things with Knollwood get nasty?"

"No. It's too risky. If he sees you, he'll bolt. We won't get another chance. I'll have to handle it on my own." Again, Rem averted his head, nagged by the persistent feeling he was being watched. But all he saw were revelers drinking and dancing. Nothing appeared amiss.

"How are you going to find out if Knollwood had a hand in the sinkings?" Boyd was asking.

Rem turned back to face his friend. "That depends on the conversation he and I have. I'll take it as it comes."

"If he's armed—" Abruptly, Boyd halted.

Senses already heightened by suspicion, Rem jerked about at Boyd's unexpected lapse and odd expression. Following his friend's mesmerized gaze, Rem prepared to strike, a tiger stalking his prey.

"Hello, gentlemen." The surprising "prey" glided over, lingering beside their table. "Can I get you anything? Another round of drinks, perhaps?"

Rem started. A woman? Impossible. Boyd never reacted this dramatically to women, least of all one of Annie's girls. Catching another glimpse of Boyd's face, Rem hastily altered his opinion.

There was an instant of charged silence. At last Rem cleared his throat and replied, "Another round of drinks would be greatly appreciated." More silence. "Have we met?" he tried next, wondering if Boyd were ever going to snap out of his reverie.

"No, I don't believe so." Cynthia shook her head. "I've only been"—the barest of pauses—"working at Annie's for a week. My name is Cynthia."

"A pleasure, Cynthia." By this time Rem was having trouble containing his amusement. Cynthia was an extremely lovely, soft-spoken woman of perhaps two and twenty, who looked more like a gently bred lady than a courtesan. And Boyd, Rem's rugged, hard-edged friend, who liked his women sturdy and seasoned, was staring at her as if she were a priceless painting—one he would give anything to possess. "Permit me to return your introduction," Rem continued. "I'm Remington Worth and this is Boyd Hayword. You'll probably be seeing quite a bit of us. We're frequent guests at Annie's." To Rem's surprise, his final words elicited a flicker of anger in Cynthia's eyes, one that dissipated so swiftly that a less observant man would have missed it.

"Mr. Hayword. Mr. Worth …" Cynthia stumbled over Rem's name. "Forgive me. Annie mentioned you were titled. How shall I address you?"

The distaste tinged her tone much as it had her eyes, subtly, yet definitively. Interesting.

"Titles have no place at Annie's," Rem assured her. "Feel free to use my given name."

"Very well." Cynthia inclined her head toward Boyd. "Does that apply to you as well, sir?"

At last Boyd found his tongue. "It most assuredly does, as I have no title to boast."

The genuine humility of Boyd's response struck home. "I see." Cynthia's expression softened. "Well then … Boyd, can I offer you anything besides that drink?"

"Only the gin … and perhaps your company." Boyd might have been requesting a maiden's first dance, so honorable was his tone.

A tinge of color rose to Cynthia's cheeks. "I'll see to the gin right away. The company we can discuss later."

"You'd best toss down that drink in a hurry," Rem commented when Cynthia was out of earshot. "You need it."

"What?" Boyd was still gaping.

"She won't disappear, Boyd. She'll be back."

This time Rem's sarcasm penetrated Boyd's fog. "Lord, she's beautiful," he muttered. "Too beautiful to be—" He broke off.

"I agree. She also appears somewhat taken with you."

"I wonder what the hell she's doing here?" Boyd scowled. "Surely such a woman could seek another means of employment."

"You really are smitten, aren't you?" Rem asked in surprise. "I've never seen you like this."

Boyd regarded Rem with probing intensity. "Really? Well, I've seen *you* precisely like this—every time we speak of Samantha Barrett. The difference, my friend, is that I'm honest enough to admit there's a void in my life … which is more than I can say for you." Boyd gripped the table. "I'm searching, Rem. As I've said in the past, I need more than the satisfaction of knowing I've dedicated my life to England. I need to care for someone, and for that someone to care for me. I need to leave my personal mark on this world … to have a family, a foundation."

"All of this with a winsome courtesan you've just laid eyes on for the first time?"

"No. All of this with a woman I can love."

A dark cloud passed over Rem's face. "You sound like Samantha. Coming from her, I can understand it. She's a romantic child. But you, Boyd? What is this sudden preoccupation with falling in love?"

"It isn't sudden. Nor should it only be *my* preoccupation." Exasperated, Boyd shook his head. "You're so damned stubborn, Rem; so determined to keep your scars raw, never allowing them to heal. Is self-protection really worth all that?"

"For me, yes."

"Well, it isn't for me."

"What about Boydry's?"

"What about it? It's a bloody tavern, Rem, not a person. I set it up to suit the Admiralty, and you know it. I'd much prefer operating a coffeehouse with sober, respectable patrons than a dilapidated pub in the worst section of London."

Their discussion ceased as Cynthia returned, setting two mugs on the table. Vaguely, Rem was aware that snatches of conversation were transpiring between Cynthia and Boyd, but the majority of his attention was claimed by a resurgence of the powerful warning sensation that plagued him earlier. Dammit. Something was wrong.

This time he swiveled totally about, boldly scrutinizing the room.

"That's the second time you've done that since you arrived," Boyd murmured when Cynthia had gone.

One corner of Rem's mouth lifted. "I'm glad to see you're still alert … despite your budding infatuation."

Boyd didn't smile. "What is it?"

"I don't know. Nothing probably. I just have this nagging feeling I'm being watched."

"Were you followed?"

Rem frowned. "I don't think so. In truth, I was so rushed, I didn't pay much attention."

"I wouldn't worry too much about it," Boyd replied, scanning the room. "Anyone who followed you to Annie's would assume you're merely enjoying the entertainment."

The person who'd followed Rem was assuming exactly that.

Sammy, just moments ago, had realized what sort of establishment she was observing. Shocked and hurt, she'd crept closer, peering inside to convince herself that Remington was, indeed, a patron. Seeing him flash his dimple at the woman who was handing him a drink, Sammy's eyes filled with tears. Not only was he frequenting this seedy brothel, but he had deceived her about the purpose for his hasty departure from the opera. What kind of hero, conventional or not, cavorted with prostitutes, and lied, as well?

The untainted entity of Sammy's blind faith fragmented … a bit. Still, she refused to allow it to shatter completely. As a heroine, it was up to her to reform her hero.

Now, if she only knew precisely how to go about it …

Pensively, Sammy paced the length of the shadowy street. She'd never lain with a man; these women were proficient at it. Remington was deterred by her inexperience. He didn't want her; yet he didn't want her to lie with another. So, how could she gain the experience he obviously sought without angering him? This was all dreadfully confusing.

" 'Ey, love! What've we 'ere? A little jewel, I'd say!"

The slurred male voice cut into Sammy's thoughts.

"Pardon me?" She blinked into the darkness.

"Look, Blake! We've found ourselves a regular lady, we 'ave!"

Three unkempt, burly men loomed before her.

"Whatcha lookin' fer, yer highness? Yer coach?"

A tight knot of fear formed in Sammy's stomach. Furtively, she looked about, praying for another person to call out to. But the shoddy street was deserted.

Instinctively, she backed off.

"Where ye goin', m'lady?" The first man stalked forward and snatched her wrist. "We 'aven't 'ad the chance to impress ye yet!"

"Please," she whispered, "let me go."

"Ah, now is that nice?" He pulled her against him, so close she could smell the alcohol on his breath. She shuddered. "Ye're a good lookin' little thing, ye know?" He traced the top of her bodice. "Real good-lookin'."

"Stop it!" Sammy began to struggle. "Unhand me at once!"

"Unhand 'er!" the second stalker mocked. "Well, maybe the lady prefers t' entertain in private, Gates. What do ye say we find out?"

"No!" Wildly, Sammy fought against her unyielding captor. He dragged her with him as if she weighed nothing, with only an occasional grunt to indicate he was aware of her struggles.

"Feisty, ain't she? 'Ope she's as good when we get 'er 'ome," the third derelict chimed in.

"Gates, just what do you think you're doing?" A clear female voice rang out through the night.

Sammy's captor came to a dead halt. "Cynthia?"

"I asked what you were doing!" Cynthia walked purposefully toward them, her eyes ablaze.

"We're just 'avin' a little fun, that's all."

"With one of Annie's girls? You know better than that!"

Gates's eyes bulged. "This 'ere's one of Annie's? But she looks like—"

"I don't care what she looks like! Do you want me to march in there and tell Annie that the three of you are abducting her newest employee? If so, I will—and then I wouldn't dare show my face at Annie's again, if I were you."

"'Ell, no!" the third man cut in hastily. "Ye know we don't mess with Annie's girls. We just didn't know." He averted his head. "Let 'er go, Gates," he ordered his friend, who was still clutching a white-faced Samantha. "Now. My favorite woman works at Annie's."

With a muttered oath, Gates thrust Sammy at Cynthia. "First you, now 'er. Cynthia, tell Annie she should start hiring girls that look like whores, not blue bloods." He turned his back. "Let's go," he muttered to his friends.

Sammy waited until they'd disappeared before she collapsed. Leaning against the brick wall behind her, she began to shake uncontrollably. "Thank you," she whispered.

"You're welcome." Gently, Cynthia steadied Sammy's trembling shoulders. "Are you all right?"

"I think so … thanks to you."

"What on earth are you doing here?"

"I'm … that is …" Sammy closed her eyes. "It's too complicated to explain."

"Try me. I'm a good listener."

Opening her eyes, Sammy regarded her rescuer. "You're the one who was serving him his drink," she blurted out.

"Who?"

"My …" Sammy paused. What could she call Remington? He wasn't her husband, nor even her betrothed. In fact, he regarded her as a burdensome child. And she certainly couldn't explain to this … woman that Remington was her hero. "The gentleman at the far table. Remington Worth. The Earl of Gresham," she said at last.

"Ah, I see." A small smile played about Cynthia's lips. "You're concerned about your man's fidelity, are you? Well, I wouldn't take his visits here too much to heart. I'm sure he places you on the appropriate pedestal—his chaste and precious possession. Unfortunately, he, like all men, are governed primarily by their sordid needs. Sex is their compulsion, indulging in it their God-given right."

"If you feel that way, why do you provide it?"

Cynthia's eyes glittered with suppressed emotion. "The answer is ugly—I assure you, you don't want to hear it."

"What is it I don't want to hear? That you've chosen to service men for a living?"

"*Chosen?*" Bitterness clogged Cynthia's throat. "Do you honestly believe I've *chosen* this sort of life? No, genteel lady, my vile job was thrust upon me."

"You're forced to be with men?" Sammy was horrified.

"I told you the truth was ugly."

"How deplorable! I never imagined …" Reflexively, Sammy squeezed Cynthia's hand, totally forgetting her own harrowing ordeal in lieu of this poor woman's plight.

Cynthia stared down at Sammy's smooth hand clasping her own work-worn one, a blunt reminder of the differences in their stations, the futures that awaited them. Suddenly all the repressed pain of the past weeks converged and exploded, sliding down Cynthia's cheeks in a bitter flow of tears. "Forgive me … I don't normally weep in front of total strangers."

"I'm not a stranger—you just saved my life," Sammy reminded her. "And I, too, am a good listener."

Bleakly, Cynthia studied Sammy's earnest face. "You're a sheltered, innocent little thing. Nobly bred, of course. My story is not for your ears."

"Who forces you to service these men?" Sammy demanded.

"Circumstances. The unshakable power of the nobility."

"Cynthia … that is your name, isn't it? I heard that horrid"—she shuddered—"Gates person call you by it." Waiting only for a nod, Sammy continued, "I cannot deny my naiveté nor my heritage. But being titled does not preclude having a heart. I'd like to help. Truly."

"There's nothing you can do. The damage has already been done."

"Damage? What damage?" Sammy gripped Cynthia's hand tightly. "Tell me."

"Very well, *my lady.*" Cynthia took a deep, shuddering breath. "I was born to a decent, hardworking family whose only misfortune was to be poor. Early on, I was encouraged to strive high, to be the first to emerge from my parents' poverty. To that end, I studied incessantly. I was elated when my hard work paid off. After but one application, I was hired as a governess at a magnificent estate in Surrey. The gentleman who hired me was wealthy, titled … and very solicitous." Cynthia gave a hollow laugh. "How naive I was! I believed he was the kindest of men, devoted to his wife, interested in his children's well-being, and therefore in my suitability."

"He wasn't?"

"Oh, he was interested in my suitability, all right … but in the bedroom, not the nursery."

Sammy gasped. "He made advances?"

"He raped me."

All the color drained from Samantha's face. "Dear God. What did you do?"

"What could I do? I cried until I was hollow and dead inside. Then I packed and left."

"Who is this man? Surely he was arrested, or punished in some manner."

"As I said, you're a sheltered, innocent child. No, he wasn't punished; I was. He? He came to my room mere hours later, stunned to find me packing. He assured me there was no reason for me to leave, that I'd pleased him enormously and that I could continue to do so. How proud he looked, as if he were bestowing upon me the greatest of honors.

"When I became hysterical, sobbing out my hatred, my intentions to seek out another job at once, he laughed in my face. He then assured me that, after he was finished spreading the word of what a common trollop I was, no respectable family would hire me. He was right. Time and again I was turned away … as if I were unwanted refuse of some kind."

"What about your family?"

"My mother is gone now. My father is old, and very set in his ways. He wouldn't even listen to me."

"He thought you were lying?"

"It didn't matter. The end result was the same. I was ruined. What was done could not be undone. Then there was the matter of money. We had none. My wages as a governess was our only hope—a hope I had extinguished. My father couldn't bear the sight of me ... and I couldn't bear the guilt. So I ran."

"To Annie's?"

"Not right away. Not until I recognized the truth ... that, thanks to what that *nobleman* did to me, Annie's is all I'm suited for."

"Oh, Cynthia, don't say that." Sammy dashed the tears from her cheeks. "How long have you worked here?"

"A week ... the most torturous week of my life."

"Well, it's over now."

"Another week will begin."

"Not here it won't. At least not for you."

Cynthia blinked. "Pardon me?"

Sammy seized Cynthia's sleeve. "You're coming home with me."

"I'm what? But I don't even know you!"

"My name is Samantha Barrett. I'm in London for my first Season. I'm staying with my aunt Gertrude. I have a brother named Drake, a temporary guardian named Smitty, a puppy named Rascal, and a collection of books as long as this street. What more do you need to know?"

"Why would you do this for me?"

"Because I like you. Because you saved my life. Because I hate what you've endured. Because it causes me great heartache to think of you forcing yourself to lie with men you care nothing for. Are those reasons enough?"

Cynthia shook her head in disbelief. "Does the Earl of Gresham know what he's getting himself into?"

The light in Sammy's eyes dimmed. "Evidently, whatever he's getting himself into tonight doesn't involve me."

"You're in love with him."

"Hopelessly."

"You're a fool."

"Definitely."

"Perhaps I will go home with you after all, Samantha," Cynthia decided on impulse. "I begin to see that you need help as much as I do. By accepting your kind offer, I'll be able to offer *you* the benefit of my insight."

"Wonderful! Can you leave right away?"

"Let me talk with Annie." Cynthia glanced curiously up and down the deserted street. "Is your carriage around back?"

"My carriage? Oh, goodness, I have none!"

"Then how did you get here?"

"In Remington's phaeton."

"He allowed you to accompany him to—"

"He didn't know. I hid."

Cynthia threw back her head and laughed. "Remington Worth has quite a challenge ahead of him." She drew Sammy to the door of the brothel. "Stand right here. That way I'll be able to see you, but your earl won't. Once I explain the situation to Annie, she'll arrange a ride for us."

"Will she be angry?"

"No. Contrary to what you might believe, the women here are far more honest and straightforward than the men who visit them. Many do this only as a means of survival … and Annie knows it. She's very shrewd. And, while I never told her exactly what happened to me, I'm sure she suspects. She won't stand in my way."

"Go ahead, then. I'll wait."

"Don't wander," Cynthia warned.

"Don't worry, I wouldn't even consider it." Sammy huddled nervously against the door.

Twenty minutes later Cynthia and Sammy were settled in a carriage, speeding toward the fashionable West End of London and Abingdon Street.

"What will you tell your aunt?" Cynthia asked curiously.

"Something loud enough for her to hear. But Aunt Gertie won't be my problem. My problem will be Smitty."

"Smitty?"

"The guardian I spoke of—a trusted servant and family friend. My brother appointed him to watch over me ... at least for the duration of the Season."

"Where is your brother?"

"In Berkshire. His wife is about to deliver their second child."

"And this Smitty won't approve of me?"

"Smitty won't even approve of me if I tell him where you and I met. He is terribly conventional ... but he has the most loving heart. I'll tell him as much of the truth as I dare." Sammy tapped her chin thoughtfully. "He knows I attended the opera tonight. Therefore, I came upon you in Covent Garden, weeping. We spoke. You told me that your employer had made improper advances, forcing you to flee. Smitty's protective instincts would never permit me to turn you away."

"Samantha ..." Cynthia fingered her plain frock. "What will I do at your Town house? I detest being idle. And I refuse to accept your kindness as charity. Is there no position open? A laundress, or a chambermaid?"

"That's it!" Sammy sat bolt upright.

"What's it?"

"Millie—my lady's maid!" Impulsively, Sammy hugged Cynthia. "Just tonight she begged me to allow her to return to her customary position in Hampshire. She loathes her job in Town. But Aunt Gertie would never permit her to leave unless I had a suitable replacement. Well, now I do!"

"You want me to be your lady's maid?"

"In name only," Sammy assured her. Rushing on, she added, "Would you mind very much? I don't really need a maid, but I do need a friend. You were right—I have been sheltered. There's so

much I don't understand, so many questions I have about men. Alexandria would answer them, but she's at Allonshire birthing a child.
And there's no other woman I can talk to." Sammy paused only to
inhale. "Anyway, since my lady's maid spends so much time with me
… well, it would give us a chance to get to know each other, to share
confidences."

A soft smile touched Cynthia's lips. "Samantha—pardon me—
my lady," she corrected herself, this time with a twinkle. "I would be
honored to accept the position."

NINE

The fog clung to Petticoat Lane, making the already menacing alley appear even more daunting, especially at the ungodly hour of 3 A.M.

Rem turned his collar up higher, ignoring the disreputable characters who stared at him from concealed corners, sizing him up as cohort or prey. Keeping his step purposeful, Rem's fingers slid into his pocket, closing around the pistol that was securely secreted there, ready to be extracted in a flash.

Reaching the designated area, he stopped.

"Lookin' fer someone, are ye?" An unsavory boy of no more than ten approached Rem, an ugly blade in his hand.

"Perhaps." Rem stared the urchin down.

"'Ave ye got money?"

"None."

"A watch, then?"

"No."

"Ah, come on"—the blade glinted—"surely ye must 'ave something in those pockets. Maybe I should 'ave a look … ?"

"I'll save you the trouble. The only thing I have in my pockets is this." In a heartbeat the pistol was leveled at the boy's chest. "Now, are there any other questions?"

His eyes wide, the boy backed off, shaking his head. "No. No questions. I meant no 'arm. J'st lookin' for a shillin' to feed myself, is all."

"Fine." Rem groped at his coat with his free hand and tossed a shilling at the boy's feet. "Go get yourself a meal … honestly, for a change."

Before Rem's words were out, the boy had snatched up the coin and bolted.

"Gresham?"

The gravelly voice came from beside Rem's elbow.

Veering abruptly, Rem aimed the pistol at the stranger's heart.

"Now, now, put that away," the stout man instructed calmly.

Pudgy. Unruly gray hair. Pale blue eyes. Of middle years. Goddfrey's description clicked in Rem's mind, leaving no doubt as to whom he was addressing.

"Knollwood." Rem tucked his pistol away. "I see you made it."

"I don't forget business appointments. I also don't believe in procrastinating. You wanted to see me. What can I do for you?"

"I need money."

"So I've heard." Knollwood took out a snuffbox, fingering it thoughtfully. "What makes you think I can help you?"

"I've heard tell that you're extremely liberal when it comes to loans."

"On occasion, yes. It depends on what the loan is for and how certain I am it will be repaid."

"It's for a ship, and I always repay my debts."

"A ship?" Knollwood's brows rose. "What sort of ship?"

Rem lit a cheroot, slowly exhaling into the night. "It's no secret that quite a few British ships have disappeared these past months. Many of them belonged to colleagues of mine. Knowing them as I do … well, let's say that instinct tells me carelessness played a big part in the losses."

"You believe you can manage things differently, I presume?"

"I believe that if I commission a ship, see it built to my specifi-cations, and supply it with my own captain and crew, I can not only avoid the disastrous fate these other ships have suffered, but make a fortune in the process—for myself *and* for you."

Knollwood's beady eyes gleamed. "Quite an undertaking."

"Are you interested?"

"I might be." Knollwood flipped open his box and pinched a healthy portion of snuff between his fingers. "How would you man-age to earn this fortune?"

"Think about it. Merchants are terrified to send their goods, for fear of losing them all. Let's say my ship traverses the seas once, twice, several times without incident. How much do you think merchants would pay to ensure that their cargo was carried on a consistently reliable vessel? My profits would soar. I could use them to purchase additional ships. Why, the investment could result in a whole fleet that would put all other fleets out of business."

"You're getting a bit ahead of yourself, Gresham. What happens in the meantime? It will take months until your fleet has established a reputation—preceded by months, maybe years, for it to become a fleet. How is my loan going to be protected? How do I know you'll be able to repay me? And what if your instincts are wrong and your so-called superior ship sinks like all the others?"

"I'm not a fool, Knollwood. I'll insure my vessel with a portion of the money I borrow. Your funds will be secure."

"It's a time of high risk."

"True. But it's also a time of high reward. If my intuition is wrong, you'll be repaid and I'll be bankrupt. However, if it's accurate, I'll be rich and you'll be richer."

"We have yet to discuss my terms."

"Whatever they are, I'll meet them. As I'm certain your sources told you, I've run out of options."

"How badly do you want this money?"

"You know the answer to that."

"How much will it take to buy and insure your ship?"

"I want more than my investment requires. I want enough to maintain my status—and my reputation—with the *beau monde*."

"How much?"

Rem thought of Goddfrey. "Two hundred thousand pounds."

"An outrageous sum." Calmly, Knollwood inhaled his snuff, then snapped the lid shut. "I assume you're willing to sign a note?"

"Of course."

"Without even knowing my terms?"

"Yes."

"You're that confident?"

"I am."

Knollwood nodded. "All right, Gresham. I'll need a few days to amass such a huge sum of money. Meet me here Monday night, same time. I'll bring your loan … and the necessary papers. You bring a quill to inscribe your name."

"Very well." Rem ground the cheroot beneath his heel. "You won't regret this decision. Others fail. I don't."

An ominous silence. "That remains to be seen, Gresham."

Knollwood disappeared into the night.

"My butler said you were here." Rem closed the sitting room door behind him. "Do you have so little faith in my ability to defend myself that you were worried … or is there some other reason you couldn't sleep?"

Boyd scowled. "Very funny."

"Your Cynthia did vanish rather suddenly, didn't she?" Rem strolled across the room and lowered himself into a chair. "It certainly altered your plans for the evening."

"I had no plans."

Rem cocked a disbelieving brow.

"All right, then. I had plans. Apparently, Cynthia didn't. In any case, I'm not here to discuss my romantic encounters, or lack of them."

"You really *are* upset, aren't you?" Rem stoked the fire, trying to oust the chill from his bones.

"Not upset. Stymied. Obviously, I read her signals all wrong."

"I don't think so … since I read her signals the same way you did." Rem cleared his throat. "Perhaps Annie had already committed Cynthia elsewhere for the evening."

Boyd gripped his chair arms so tightly his knuckles turned white. "Can we change the subject? I didn't come out at five A.M. to speculate about Cynthia's actions, or her whereabouts."

Lacing his fingers behind his head, Rem nodded. "My meeting with Knollwood." With calm precision, he recounted the details.

"Evidently, he didn't harm you. Did he threaten you?"

"No … at least not yet. But remember, he hasn't handed the money over either. I'm certain the threats will come once he owns me."

"I don't doubt it." Boyd squinted as the first patch of early morning sunlight seeped through the window, a reminder that it was nearly day. "Do you plan to handle this one alone, too?"

Rem shook his head. "No. I plan to find out if Knollwood will offer me his own personal insurance policy."

"Meaning?"

"Meaning, will he promise to make certain my ship remains safe, my venture secure, in exchange for an immense additional sum? If so, he's our man."

"Ah, I begin to see. You think he's been blackmailing men into buying his protection."

"Um-hum. And convincing those who are reluctant to do so by providing firsthand demonstrations of what will happen if they refuse to comply," Rem added.

"Interesting speculation. Now, what if Knollwood doesn't offer you this unique opportunity?"

"Then he's merely a bloodsucking, heartless parasite, rather than a mass murderer." Rem calmly crossed one leg over the other. "To answer your original question, I want Harris and Templar ready to grab Knollwood immediately after I meet with him Monday night." Rem's eyes gleamed with the triumph of ensuring justice would soon be served. "At which point, the 'terms' of my agreement with Mr. Knollwood will alter ... as will the person dictating them."

Muffled laughter intruded on Sammy's last remnants of sleep, coaxing her eyelids to open. At first she wasn't certain where the sound came from, only that it was close by. Curious, she sat up in bed ... and smiled.

Romping on the floor, both buoyant and panting, were Rascal and Cynthia. They were evidently in the middle of a competitive bid for Cynthia's stocking, one end of which was tightly clenched in Cynthia's hand, the other firmly fixed between Rascal's small but effective teeth.

"I'd let you have it, honestly," Cynthia was promising between chuckles. "But it's my best pair. Can I substitute a different one, perhaps?"

Rascal wagged his tail cheerfully, but made no attempt to relinquish the garment.

"Don't humor him, Cynthia." Sammy climbed out of bed. "He's entirely too spoiled as it is." She snapped her fingers. "Drop it!"

Rascal eyed Sammy, apparently debating which meant more, his mistress's affection or his new possession.

The decision, thankfully, never needed to be made.

"Oh, you're awake, my lady." Millie pressed open the door and inched in, carrying a tray of hot chocolate and scones.

Seeing his opportunity, Rascal bolted down the hallway, stocking in mouth.

"I'm sorry, Cynthia." Sammy rolled her eyes to the heavens. "Rascal is well-named—he's still as devilish as the day I got him."

"He's precious."

"He's impossible." Sammy sighed. "But luckily for him, I happen to adore him. I'll replace your stockings."

"Pardon me, my lady …" Millie still hovered in the doorway, looking bewilderedly from the fleeing pup to his mistress. "I brought your breakfast—Cook thought you'd be tired after your evening at the opera. But I didn't know you had a guest. I have only enough for one."

"It's not your fault, Millie," Sammy hastened to assure her. "Cynthia spent the night unexpectedly." Already Millie's eyes were growing suspiciously damp. The last thing Sammy needed right now was for her maid to dissolve into a customary round of tears. "This is my friend, Cynthia. Cynthia, this is Millie"—Sammy shot Cynthia a meaningful look—"my lady's maid."

Cynthia nodded her understanding. "Nice to meet you, Millie."

Millie curtsied, nearly upsetting the tray. "Oh dear!" She steadied the rattling china and sped across the room to deposit the tray on Sammy's nightstand. "I'll get more," she blurted, backing from the room. "Food, I mean. I'll only be a moment. I'll be right back. It's nice to meet you, too, ma'am." Like a terrified rabbit, she bolted.

"Do you see what I mean?" Sammy asked, noting the spark of amusement in Cynthia's eyes.

"I do."

"Well, we'll soon remedy that. After breakfast, you and I will talk to Smitty and everything will be resolved."

"Surely you don't think I should go with you to consult your guardian."

"Why not? It's your life we're discussing."

"But I'm just—"

"You're not *just* anything, Cynthia." Sammy seized her new friend's hand, dragging her over to the looking glass. "You're a beautiful, sensitive woman who's been scandalously mistreated. Stop demeaning yourself—I won't have it."

Cynthia stared at her reflection, her dark eyes wide, vulnerable. The pristine night rail Samantha had loaned her billowed about her slender form, seeming to mock her by its very presence. Her masses of wheat-colored hair were disheveled, draped about her shoulders. How did she look?

Like a whore.

Unable to bear the shame, Cynthia lowered her eyes. "It's ironic. What happened to me wasn't my fault, and I know it. I despise the man responsible, and all the men who have followed in his wake. But when all is said and done, they've managed to reduce me to exactly what they believe me to be—a common prostitute." She wrapped her arms about herself and averted her head. "The only emotion left inside me is enmity; I hate them … and I hate myself."

"You saved my life," Sammy returned in an unsteady voice. "Not many women would have risked their own safety to protect a total stranger. How can you doubt your worth?"

"Women judge other women differently than men judge them, Samantha. And since it's men's opinions that matter, I'm unworthy for any decent life, and unfit company for you."

"Not all men think like that."

"I beg to differ with you, my naive friend. Men relegate women to two varieties, each separate, but necessary: a chaste paragon on their arm and a skillful whore in their bed. No woman can be both."

"Drake's not like that. He loves Alex."

"And keeps only unto her?" Cynthia returned sardonically.

"Yes."

"You're a fool."

"You're wrong."

Cynthia gave a shiver of distaste. "I can't imagine ever marrying. Why would any woman *choose* to condemn herself to a lifetime in her husband's bed, subjecting herself to his lust, night after night?"

"Alex says making love is wonderful."

"Making love?" Cynthia gave a bitter laugh. "Is that what you call it?"

"When you care for someone, yes." Sammy perched on the edge of her bed. "You're right about my being naive, Cynthia. I am. I don't profess to know firsthand what it's like to lie with a man. But I do know that when you're in love, you merge with your hearts as well as your bodies. You join in passion and tenderness, not lust. I see the wealth of feeling in Drake's eyes when he looks at Alex … and in hers when she looks back."

"Tenderness." Cynthia spoke the word as if it were foreign. She fell silent, her fingers knotting in the folds of her night rail. "Samantha," she asked suddenly, "that man your earl was sitting with … who was he?"

"What?" Sammy blinked.

"The other person at the table with Lord Gresham, do you know him?"

"I don't think so. But then, all I saw was Remington." Sammy pursed her lips, trying to remember. "Now that you mention it, yes, I do recall another gentleman. He didn't look familiar … at least not from the quick look I got. Why?"

"Oh, he and the earl seemed mismatched, that's all. I would never have suspected they'd be friends."

"Are you certain they were?"

"Yes. They were far too relaxed and informal with each other to be anything less." She paused. "His name was Boyd … Boyd Hayword."

"Boyd? Oh! He must be the tavern keeper of the establishment where I met Remington. It's called Boydry's. I seem to recall a stocky man serving drinks when I first dashed in out of the rain. It was probably he." Sammy studied Cynthia thoughtfully. "Did the two of you speak?"

"Only briefly." Again Cynthia averted her eyes. "What on earth am I going to wear to meet your guardian?"

"Don't worry, we'll find something." An inner voice told Sammy to drop the subject of Boyd, at least for now. Rising, she went to the wardrobe and began browsing through her morning dresses, determined to give Cynthia's battered trust some time to heal. But Sammy was wise enough—and perhaps objective enough—to understand that Cynthia needed far more than mere time in order to truly recover from her devastating scars; she needed love.

"This gown is perfect." Sammy flourished a modest, Devonshire brown morning dress.

"Oh, I couldn't!"

"Of course you could. It's far too muted for my coloring anyway—it makes me look drab and melancholy. On you— with your pale skin and light hair—it will look magnificent!"

"But I should wear a uniform or—"

"You will." Sammy grinned. "*After* we procure your new position. To that end, let's impress Smitty with your breeding and beauty—it makes every heroine that much more appealing." Wisely, Sammy indicated the row of Gothic romances lined up beside the window. "Now let's hurry and don our clothes before Millie returns. Who knows? If we manage to dress ourselves without her assistance, we might even see Smitty before nightfall."

"Good morning, Smitty."

Cheerfully, Sammy tugged Cynthia into the sitting room where Smitty was worriedly pacing.

"Lady Samantha—your maid said you wished to see me. Is anything amiss …?" His voice trailed off as he saw the woman standing beside his charge.

"To the contrary." Impatient to set things right, Sammy blasted into her story. "Smitty, this fine young lady"—she thrust Cynthia forward—"is the answer to all our problems."

Smitty's brows rose. "I wasn't aware we had any problems."

"That's because I've spared you—and Aunt Gertie—the distressful details."

"What details?"

"Millie. She hates it here. And, quite frankly, she's a horrendous lady's maid. It's not her fault, of course. She wasn't trained to attend the family, only to assist the other servants. Still, I couldn't honor her request for reinstatement at Aunt Gertie's Hampshire manor—not until I had a suitable replacement. Well, now I do." Pausing only to gulp in some air, Sammy raced on, "Smitty, this is Cynthia ..." She hesitated, glancing quizzically at her new friend.

"Aldin," Cynthia supplied in a whisper.

"Miss Aldin." In what was fast becoming a habit this Season, Smitty withdrew his handkerchief and dabbed at his forehead.

"Cynthia and I met at Covent Garden last night. I believe it was fate."

"Fate?"

"Yes ... you see, not only do we need Cynthia, but she needs us as well. So, it's perfect."

"Where are you from, Miss Aldin?" Smitty inquired politely, trying in vain to make some sense of the conversation.

"From just outside London, sir."

"Cynthia is highly educated; she was trained to be a governess."

"Then why is she seeking employment as a lady's maid?"

It was the question Cynthia had dreaded and Sammy had anticipated. With all the gentle sincerity in her heart, Sammy addressed it.

"When Cynthia and I met, all she was seeking was solace. I was the one who insisted she come home with me. You see, Smitty, her previous employer insulted and mistreated her. I won't even mention the unspeakable advances he made, nor the subsequent damage he did to her reputation. Suffice it to say she was horribly, horribly wronged … and it's up to us to make it right." Sammy's eyes pleaded her case. "I told her how kind you were, how mortified you'd be that an innocent woman could be so ill-used. And I offered her a position as my lady's maid. The idea was totally mine, not hers."

Smitty did indeed look mortified. "I'm appalled that Miss Aldin has been subjected to such abuse," he began. "However, my lady, I must point out—"

"She saved my life."

That stopped him. "Pardon me?"

"She saved my life." Sammy's mind was racing as she desperately sought a way to tell Smitty the truth, without implicating both Cynthia and herself. "When the opera concluded, Lord Gresham went to arrange for his phaeton to be brought around. I grew impatient and strolled off."

"Alone?" Smitty looked ill.

"Yes. 'Twas stupid, I know, especially in light of what occurred. I was accosted by a band of ruffians. Heaven only knows what they intended—"

"Where was the earl?" Smitty interrupted in a croak.

"He had no notion of my whereabouts." That much was indeed true. "As luck would have it, Cynthia was walking nearby, grappling with the bleakness of her future, when she heard my muffled calls for help. She interceded, made enough of a scene for the scoundrels to panic and flee." Sammy's shudder was as genuine as her next words. "I hate to think what my fate would have been had she not arrived."

Smitty swallowed convulsively. "Miss Aldin … you have my heartfelt gratitude." He bowed. "It would be an honor to have you stay on as Lady Samantha's personal lady's maid."

"Sir," Cynthia rubbed her damp palms together, "I feel you should know that, given the circumstances, I have no references."

"I've just received the only reference I need." Smitty's voice was gruff with emotion.

"Thank you, sir … I promise you won't be sorry."

Sammy was less formal, throwing her arms around Smitty's neck. "Thank you," she whispered. "Oh … Smitty?" she said in a normal tone. "Will you speak to Aunt Gertrude for us? That way I can go tell Millie the wonderful news right away, and help her pack. Cynthia spent last night on my settee. I'm sure she'd prefer moving into her own room."

A twinkle of amusement flashed in Smitty's eyes. "I'll speak to your aunt, my lady. As for young Millie, I'm certain you'll have her on her way in less than an hour."

Fifty minutes later Millie was hastened into a waiting carriage, still calling thank-yous over her shoulder as the horses sped off for Hampshire.

"Done," Sammy announced, closing the door behind her. "Now let's get you settled."

"Do you always do things this way?" Cynthia asked as they climbed the stairs.

"What way?"

"Like a tempest. A delightful tempest, mind you, but a tempest just the same."

Sammy flashed Cynthia an impish grin. "Yes."

"I was afraid of that."

"We have two days to get you accustomed to your new position. Monday night you'll make your first official appearance as my chaperon."

"Monday night?"

"Yes … we're going to Vauxhall."

"Who is 'we'?"

"You, Remington, and I."

Cynthia halted on the second floor landing. "You're not serious."

"Of course I am. You're my companion, remember? Certainly you didn't think my escort and I would be permitted to go out alone, unchaperoned? Why, Millie accompanied me everywhere."

"That's not the point, Samantha. Lord Gresham knows who—*what* I am. He met me at Annie's."

"Good. Then when he realizes you've abandoned Annie's in favor of my more desirable company, perhaps he'll do the same. Besides"—Sammy placed a conspiratorial finger across her lips—"you'll be overseeing us only as long as it takes to quiet the tongues of Vauxhall's gossips."

"You're not thinking of going off alone with him, are you?" Seeing the triumphant expression on Sammy's face, Cynthia shook her head emphatically. "You're making a big mistake, Samantha. I mean it. You're playing a dangerous game … with rules you don't even know."

"Remington wouldn't hurt me."

"He would and he will."

"Then you'll just have to come along."

"So I can protect you?"

"No, so I can prove you wrong."

Vauxhall's thousands of colored lamps illuminated the grove and its surrounding pavilions, bathing the gardens in an ethereal glow.

Sammy had never seen anything more romantic in her life.

"Oh …" she breathed, alighting from the carriage. "It's breathtaking. And listen! The concert is under way—do you hear the musicians?"

"Yes, imp, I hear them." Tenderly, Rem tucked Sammy's arm through his. In truth, he was having trouble concentrating on anything but Samantha. She'd pervaded his thoughts since Friday, eclipsing everything—even his mission—from view. It was frightening. To lose his focus would be insane. Yet, deny it though he would, Rem could feel himself weakening, unable to recall that his sole purpose for pursuing Samantha was to discover how much she knew about the disappearing ships.

If the pull between them continued to intensify, his mission and Samantha's innocence would both be in jeopardy. Rem was acutely aware of the disastrous possibilities, just as he was aware that he was all wrong for Samantha, that what she needed wasn't inside him to give. But, God help him, he couldn't stay away. And now, immersed in her beauty, watching the rapturous expression on her face, he wondered if he even wanted to try.

Rem cleared his throat, but not his head. "Millie is still in the back seat of the carriage. I'll help her alight. Then we can get some punch and go for a stroll."

His words snapped Sammy out of her reverie. "Millie's gone," she blurted out.

"What?"

"She's gone. I sent her back to Hampshire. She hated it here."

Rem's brows drew together in puzzlement. "Well then, what specter darted into the rear of my carriage just before we departed?"

"My new lady's maid."

"Oh. Fine. Then I'll help your new lady's maid alight." With a mock bow, Rem turned back and extended his hand.

Cynthia climbed down unassisted. Raising her chin, she met Rem's gaze with a combination of cynicism and resignation.

"Remington, this is Cynthia. Cynthia, Lord Gresham."

"My lord." Without averting her eyes, Cynthia curtsied.

Recognition was instantaneous, even before Rem heard the name. "Cynthia," he repeated, nodding politely.

"Yes, I was very fortunate to find Cynthia," Sammy continued, watching Rem's expression. "She was unhappy at her previous position. I hope she'll find this new one more to her liking."

"I see." Years of training served Rem in good stead. Not a flicker of surprise or censure registered on his face, in his voice. "Well then, shall we?" Once again he offered Sammy his arm.

Sammy sensed Rem's change in mood immediately, and her heart sank. Was he upset because she had hired a courtesan to be her maid, or because she wasn't more like one herself?

"Are you thirsty, imp?"

"Yes, I suppose."

Gently, he caressed her cheek. "Don't sound so forlorn. Vauxhall boasts an abundance of punch." He gestured toward the closest pavilion. "I'll be but a moment."

"He recognized me," Cynthia said, the instant she and Sammy were alone.

"Of course he did. Did you doubt it? Now, hurry."

"Hurry?"

"Yes. Wander off by yourself—quickly, before Remington returns. I want some time alone with him."

"Samantha—"

"Cynthia," Sammy's chin set stubbornly, "I know you have my best interests at heart. But it's *my* heart I must listen to, not yours. Please ... go."

Still Cynthia hesitated. "If you need me, call out. I'll race back and—"

"I won't need you."

There was nothing more Cynthia could do but comply. "All right." With a resigned sigh, she turned and walked away.

"Where is your new maid?" Rem's deep baritone reached Sammy's ears a scant moment later. Handing Sammy a cup of punch, he scanned the area.

"I asked her to leave us alone."

His dimple flashed. "Did you? In those words?"

"Yes."

"And now that we're alone?"

"I'd like to go wherever it's most private."

"Samantha ..."

"I want to enjoy your company, Remington ... to talk."

He brought her fingers to his lips. "Whenever you and I are alone, talking is the farthest thing from my mind. I can't promise this time will be any different."

She smiled. "I'm glad."

Lover's Path was wickedly deserted, the fragrant aroma of the garden their only companion.

"Have I told you how breathtaking you look tonight?" Rem murmured, guiding Sammy along.

"No, but please do."

Heatedly, Rem surveyed the low-cut bodice and flowing layers of her bottle-green gown. "That color makes your eyes glow like rare pieces of jade."

"I wore it intentionally," Sammy confided, her cheeks flushed with pleasure. "So you would look at me the same way you did at Almack's … the last time I wore green."

Rem chuckled. "And have I disappointed you, my honest romantic?"

"No."

The intimate silence that followed made Sammy's heart pound with fevered anticipation.

Her hope was shattered by Rem's next question.

"When did you meet Cynthia?"

Sammy tensed. "Several days ago."

"Really? Smithers must have been tremendously impressed by her references."

"Why do you say that?"

Casually, Rem sipped at his punch. "Because she's a veritable stranger. And you're his most precious charge."

"Are you mocking me?"

"Never. I'm only stating the truth. Your brother's valet is very protective of you—which is why you were entrusted to his care to begin with."

"Actually, Cynthia is almost as protective of me as Smitty is."

"Why is that?"

"She thinks I'm too innocent for my own good."

"I'm not surprised."

Sammy halted, turned to face him. "What does that mean?"

Stopping beside her, Rem tossed off the remains of his drink.

"Why don't you like Cynthia?"

"I don't know her well enough to like or dislike her. Neither, for that matter, do you."

"You're wrong, Remington. I'm not nearly as naive as you think I am."

Another silence.

"When will you stop viewing me as a child?" Sammy tilted her face up to his.

Rem smiled, traced his forefinger down the bridge of her nose. "I never viewed you as a child, imp. A very beautiful, very romantic distraction, perhaps; but never a child."

"You know what I mean. I'm certainly chaste and untutored compared to your other women."

Rem chuckled. "A very forthright distraction," he amended.

"Would you prefer me to be coy?"

"I prefer you just as you are."

"Even if I'm not like the women at Annie's?" The minute the words were out, Sammy wanted to kick herself.

Fiercely, Rem seized her shoulders. "What do you know about Annie's?"

"Cynthia told me," she managed, chilled by the fury in his eyes.

"So you know where your lady's maid originated."

"She's not like them. She's ... different."

"Samantha—"

"Please don't patronize me, Remington. She *is* different. As for Annie's, I knew what a brothel was long before I met Cynthia. One needn't frequent them to know they exist. What I don't understand is, why do *you* frequent them? With scores of women like—what was that stunning marchioness's name—Clarissa …? With an abundance of Clarissas anxious to sample your charms, why do you visit Annie's? Is it the feeling of anonymity that appeals to you? Is it the sense of detachment? Or is it the variety? I assume you grew used to diversity when you served in the Royal Navy."

Abruptly, Rem's anger transformed to amazement. "I can't believe we're standing here discussing—"

"Why not? I want to understand what draws you to a woman. Is it experience? Then why do you object to my gaining some?"

"Because you're not like Annie's girls. Nor like the women I met at sea."

"If I became like them, *then* would you want me?"

Rem knocked their drinks to the ground and caught Sammy's face between his hands. "Is that what this is all about? You don't think I want you?"

"Do you?"

"So much that it terrifies me."

Sammy stepped closer. "Show me."

"I'm not sure I'll be able to stop."

"Oh, Rem …" With a dreamy sigh, she leaned against him, twined her arms about his neck. "Don't you know by now that I don't want you to stop?"

Restraint snapped.

Days of unsatisfied need converged in Rem's gut, pounding through his loins and obscuring his judgment … if he ever had any where Samantha was concerned. His hands left her face to clamp her waist, dragging her closer, until there was nothing between them but the hindering layers of their clothing. Slowly, maddeningly, he lowered his head, covered her trembling mouth with his, parting her lips to accept the intimate invasion of his tongue. Her response was instant and ardent. She whimpered softly, tightening her hold about his neck and melding their tongues in an innocently seductive act that nearly brought Rem to his knees.

Somewhere in the distance a bell sounded, a silvery echo through the garden. On its heels, a bright cascade of multicolored light infused the sky with a magical glow.

"The fireworks are beginning," Rem murmured, tangling his fingers in the glorious sable waves of Sammy's hair.

"Really? I thought they'd already begun." With a siren's smile, she traced his lower lip with the tip of her tongue.

"Christ, Samantha ..." he muttered, "I'm only human. Do you have any idea what you do to me?"

He didn't wait for her answer.

She never intended to give one.

Burning with a fire all its own, their kiss exploded into passion. Preliminaries cast aside, Rem possessed Samantha fully, crushed her in his arms until neither of them could speak. He absorbed her shiver, tasted as well as felt the innocent awakening of her body. Her breasts swelled against his chest, her nipples hardening through the confines of her gown. Gliding his hands down her back, he cupped her bottom, lifted her against him purposefully, determined that she should experience the full extent of his desire. Half expecting her to recoil with horror, Rem was stunned when Sammy tightened her embrace, pressed her body closer to his ... and severed yet another filament of his control.

"Samantha ..." Her name was a harsh rasp from deep in his chest, his lips leaving hers to burn urgent kisses on her cheeks, her neck, the graceful column of her throat. The scent of flowers was all around them, fragrant and sweet—as sweet as his mouth on her skin, the seductive words that spilled from his soul, unchecked and uncensored. "I want you ... you can't know how much. In my bed, naked, pleading for me to make you whole. I want you under me, wrapped around me, crying out my name again and again." He moved his hips seductively against hers. "Not want you? Feel me, Samantha, and know how wrong you are."

Sammy's eyes slid shut, her entire being concentrated beneath her throbbing senses. She arched her back, silently begging for more, wanting to drown in the hypnotic spell Rem was weaving.

With shaking hands, Rem eased her deeper into the shadows, unfastening the tiny row of buttons down the back of her gown. Discretion be damned, principles be damned, missions be damned. Nothing mattered but having this woman. Now. Now.

Desire pounding through him in a relentless surge, Rem tugged Samantha's gown and chemise down to her waist, aroused nearly beyond bearing by her eager attempts at assistance. He raised his head, the faint moon glow enough to reveal the incomparable treasures he'd just bared for the first time.

Rem's breath actually lodged in his throat, tenderness momentarily taming passion. Mesmerized, he stared down at her breasts, moved by an emotion he didn't quite understand, one that unfurled like warm mists of smoke in his chest. She was beautiful, so beautiful, and so very trusting, waiting for him to touch her, offering him anything he wanted.

God, if she only knew how badly he wanted.

"Am I all right?" Sammy whispered, her eyes as soft as the grass beneath their feet.

"All right?" Reverently, Rem caressed her with light, feathery strokes of his fingertips, reveling at her warm, responsive flesh, the quiver that raced through her, the never-before-touched splendor beneath his hands. "You're perfect. More than perfect. You're every exquisite fantasy a man envisions." Slowly, he lowered his mouth, acutely attuned to her response as he brushed his lips against the warm curve of her breast. Her soft sigh, the acceleration of her heartbeat rippled through him, and he grew bolder, tracing the sensitive outline of her nipple, nuzzling its taut peak, finally surrounding it with his lips and tongue.

Sammy cried out, her legs buckling as dizzying sensations coursed through her blood in pulsing bursts. "Remington …" If there were other words to say, she couldn't imagine what they were. Nothing could describe this shattering feeling, this all-encompassing storming of the senses. She never, never wanted it to end.

Scooping her into his arms, Rem carried Samantha to the nearby bench, lowering her gently, half covering her with himself. "This is madness, imp," he murmured, taking her mouth in a long, drugging kiss, caressing her swollen breasts. "Anyone could discover …"

His words of caution dissipated the instant her soft hands slid inside his jacket and beneath his shirt. Everything inside him went rigid, aching, as she unbuttoned first his waistcoat, then the shirt, tugging them away from his skin.

"I want to touch you," she breathed, smoothing her palms over the powerful muscles of his chest, gliding her fingers through the dark hair that curled on it. "Is that all right?"

"Christ, I want your hands all over me," he rasped, his whole body shuddering at the erotic contact.

Sammy watched him, her eyes wide with wonder and joy. "You're even more magnificent than I imagined." She leaned up to kiss his throat. "And I did imagine, Rem … just as you did."

A harsh groan rumbled from his soul. "Sweetheart … you're killing me." His hands grew more feverish on her breasts, his mouth following in their wake. He pressed her down onto the bench, lost to the craving that was stronger than he. She was scented heaven beneath him, warm and soft and willing, and no amount of reason was going to make him stop. His lips closed around her nipple, tugging at it once, twice, then rhythmically until Samantha whimpered, feverish with a need she'd never envisioned.

"Remington …" She shifted restlessly. "Please …"

Her plea blazed through him like a brushfire. "Ah, Samantha ... my beautiful Samantha ... do you really know what it is you're begging me for?" God, he wanted to tear off her gown and bury himself inside her. It was beyond need; it was compulsion.

"Yes, I do." She caressed the broad expanse of his shoulders, staring up at him through trusting eyes that were misty with passion. "I've known from the instant we met that I was going to belong to you. Make love to me."

They were the most beautiful words Rem had ever heard. Also the most sobering. He gazed down at her, half naked in Vauxhall's very public gardens, and guilt reared its ugly head. Guilt, mixed with that strange new emotion in his chest and some very old, very ingrained truths about himself. What the hell was he on the verge of doing? "No."

Sammy blinked. "No?"

His breathing ragged, Rem hoisted himself to a sitting position, resolutely pulling up her gown and chemise and refastening them.

"Why?" she demanded in a tiny whisper.

"Because you're far too precious, that's why."

"Far too precious for what?"

"For a quick tumble on a bench at Vauxhall. For a quick tumble anywhere."

Silently, she watched him rebutton his shirt. "To me, it wouldn't have been a quick tumble," she said at last. "But you already know that. Just as I know that it's not merely my vulnerability you're so driven to protect." Gracefully, she stood, smoothing her hair back into place.

"Isn't it?" Rem's tone sounded wooden.

"No. 'Tis your own vulnerability as well." Sammy's eyes were filled with sad resignation. "You see, Rem, for the first time in your life, this wouldn't have been a quick tumble for you either."

TEN

Knollwood was already waiting.

Keenly aware of Templar and Harris concealed nearby, Rem headed toward the orange glow of Knollwood's cheroot, forcing everything but the confrontation ahead from his mind. Samantha's words still haunted him with their uncanny insight, resurrecting memories long since buried. Her reference to his staunch attempts at self-protection wasn't a revelation—Lord only knew how many times he'd heard it from Boyd—but from Samantha's lips the words were different, more profound. Boyd was his closest friend, the one who'd shared his pain, been there when the wounds were inflicted. But Samantha was … different.

Rem needed to be alone, to probe into his own needs and motivations. But later, after Knollwood had been dealt with.

"Gresham. You're late. I thought maybe you'd changed your mind."

"Hardly." Rem glanced at his timepiece. "It's seven minutes past three, Knollwood. I had to conclude my evening plans and slip away. Oh, and stop for this." He brandished a quill. "You did say to bring a writing implement?"

"I did." Knollwood blew a ring of smoke over Rem's head. "Are you ready to use it?"

"Did you bring my money?"

"*My* money, Gresham, *my* money." Knollwood snapped open a small leather bag, exposing piles of neatly stacked bills. "Your loan, but my money. Don't forget that."

"I won't." Making a quick mental assessment, Rem concluded that the full amount was there. "All right. Where's the note you want me to sign?"

"Right here." Knollwood reached into his pocket and withdrew a single sheet of paper. "Sign at the bottom."

"After I read what I'm signing." Rem scanned the document, unsurprised by the exorbitant amount of interest Knollwood was demanding. "My instincts had better not fail me," he muttered just loud enough for Knollwood to hear. "These terms are outrageous."

"You're reconsidering your original intentions?"

"No. I still believe my ship will succeed. I'll find a way to ensure it will."

"How?"

"That's my problem." Rem paused. "Unless you have a suggestion. In which case, I'm listening."

Taut with anticipation, Rem awaited Knollwood's next, all-important response.

"I'm a businessman, Gresham, not a prophet." Knollwood jabbed his finger at the signature line. "Now, pen your name. Unless you don't want the funds after all."

Studying Knollwood through narrowed eyes, Rem had his answer. The despicable parasite wasn't the national culprit they sought. Evidently, he wasn't astute enough to pull off so sophisticated a scheme.

Rem scrawled his name and shoved the document back at Knollwood. "Here. Now my money."

Thrusting the bag into Rem's hands, Knollwood didn't release it until the note was safely tucked in his waistcoat. "I'll be in touch," he promised, relinquishing his grip on the bag's handle. "Soon. And Gresham ... I'm sure I don't need to remind you not to do anything stupid. I always keep abreast of my business associates ... and their friends."

"I don't doubt it."

"Speaking of which—how is Lady Samantha Barrett faring these days?"

Rem's guts clenched.

"She's a beauty, Gresham. Fresh from the schoolroom, too. Quite a change from your usual sort. She must be an avid learner in bed."

"You filthy bastard." Rem's cool veneer dissipated in a heartbeat. Lunging forward, he grabbed Knollwood by the throat. "If you ever even mention Samantha's name again, I'll break every bone in your despicable body."

"Let me go, Gresham," Knollwood rasped.

Rem's thumb depressed on Knollwood's windpipe. Vehemently, he averted his head, calling, "I've had all I can take. Templar, Harris—get this scum out of here."

On the heels of Rem's command, the sound of rustling trees and thudding feet split the night. Before Knollwood could move, Templar had a gun pointed at his head.

"B-But you came alone," Knollwood stammered at Rem.

"No, I just happen to know what hiding places your men don't check." With a chilling expression, Rem released his hostage.

Knollwood rubbed his neck with shaking hands. "I'll lessen the payments. And increase your time to pay them."

"Really? How reassuring." In one casual, adept motion, Rem extracted the note from Knollwood's pocket, tearing it once, twice, three times, and scattering the pieces to the wind. "Payments? What payments?"

"What do you want, Gresham? The money?"

"Don't flatter yourself, Knollwood. If all I wanted was your money, I needn't have gone to so much trouble. I'd just have taken it."

"Then what do you want?"

"To put you somewhere far away from your poor, unsuspecting prey."

Sweat broke out on Knollwood's forehead. "On what grounds? It's your word against mine. You just destroyed the only evidence you had, you fool."

"Did I? How clumsy of me." Rem tapped his chin thoughtfully. "Harris, do you think we might produce some additional evidence, since I just impulsively shredded my own?"

"I think so." Harris's pistol flashed as he carefully backed up Templar.

"Good. That eases my mind quite a bit."

"What evidence?" Knollwood demanded. "Who the hell are these thugs anyway?"

"Oh, did I neglect to introduce you? How tactless of me. Meet Templar and Harris, two of Bow Street's finest runners. They have scores of witnesses who can attest to your vast number of crimes, plus a multitude of papers to substantiate the witnesses' claims. As luck would have it, both Templar and Harris are also personal favorites of the Bow Street Magistrate ... to whom, incidentally, they are about to deliver you."

"You bastard. And what about my money? Are you going to turn that in, too?"

"*Your* money? Don't you mean *my* money?" Rem shook his head. "How quickly you forget."

"You're going to keep it, aren't you?" Knollwood made a dive for Rem, one that was quickly checked by Harris's iron grasp and the cold steel of Templar's pistol against his head.

"Careful, gentlemen," Rem cautioned, never flinching. "We wouldn't want to injure Mr. Knollwood. Then he couldn't enjoy his long stay at Newgate." He gestured for his men to take Knollwood away. "Oh, and don't worry about your money, Knollwood. I promise to put it to excellent use."

"It's done?"

Boyd unlocked the front door of Boydry's and opened it just enough for Rem to slip inside.

"Yes … Mr. Knollwood won't be blackmailing anyone for a long, long time."

"And? Did he offer you the incentive you suspected?"

"No. Another impasse."

Boyd sighed. "I was afraid of that." He poured two glasses of gin. "Where are Harris and Templar?"

"Delivering Knollwood to Bow Street. Once he's been handed over, they'll join us here." Rem placed the leather bag on Boyd's counter and flipped it open. "May Knollwood spend one year rotting in Newgate for every pound in this bag."

"What are you going to do with the money?"

Rem snapped the bag shut. "Effect a little justice of my own. It's but a fraction of all Knollwood's taken, but perhaps it can restore one man's dignity."

"You're going to pay off Goddfrey's debts." It was a statement, not a question; one Boyd didn't need answered. He knew his friend's mind, just as he knew Rem would try his damnedest to make certain Goddfrey never knew how the funds were repaid.

"You know where Goddfrey is staying?"

A nod. "I do. A missive informing him of Knollwood's capture will be on its way in an hour. In the interim, we're right back where we started." Tucking the leather bag away, Rem lit a cheroot and took an appreciative swallow of gin. "Unless, of course, Templar and Harris have anything to report. Or Johnson—have you checked on him?"

"More than once. The docks have been quiet," Boyd replied. "But then, so have the seas. Whoever's running this scheme has decided to be cautious."

"I'm not surprised. He doesn't want to be caught."

"What about the companies our men checked out? Did their records provide any clues?"

"We'll find out as soon as Harris and Templar get here. I don't expect major revelations, though. If they'd uncovered anything significant, either you or I would have heard from them."

Boyd cleared his throat. "What about Samantha?"

"What about her?"

"Did you learn anything from her?"

The irony of the question almost made Rem laugh aloud. "Quite a bit. None of it, however, had to do with the missing ships."

"What did it have to do with?"

"Me." Rem regarded the glowing tip of his cheroot. "Evidently, she shares your opinion that I'm running from myself."

"How much have you told her?"

"Nothing."

"Startling, wouldn't you say?" Boyd sat down beside his friend. "You've known how many women—each one more worldly and sophisticated than the last? Yet not one of them has seen beneath your accomplished veneer. And now this very young, very innocent girl bursts into your life and in a matter of days understands you better than you understand yourself." Boyd paused, praying the significance of his words would sink in. "She obviously cares a great deal about you."

"Obviously."

"Are you ready to admit you care in return?"

"I admitted that days ago," Rem returned in a strangled tone. "It's what I plan to do about those feelings that plagues me. Hell, Boyd," he shook his head in disbelief, "I lose my mind when I'm with her. I act like an uncontrolled youth, forgetting everything: who she is, who I am, what I'm supposed to be doing. I can't let this happen."

"Why? Because she's a possible link to our mission? Or because she's a threat to your carefully guarded heart?"

"Both."

"At least now you're being honest. Not only with me, but with yourself."

"My personal feelings aren't the issue. Unless Templar and Harris turn up something, we have no source of information but Samantha. ...I can't stop seeing her." Rem met Boyd's knowing gaze, and his jaw set. "All right. My personal feelings *are* the issue. I don't *want* to stop seeing her."

"Then don't. She's a beautiful, warm, loving young woman. Perhaps she can give you back a bit of what you've lost."

"And what will I take from her in return?"

"What will you deprive her of if you walk away?"

"Pain. Hurt. Social ruin."

"Do you think she'd escape unscathed if you ended it now?" Boyd put in quietly. "I'm not prying, Rem, but it sounds as if things have progressed beyond casual conversation and a perfunctory kiss on the hand."

Rem's silence answered his question.

"Think about it, Rem. I understand you're trying to be honorable. But Samantha's chastity is not all that's at stake here."

A corner of Rem's mouth lifted. "According to Samantha, my concern is not for her virtue, but for my own self-protection."

"She's a very astute young lady."

"Dammit, Boyd!" Rem's smile vanished. "Why have you undergone such a complete change of heart? Am I now the only one who recognizes what Samantha stands to lose?"

"No. But circumstances have changed ... *feelings* have changed. Remember, there are all kinds of losses. Perhaps Samantha perceives physical innocence as less painful to relinquish than emotional austerity."

"Perhaps Samantha is too naive to know what losing her innocence would mean to her ... and her family. She's so damned trusting, living vicariously through one of her novels, seeing only the best in everyone." Abruptly, Rem remembered something Boyd should know. "Which reminds me, Samantha has a new lady's maid."

"Oh?" Boyd's expression was quizzical.

"It's Cynthia."

"Cynthia?" Boyd started. "Annie's Cynthia?"

"One and the same."

"What is she doing with Samantha?"

"I told you—she's her lady's maid. Apparently, they met several days ago. Cynthia told Samantha she hated working at Annie's. Samantha offered her an alternative."

"So Samantha knows about Cynthia's former occupation?"

"Yes, my avenging romantic told me so herself, defended Cynthia as if they were old friends."

"I see." A spark kindled in Boyd's eyes. "Interesting."

"I thought you might say that."

A noise at the door interrupted them.

Cautiously, Boyd waited until he'd heard the customary signal required from his after-hours guests. Three knocks … a pause … two knocks more. Satisfied, he rose to admit Templar and Harris.

"Knollwood's at Bow Street," Templar announced, shedding his coat. "From there he'll go to Old Bailey, then Newgate. We won't be seeing that cur for a long, long time."

"Good." Nodding his approval, Rem handed each man a wad of bills.

"Is that from Knollwood's booty?"

"No, from mine. Knollwood's funds are being put to another use. One that needn't concern you."

The men knew better than to pry.

"This might be the only money we see," Harris announced, helping himself to a drink. "We don't have a damned thing for you, Gresham."

"I'm not surprised." Rem tossed off the remains of his gin. "You shouldn't be either. Whoever's sinking these ships isn't stupid. Nor is he anxious to get caught. It's up to us to be shrewder and more persistent than he. How many companies have you visited?"

"Four companies, three merchants. All with impeccable records."

"That leaves at least six more companies and an equal number of merchants to investigate. You should have something for me by Wednesday night."

"Two days?" Templar blanched.

"Two days." Rem replenished his drink. "I don't pay you to dawdle, Templar. I pay you to work—hard. So"—Rem lifted his glass—"shall we say Annie's? Wednesday night, two A.M.?"

Harris and Templar exchanged glances. Resignedly, they nodded. "We'll be there, Gresham."

By the time Sammy arrived at Carlton House Wednesday night, she no longer wanted to view the Prince Regent's palatial mansion or take part in the enormous gathering within. Her head throbbed from idle chatter, her heart ached with loneliness, and her mind screamed with frustration.

She hadn't heard a word from Rem since their broodingly silent carriage ride home from Vauxhall two nights past. She missed him dreadfully, found herself searching the crowds for him at every ball she and Aunt Gertie attended. He'd not been present at a single one, and there had been countless. Carlton House was her third stop this evening—and definitely her last.

"Samantha ... what a delightful surprise!"

Clarissa's insincere greeting accosted Sammy like a bucket of ice water. Fervently, she wished she were anywhere but here. "Good evening, Lady Sheltane," she returned, forcing a smile.

"Please, call me Clarissa. After all, we're both friends of Rem's, aren't we?"

Sammy flinched. "Did the marquis accompany you tonight ... Clarissa, or is he still ailing?"

"He's still not well, poor dear. But he did manage to meet with your brother again regarding my yacht. Oh, it should be splendid."

"I'm sure." Where oh where was Aunt Gertie?

"Samantha! It is you! I thought I saw your lovely face brighten the room a moment ago."

"Stephen." Sammy wanted to throw her arms around Viscount Anders's neck. "I'm so happy to see you."

The warmth of her greeting seemed to please him immensely. "The pleasure, *petite fleur,* is all mine. May I have the honor of this dance?"

"Of course."

He glanced at the marchioness. "Clarissa, will you excuse us?"

"But of course, Stephen. I'd never stand in the way of so handsome a couple." Clarissa's face was the picture of innocence.

Stephen guided Sammy onto the dance floor, keeping her hand securely in his. "I've missed you."

"It's only been a few days." Sammy scanned the ballroom quickly. Rem was nowhere in sight.

"It feels much longer. I looked for you at every ball I attended. Where were you?"

"I …" An inner voice warned Sammy to be cautious. She suspected there was no great love between Stephen and Rem. "I haven't been out much. My lady's maid left me and I've been training a new one."

"I see. Well, I'm delighted. I feared you'd been swept off your feet by some unworthy rogue." Rem's name hung between them. "I hope your appearance tonight means you're ready to resume enjoying your first Season."

"Yes, of course."

"Have you had the opportunity to see all of Carlton House?" Anders inquired as the strings fell silent.

"No, but—"

"Let me take you on a tour, then; it's really quite spectacular."

"Well, I ..." What choice did she have? He was already leading her through the sky-lit vestibule and beyond. Most of the rooms were brimming with people, Sammy noted in relief. And at least she needn't face Clarissa.

It was on their way back to the party that Stephen managed to get her alone, in a small corner of the hallway. "Samantha ... I haven't been able to stop thinking about you." His knuckles grazed her cheek. "Do you have any idea how beautiful you are?"

Sammy drew away. "Please, Stephen, you're embarrassing me."

"I'd like to do much more than speak the words, if you'll let me."

"There are scores of people about," she protested, inching backward.

"We can go somewhere and be alone."

"I don't think—"

"I'll go as slowly as you want me to."

"I think the lady is saying no, Anders."

Rem's voice was quiet, but lethal.

Sammy's knees began to shake.

"My conversation with Lady Samantha does not concern you, Gresham. Kindly go off and seek entertainment elsewhere."

"I'd like to break your jaw," Rem responded calmly. "Say the word, and I shall."

"Remington—don't." Twin spots of red stained Sammy's cheeks. "Please."

He took in her expression and nodded. "Very well. But I do insist on escorting you back to the party."

"When did you become so gallant?" Anders mocked.

"Stephen, don't make a scene, please." Sammy lay her hand on his arm. "I think it's best if I do go back to the party. Aunt Gertie will be looking for me anyway."

"As you wish." Stephen bowed stiffly, his icy gaze fixed on Rem. "We'll talk another time."

"Yes, fine." Gathering up her skirts, Sammy made her way to the ballroom.

"Samantha."

She stopped, inclining her head slightly. "What is it, Remington?"

"We need to talk."

"About what?"

Rem inhaled sharply. "What the hell were you just doing?"

"Conversing with Viscount Anders."

"You mean flirting with him."

"I don't flirt, my lord. You of all people know that. Remember? You're the one who told me how forthright I was."

Despite his anger, Rem's dimple flashed. "I remember." His gaze fell to her lips. "I remember many things."

Her flush deepened. "May I go in now?"

"Only to say good night."

"What?"

"I'm taking you home."

"But—"

"Don't argue with me. Just tell your aunt I'm taking you home."

Sammy studied him uncertainly. "Why?"

"Because neither of us wants to be here. And because I need to talk to you."

"All right."

Several minutes later, Sammy sat rigidly in Rem's luxurious carriage, desperately trying to calm herself. She must act casual, nonchalant, as if she hadn't spent the past forty-eight hours yearning for this man. It was imperative that she keep her anxiety carefully concealed.

"Why are you so uneasy, imp? You've been alone with me before."

So much for concealment.

"After Monday ... I feel uncomfortable."

"Why?"

"Because"—she averted her eyes—"I'm well aware that you un-dress and ... touch women with great regularity. But it was my first such experience with a man. And, in the wake of our encounter, I'm not certain how to behave."

"Come here."

"What?" Her chin came up.

"I said, come here." Rem reached over and lifted her onto his lap. "God, I've missed you." Hungrily, he buried his lips in hers, his kiss burning with passion and jealousy and a touch of anguish.

"Is this because of Stephen?" Sammy managed.

"No." His mouth was on her neck, her throat. "Not that I didn't want to kill him. I did. But this is because of us." He tugged down her sleeve, bathing the smooth curve of her shoulder with his tongue. "Because the very thought of you with another man—*any* other man—is untenable. Because you're mine. Because I'm so bloody tired of fighting a battle that was lost the moment we met. Because if I don't have you I'll die." He pressed his face against the hollow between her breasts. "Are those reasons enough?"

"Yes," she breathed, threading her fingers through his hair. "Oh, Rem, I've missed you, too. I couldn't stop thinking about Vauxhall, and what happened ... what almost happened—"

He silenced her with his mouth, pressing her to the velvet cush-ion of the darkened carriage, following her down.

Words evaporated into nothingness, and the reality that time was short, their destination imminent, became insignificant next to the relentless need pulsating through them.

Rem was ruthless in his seduction, driven by demons he didn't recognize and an emptiness he could no longer face. He unfastened the buttons of her gown, kissing each inch of skin he bared, worshiping the upper slope of her breasts with his mouth.

It wasn't enough … for either of them.

With one harsh tug, Rem pulled her bodice lower, freeing her breasts to his gaze, his touch. With burning eyes, he watched her nipples tighten, until, when he could bear no more, he slid his arm beneath her waist and lifted her to him, lowering his mouth to the beckoning peaks and taking what Sammy so willingly, wholeheartedly, offered.

Nothing had ever tasted this sweet. The untainted beauty of Samantha's body, the natural sensuality of her response, stoked the flames coursing through Rem's blood. He didn't give a damn if the whole world disintegrated around them. He wanted Samantha. Here. Now. This instant. With every fiber of his being.

Damn Anders to hell. Damn any man who tried to claim her. She was his—*his*—and he needed to brand her so completely that there would never be any doubt of that fact.

His fingers glided up her leg, beneath her gown, over the silk of her stocking. She was trembling; so was he. The carriage jostled, and his hand slid farther up the soft contour of her thigh. "I've got to touch you," he muttered against her breast. "I've … got … to."

Sammy's fingers sifted restlessly through his hair, holding him to her. "Yes … that feels so … oh, Remington." She caught her breath as his fingers neared their mark, teasing the sensitive curve where her thigh ended.

"Let me …"

"Yes …"

"I've got to …"

"Yes."

"Samantha …" His most intimate caress followed on the heels of her name, causing her breath to erupt in a harsh sound of pleasure.

"Oh, Rem ..."

"God ..." Rem closed his eyes, tenderly claiming the warm wetness that belonged to him ... only him. Slowly, gently, he entered her with one finger, groaning aloud at the tight, clinging resistance that greeted his touch. "You're perfect," he told her huskily. "Perfect."

"Kiss me," she managed, quivering from head to toe. "Please ..."

He covered her mouth with his, taking her with deep, lusty strokes of his tongue, his finger moving tantalizingly in and out, in a rhythm that made them both wild.

"I want to be inside you," he rasped against her parted lips. "God, I've *got* to be inside you."

"Remington ... what's happening?" Sammy choked out, her body tightening, crying out for some unknown release.

"It's all right, sweetheart. Let it happen," he replied, determinedly mastering his own body's urgent need. "Let me give this to you ..."

The carriage jolted to a halt.

"Remington ... please ... don't stop," she pleaded.

"I won't. I won't." He didn't give a damn where they were.

"My lady?" Cynthia's purposeful voice penetrated the privacy of the carriage walls. "Is that you?"

Sammy's eyes flew open, filled with fear and smoky passion and unfulfilled need. "Oh ... I ..."

Rem wanted to choke Cynthia with his bare hands. "Dammit. Dammit to hell." He gritted his teeth, simultaneously striving to bring his own body under control and to soothe the panicked, heightened sensations of Sammy's. "God I'm sorry," he whispered, his fingers still damp with her response. "Samantha, I ..." He didn't know what to say. Maybe there was nothing he could say. "It's all right, sweetheart." Swiftly, he hauled himself upright, tugging up her bodice and smoothing her gown. "No one will know."

Her expression tore at his heart. "I don't care who knows. I feel so ... I ache."

"I know you do, love. So do I."

That seemed to surprise, and distract, her. "You do?"

He chuckled, despite the screaming need for release that tore at his loins. "More than you could ever imagine." He stroked her hot cheek with his knuckles. "I'll explain to you another time ... when we finish what we just began."

She searched his face intently. "*Will* we finish what we just began?"

"Yes." Even as he uttered the vow, Rem knew he intended to keep it. Neither of them could retreat from this madness, return to being the people they were before. It was too late ... for both of them.

Soberly, Rem reached around to button her gown. "The next time you're in my arms, I promise to bring you every exquisite pleasure you've ever dreamed of, fulfill aches you never even knew you possessed."

"When?"

His eyes smoldered. "The instant I get you alone." He framed her face between his hands, kissed her softly. "Will you be all right?"

"Not nearly as all right as I will be next time."

His body leaped at the suggestive gleam in her eye. "Samantha—"

"My lady? Are you well?"

"Yes, Cynthia, of course I'm well," Sammy snapped loudly enough for her friend to hear. "I'll be out in a minute."

"I'm going to throttle your new maid," Rem muttered.

"I'd better go." Sammy eased away reluctantly.

"Till tomorrow, imp." He pressed his lips to her palm.

"Remington ..." Sammy stared at his mouth as it caressed her fingers. "Until we find the time we need to be alone ... until then"—she raised her chin, candidly uttering her solemn proclamation—"I don't want you with other women."

Rem didn't mock her as she'd feared. He didn't even smile. "Your fate is sealed, my lady," he murmured huskily, his breath warm against her skin. "Since that night at Boydry's, I haven't been with another woman. I haven't even wanted one. Only you."

"Not even at Annie's?"

"Not even at Annie's."

"I'm glad." Sammy's smile was radiant, her belief instant and absolute.

Humbled by her faith in him, Rem felt that now-familiar emotion unfurl in his chest. "Go, love." He leaned across to open the carriage door. "Before your Cynthia has my head."

Sammy nodded, dazedly accepting the waiting footman's assistance in alighting, profusely thanking the stupefied servant for his exceptional efforts. In truth, she wanted to hug the man … and everyone else for the gift she'd just been given.

Her elation did not extend to Cynthia.

Waiting only until Rem's footman had abandoned his post, Sammy confronted her friend, mincing no words.

"What exactly did you think you were doing?"

"Saving you." Cynthia gestured toward the Worth family crest, emblazoned on the gleaming carriage side. "It's obvious who brought you home. It's not hard to imagine what was going on in there." She scrutinized Sammy's disheveled appearance. "It appears I didn't interrupt a moment too soon."

More exasperated than embarrassed, Sammy headed toward the house. "Right now, I'm far too ecstatic to be angry," she called over her shoulder. "However, when my feet touch the ground, I have a few things to say to you."

She disappeared into the entranceway.

Cynthia inhaled sharply, frustrated and worried over Samantha's naiveté. Naught but pain could result from the preoccupation her young mistress had with the Earl of Gresham. Yet Samantha refused to see the reality of where her adoration was heading. Well then, it was up to her to intervene, Cynthia thought, before it was too late.

Taking advantage of her unexpected opportunity, Cynthia stalked forward and yanked open the carriage door. "I'd like a word with you, my lord."

Rem leveled his cool gray stare at her. "That would probably be wise. Perhaps you could explain your rather curious display of morality."

"I know what you think of me, Lord Gresham. In truth, I couldn't care less. But Samantha is a different situation entirely. I want you to leave her alone."

"You've known her several days, and are already prepared to assume the role of her protector?"

"Why not? You've known her but a scant time longer and are already prepared to assume the role of her seducer." Cynthia bristled, too angry to remember her station as a servant. "Go back to Annie's, my lord. At least there you can be honest about your intentions. And no one will get hurt."

"While we're on the subject of Annie's, why are *you* no longer there?"

"I owe you no explanation."

"Or perhaps I should ask why you began working at Annie's in the first place?"

"My choices are my own. They concern no one but me."

"I beg to differ with you. As long as you're employed by Samantha, your choices concern me as well. And Cynthia … I'm very adept at finding out what I want to know."

Cynthia began to tremble beneath Rem's implicit threat. "You're all alike, aren't you? Domination and conquest are all you care about. Well, do your worst, my lord—I have nothing more to lose. But Samantha does. And I'll be damned if I'll stand by and let you reduce her to the life of a whore." Gathering up her skirts, Cynthia turned away. "Good night, Lord Gresham … I'm sure Katrina will be more than happy to minister any lingering needs you might have."

Watching Cynthia's retreating back, Rem mulled over the altercation that had just occurred. He couldn't help but admire the woman's blatant and genuine loyalty for Samantha, nor could he ignore her obvious breeding and refinement. A whore? Doubtful. Boyd was right—there was more here than met the eye. Samantha's new maid was fast becoming an engrossing enigma of her own.

Somewhere in the distance, a clock chimed two, reminding Rem he had an appointment to keep.

"Badewell?" he called to his driver, leaning out the carriage window. "Let's be off to Annie's."

A moment after Rem's carriage disappeared down Abingdon Street, the Barrett's front door clicked shut.

ELEVEN

"I won't stop seeing him."

Sammy raised her chin defiantly, confronting Cynthia in the privacy of her own bedchamber.

"I know you care for him, Samantha. And you *believe* he cares for you. But—"

"He does care for me. Probably more than even he knows."

Cynthia sighed. This was turning out to be more difficult than she'd expected. "We haven't known each other very long, Samantha. There's really no reason why you should trust me—"

"I trust you implicitly," Sammy interrupted. "This has nothing to do with trust. It has to do with love." She took Cynthia's hands in hers. "I love him, Cynthia. I've loved him from the first moment I saw him."

"How can you love a man you hardly know?"

Sammy smiled. "But I do know him. Somehow I've always known him."

"In your dreams."

"In my heart." Sammy chewed her lip, trying desperately to make Cynthia understand. "Cynthia, I truly believe that for every woman, fate has created the right man. I know you think I'm a fanciful child … that, of course, is your right. But I've watched Alex and

Drake, so I've seen what love is. I also remember Drake's life before Alex, so I've seen what loneliness is, as well. Please believe me, I'm not as much a child as you assume I am. A romantic, perhaps, but not a child. And since that rainy night in Boydry's when I first laid eyes on Remington, I've never doubted that I was destined to belong to him, and he to me."

"You've been reading too many of your romantic novels." Cynthia gestured at the books scattered about the room.

"Oh, no, Cynthia. My books bring me hours of pleasure."

"But apparently they're also putting foolish ideas in your head. Ideas that transform your earl into a hero and you into his damsel in distress. *That* is a big mistake."

"You're wrong," Sammy denied fervently. "My books feed my romantic nature, but they aren't responsible for my feelings for Remington. You see, Cynthia, despite a mutual affinity for mysterious adventures and a high regard for happy endings, I have very little in common with my Gothic heroines. They are sensible and serene, prone to tears, and inclined to swoon at the drop of a hat. And while Lord knows I've tried, I cannot seem to be either sensible or serene. I detest crying in public and I absolutely never faint. Instead, I'm impetuous and passionate and far too forthright about what I think and feel to suit the tastes of a true Gothic heroine. And, although Remington is protective and strong, and comes to my rescue whenever I need him, he's far too much of a rake and a womanizer to resemble a staid Gothic hero. But it matters not. He's *my* hero nonetheless. As I am his heroine."

Cynthia slapped her palm on the dressing table, utterly frustrated. "You thwart me at every turn, don't you? How can I open your eyes to the truth?" She hesitated, studying Sammy's unyielding stance. "I don't want to hurt you, Samantha."

"Hurt me?"

"Yes, by forcing you to see your earl for the duplicitous rogue that he is."

"Remington has been nothing but honest with me."

"Has he? Even about other women?"

"He hasn't been with another woman since we met."

Cynthia gave a derisive laugh. "Is that what he told you? And you, of course, believed him." She seized Sammy's shoulders, desperate to make her face reality before it was too late. "Think about it, Samantha. A handsome nobleman like Lord Gresham? Saving himself for you ... no matter how long that might take?"

"Remington wouldn't lie to me."

"Really? Then why was he at Annie's the night you and I met?"

"He had a business meeting."

"And did he have another meeting tonight?"

"What?"

"Where do you think he was going after he failed to ravish you in his carriage? Home? To his lonely bed? He was going to Annie's."

Sammy's eyes widened. "No."

"Yes. I myself heard him instruct his driver to take him there." Cynthia wanted to weep at the spasm of pain that crossed Sammy's face. "I'm sorry, Samantha." Her hands gentled on her friend's shoulders. "I wish I were wrong. I wish everything you believe could be so. God, how I wish that." A tremor of emotion made her voice break. "But I won't let him do this to you. I couldn't prevent what happened to me, but perhaps I can save you from suffering the same fate; indeed, a more severe one. At least in my case, I was taken by force, so I was spared the knowledge that I was a willing participant. If Remington Worth should take you to his bed, you'd go eagerly, like a lamb to slaughter. Could you face yourself the next day knowing you were but a pawn in his scheme of seduction?"

Throughout Cynthia's speech Sammy remained silent, pondering the significance of her maid's words. Now she straightened, met Cynthia's gaze with sympathy and candor. "Remington's not trying to seduce me, Cynthia, any more than you're trying to hurt me. In your own way, you're each trying to shelter me ... in areas that, much as you believe otherwise, I don't need sheltering. Perhaps Rem is going to Annie's tonight. But if so, it's not for a sexual liaison. Why am I so certain? Because he would have told me so directly. I have no claims on his fidelity, only on his feelings. To answer your question, yes, I could live with myself if I went to the bed of the man I love. And I hope with all my heart that someday you'll be able to say the same."

"I don't believe in love. Nor would I ever knowingly embrace social ruin, the way you seem determined to do."

"Social ruin? Why would I be ruined?"

Cynthia shook her head in disbelief. "Even among the working class, for an unwed girl to relinquish her innocence is appalling. In the *ton?* Need you ask? If you lie with a man out of wedlock, you'll be labeled a common trollop!"

"Not if I wed the man with whom I share my innocence."

"Wed the ..." Cynthia inhaled sharply. "Samantha, do you honestly believe you are going to marry Remington Worth; or rather, that he is going to marry you?"

"Of course."

"Has he actually spoken of matrimony?"

"Not yet."

"Then what makes you think he will?"

Sammy lay her hand over her heart. "This."

"So you're going to lie with the earl because of some romantic misconception that, in the glowing aftermath of your union, he'll feel compelled to propose marriage?"

"No. I'm going to lie with the earl because I love him. And the earl's going to propose because he loves me." Sammy smiled as she summed up the obvious.

"I see." Cynthia didn't smile back. "Will you promise me one thing?"

"If I can."

"Before you enact your sentimental plan, will you make sure Lord Gresham's intentions concur with your own?"

A faraway look appeared in Sammy's eyes. "All right. I'll make certain Remington and I understand each other completely."

"Rem. I'm glad you're here. I was getting concerned." Boyd glanced down at his timepiece, which read nearly half after two.

"I was unexpectedly detained. I apologize, gentlemen." Rem slid into his chair, addressing Boyd, Templar, and Harris.

Boyd's eyes narrowed on Rem's face, but he did not pursue the subject. "Another British ship went down."

"When?" Rem was instantly alert.

"The Admiralty got word late this evening. They couldn't locate you, so they delivered the message to Boydry's."

"What details did they provide?"

"Not many. Their information is still sketchy. Apparently, the vessel was en route to Canada. It was last seen in the far waters of the English Channel. As for its cargo—it was varied in content and belonged to several different merchants."

"I'll get that data for you," Harris chimed in. "You'll have the names of the merchants and exactly what each one was transporting by morning."

"The ship was part of Anders's fleet," Boyd continued. "Evidently, it was one of his prize brigs."

"Judging from his records, he's hurting pretty badly. This loss is going to cripple him," Templar added.

Boyd cleared his throat. "The missing brig was built by Barrett Shipping."

A muscle tightened fractionally in Rem's jaw. "I see."

"Harris and I are going directly to the docks from here, Gresham," Templar informed him. "We've reached a dead end everywhere else. Maybe we can learn something useful from the wharf rats."

Rem frowned. "You checked out the other companies we discussed?"

"Yes, all of them. The merchants, too."

"And?"

"Nothing was amiss in any of their records."

"All right." Rem nodded. "Do as you suggested. Poke around at the docks and see what you can find out. In the interim, I'll have a chat with the Viscount Anders and the Duke of Allonshire."

"Is there anything else or should we get started?"

"Get started."

Harris's chair scraped the floor. "We'll be in touch."

Boyd waited until the Bow Street men had left Annie's before he spoke. "Don't assume the worst, Rem. The fact that Barrett Shipping built the missing brig doesn't implicate them. There's no evidence that the ship's construction had anything to do with its disappearance."

"I know that. I just wasn't anticipating a discussion with Drake Barrett at this particular time. It's going to be damned uncomfortable, given the circumstances, for me to face him. Hell, I'm not even sure I can look the man in the eye."

"Your conversation won't pertain to Samantha or your relationship with her."

"Unless her brother brings it up. Aren't you the one who told me how rampantly gossip travels?"

Boyd weighed that possibility in his mind. "What will you tell him?"

"As little as possible."

"Nothing tangible has actually occurred … has it?"

Rem met Boyd's questioning look. "Not yet."

The inference sank in.

"Moreover," Rem continued, "with Alexandria about to deliver a child, I'm not even sure Allonshire will see me."

"Why not begin with Anders, then? He's right here in London, isn't he?"

"He certainly is. I had an altercation with him not two hours past."

Boyd looked surprised. "I know you don't particularly like or trust the fellow. But I didn't know you were openly hostile toward each other."

"We weren't. We are now."

"Why?"

"He made some unwanted advances to Samantha."

"Unwanted? By whom?" Despite the seriousness of tonight's news, Boyd's lips twitched.

"By Samantha ... and by me."

"I see. Well, the knight-in-shining-armor role is becoming a habit with you. At least where Samantha Barrett is concerned. One would almost think you were saving her for yourself."

"One would be right."

Boyd's smile faded. "Rem—"

"Not now, Boyd. My feelings about Samantha are too complex for a two-minute discussion. We'll delve into them another time. Right now, we have work to do."

"What will you tell Samantha about your meeting with Allonshire?"

"I can't keep it a secret; she's too close to her family. I'll continue with my original story about attempting to settle some financial difficulties. I'll tell her I managed to borrow a respectable sum of money and want to commission the building of a ship."

"And will you tell the same to Allonshire?"

"I don't know. That all depends on what he tells me." Rem rubbed his palms together. "The day we rode through Hyde Park, Samantha mentioned Goddfrey's name, as if she thought he might have some information that could solve the mystery of the missing ships. I have yet to figure out what precipitated her comment."

"But you don't think Goddfrey's involved."

"No, I don't. But perhaps Allonshire does. Samantha seemed terribly nervous when she inadvertently let the viscount's name slip in my presence. I couldn't help but think she might have been privy to a conversation she was told not to repeat."

"Which leads us back to Allonshire."

"Exactly." Rem stood. "When I left Carlton House, Anders was still at the party. I assume he'll be abed until midday ... unless he's awakened by word of his missing ship. I'll get some sleep and call on him at noon. I'll also send a message to Allonshire, requesting a few minutes of the duke's time. Berkshire is only an hour's drive. If Drake agrees to see me in the late afternoon, I should have some answers by nightfall."

"Rem, before you go ..." Boyd rose slowly, obviously uncomfortable with his next question. "Did Samantha happen to mention Cynthia at all?"

"Ah, Cynthia. I'm glad you brought her up." Rem leaned toward his friend. "I had a very interesting chat with Samantha's new maid this evening."

"A chat? About what?"

"Evidently, Cynthia has appointed herself Samantha's conscience. She warned me in no uncertain terms to stay away from her mistress and to leave her virtue intact."

Boyd blinked. "I see."

"That doesn't surprise you?"

"No. I'm not sure why, but it doesn't. There's something about that woman ... I don't know what it is. All I know is that she doesn't belong at Annie's and that she's more a lady than a whore."

"I agree."

"You do?"

"Wholeheartedly. I also think that the only person Cynthia has entrusted with the true details of her background is Samantha. We could question Annie, but my guess is she knows as little as we do."

"The other night you mentioned that Samantha defended Cynthia to you—I take it that means she's fond of her?"

"Definitely."

Again Boyd hesitated.

"Why don't you pay Cynthia a visit?" Rem suggested casually. "She was quite taken with you that first evening."

"She was polite, nothing more. I assume she treats everyone that way."

Rem chuckled. "A poor assumption. She lambasted me quite thoroughly tonight, with a razor-sharp tongue. No, I should say that your Cynthia leans toward honesty in her treatment of men."

"Still … I wouldn't want to make her uncomfortable or jeopardize her new position."

"From what I witnessed, Cynthia's position is secure. Moreover, I'm certain she's granted a day off."

Boyd nodded. "True."

"Do it."

"You don't think Samantha would mind?"

Again Rem's dimple flashed. "I think Samantha would find it stirringly romantic."

"All right then." Boyd visibly relaxed. "You know, Rem, if I didn't know better, I'd swear Samantha Barrett was converting you to her way of thinking. You're becoming quite the romantic yourself."

"Rem?" Katrina strolled cautiously over to their table. "I thought it was you back here."

"Hello, Katrina." Rem gifted her with a dazzling smile. "It's good to see you."

"Is it?" She fingered the folds of her gown awkwardly. "I was beginning to wonder. It's been ages."

"I'm hardly a stranger. Why, I've been at Annie's twice this week."

"You know what I mean." Katrina's brilliant blue eyes were veiled with questions. "Are you leaving already?"

"Yes, sweet, I am." Rem's voice was gentle.

"Could I convince you to stay?"

Even as Katrina spoke, gazed at him with explicit promise in her eyes—a promise he once would have savored—it was Samantha's face Rem saw, Samantha's words he heard issuing her enchanting request. *Remington ... until we find the time to be alone ... until then ... I don't want you with other women.*

On the heels of Rem's memory came the irrefutable realization that the reply he'd given her was the truth. He didn't want another woman. Only Samantha.

"Katrina—" he began.

"There's someone special, isn't there?" It was a statement, not a question.

Rem answered anyway. "Yes, there is."

Katrina managed a smile. "She's a lucky woman." Raising up, she kissed his cheek, murmuring, "I'll miss you, Rem." With an audible swallow, she turned away. "Now, if you'll excuse me, gentlemen, I have work to do."

"Christ, Boyd," Rem shook his head, staring after Katrina's retreating figure and looking more vulnerable than Boyd had seen him in years. "What's happening to me?"

"You know what's happening to you, Rem. But if you need me to say the words, I'll say them for you. You're falling in love with Samantha Barrett."

Sammy was thinking much the same thing. She'd seen the look in Rem's eyes when he'd held her, felt the tremor in his hands on her skin. He was starting to fathom the significance of what was destined to be. And she could hardly wait.

Smiling, she rolled onto her side, savoring the last filaments of night. Alone in her romantic cocoon, Rem was already hers.

She must have slept. The next thing she knew, sunlight was streaming insistently through her bedroom window, demanding that she open her eyes. Sammy ignored it, snuggling back into the covers and tugging a pillow over her head. It was too soon to part with the night's exhilarating dreams.

The commotion from the lower level changed her mind.

A series of opening and closing doors ensued, followed by hurried footsteps and anxious, murmuring voices, intruding on Sammy's pleasant reverie. She sat up, the clock beside her dressing table telling her that it was only a few minutes past nine; far too early for visitors or appointments of any kind. Something was amiss.

She slid out of bed, washed and dressed in record time. Cynthia wouldn't be in for at least an hour, and there was no point in summoning her. All Sammy wanted was to get downstairs and find out what was causing the excitement.

Smitty collided with her in the hallway.

"Lady Samantha, forgive me, I didn't see you." His mouth was drawn, his expression grim.

"What's happened, Smitty? What's wrong?"

He hesitated.

"Is it Alex? Is the baby coming?"

"No, my lady. The duchess and her unborn child are well. As of yet there are no signs that the birth is imminent."

"Is it Drake, then?" Sammy tried next. When Smitty didn't answer immediately, she panicked. "Is he ill? Hurt?" She seized Smitty's hands. "Tell me what's wrong!"

"Physically your brother is fine, my lady. It's nothing such as that. It concerns Barrett Shipping."

"Barrett Shipping?" Sammy's focus shifted abruptly. "Did we lose another vessel?"

"We did."

"Which one?"

"A brig. Not one of our fleet, thankfully."

"But one we constructed?"

"Yes."

"Was anyone hurt, Smitty?"

"It doesn't look good, my lady. The crew was small, but none of them has been spotted. Nor has the ship or its cargo been recovered."

"Have we any clue as to what happened?"

"None. His Grace is terribly upset, and determined to find out what occurred. He's launching a full-scale investigation."

"I'm not surprised." Sammy nodded thoughtfully. She felt so helpless, so ineffectual. All her life Drake had been there for her. Now was her chance to be there for him.

Goddfrey.

The name sprang to mind, along with the realization that she'd never found the viscount to question him. "This brig ... it didn't by any chance belong to Viscount Goddfrey, did it?" she blurted out.

Smitty looked startled. "Why, no, my lady, it didn't. In fact, it belonged to Viscount Anders."

"Stephen?" Sammy's brows rose in surprise. "Oh, he must be devastated. I'll go to him at once."

"It's barely nine o'clock, Lady Samantha. Hardly a proper hour to call on a gentleman."

"Smitty," Sammy gave him an exasperated look, "the viscount just lost his ship. I'm not paying a social call, I'm offering my support. But if it will ease your mind, Cynthia will accompany me."

"Well ..." Smitty frowned.

"Thank you for understanding," Sammy said quickly, already scurrying up the stairs to alert Cynthia. It had just occurred to her that, in the process of comforting Stephen, she might learn something of Goddfrey's whereabouts. "I'll be home before you have time to miss me."

"This Viscount Anders—is he another of your beaux?" Cynthia questioned curiously as their phaeton raced toward the docks.

"Perhaps in his mind. Not in mine," Sammy replied.

"Yet you're rushing to his side."

"No, I'm offering him friendship. Besides," Sammy's eyes sparkled, "I might learn something from him ... something that could help Drake."

"Ah, your Gothics again."

Sammy shot her a sidelong glance. "I just happened to recall that it was Stephen I first heard discussing Lord Goddfrey's dilemma."

"Who is Lord Goddfrey?"

Sammy filled Cynthia in on what she'd overheard at her first Almack's ball and subsequently at the dock. "Stephen might know where Lord Goddfrey is. If so, perhaps that will lead us to the truth. Then all would be well and Drake would be out of danger."

Cynthia rolled her eyes. "Samantha—"

"We're here. Come." Sammy sprang from the barely still phaeton, dragging Cynthia along with her.

"This is even more odious than Shadwell!" Cynthia surveyed London Dock with distaste.

"You'll get used to it. I've been here countless times, so I barely notice the riffraff anymore. Besides, we have no choice. This is where the warehouses are located. Now all we need to do is find Stephen's."

"How do you know he's at his warehouse and not his home ... in his bed, for that matter? It's only mid-morning."

"Because he's just lost a ship. If Drake's received the news, so has Stephen. He'll rush right down to his warehouse to get the full details. There it is!" Triumphantly, Sammy pointed to a corner building with the sign ANDERS SHIPPING COMPANY. "I'm going in. You wait here."

"Just a minute." Cynthia stayed Sammy with her hand. "You're not going in there alone."

"It's possible that Stephen will refuse to confide in me ... but he'll certainly refuse to do so if I bring a chaperon. I'll be fine, Cynthia. Just wait here. If I need you, I'll yell." She grinned. "The way you suggested at Vauxhall."

"And we both know how that evening turned out," Cynthia muttered. "Very well. I'll stand guard."

Sammy marched up to the door and knocked.

"Yes?" A ruddy-complexioned foreman opened the door.

"Good morning. I'm here to see Viscount Anders. I realize I haven't an appointment, and it is a bit early, but I do hope he's in and he can see me."

The man scratched his head, drinking in Sammy's delicate curves and earnest expression. "He's here. As for seeing you … who are you?"

"Forgive me, sir." Sammy curtsied. "I'm Samantha Barrett, a friend of the viscount's."

"A friend, huh?" The foreman grinned, watching Sammy's formal curtsy as if uncertain exactly how to respond. Ultimately, he shrugged. "Well, come in, little lady. You might be just the medicine Anders needs today."

Sammy's guide led her through the warehouse, stopping before a heavy wooden door. "That's his office. Good luck."

"Thank you, sir." Sammy knocked.

"Who is it?" a slurred voice called.

"Stephen? It's I … Samantha."

Silence, followed by a murmur of male voices and the muffled sound of drawers closing. An instant later Stephen himself opened the door.

"Samantha?" He stared at her from beneath red-rimmed eyes, his rumpled clothing the same attire she'd seen him in at Carlton House. Evidently, he'd been up all night.

"I heard what happened. I came to see what I could do." A movement from inside the office caught Sammy's eye. "Have I come at a bad time?"

"No … of course not. I appreciate your visit more than I can say. Forgive me for forgetting my manners." He drew her inside.

"Arthur, may I present Lady Samantha Barrett. Samantha, Arthur Summerson." He cleared his throat. "Arthur is a fine merchant. ...He lost valuable cargo on my missing brig."

"Lady Samantha, I'm honored." The stocky, balding man bowed, his eyes meeting Samantha's.

It was all she could do not to cry out her distress.

Arthur Summerson was the man she'd seen chatting with Lord Hartley the morning she'd investigated the docks dressed in her gardener's clothes; the man who'd stared at her as she made her way through the warehouse walls disguised as a boy. She recognized him at once, as well as his name—it was the one Lord Hartley had used in addressing him. The question was, would he recognize her?

If he did, she would die.

"Mr. Summerson." Forcing a smile, Sammy fought the urge to dash back out the door.

For a fleeting instant Summerson's eyes narrowed, a quizzical expression in them. "Have we met before, my lady?"

"I don't believe so ... but it is possible, sir. My brother owns Barrett Shipping."

"Ah ... you're Drake Barrett's sister." Fortunately, that realization seemed to satisfy Summerson's doubts, "I imagine your brother is troubled by this loss. After all, it was his ship that sank."

"Drake is upset by all the losses, whether they involve his ships or not," Sammy defended instantly. "Frankly, however, all the Barrett vessels are constructed with the finest materials and by the most capable men. So it is puzzling indeed that any of our brigs would go down."

Summerson cleared his throat roughly. "Yes ... of course, I quite agree. Barrett Shipping is a fine, reputable firm. Well, Anders, I'd best be on my way. Keep me abreast of any news you might hear."

"I certainly shall," Stephen assured him.

"Lady Samantha, it was a pleasure."

"I'm sorry we had to meet under such disagreeable circumstances, Mr. Summerson. I hope you recover all that is lost."

"As do I. Good day."

"Forgive me, Stephen," Sammy apologized when they were alone. "I didn't mean to be so defensive."

Stephen waved away her apology, pouring himself a brandy. "You were defending your family's business. I understand completely." He tossed off his drink, then gave her a measured look. "Dare I hope that your visit means you've changed your mind about us?"

"There is no 'us,' Stephen. You're my friend, nothing more. But friends care about each other. They also help each other, if need be."

"I see. So you're here to offer your assistance?"

"And to elicit yours."

"Mine? In what manner?"

Sammy ran her fingers along the edge of Stephen's walnut desk. "Viscount Goddfrey. What do you know of his circumstances?"

"Goddfrey?" Stephen's brows rose in surprise. "Only that he's endured great financial losses; losses that forced him to flee from London in order to save face. Why?"

"Do you know where he went?"

"No." Stephen frowned. "Why are you so interested in Goddfrey? You're not involved with him, are you?"

"Involved with him?" Sammy blinked. "No, Stephen. I never even met the man. I only thought perhaps he knew something about the missing ships ... and that what he learned had forced him—or frightened him—away."

The frown faded from Stephen's face. "I see. You're investigating on behalf of your brother, are you?"

Sammy's face fell. "Am I so obvious, then?"

"No, *petite fleur,* you're not obvious ... only adorably forthright. I find your family devotion quite touching." He moved toward her. "Now, if I could only convince you to extend that devotion to me."

"Is there anything"—she held up a restraining hand—"other than *that,* I can do to help?"

He grinned. "You've already brightened my mood considerably with your visit. Despite your maidenly qualms, I shan't give up hope."

"I—I'd best be going." Sammy inched toward the door, wondering where to turn now. She'd gotten nowhere with Anders. And she dared not stay—not when he was looking at her like a hungry lion about to pounce on its dinner. "Well, good-bye, Stephen."

She nearly knocked Cynthia down in her haste to leave.

"Are you all right?" her maid demanded.

"Yes. Just as uninformed as I was prior to my visit, but fine."

"Good. Let's go home." Scarcely had Cynthia taken a step, when she came to a grinding halt.

Curiously, Sammy followed Cynthia's stare, spotting the sandy-haired, powerfully built man approaching them. He stopped, his eyes on Cynthia.

"Hello." He shifted uncomfortably. "I'm not sure if you remember me. We met the other night at"—the slightest of pauses—"a coffeehouse."

The wall of Cynthia's self-protective reserve seemed to waver. "I remember. Boyd, isn't it?"

His entire face broke into a smile. "Yes, Cynthia. It's Boyd." Belatedly, he glanced at Samantha. "Oh, forgive me. We haven't met. I'm—"

"I know. Boyd." Sammy shot him an impish grin. "You're the tavern keeper at Boydry's, my sanctuary from this Season's first storm. You're also a friend of Remington's. I'm glad to meet you."

If Sammy didn't know better, she'd swear Boyd already knew who she was. She'd also swear he was fighting back laughter. But he'd have no way of knowing her, and a man as rugged as he wouldn't find a green girl like her amusing. "My name is Samantha Barrett," she offered.

"Rem speaks of you often. I'm delighted to meet you."

"He does?" Sammy lit up like a ray of sunshine.

"He does." Boyd's chuckle was genuine. "He also mentioned that Cynthia had sought employment with your family."

"I'm sure Lord Gresham had a few other choice words to say about me," Cynthia interjected dryly. "None of them flattering."

"You're wrong."

"Not necessarily." Rem's voice cut through the morning air. With barely leashed fury, he stalked over, his anger a palpable entity that loomed closer with each step. "What the hell are you doing alone at the docks at this ungodly hour?" he demanded without preliminaries. His steely gaze was fixed on Samantha.

It was Cynthia who answered. "Samantha had an appointment. I accompanied her."

"An appointment." His eyes bore into Sammy's soul. "With Anders? Before noon? You didn't mention it a few hours ago when you were in my arms."

"Christ, Rem ..." Boyd's head snapped around at Rem's unprecedented display of jealousy.

Rem ignored his friend. In fact, he didn't even see Boyd, or Cynthia for that matter. All he saw was Samantha ... with that bloody bastard Anders.

"Stephen lost another ship, Rem. One of ours." Sammy's heart pounded wildly in her chest. Rem was jealous. Jealous, livid, and harshly possessive. She was ecstatic.

"Really? And did the two of you console each other?" Rem's tone was lethal.

"No, as a matter of fact, we had a business meeting."

"A business meeting." He repeated the words with the same utter contempt as if she'd just confessed to a heinous crime.

"Yes." Sammy was playing with fire and she knew it. Yet something propelled her forward, some innate knowledge of the man she loved. "A business meeting ... much like the one Cynthia overheard you directing your coachman to a few hours ago, at Annie's."

A charged silence surged between them.

"Samantha ..." Cynthia lay a hand on her arm. "Perhaps we'd best go home ..."

"No." Rem reached forward and seized Sammy's elbow. "I want to talk to you. Now." Without waiting for a reply, he dragged her off to a private spot a short distance away from the others. "What the hell was that all about?"

"Which 'that'? My visit to Stephen's warehouse or your visit to Annie's brothel?"

"It *was* a business meeting, Samantha."

"So was mine."

"Concerning what?"

Sammy hesitated. "I had some questions," she hedged at last.

"Questions for Anders? Pertaining to what; his missing ship?"

"Yes." Her shoulders sagged. What was the use in evading Rem's inquiries? Anders had guessed what she was up to. She might as well be honest. "I had hoped Stephen could tell me where Viscount Goddfrey was living. He couldn't. And it no longer matters."

Rem's eyes narrowed on her face. "Why did you want to find Goddfrey?"

"Last week at Almack's I overheard Stephen talking about Goddfrey's terrible losses, his precarious financial state and his subsequent disappearance. I thought perhaps the viscount might be somehow involved in the sinkings. Evidently, I was wrong." She sighed. "I was only trying to help Drake."

"What did Anders tell you?"

"Very little. Only that he didn't know Lord Goddfrey's whereabouts, but that the viscount had fled in order to avoid a personal scandal."

"And then?"

"Then I left."

"Are you trying to tell me Anders made no advances?"

"Oh, he did. But I rejected them." Sammy inclined her head, a mischievous light coming into her eyes. "And you? Are you trying to tell me that not one of Annie's women made any advances?"

Rem stared at Sammy for a long, electrifying moment. Then he smiled—a slow, seductive smile—sliding his hand beneath the heavy sable mane of her hair. "Oh, one did. But I rejected them." He cupped her face. "All I could see was you." He bent his head, took her mouth with tender ferocity. "All I want is you."

Oblivious to the bustle of activity around them and the prying eyes of the world, Sammy twined her arms around Rem's neck, standing on tiptoe to deepen his kiss. "When?" she breathed.

"Constantly. Relentlessly. Until I'm burning with it."

Sammy began to tremble. "No … I meant when can we be together?"

He nibbled lightly at her lower lip, running his warm fingers up and down her bare arms. "Right now, if I had my way. But that might cause quite a scandal … even in so unsavory a place as this."

"Will you find a way?" She gazed up at him with those melting, trusting green eyes.

"If I have to move heaven and earth, yes."

In that instant Sammy had to bite her lip to keep from blurting out how much she loved him. But her heart cautioned her that Rem was not yet ready to hear those words.

"Boyd and Cynthia will be worried," she murmured.

"Oh, something tells me they don't mind our absence."

Sammy's ecstatic smile made her glow like the dawn. "Is Boyd as intrigued by Cynthia as she is by him?"

"Without a doubt."

"Oh, Rem, wouldn't that be wonderful? Cynthia so badly needs a man she can trust. After what happened …"

Rem studied Sammy with quiet insight. "Cynthia's endured great pain at a man's hands, hasn't she?"

That much, at least, Sammy could disclose. She nodded. "Have you and Boyd been friends for long?"

"Over a decade. We served in the navy together."

"I see." Sammy did see. If Boyd had been by Rem's side all these years, then he would understand Rem's staunch need for autonomy … and his vehement resistance to allowing anyone into his heart.

Storing that information away for later, Sammy merely said, "Boyd seems like a fine man."

"He is. The finest."

Nearby, one dock worker called out to another, readying a heavy crate to be hoisted aboard a ship.

"I'd best take my leave." Sammy dropped her arms to her sides in an action that was charmingly reluctant. "Will I see you later today?"

Later today.

Rem's stomach clenched. Later today he'd be meeting with Samantha's strong-willed brother, the brother who would call him out in a minute and shoot him dead if he knew what Rem intended for Samantha.

But Rem's will was equally strong. No one was going to stop him. Not from fulfilling his mission.

Nor from taking Samantha Barrett to bed.

"Yes, imp, you'll see me later. You have my word."

TWELVE

"Who is it?"

"It's Gresham. We need to talk."

Yanking open his office door, Anders eyed Rem with undisguised hostility. "Really? What about?"

Rem scrutinized the viscount's disheveled appearance, making no attempt to hide his own dislike. "Samantha."

"Samantha?" Anders's jaw tightened. "In that case we have nothing to discuss."

"You're wrong." Rem caught the door a split second before it slammed in his face. Thrusting it open, he stepped brazenly into Anders's office. "Now, we can either have this disagreeable conversation in private, or in full view of your workers. The choice is yours."

A charged moment ticked by, then Anders moved stiffly aside. "Suit yourself." He walked over to the sideboard and poured himself another drink. "You'll forgive me if I don't offer you one."

"This isn't a social call." With a swift, nearly imperceptible shift of his head, Rem scanned the office, affirmed that it was empty save the two of them. Then, kicking the door shut, he got right to the point. "Your behavior at Carlton House was reprehensible."

"*My* behavior? I wasn't the one who made a scene."

"I wasn't the one who prompted it."

With a mirthless laugh, Anders tossed off his drink. "You're questioning my morals? You, who have none of your own?"

"We're discussing your morals only as they pertain to Samantha. Otherwise, quite frankly, I don't give a damn who you bed."

"'Tis your mind in the gutter, Gresham, not mine … an amusing fact, considering that yours are the contemptible actions here. After all, it wasn't I who whisked Samantha away—not once, but twice—at an Almack's ball. Nor was it I who returned her, breathless and out of sorts each time." Anders refilled his glass. "No, Gresham, if anything, I intend to maintain Lady Samantha's respectability … and her innocence. Which is more than I can say for you."

Blood began to pound through Rem's temples. Resolutely, he steeled himself, curbing his possessive fury with great effort. He had to stay calm. There was too much at stake. "Are you trying to tell me you're not plotting ways to get Samantha into your bed?"

"No, I'm not telling you that at all. I can hardly wait to make Samantha mine. However, I intend to place a wedding ring on her finger first."

Every muscle in Rem's body went taut to breaking, rage exploding inside his skull in a violent surge. "What makes you think Samantha wishes to marry you?" he managed between clenched teeth.

Anders's eyes glittered brittlely. "I'm titled, eligible, and more than willing to give the lady anything she desires. I intend to ask the duke for her hand within the month." Triumphantly, Anders raised his glass in mock tribute to himself, and his future. "I've enjoyed successful business dealings with Drake Barrett for many years … I see no reason why this one should be any less fruitful."

Rem had to swallow the bile that rose in his throat. This smug blackguard was describing his precious, unsuspecting Samantha as a business acquisition. The same blackguard, however, was also providing him with just the opportunity he'd hoped for—and now seized. "I hear you just lost another brig."

Suspiciously, Anders's eyes narrowed. "Where did you hear that?"

"The news is hardly a secret."

A reluctant pause. "True," Anders conceded at last. "'Tis a heinous tragedy; a fine ship—constructed by Barrett Shipping, incidentally—a small crew, but valuable cargo."

"This is your third loss, is it not?"

"Unfortunately, yes ... why?"

Casually, Rem shrugged. "A moment ago you proclaimed your intentions to wed Samantha Barrett. I only wondered how you'll provide for her with a third of your fleet gone."

"Such gallantry! Why, Gresham, one would almost think you yourself had personal designs on Samantha."

Watching Anders's lips curve into a condescending smile, Rem knew at once his ruse had worked. The insipid viscount had just come to the erroneous conclusion that Rem's questions were rooted solely in jealousy—precisely the conclusion Rem had hoped he'd reach.

"I hate to disappoint you, Gresham, but I'm a very wealthy man. As to my fleet—I collected insurance money for the first two vessels. It will take some time, but I'll do the same for the third."

"Yes, but how will you continue to operate Anders Shipping? Insurance rates have soared due to the number of missing British ships. I shudder to think what this new loss will mean for you. Won't it cripple your business?"

"Far from it. My business is thriving."

"I see." From the Bow Street reports, Rem knew otherwise. Of course, Anders's lie was most likely an attempt to salvage his pride. Still ... "How fortunate. I wonder how many of your merchants can make the same claim."

"Your concern is touching. But fear not. Even if the merchants become reluctant and my shipping trade decreases, my income will continue to flourish. I have many investments, all of which yield high profits. Anders Shipping is but one of them. When Samantha becomes my wife, she will assume the life of luxury both you and I agree she deserves. All her whims will be indulged"—Anders cocked a meaningful brow—"both in bed and out."

That did it. Though he understood he was being deliberately goaded, Rem knew if he didn't get out of here soon, he was going to tear Anders apart limb from limb.

"Stay the hell away from Samantha," he ground out, his menacing tone conveying the magnitude of his threat. Flinging open the door with such force it was nearly torn from its hinges, Rem stalked out, unable to bear being in the viscount's presence one second longer. "Don't make the mistake of ignoring my warning, Anders," he cautioned over his shoulder. "Or I vow, you'll answer to me."

He didn't wait for a reply.

"Good afternoon, Lord Gresham. We received your message. The duke is expecting you."

Humphreys, Allonshire's portly butler, acknowledged Rem with a slight bow. "I'll show you to his study."

"Thank you, Humphreys."

Rem had visited Allonshire on but several occasions, and never during the past few years. He'd forgotten how palatial an estate it was. Gilded ceilings and elaborate statues decorated the entranceway, and priceless paintings hung on the walls, stretching as far as the eye could see. Hundreds of rooms on just as many acres defined the Gothic manor, bespeaking both great wealth and great power. Indeed, Allonshire was as formidable as the man who owned it.

Soberly, Rem followed Humphreys through the marble corridor, contemplating his impending challenge: the interrogation of Drake Barrett. The task wouldn't be an easy one. Allonshire's astute, imposing master was not a pompous dolt like Anders. His strong-minded cunning wouldn't blind him to what Rem was about, nor deter him from the realization that Rem's questions were motivated by more than mere curiosity. With the secrecy of his mission at stake, Rem cautioned himself to tread carefully when broaching the subject of the missing ships.

And when broaching the subject of Samantha.

That reminder incited all Rem's protective instincts, and intensified his resolve threefold. His original vow to drown in Samantha's company for no more than four days was long since cast aside, obliterated in a tidal wave of desire so powerful it stripped reason away. And despite her brother's anticipated and justifiable rage, despite her innocence, her tender heart … despite the insanity of it all, Rem was going to have her.

"Your Grace … Lord Gresham," Humphreys announced.

Drake Barrett turned from the window, leveling his probing gaze on Rem. "Hello, Gresham."

"It's been a long time." Rem extended his hand. "Nearly a year, if memory serves me correctly." Upon close inspection, Rem could see the family resemblance: the thick black hair, the startlingly green eyes, the chiseled, aristocratic features. But where Samantha was soft, delicate—from the velvety meadow-green of her eyes to the fine bones of her face and her slender shape—Drake's features were hard, arrogant, his eyes fiery emeralds, the lines of his face harsh, his shoulders broad, muscled from years at sea. A formidable opponent indeed.

"Since last Season to be exact," Drake agreed, shaking Rem's hand. "The final ball at Almack's." He indicated a large, tufted chair. "Have a seat and we'll get to the purpose of your visit. What can I offer you?"

Noting the nearly empty glass of brandy on Drake's sideboard, Rem replied, "Brandy would be fine."

"I'll see to the earl, Humphreys," Drake informed his butler. "That'll be all for now."

"Very good, Your Grace." Humphreys turned to go.

"Oh … Humphreys?" Drake looked up, ran an agitated hand through his hair. "You'll call me if I'm needed?"

"Of course."

Rem watched the exchange with interest, taking in Drake's unsettled state and unsteady hand. Evidently, something was troubling the duke.

"You seem distressed," Rem commented, leaning back in his chair. "Is it the ship that just went down?"

"Hmm? Oh, the ship." Drake handed Rem his drink and began to pace restlessly about the room. "Of course I'm deeply concerned by the loss. I've arranged a thorough investigation to determine its cause." He tossed down the remaining contents of his own glass. "As for my agitation, you'll have to forgive me. I am a bit out of sorts. My wife is in the process of gifting me with our second child." He tilted his head back, staring at the ceiling as if seeing through to their second story bedchamber. "I'd almost forgotten how unbearable it is to see her in pain," he added softly.

Rem started to rise. "Forgive me. This is obviously not the time to discuss business. I'll come back after—"

"No." Drake gestured for Rem to remain. "A diversion would be welcome, I assure you. Besides, I've been asked"—a corner of Drake's mouth lifted—"actually, ordered to leave Alex's room."

"By a midwife?"

"No, by Alexandria herself. Evidently she feels I'm more hindrance than help." Drake grinned. "My duchess is a tyrant, Gresham. The idea that I rule her is questionable at best. And, as if that notion alone weren't humbling, she's managed to pass her winsome brand of defiance on to my son. At two years of age, Gray is a little devil who upends the whole household, then flashes me one of Alex's angelic smiles and I relent." Drake shook his head, his expression baffled and tender all at once. "For a man who's used to intimidating all he meets, it's unnerving as hell."

Rem was stunned by two distinct and simultaneous realizations: one, he completely understood the emotions Drake was describing, and two, the tightness constricting his chest was not disdain, but envy. "Unnerving as hell," he murmured in agreement.

"Pardon me?"

Coughing discreetly, Rem forced himself back to coherence. "It's difficult for me to envision Alexandria as a tyrant. From what I've seen, she's a beautiful, charming woman."

"True. She's also an opinionated, outspoken hellion who has turned my life upside down since the day she burst into it three years past. And I wouldn't trade a moment of our time together for all the riches in the world." Self-consciously, Drake rolled his empty glass between his palms, dispelling the conversation's sentimental tenor. "In any case, it will do me good to concentrate on business for a while—which I assume is the reason you're here. You certainly didn't come all the way to Allonshire to hear me ramble on about my family." Drake perched at the edge of his desk. "What's on your mind?"

In truth, what was on Rem's mind at that moment was Samantha's description of her brother's marriage. Love, she'd said. Well, perhaps she was right. Certainly Rem had never witnessed such tenderness from Drake Barrett, never even suspected he was capable of it.

"Do you intend to tell me why you wished to see me?" Drake prodded.

"Of course." Sipping his brandy, Rem berated himself for his lack of concentration. This was not the time to lose control. "I'm considering making an investment. I wanted your opinion on it."

"*My* opinion?" Drake's brows rose. "Why?"

"Because it involves purchasing a ship. Or rather, commissioning one to be built."

"You're going back to sea?"

"Not in any official capacity, no. I'm looking for a merchant brig, not a warship."

"I see." Drake set down his glass. "What kind of vessel did you have in mind?"

"One large enough to transport extensive amounts of cargo, yet fast enough to reach her destinations more swiftly than all her competitors."

"Is that all?" Drake looked vastly amused. "Just a five-hundred-ton runner laden with three decks of cargo that can traverse the seas in the blink of an eye."

"Exactly." Rem leaned forward. "And one other thing. She has to be immune to the disastrous fate so many English ships have suffered these past months."

Instantly, Drake's smile vanished. "Guarantees such as that I cannot offer."

"How do we ensure that you can?"

"What the hell kind of question is that?"

"The kind of question I ask before I commit tens of thousands of pounds to an investment. The kind of question asked by a cautious man who wants some assurances."

"I presume you're considering Barrett Shipping for the construction of this superior vessel of yours?"

"You presume correctly."

"Our record stands on its own."

"Really?" Rem inclined his head. "Wasn't yesterday's loss your second in the same number of months?"

"It was." A muscle worked in Drake's jaw. "And if you're implying that the losses were caused by poor workmanship or inferior materials, then I suggest you leave my home."

"I'm not implying anything." Rem finished his drink, unbothered by Drake's show of temper. "I'm merely trying to protect my investment."

"My company doesn't require any defense, and I don't require your business." Drake came to his feet.

"If I thought you did, I wouldn't be here." Rem held out his empty glass. "Another brandy, if you will, Your Grace."

Reluctant admiration flickered in Drake's eyes. "You're an insolent bastard, you know that, Gresham?"

"So I've been told."

Chuckling, Drake took the glass and refilled it. "Very well. What do you want to know?"

"I won't insult you by questioning your choice of workers. But I will ask what materials you use and what final steps you take to inspect your vessels prior to declaring them fit for sailing."

"Fair enough. Our ships are painstakingly designed, then constructed under strict supervision and to precise specifications in our own yard. We use the finest wood and canvas money can buy, not to mention the highest quality iron for our guns. Our engineers, machinists, and carpenters are unsurpassed in their abilities and are instructed to spare no expense in building consistently superior vessels. No corners are cut, ever, not in design, construction, or inspection. Once the ships are completed, I have my men scrutinize every deck for ill-fitted planking, check every sail for slack rigging and poor stitching ... right down to the smallest topgallant. I personally test each and every ship for seaworthiness. Is that procedure satisfactory enough to suit your needs?"

Rem raised his glass in tribute. "I'm impressed. Truly, I am. What you've just said will certainly influence my decision. I have a strong feeling I'll be doing business with you."

"That depends upon whether or not I choose to do business with you."

"Touché." Rem's eyes twinkled. "Then I return the favor. Go ahead and interrogate me—I'll answer any questions you have."

"All right." Drake lounged against his desk in a deceptively relaxed stance. "I hear you're short of funds. How do you plan to pay for this ship?"

Rem grinned broadly. "I'm happy to see you're thorough, Allonshire. It reassures me that my investment is in good hands. To answer your question, my business reverses were temporary. I've recouped all my losses. I can summon my banker here to verify my words, if you require proof."

"No. Your word is satisfactory." Drake's eyes narrowed. "What are you really up to, Gresham?"

"Meaning?"

"Meaning this sudden urge to purchase a merchant ship. Meaning this business risk you're plunging into so impulsively. It's not at all like you. Your style has always been to scrupulously invest money while otherwise attending parties and bedding women. Why the change?"

Coolly, Rem shrugged. "Perhaps I'm bored. Or perhaps my instincts tell me this is a perfect way to scrupulously invest my money, as you put it. I know ships, Allonshire. Better than anyone else you do business with, I trust. Maybe it's time to put that knowledge to use." Rem arched a brow. "And you must admit, you and I would make an extraordinary team."

"We would indeed." Drake nodded. "I don't admire many men, but I find myself developing a grudging respect for you. Perhaps we can work well together at that." Broodingly, Drake stared into his glass. "Parrying aside, I think we should discuss the ongoing problem of the missing ships. The threat is very real, worsening, it seems, every day. I must admit I'm worried. Since I'm certain that, at least in the case of Barrett Shipping, carelessness is not a possibility, it makes me strongly suspect that terrorism is the true culprit here. That's not a pretty thought, not only for the shipping industry, but for all of England."

"I agree."

"As I mentioned earlier, I've hired a team of men to look into the situation. If you and I decide that my company will be constructing your vessel, I'll make certain to keep you apprised of what I learn."

Although he'd never actually suspected Drake was involved in the sinkings, Rem found himself impressed by the depth of the man's integrity. "I'd appreciate that. And now I'd like to officially commission Barrett Shipping to design and build my brig."

For a moment Drake's eyes delved into Rem, seemingly in search of something not readily perceived. Then he rose, extending his hand. "We have a deal, Gresham."

Rem clasped Drake's hand. "We'll meet next week to discuss my specifications—*after* your child is born."

"Yes." Drake smiled faintly. "It's an incredible feeling, having a child of your own. I still remember the first time I held Gray. It was as if a part of me had merged with a part of Alex and formed this extraordinary little being who looked up at me as if heaven itself should bow to my command. The surge of love, of protectiveness, was staggering. It still is. I'd give my life for my son ... and for all his sisters and brothers yet to come." Once again Drake glanced upward. "If only Alex didn't have to suffer so ... it twists a knife in my gut. God, how I wish I could take her pain."

Rem felt that odd constriction in his chest. "You love Alexandria very much."

"More than I ever believed possible." Drake gave a self-deprecating laugh. "I wasn't much of a believer in love until Alex exploded into my life. In fact, I wasn't much of a believer in anything; didn't give a damn for anyone. Except the sea. And Sammy." Drake's brow furrowed as a sudden thought struck him. "Speaking of which, I want to thank you, a bit belatedly, for the excellent care you took of my sister."

Rem nearly leapt from his chair. "Pardon me?"

"Samantha." Drake shot Rem a quizzical look. "Smitty told me you rescued the two of them from the storm their first night in London."

"Oh ... yes. 'Twas nothing. In fact, I'd nearly forgotten."

"I'm sure you barely recognized Sammy; when you last saw her, she was a child."

Warning bells sounded in Rem's head. "True. She's become an enchanting young lady."

"Young is right. Too young to be let loose among the lechers of the *ton*. I sent her off to London under Smitty's watchful eye so that she could indulge in her first Season. I feel guilty as hell for not accompanying her, but I couldn't bear to leave Alex ... not with the baby's birth so imminent. Still, I'm bloody worried about Samantha. She's too damned open and trusting, and sheltered—my fault, I suppose. But being seventeen years her senior, I've always protected her from the world's ills ... in many ways a father more than a brother."

"I can understand that."

Something of Rem's tension must have conveyed itself to Drake. He inclined his head sharply, eyes narrowed on Rem's face. "Have you had occasion to see Sammy since that night at the tavern?"

Careful, Rem cautioned himself. "Your aunt Gertrude has been escorting Samantha to all the Season's grand balls and soirees. They were in attendance at Almack's, Carlton House, and at least several other parties that come readily to mind."

"I see. So you noticed her at these gatherings?"

"I did."

"Did you dance with her?"

Rem nodded. "She's delightful."

"Yes ... delightful and innocent. Thoroughly innocent. Perfect prey for an immoral blackguard ... wouldn't you agree?"

"Definitely."

"I'd kill any man who touched her. Surely you can't blame me for that?"

"I don't blame any man for doing what he must," Rem replied, calmly meeting Drake's gaze.

"I'm glad to hear that, Gresham. Very glad."

"Your Grace?" Humphreys' knock was loud and purposeful.

Drake reached the door in two strides and yanked it open. "Is it Alex?"

"Yes." Soberly, Humphreys nodded. "The duchess asked me to give you a message. She would like to remind you that all women, no matter how young, dislike being kept waiting by the most important man in their life—especially once they've made an entrance."

Already halfway down the hall, Drake came to a screeching halt. "What?"

A broad grin erupted on Humphreys' face. "You have a daughter, Your Grace. Congratulations."

"A daughter." Drake's throat worked convulsively. "Alex ... is she ...?"

"The duchess herself spoke to me. She's tired, but splendid. And a bit impatient."

Running a shaking hand through his hair, Drake looked dazedly at Rem. "I've got to go to her. Gresham, I—"

Rem waved Drake off. "My best to all of you. Now go. Your family awaits. I can see myself out."

"I'll show Lord Gresham out," Humphreys dutifully offered.

"Yes ... fine ..." Drake had reached the staircase and was taking the steps two at a time. "We'll pursue our plans for your brig soon, Gresham," he called, disappearing around the second floor landing.

Strangely pensive and out of sorts, Rem followed Humphreys to the front door, then strolled out into Allonshire's expansive gardens. He felt he'd just been privy to an intensely personal and emotional moment in the life of a man who wasn't given to sentimental displays. And Rem couldn't deny that it had affected him ... in a way he'd sworn never to be affected.

And what of Samantha?

Drake had vowed to kill any man who touched her, and Rem didn't doubt that he would, nor blame him if he did. Everything the duke had just said about his beautiful, trusting sister was true, and Rem knew he should be plagued with guilt for what he intended.

Why wasn't he?

Lord knew, he was many things, but never unprincipled. Even in serving his country, he was vehement in attempting to see that the innocent remained unharmed. Yet in this case he was knowingly taking a virgin to bed, forever altering her life, but still unable to walk away before her ruin was realized. Worse, unable to see their impending union as anything but inevitable. Why?

You know what's happening to you, Rem. Boyd's pronouncement reverberated loudly in Rem's head. But if you need me to say the words, I'll say them for you. You're falling in love with Samantha Barrett.

A new kind of terror gripped Rem. Boyd was right.

"Hullo."

The small voice seemed to come directly from Allonshire's flower bed. Rem blinked and looked down.

A handsome tot, whose brilliantly green eyes and black hair identified him instantly as Drake's son, grinned up at Rem.

"Well, hello." Rem squatted beside him, wincing as the child yanked a fistful of marigolds from the ground. "You must be Gray."

The boy nodded sagely, pulling up two more handfuls of flowers.

Clearing his throat, Rem looked about for the boy's governess. He had little experience with children and no idea how to handle the boy's destructive sport. Unfortunately, the gardens were deserted, save the two of them.

"May I ask why you're ripping up this lovely flower garden?" Rem inquired at last.

Gray looked at his grimy fist and nodded effusively. "Pretty flowers. Bright colors."

"I agree." Once again, Rem scanned the area. "Where is your governess?"

Triumphantly, Gray pointed to the mansion. "Reading."

"Reading? Why isn't she with you?"

"She thinks I nap."

Rem's lips twitched. "You're telling me that your governess thinks you're napping? Then perhaps you should be."

"No." Gray shook his head vehemently. "No nap. Flowers." Another handful of stems were torn from their grassy bed.

"Why, Gray?" Rem lifted the boy's chin, stared into his intense eyes. "Why flowers?"

"Mama's in bed. She's giving me a brother." He grimaced. "Or a sister." Holding up the mangled bunch of marigolds, he proudly announced, "I give her flowers."

Perhaps it was the afternoon sunshine that made Rem's eyes sting. "I see. Well, I'll tell you something, Gray. Your mama is very lucky to have such a thoughtful son. I'm sure she'll think those are the most beautiful flowers she's ever seen." Smiling at the rapturous expression on the little boy's face, Rem leaned conspiratorially forward. "And do you know what? I think now would be the perfect time to give them to her. In fact, I can't think of a more perfect time."

"I go." Half the flowers fell as Gray struggled to his feet, but Rem suspected Alexandria wouldn't mind their absence. Nor would she mind the glaringly conspicuous bald patch amid Allonshire's otherwise perfect garden. The gift she was receiving was far more precious.

"'Bye." Gray smiled again, and Rem could well understand how that impish grin would melt Drake's heart.

"'Twas a pleasure." Rem solemnly extended his hand. "Incidentally, my name is Rem."

Soberly, Gray shook the proffered hand. "'Bye, Rem." He turned to go.

"Oh, Gray?"

Gray inclined his head quizzically.

"How do you feel about your aunt Samantha?" Rem asked.

Gray's eyes lit up. "Aunt Sammy!"

"She's very special, wouldn't you say?"

An emphatic nod.

"And she adores your papa, doesn't she? Follows him around, looks up to him … that sort of thing?"

"Aunt Sammy says Papa is a … a …" Gray screwed up his face intently, thinking. "A hero!" he exclaimed suddenly.

Warmth seeped through Rem at the characteristically Samantha-like term. "Yes, Aunt Samantha definitely thinks your papa is a hero. Do you know why?"

Shaking his head, Gray waited.

"Because he's her big brother, that's why. And nothing's more special to a girl than her big brother."

Gray's eyes widened.

"Trust me, Gray," Rem advised confidentially. "If you get a brother, it'll be nice, but there's nothing as wonderful as having a little sister who thinks you're the most wonderful person in the whole world. If I were you, I'd wish real hard that your mama gives you just that—a sister who loves you as much as Aunt Samantha loves your papa."

Squeezing his eyes closed, Gray's fist tightened on his flowers. "I'm wishing."

"Good. Now hurry home and see if your wish came true." Quick as a wink, Gray sprinted off toward the manor.

Alexandria Barrett turned her head at the sound of her bedchamber door opening. A soft smile touched her lips as her eyes met her husband's. "Finally."

Gingerly sitting on the edge of the bed, Drake leaned over and reverently kissed Alex's face; her forehead, her cheeks, her lips. "After the unceremonious way you tossed me out, I wasn't sure I was welcome."

"Have you seen her?"

"No. I wanted to see you first." He cupped his wife's face between his palms. "Are you all right?"

"Would you have it any other way?" Alex lay her hand on his jaw.

"No."

"I'm fine. And so is our daughter."

"Thank you, princess." Drake gathered Alex tenderly in his arms. "Thank you for our daughter."

"Another princess," she murmured, a catch in her voice. "Will you withstand it?"

"Gladly."

"I love you, Drake."

"You're my life," he said simply.

"Pardon me, Your Grace." Molly, Alex's lady's maid, poked her head in the room. "Evidently the new babe is hungry. Would you like me to—"

"Bring her to me." Disengaging herself from Drake's embrace, Alex pushed herself to a sitting position.

"But Your Grace—"

"We've discussed this, Molly. Time and time again. The duke and I feel as strongly as we did two years ago when Gray was born. I will feed my daughter. Now would you please bring her in so she can meet her father?"

With a resigned sigh, Molly nodded.

"Princess, are you sure you're not too tired?" Drake traced the dark circles under Alex's eyes with a gentle finger. He still couldn't believe that his tiny, fragile-looking wife was capable of enduring the rigors of childbirth.

"I'm sure." Eagerly, Alex reached out as Molly returned with a small, wailing bundle. Lovingly, Alex took her newborn daughter into her arms, then proudly displayed her to Drake. "Look at her. Isn't she beautiful?"

A muscle worked in Drake's jaw as he gazed into his daughter's fathomless gray eyes—Alex's eyes. Slowly, he lifted her from Alex's arms into his own, cradling her tiny, fuzzy head in his hand. An explosion of pride, protectiveness, and love erupted inside him, so powerful it nearly brought him to his knees. "Hello, little one," he said in a rough whisper.

Instantly, the baby stopped crying.

"Oh Lord." Alex rolled her eyes. "Another woman has fallen prey to your fatal charm."

"Evidently not." Drake chuckled as the crying resumed. "Or at least not in lieu of nourishment." He waited for Alex to lower her night rail before reluctantly shifting the baby back into her mother's hands.

Crooning softly, Alex cradled their daughter to her breast, smiling as the infant greedily latched onto her nipple and, with great enthusiasm, began to suckle. "You're a fast learner, my love," Alex murmured, kissing one flailing fist.

Alex was readjusting her night rail, the baby sound asleep in the crook of her elbow, when Gray exploded into the bedchamber. "Mama, do I have a sister?"

"Forgive me, Your Grace." Miss Hutch, the Allonshire governess, appeared, flushed and panting, beside her charge. "I put the young marquis down for a nap. I had no idea—"

"It's all right, Miss Hutch." Alex's lips twitched. "Gray may come in. You and Molly are both free to go."

"Yes, ma'am."

"Do I, Mama?" Gray rushed to Alex's bedside, his eyes glued to the tiny form beside his mother, his hands tightly clasped behind his back.

Alex laughed. "Now that's quite a change! I thought only a brother would do."

"No, Mama. I want to be a hero. Like Papa. So I need a sister."

Alex and Drake exchanged baffled looks. "Then rest easy," Alex assured Gray. "You are indeed a hero. Meet your sister."

Gray's eyes opened wide with wonder as he stared down at the peaceful, angelic face. "She's little."

Drake chuckled. "She'll grow, son."

"She's pretty. What's her name?"

Tenderly, Alex rumpled Gray's hair. "Papa and I are still discussing—"

"Bonnie."

Alex blinked. "What?"

"Her name. It's Bonnie. 'Cause she's pretty. I choose, 'cause I'm her hero."

A maternal gleam flashed in Alex's eyes. "Bonnie. It is a lovely name. Drake?" She inclined her head.

"I'm her hero. I choose," Gray insisted.

A rumble of laughter erupted from Drake's chest. "Very well. Since you insist you're the hero—"

"Not *the* hero, Papa. Bonnie's hero. Same as you're Aunt Sammy's."

"Ah." Drake's brow furrowed as he tried to deduce what had prompted Gray's surprising analogy.

"Here, Mama. For you." Remembering his gift, Gray yanked his hand from behind his back and thrust the bunch of wilting marigolds at Alex. "'Cause you made me a hero."

Alex stared from the droopy flowers to Gray's earnest face, tears filling her eyes. Drawing her son forward, she kissed his cheek and took her bouquet. "Thank you, Gray. They're the most beautiful flowers I've ever received. You really are a hero."

"Just like Rem said."

"Rem?"

"The man. He told me Papa was Aunt Sammy's hero. He told me to wish for a sister so I could be a hero, too."

"I see." Drake grew thoughtful. "When did you see this gentleman?"

"In the garden. Just now."

"Rem ... Remington Worth?" Alex questioned Drake. "Is that who your business meeting was with?"

Drake nodded. "He commissioned Barrett Shipping to build his brig."

"I didn't know he had a fleet."

"He doesn't. This will be his first ship ... an odd time to be taking such a risk, considering the unsettled status of British waters. I fully intended to delve a bit further into the reasons behind his unexpected purchase. However, given the circumstances, I hadn't the chance. I bolted the moment Humphreys broke in to tell me ..." Drake's voice trailed off.

Alex understood at once. "Lord Gresham was with you," she finished quietly. "Gray ..." Hooking a forefinger beneath her son's chin, she asked, "Did you mention to the gentleman—Rem—that you wanted a brother?"

"Yes, but he was right. I don't want one now. I want Bonnie."

"I know, darling. And you have Bonnie. We all do." Alex inclined her head in Drake's direction. "What a sensitive thing for the earl to do."

"Yes, it was, wasn't it? I'll have to remember to thank him. I think."

"You think?"

"I'm not sure why, princess, but I have a nagging feeling that my association with Gresham is going to be a turbulent one. Oh, he's charming as hell. Intelligent, too. Still ..." Drake shook his head, bemused. "Underneath all that inherent charm, I sense a core of calculated planning and rigid discipline; almost as if I were the fly and he the spider preparing to snare me in his web."

"He sounds a great deal like you," Alex commented dryly.

"True." Drake didn't smile. "But there's one difference."

"Which is?"

"I know my motives. I have yet to figure out his."

THIRTEEN

Rem never considered going home. Totally off balance, his emotions raw and unsettled, he ordered his driver to take him directly to Abingdon Street. To Abingdon Street ... and Samantha.

"Good day," he greeted the Town house butler. "Please tell Lady Samantha the Earl of Gresham is here to see her."

Hatterly didn't budge. "Is she expecting you, my lord?"

"Actually, no. I've come directly from a business meeting and had no opportunity to alert her to my imminent arrival. But I'm certain she'll receive me."

Hesitating an instant longer, the butler shrugged. "Follow me, my lord."

As they approached the sitting room, Rem heard the sound of melodic laughter. Samantha's laughter. Like a haven from the storm, it beckoned him, offering him the solace he craved, the cause and the cure for his inner turmoil.

The butler had not yet completed his formal announcement of Rem's arrival when Rem strode into the room, nearly tripping over the carved armchair that held Cynthia and her needlepoint.

"What the ...?" Rem's glance slid from Cynthia's startled face to the room's large settee, which currently held Samantha and Viscount Anders ... several feet apart, but beside each other nonetheless.

"Remington!" Sammy's eyes lit up as she rose to greet him. "I didn't expect you."

"Evidently not." Rem's fists clenched at his sides and he counted slowly to ten, simultaneously planning the viscount's sudden, violent demise. "If you recall, I did say I'd be here late this afternoon."

"You said you'd see me later today," she corrected, glancing uneasily from Rem to Stephen. "You never mentioned what time, nor that you intended to visit me at home." Attempting to defuse the tension permeating the room, she smoothed the folds of her gown and walked toward Rem. "But I'm delighted to see you. May I offer you some refreshment?"

"Why is the viscount here?"

Sammy wet her lips with the tip of her tongue. She should have known better than to think Rem would make this easy, she realized. "Stephen only just arrived. He came to … that is …" Self-consciously, her fingers flew to the heavy gold and diamond necklace at her throat.

The viscount stood in one fluid motion. "I brought Samantha a small token of my esteem, Gresham," he said with a smug smile. "It looks lovely on her, does it not?"

Rem's icy gaze dropped to the glittering gems. "Yes. Very lovely. And very costly."

"Samantha is more than worth the cost, no matter how high."

"Please, Stephen, you're embarrassing me." A faint tinge of color stained Sammy's cheeks. "And, if you recall, I also told you the necklace was far too extravagant."

"Nonsense, my dear. 'Tis but a mere trinket." Anders straightened his waistcoat. "I'll take my leave now. But rest assured, I'll be calling again tomorrow."

"Good day, Anders." Rem's voice was menacing.

"Cynthia, would you show the viscount to the door, please?" Sammy asked.

For the first time, Cynthia spoke. "I really don't think—"

"Please, Cynthia." It was not a request.

"Fine. I'll be but a moment." Cynthia's eyes flashed Sammy a warning.

The instant they were alone, Rem caught Sammy's elbows, dug his fingers demandingly into her skin. "Take it off."

"Pardon me?"

"The necklace. Take it off. I don't ever want to see you wearing it again."

"Remington—"

"Samantha, I'm going through a gamut of emotions right now, none of which I'm enjoying. I want to kill Anders in cold blood, smash that necklace into a thousand fragments and haul you off somewhere where Anders will never find you again." Rem ravaged her with his eyes. "I need and I ache and I hurt."

"So you came to me," she whispered, tenderness softening her features. "Thank you, Remington." She lay a trembling hand on his jaw. "I'd want it no other way."

With a muffled oath, Rem dragged her into his arms, kissing her with a clawing, bottomless hunger. The raw vulnerability that had accompanied him from Allonshire merged fiercely with the primal possessiveness now raging through his blood. He wanted to absorb her into himself, ease the gnawing ache in his soul with the sweet balm of her body, bury his pain, his jealousy, and his bewilderment deep inside her, along with his seed.

Sammy twined her arms around his neck, standing on tiptoe to lean into his kiss and give him hers. Her tongue glided into his mouth, stroked slowly along his, then ran lightly over the tingling surfaces surrounding it.

Cupping her soft bottom, Rem lifted Sammy up and against him, hard and fast and fully, pressing his rigid arousal between her thighs in such a way that it burned right through the ineffective barrier of her gown.

"Rem …" Half moan, half sigh, it was enough, when combined with the inadvertent, tantalizing motion of her hips, to strip away the last of Rem's control.

"Christ … I want to lock that bloody door and take you right here. Right now. On the floor." Rem rasped the words into her parted lips. "I couldn't even make it to a bed, that's how badly I want you. Samantha …" Kneading her buttocks through the layers of silk, Rem urged her closer, melding their lower bodies into one. He rocked his hips against hers, delving as deep into her softness as their clothing would allow, so frantic to brand her that he was shaking. "Tell me you want me," he demanded hoarsely. "Say the words."

"I want you," she managed. "So much, Rem."

"Only me."

"Only you."

Rem lifted his head, stared into her magnificent jade-green eyes. "I can't wait anymore."

Not even a whisper of fear crossed Sammy's face. "I don't want to wait. Please, Rem, find a way."

He felt her heart pounding against his. "Samantha …" There was so much to say, and no words with which to say it.

"The necklace means nothing," Sammy tried, mistaking Rem's silence for brooding. Easing out of his embrace, she reached behind her neck to unclasp it. "I'm not even certain why Stephen gave it to me."

"Oh, I know exactly why he gave it to you."

"You're suggesting that Stephen used the necklace as a tool to win my affections?"

"Among other things, yes."

"Then he failed miserably. It's your arms I want around me—not his diamonds. So please don't feel badly."

"I don't feel badly—I want to kill him."

Placing the necklace on a nearby table, Sammy said, "I'll return it. The next time I see Stephen."

"The next time … and the last time," Rem instructed her. "To-morrow when the viscount comes to call, I want you to inform him that you can no longer receive his visits, or his gifts. From now on you'll see each other only in public."

"I assure you, Lord Gresham, Viscount Anders was a perfect gentleman," Cynthia said coldly, hovering in the doorway. "In fact, I would venture to say that his intentions are far more honorable than yours."

"Cynthia, stop it," Sammy directed instantly, sensing Rem stiffen.

"The viscount has taken his leave," Cynthia reported in clipped tones.

"And so have you," Sammy returned. "Please excuse us."

"I don't think you and the earl should be left unchaperoned."

"Well, I do." Sammy raised her chin decisively. "And, should Smitty chastise you for abandoning your post, I take full responsibility for my actions. Please, Cynthia," she added, her gaze appealing, seeking her friend's understanding. "Trust me, if not Remington."

A flicker of tenderness softened Cynthia's dark eyes. "Very well, my lady. I'll await you in your bedchamber."

Rem watched Cynthia's departure, frowning. "She's so damned convinced I mean to hurt you."

"It isn't you. It's men."

"Then why not Anders?"

"Because she knows I care nothing for Stephen, so I'm not vulnerable to his charms." Gently, Sammy lay her palms on the front of Rem's waistcoat. "Whereas you …" She reached up to kiss his chin.

With a will of their own, Rem's arms closed around her, enfolding her against his chest. "Whereas I," he interrupted, "am so bloody possessive that I cannot bear the sight of another man giving you gifts. Or you accepting them."

"I should never have taken the necklace," Sammy murmured, inhaling Rem's wonderful masculine scent. "Nor would I, had Stephen not been so insistent. I'm terribly inexperienced at rejecting men while sparing their feelings."

"Damn his feelings."

"Rem ... I simply didn't know what to say. By the time I'd found my tongue, the necklace was fastened and Stephen was beaming from ear to ear." Sammy tilted her head back to gaze into Rem's smoky gray eyes. "I understand your bitterness; truly I do. But in this instance, it's totally unfounded. I do not require lavish gifts. In fact, I don't require any gifts at all." She stroked the hard line of his jaw. "In truth, a mere smile from you would be preferable to a deluge of gems from other men. So please don't berate yourself."

"Berate myself?" Rem was totally at sea.

"I'm aware of your financial difficulties; you confided in me at the opera, remember? And I admire your relentless attempts to overcome the situation. Why, just this week you had two business meetings at Annie's. Surely something lucrative will come of those." Sammy's voice rang with conviction. "In any case, I want you to know I have faith in you. I know in my heart all your efforts will pay off and your luck will change very soon. I want that for you ... desperately, but only because you want it for yourself. To me, it matters not. Rich or poor, you'll remain a hero. *My* hero."

For a moment Rem said nothing. Overcome, he just stared down into Samantha's earnest face, humbled by the selflessness of her words. Samantha thought his jealousy stemmed from the fact that he couldn't afford to heap expensive gifts upon her like her other suitors. And she was consoling him, telling him his monetary status wouldn't alter her feelings, assuring him he would soon recoup his losses, but that, should he not, her heart would remain his.

Too moved to speak, Rem turned his lips into Sammy's palm.

"I meant every word I just said," she reiterated, assuming his continued silence implied skepticism.

Slowly, Rem raised his head. "Did it ever occur to you, imp, that my jealousy has nothing to do with money and everything to do with you?"

"To some extent, yes. You did make it clear that you don't want me with other men. But you already know you have nothing to fear on that score. As I told you, I don't want other men. So naturally I assumed—"

"Even if they want you?"

"Even if they want me." Her eyes twinkled. "And even if they're incomprehensibly affluent."

Rem's dimple flashed. "No gifts, you said. Does that mean I needn't take you to Hatchard's again?"

"No, it definitely does *not* mean that," she teased back. Abruptly, her laughter faded. "What it does mean is that you needn't agonize over your lack of funds. Your *temporary* lack of funds," she corrected herself. "One of your investments will prosper, you'll see." Another radiant smile lit her face. "Heroes always prevail."

Heroes. Investments.

Abruptly, Rem remembered he had important news for her. "You may be right about one of my investments proving successful. I entered into a business arrangement today that I think will be a long and profitable one."

"Oh, Rem, that's wonderful!"

"I think you'll be interested to learn more about it, not to mention the name of my colleague."

Sammy's brows drew together quizzically. "Why? Do I know him?"

"Quite well."

"Who is it?"

"The Duke of Allonshire."

"Drake?" Sammy clapped her hands together. "You met with Drake today?"

"I did. But before I tell you the details, there's a small bit of news I think you'll want to know." He grinned. "You're an aunt again, imp. As of approximately two hours ago you have a niece."

"A niece!" Sammy clutched Rem's forearms. "Is the baby well? Is Alex well? What's the baby's name? Who does she look like? How did Gray take the news? Is Drake ecstatic? Is Alex exhausted? Is Humphreys telling all the world yet? Does Smitty know?"

"Enough!" Rem's shoulders were shaking with laughter. "I can scarcely remember your questions, much less think of answers to them. My information is sketchy at best; I left the moment your brother received the announcement."

"Received the announcement? Wasn't he at Alex's bedside?"

"No. Evidently, Alexandria felt things would go easier if Drake weren't present."

"In other words, he was a nervous ninny and Alex tossed him out."

"Precisely. I *can* tell you that both baby and mother are well, and your brother is euphoric. If my suspicions are correct, your nephew—whom incidentally I met and found to be a thoroughly enjoyable little lad—is thrilled with his new sister, long having abandoned the foolish notion of wishing for a brother. Your butler, Humphreys, did appear to be bursting with pride, so I assume he began notifying the world of the babe's arrival immediately following my departure. As for Smithers, I rode here directly from Allonshire, so, unless someone's carriage is faster than mine, your brother's valet couldn't possibly have received the news yet. Lastly, so far as the infant's name and physical attributes, I wasn't told." Rem paused to inhale deeply. "Have I covered everything?"

"Oh, yes! Oh, Rem how wonderful!" Sammy threw her arms around his neck. "I'm so happy … I can't wait to meet my new niece!" Leaning back, Sammy smiled delightedly up at Rem, a magnificent idea dawning in her eyes. "Would you take me to Allonshire?"

"Sweetheart …" Rem hesitated, trying to think of a way to present the reality to his naive Sammy. With her customary exuberance, she could see naught but the rightness of his accompanying her to her brother's house.

He, fortunately, could see beyond.

"Samantha." He caught her hands, easing her away from him. "I don't think Drake would think kindly of my escorting you to his home."

"But you said you're conducting business with him … surely you must be on good terms?"

"I am and we are. I've commissioned Barrett Shipping to construct a brig for me."

"You did?" Sammy chewed her lip, perplexed. "But how will you pay for it?"

A brief pause. He hated lying to her. But to tell her the truth meant to justify his original lie, which in turn meant to jeopardize his identity and his mission. "I managed to secure a loan."

"Why do you want a brig?"

"I plan to begin my own fleet. Hopefully, my ships will succeed in safely traversing British waters."

"I see. And is Drake enthusiastic about the idea?"

"He appears to be, yes."

"Then why won't you escort me?"

"Imp, we're talking about your brother. A man who protects his family like a wild animal protecting his pack. All I did was mention I'd seen you at a party or two, and he coiled to strike. Imagine his reaction if I appeared at your side for a family visit."

Color suffused Sammy's cheeks. "What did he say?"

"Oh, a few pointed comments about my reputation … and a few others about your innocence. He subtly—but emphatically—warned me to stay away from you."

"Did you tell him that we—"

"I told him nothing."

Sammy sagged with relief. "Then there's no reason why you can't accompany me to Allonshire."

"There's every reason why I can't accompany you to Allonshire, sweet." Rem trailed his fingers up the side of Sammy's neck, feeling her inadvertent shiver. "Samantha, I want you. Every nerve ending in my body is screaming to be inside you. And you want me. It's in your eyes, your touch, the intimacy of your gestures. Drake is one of the most astute men I've ever met. Do you honestly believe we could hide this"—Rem brushed his lips slowly, heatedly across hers, capturing her soft sigh with his mouth—"from him?"

Anxiety clouded Sammy's face, another worrisome thought intruding. "Rem, you're not changing your mind? I mean, you haven't decided not to ..." She blushed.

Brushing wisps of sable silk from Sammy's nape, Rem smiled at her enchanting honesty. "I couldn't walk away from you if my very life depended on it," he replied huskily. "Not for your brother. Not for anyone. Does that satisfactorily answer your question?"

"Yes." Relief surged through her.

"However," Rem rubbed his thumb across her moist lower lip, "that doesn't mean I should flaunt my desire for you in Drake's face. I admire the man. And he and I are working together, yes. But working with me is one thing. Approving of my involvement with his little sister is quite another."

"I'm a grown woman," Sammy defended hotly.

Rem's smile made her bones melt. "Yes, imp, I know." He buried his lips in hers for another long, drugging kiss. "God, how I know."

"Very well," Sammy acquiesced, languorous and dreamy. "I'll make arrangements to visit Allonshire myself. Smitty will escort me first thing tomorrow morning ... if I can restrain him that long. He'll be nearly as eager to hold the new baby as her father is."

"Be back by nightfall," Rem murmured, kissing the fragrant hollow behind her ear.

"Nightfall?" Sammy wondered if her legs might give out.

"Um-hum. Be dressed by nine. My carriage and I will arrive then. There are a host of balls and soirees we'll be attending." Rem nuzzled her neck, his breath hot, explicit. "And, imp? Forget what I said about keeping me fashionably waiting. This is one night I want you to be ready for me. Very ready for me."

Samantha's eyes slid shut, liquid heat coursing through her in wide rivers of trembling need. "Tomorrow?"

"Yes."

"Rem … how will you manage …?"

"Trust me."

"I do."

"Good." Ever so slowly he released her, bringing her fingers to his lips. "I suggest you retire early, my lady. I don't expect you'll be getting much sleep tomorrow night."

FOURTEEN

White's was bustling with activity—the perfect release for Rem's restless energy. He strolled into the card room, thinking how beautiful Samantha had looked when he'd left her, flushed and impatient, eager to retire early so the morning would arrive that much sooner. The morning … together with her visit to Allonshire … and the dark magic of the night to follow.

Tomorrow at this time Samantha would be his.

Just the thought of her in his bed, in his arms, made Rem's entire body harden, throb with an intensity that was as foreign to him as the tenderness that accompanied it. He wanted their lovemaking to be exquisite, perfect, everything Samantha had envisioned it to be. He wanted to join his body to hers, to thereby fulfill all her fantasies, make her every dream a reality.

He wanted to be the hero she insisted he was.

And he knew just the way to do it.

"Gresham, hello. Quite a surprise, seeing you here. We didn't expect you." The Marquis of Gladdington gestured to Rem as he rose from the whist table. "But I, for one, am delighted you arrived. You're most likely the only sober fellow in the room. Care to join this evening's game?"

"Is it my superior skill you require or my as-of-yet unsquandered funds?" Rem chuckled, strolling over.

"Both," Gladdington responded cheerily. "Also, if you glance at the Betting Book, you'll note that your latest conquest is in dispute."

Rem stiffened. "My latest conquest?"

"Of course. The only time you're ever conspicuously absent from White's for any period of time is when you're ... er, diverted by a particular lady. And, as we haven't seen you in nearly a week, we're trying to guess who she might be this time."

"I sincerely hope no one had the poor judgment to risk offending any of White's patrons," Rem commented, reversing his steps and heading toward the infamous Betting Book.

"Offend us? Why ... is your current paramour one of our wives?" Gladdington chuckled.

"Hardly. But I'd best see whose names are penned lest I be challenged to a duel without cause."

In truth, Rem wasn't the least concerned with the upset of his peers, nor did he give a damn whose names were mentioned. But Gladdington's taunt had just spawned an uneasy worry that he had conveniently eluded these past few emotion-charged days.

Gossip.

He and Samantha had been seen together, not only for a casual dance at Almack's and an innocent chat at Carlton House, but as a twosome: a covert ride through Hyde Park, an evening at Covent Garden Theater, Lover's Path at Vauxhall ...Lord alone knew who had spotted them. Not to mention how many tongue-wagging biddies had spied his phaeton arriving at the Barrett Town house. Dammit, how could he have been so careless? Somewhere in the back of his mind he'd dismissed the notion as preposterous, assuming the *beau monde* would scoff at the idea of a notorious rake being sexually involved with a total innocent. Hell, he'd scoffed himself not a fortnight ago. But if anyone thought otherwise—if rumors had spread—he would kill whoever had started them.

Whatever names were penned in that damned book, they'd bloody well not be Samantha's.

Expediently, Rem scrutinized the pages. The speculations were amusing, if not accurate. Clarissa's name appeared several times, followed in frequency by the delectably buxom Duchess of Ladsworth, trickling off to a diverse list of equally attractive, overtly available women, who were cited as contenders for Rem's bed. Samantha's name was blessedly absent.

Relief surged through him.

"That's quite an impressive assortment," Rem commented dryly as he returned to the card table. "Although I must admit I'm grateful as hell that Sheltane and Ladsworth are patrons of Brooks' and not White's."

"Understandable," Gladdington agreed. "But tell me, Gresham. Are you going to end our speculation and arouse our envy by telling us who your current interest is?"

Rem's dimple flashed. "I think not. I'll let the book become a bit plumper in wagers and more extensive in names before I satisfy your curiosity."

Gladdington groaned. "I was afraid you might say that. Very well, then, I suppose we'll have to settle for your superior card playing."

"Hello, Gresham." The voice was distinctly familiar, and Rem averted his head, surprised and pleased to see Viscount Goddfrey approaching him.

"Goddfrey … welcome home." Rem extended his hand.

Soberly, Goddfrey shook it. "Gladdington, I'd like a word with Gresham. Would you mind delaying your game a moment?"

"Not at all," Gladdington assured him. "There's no hurry. Our final two players are satisfying their thirst."

Goddfrey drew Rem off to a quiet corner across from White's bow window. "Thank you," he said simply.

"No thanks are necessary," Rem didn't pretend to misunderstand. "I was delighted to participate in Knollwood's downfall; he's destroyed too many innocent men. As for the message I sent you, I'm only glad I knew where to reach you. With that filthy parasite locked up, I felt certain you'd want to return to your family ... and your business."

"You were indeed correct. But my gratitude isn't limited to your missive. It also extends to your generous loan."

"Loan?" Rein's brows rose in question.

"I know you paid off my debts, Gresham," Goddfrey replied quietly. "It wasn't easy to pry the information out of my colleagues. According to them, my anonymous benefactor wanted to spare his reputation by keeping his embarrassingly vast business loss as quiet as possible. He assured them he planned to tell me he'd repaid the debt as soon as I arrived in London ... and compensated them generously for their discretion. But since he—you—obviously opted not to tell me, they eventually decided I had the right to know. I found the details very informative, as I couldn't quite remember your owing me any money at all, much less two hundred thousand pounds.

"Moreover, the most remarkable transition seems to have occurred during my absence. I've regained the trust of all my former business associates. And why? All because of the astounding profit I presumably made from my business transaction with the Earl of Gresham." Goddfrey's eyes grew damp. "There aren't words to express my thanks, Remington. And, now that my life has been mercifully restored, I intend to pay back every penny."

"You needn't repay nor thank me. The money I used wasn't mine." Rem grinned. "Actually, your thanks should go to Knollwood. His blackmail funds are what paid your debts. All I did was arrange to borrow the exact sum that I knew you owed your creditors. So, it all worked out rather nicely. Besides," Rem's grin grew broader,

"Mr. Knollwood will have no use for such a vast amount of money in Newgate, now will he?"

Goddfrey chuckled. "I suppose not."

"And I expect he'll be there for a very long time. So, as I said, no thanks or repayment are necessary. Unless, of course, you'd like to join our game and allow me to divest you of your money at the whist table."

"Someday perhaps," Goddfrey agreed, without a trace of bitterness or regret. "But not just yet. I have things to put in order and a profit to show before I'm ready to resume gambling. My priorities have changed—significantly."

"I understand. And I wish you the best of luck."

Goddfrey gestured toward the card room. "You'd best join the others. And I shall join my family." He cleared his throat. "I'll never forget what you've done for me. Should you ever need a favor, you know where to turn."

Rem watched Goddfrey go, feeling that familiar, incomparable sense of peace that always pervaded him when he'd seen justice served. The rightness made all the ugliness worthwhile.

Lost in thought, Rem returned to the card room, absently noting that the whist table was now full, save him.

"Good evening, Gresham. It's been some time."

Sliding into his seat, Rem glanced across the table and nodded cordially to the elderly Marquis of Hartley. "How have you been, Hartley?"

"Well. Quite well. It appears you and I are partners this evening."

"Excellent. We should do splendidly. I'm feeling especially lucky tonight."

"Then, 'tis a pity *we're* not partners, Gresham," an unwelcome voice responded. "I've been extraordinarily lucky throughout the day, and my good fortune promises to continue well into the evening … and beyond."

The pointed words and polished smile came from Viscount Anders.

It took Rem a split second to respond—not because he hadn't a ready answer, but because he was seriously considering knocking the smug look off the viscount's face. Quickly, he reconsidered. Making a scene was the most imprudent thing he could do. It would necessitate an explanation, which would, in turn, dredge up the cause of their rivalry and implicate Samantha in precisely the way he had vowed to avoid. Moreover, his own curiosity was now doubly peaked by Anders's appearance at the whist table. The Bow Street men had confirmed that the viscount's records proclaimed him as nearly bankrupt. Yet, in the past two days, Anders had gifted Samantha with an extravagant bejeweled necklace and was now complacently sitting in White's, prepared to enter into a potentially high-stakes game of whist.

Where the hell was this bastard getting his money?

Keeping his expression carefully blank, Rem replied, "What we have in common, Anders, is that we both play to win."

"True. How regrettable that only one of us can do so." Anders inclined his head toward Gladdington. "Deal."

"So, where have you been keeping yourself, Gresham?" Hartley inquired. "You've been conspicuously absent from the card rooms."

Rem arranged his hand. "Actually, I've just joined the ranks of the shipping community."

"Have you?" All three men looked surprised.

"Indeed. Plans for my brig are in the making. With a modicum of luck, I'll soon be reaping the profits of merchant trade." Intently, Rem studied his cards. "I'm ready to begin whenever you are, gentlemen."

"What do you know about the shipping trade?" Anders demanded.

Rem looked vastly amused. "Need I remind you that the sea was my home during the decade I served the Royal Navy? I assure you, no one can assess the potential of a ship better than I. As for trade, let's just say that I make it my business to thoroughly research a subject before I invest my money. And who knows? Perhaps with my experience, I can make my fleet immune to whatever disasters seem to be befalling England's vessels."

Hartley took out a handkerchief and mopped his brow. "Who, may I ask, is constructing your brig?"

"Barrett Shipping." Rem met the marquis's anxious gaze. "Your company is more than reputable and highly trustworthy, Hartley," he assured him. "But I've done business with Drake Barrett in the past and—"

Hartley cut Rem short. "Please, you needn't explain. Grayson Barrett was my dearest friend. His son Drake is a fine man and their company is above reproach. I harbor no resentments. I merely asked." He cleared his throat. "The brig Anders just lost … that was built by Barrett Shipping, was it not?"

"It was."

"I was afraid so." Hartley shook his head nervously. "Three of the lost ships were constructed by my company," he admitted. "The situation is terribly unsettling."

"Are we going to play whist or commiserate about our lost ships?" Anders bit out.

Testy, Rem mused, casting a sidelong glance in Anders's direction. *I wonder why.* "Fine," he said aloud. "Let's begin."

The first hand was over quickly, Rem skillfully managing to accumulate an exorbitant number of points.

The stakes were doubled.

The next hand resulted in Rem and Hartley together amassing an even greater score.

The stakes doubled again.

The tension swelled.

The evening wore on.

Rem and Hartley continued to win, and Gladdington and Anders continued to raise the stakes.

It was nearly dawn when Gladdington tossed down his cards. "I've definitely had enough." Ruefully, he glanced at his scorecard. "I shudder to think how much we've lost."

"Over ten thousand pounds, I should think," Anders replied. Calmly, he reached into his pocket, withdrawing the requisite number of bills, leaving, as Rem could see from the corner of his eye, nearly twice that number intact.

"Ah well," Anders rose, stretching, "it appears my fortune lies elsewhere today. Therefore," his gaze flickered briefly to Rem, "I'd best get some rest. I have an important social engagement this afternoon."

"Really?" Gladdington leaned back in his chair. "With young Samantha Barrett?"

Beneath the table, Rem's fingers gripped his knees.

"As a matter of fact, yes," Anders said with a meaningful smile.

"I suspected as much. At first I wondered if Gresham might be pursuing her, but I dismissed that as nonsense." He shot Rem a knowing look. "A child fresh from the schoolroom certainly isn't your style, is it?"

Rem arched a brow, seizing the opportunity he'd awaited. "Quite the contrary. What I'm attempting to do is look out for Samantha's well-being. Her brother is exceedingly concerned, and with good reason. An innocent beauty like Samantha needs to be shielded from the lechers of the *ton*."

"I quite agree," Hartley interceded fervently. "Why, Grayson's daughter is little more than a babe. I can remember the day she was born!"

"So Drake Barrett has elicited your services, has he, Gresham?" Gladdington looked thoughtful. "Well, that certainly explains your attentiveness to his sister." Casting a sidelong glance at Anders, Gladdington turned his questions to the viscount. "And what are your intentions toward Samantha? I hear tell you visited the Barrett Town house three times already this week. Is there anything you'd care to share with us?"

Hartley's head snapped around. "Anders, I didn't know you were pursuing Samantha Barrett."

"Relax, Hartley." Anders's tone was dry. "Your friend Grayson would approve. My intentions toward his daughter are completely honorable." He smoothed his waistcoat. "The way things look, Samantha will finish this Season as my wife."

Rem's chair scraped the floor loudly. "If you gentlemen will excuse me, I, too, must get some rest."

"Ah, yes. Your new business venture, Gresham." Anders's gaze narrowed on Rem's face. "When will this exemplary brig of yours be ready?"

"My plans will come to fruition as soon as possible." Rem scooped up his winnings, his jaw clenched to restrain the fury threatening to erupt. "You may rely upon it."

"Anders is doing something illegal. I'd stake my life on it." Rem shoved the end of his cravat through its loop, yanking the ends into a knot with all the venom he wanted to use on Anders's throat.

Boyd polished off his brandy, watching in amusement as Rem fumbled with his cuffs. "Are you certain you're not letting personal feelings cloud your thinking?"

"You know me better than that." Rem shrugged into his coat. "I've never permitted sentiment to interfere with business."

"You've also never been in love."

"Samantha has nothing to do with this."

Boyd gave a pointed cough.

"All right. I despise the man. If he goes near Samantha again, I'll kill him. But that has nothing to do with my suspicions."

"That's honest enough. And you certainly have reason to question the viscount's actions. With a company that's nearly bankrupt, and no other visible means of income—despite his pompous boasts to the contrary—how did he manage to pay for an elaborate necklace and satisfy losses of over ten thousand pounds at White's?"

"Precisely. That is just what I intend to find out. Tonight." Frowning, Rem rebuttoned his waistcoat. "Bloody evening clothes."

"I know you gambled till dawn, but you've gone without sleep many times before. Never have I seen you so out of sorts. What the hell is wrong with you?" When a grunt was his only response, Boyd tried another tactic. "Why not summon your valet to help you dress?"

"As you might recall from our years at sea, I'm perfectly capable of donning my own clothing," Rem snapped. "Without the aid of a valet. Moreover, the point is a moot one. I gave my valet—and all the other servants—the night off."

"Why?"

"That leads me to the reason I asked you to stop by—other than to fill you in on the situation with Anders. I need a favor."

"Anything."

"In approximately"—Rem glanced at his timepiece—"four or five hours, I shall need a diversion. I'd like you to provide it. In the interim, my gardener, who is the last of my servants to take his leave tonight, will require your assistance. I'd greatly appreciate if you'd give him whatever help he needs."

"This sounds intriguing." Boyd's eyes twinkled. "I must admit you've sparked my curiosity."

"I'm sure I have." A corner of Rem's mouth lifted. "Will you do it?"

"You know I will." Boyd waited expectantly. "Are you going to tell me what this is all about?"

"No."

"No?"

"Excluding, of course, your part in it. The rest, I'm certain, you'll easily deduce on your own."

Grinning, Boyd watched as Rem fastened his final button with a flourish. "I can hardly wait."

Samantha was thinking much the same thing. The difference was that, unlike Boyd, she knew *exactly* what tonight was about.

Knotting her palms in the silken folds of her gown, Sammy tried to concentrate on Cynthia's casual discourse rather than dwelling on the excitingly forbidden moments that hovered just beyond reach, mere hours away.

It was futile.

"These jeweled combs will set off your gown exquisitely," Cynthia commented, holding them up to Sammy's hair. "The deep purple stones are a perfect contrast to the pale lilac of the dress."

"I agree." Sammy nodded sagely, thanking her lucky stars that, unlike Millie, Cynthia was quite talented at selecting gowns and arranging hair. This particular night, Samantha was in no condition to manage on her own. Not with her hands trembling as if winter's frost had descended upon them.

Moistening her lips, Sammy glanced at the clock, her heart keeping pace with its ticking, her mind racing ahead to the wondrous adventure that awaited her.

In a matter of hours, she'd belong to Rem.

How would he manage it? she wondered, anticipation tingling through her. Where would he take her to make her his?

"Is she very beautiful?"

"Pardon me?" Sammy blinked.

"Bonnie, your new niece," Cynthia prompted, exasperated and puzzled. "What on earth is wrong with you tonight?"

"Nothing. Yes, Bonnie is precious." Hastily, Sammy brought the subject back to safe ground. "She looks just like Alex, with huge gray eyes and delicate little features." Sammy grinned. "And a powerful shout when she wants something."

"Your brother must be thrilled."

"That was the only disappointing part of the day. Drake was away from Allonshire all morning. He left for his banker's estate just prior to my arrival. Evidently, he decided to use the hours that Alex, Gray, and the baby were napping to conduct business. So, other than Humphreys, whose chest is as swollen with pride as Smitty's—honestly, you'd think the two of them had fathered Bonnie themselves—I saw no one but my new niece. And even she slept during most of our first meeting. A humbling experience, at best."

Cynthia smiled wistfully. "It must be wonderful to have such a loving family."

Sammy met Cynthia's gaze in the mirror. "It is. But things weren't always as they are now," she returned quietly. "Don't presume the tranquility you see has perpetually graced the Barretts. There are many skeletons in the family closet. Someday I shall regale you with them."

A knock sounded on the bedchamber door.

"Yes?"

"Pardon me, m'lady." The young maid curtsied. "The Earl of Gresham asked me to tell you he has arrived."

"Thank you." Sammy rose, snatching up her wrap. "Good night, Cynthia."

"Samantha—"

"Good night, Cynthia." Pausing in the doorway, Sammy's tone was as emphatic as her stance. She was in no mood for a lecture on the dangers of caring for Rem. Nor did she have any intention of allowing Cynthia to accompany her. "Please," she said softly, inclining her head in Cynthia's direction. "Not tonight."

"Enjoy yourself, my lady." Cynthia's reply was as reluctant as it was relieving.

A tiny smile hovered about Sammy's lips. "Thank you. I shall."

Rounding the second floor landing, Sammy fought the impulse to raise her skirts and dash down the stairs to the sitting room, and Rem. She counted to ten slowly, then began her descent.

Halfway down she halted, clutching the handrail for support.

Rather than doing what was proper—patiently awaiting Sammy's arrival in the sitting room—Rem was standing at the foot of the stairs watching her approach. Hands clasped behind his back, he studied her from beneath hooded lids, drinking her in like a rare and fine wine.

Sammy could feel the intimate possession of his stare burn through her, a hot brand deep inside her.

"I followed your instructions precisely, my lord," she murmured breathlessly, gliding down the final step to meet him. "As promised, I didn't keep you waiting."

"Didn't you?" Rem raised her fingers to his lips, lightly caressing her hand in a kiss as suggestive as it was brief. "It seems I've waited an eternity for you."

Trembling pleasure shimmered through her. "If you continue talking to me like that, I'll be unable to walk, much less dance."

"Then we'll have to adjourn to a bed, won't we?" He pressed his open mouth to her wrist, nudging aside the lilac silk of her sleeve.

"Rem ... don't," she whispered.

"Do you know how beautiful you are?" he questioned huskily, his tongue finding her racing pulse. "Have you any idea how profoundly you affect me?"

"I'm almost afraid to know."

"I'll show you." His fingers closed possessively around hers. "Later."

The sound of footsteps interrupted them.

Glancing up, Sammy saw Smitty approaching, his jaw set. Thankfully, she realized he was too far away to have witnessed the intimacy of Rem's greeting. Still ...

Swiftly, Sammy urged Rem toward the door. "We'd best be off—before a confrontation ensues."

"My lady, you didn't mention that you'd be going out this evening," Smitty called, scowling at Rem.

"Didn't I? I suppose I was preoccupied with Bonnie." Sammy gave Smitty her most winning smile. "In any case, Lord Gresham and I had best be on our way. He has promised to whisk me in and out of countless parties."

"Where is your aunt Gertrude, may I ask?"

"Abed." Casting pretense aside, Sammy gazed pleadingly up at her guardian. She could, in all candor, demonstrate her eagerness, though she dared not reveal its cause. "Please, Smitty. There are parties at Devonshire House and Chesterfield House, not to mention the elegant soiree at Lord and Lady Rathstone's estate, and innumerable other grand balls. You know how long I've waited for nights such as these. I realize I should be chaperoned, but no one will suspect that I'm not. Aunt Gertrude rarely stays awake past ten o'clock, anyway. After that, she retires to our carriage, where she snores the duration of the evening away." Sammy paused only to suck in air before plunging on in an attempt to win Smitty over, and to soothe his growing agitation. "The point is, no one expects Aunt Gertrude to partake in the merriment. I'll just make my usual excuses, tell everyone she was fatigued. They'll assume she drifted off for a nap. Please, Smitty, I know how you despise impropriety; but just this once, don't say no."

"Lady Gertrude actually sleeps in the carriage, while you …" Smitty withdrew his handkerchief and proceeded to mop his brow.

"Smitty …" Samantha lay her hand on his arm. "Lord Gresham will keep me safe. You have my word. Please … let me go."

Indecision warred in Smitty's eyes.

"Thank you." Sammy gave her guardian a quick, hard hug.

"All right," Smitty conceded. Roughly, he cleared his throat. "The duke would have my head."

"Perhaps." Sammy dimpled. "But I much prefer your heart, anyway."

Rem was still reeling as their carriage sprinted off into the foggy London night. "Well, imp, even Smithers is captivated by your charm." He drew Sammy against him, tenderly pressing her head to his shoulder. "I can't blame him. You're fatal, you know."

"Am I?" Sammy snuggled closer, inhaling Rem's heady masculine scent. "I hope so." A nagging thought plagued her, marring the perfection of the moment. "I've never lied to Smitty before."

"You didn't lie to him now." Rem nuzzled her hair. "You said I'd keep you safe ... and I will."

"I also said we'd be attending dozens of extravagant London balls," she reminded him.

"And so we shall."

Sammy sat bolt upright. "What? But I thought—"

Rem smoothed his knuckles over her flushed cheek. "Patience, my beautiful romantic. Patience."

She turned her lips into his hand. "Patience has never been one of my virtues, my lord."

"Nor mine, my lady. But tonight we shall both learn to exercise some." He tipped her disappointed face up to his. "By the time I take you to bed, I want you on fire for me." Slowly, hungrily, he buried his lips in hers.

With a low moan, Sammy relinquished herself to the kiss, Rem's words seeping into her like the most potent aphrodisiac. She was already on fire for him, her untutored body clamoring for more, unwilling to wait.

Avidly, she tried to deepen the kiss ... and was thwarted by Rem's maddening refusal to do so.

"Patience," he murmured softly, nibbling at her lower lip.

"But when will we—"

"Trust me. Didn't I give you my word that I'd never leave you aching again?"

"But I am aching," she said in a bewildered whisper.

Rem made a husky sound that was part laugh, part groan. "You won't be. I promise, once this night is over, you won't be. Will you have faith in me?"

Sammy stared into the mesmerizing gray of his eyes. "Yes."

"Good." He brushed his lips across hers, a whisper of sensation against her feverish skin. "Then, Lady Samantha, I suggest you prepare for a long and exhausting evening."

FIFTEEN

Long?

Endless would have been a better choice of words, Sammy rued silently, feeling her leg muscles throb their agreement.

She and Rem had finally arrived at Devonshire House. It was well after midnight, the ballroom crammed with partygoers, and Sammy was coiled tight as a spring. In three hour's time, she'd made appearances at five balls and three soirees, danced with over a dozen men, drunk enough Regent's punch to make her dizzy, and smiled until she thought her cheeks would break.

Only two things sustained her.

One was the possessive way Rem escorted her into each gathering; keeping her staunchly by his side, his hand firmly gripping her elbow, almost as if he were publicly proclaiming her as his; relinquishing her only when protocol insisted he allow other men their chance to dance with her.

The other was the constant flow of suggestive words and intimate looks Rem lavished upon her throughout the night, making everything inside her turn liquid with longing.

Sammy wondered if she could withstand the torment much longer.

"Are you enjoying yourself, imp?" Rem questioned, leading her onto the dance floor for the waltz she'd promised him.

"What?" Sammy turned dazed eyes to his.

Rem's dimple flashed. "I asked if you were enjoying yourself." Lazily, he caressed her palm with his thumb.

Sammy's heart lurched. "You're torturing me," she whispered.

"No, sweetheart. I'm heightening your anticipation."

"You're so … experienced," she blurted out, lightheaded from the punch she'd consumed, her nerves taut to breaking.

Rem chuckled, maddeningly. "And you're so innocent." His voice dropped to a seductive whisper. "I want to drown in you."

Sammy's eyes slid shut. "Can we *please* leave?"

"Soon." He whirled her around. "Very soon."

"I believe the next dance is mine."

Viscount Anders's voice was like a bucket of ice water on Sammy's heated body.

"Stephen?" She knew she sounded disoriented, but Anders was the last person she'd expected, or wanted, to see.

"Good evening, Samantha." Stephen's tone was frosty, his expression emanating irritated censure. "I hear you've cut a path at nearly every party in London."

"We have. And if you wish to speak with Samantha, you'll have to wait. This particular waltz belongs to me." Rem whirled Sammy off.

"Oh, Rem." Sammy felt all too sober as she glanced uneasily back at Stephen's furious expression. "Did you have to be so rude?"

Rem shrugged. "I loathe the man. I loathe the way he looks at you, the way he speaks to you, the way he thinks of you as his. I also distrust him. I think he's an unprincipled snake. So, yes, I had to be rude. And incidentally, as your visit to Allonshire precluded Anders from calling on you today, this is the perfect time for you to return his necklace."

"I don't have it with me."

"Tell him you'll have it delivered."

Her heart warmed by Rem's show of jealousy, Sammy stepped a tad closer, her chin just brushing his frilled shirt. "You're terribly overbearing, my lord," she murmured softly. "'Tis fortunate I prefer an overbearing hero."

Rem stared down into her beautiful, teasing face, and a jolt of desire shot through his loins. "Christ, I want you under me."

Heat surged through Sammy's body. "We can't leave now," she said weakly, wishing with all her heart Stephen were anywhere but here.

"Because of Anders." Rem's jaw clenched.

"Rem … please." Her fingers tightened within his. "It's not because I feel anything for him. But if we were to take our leave now, before he claimed the dance I promised him—"

"You promised him nothing. He assumed." It took every shred of Rem's unshakable discipline to bring his temper under control. But Samantha's honor was at stake. "You're right," he agreed flatly. "If Anders sees you leave with me, he'll assume the worst. Your reputation won't be worth a damn. So have your bloody dance with him. But tell him it's his last."

"I shall, my lord."

Rem stood stiffly by as Anders came to claim his dance.

"Samantha, you look lovely." Pointedly, the viscount ignored Rem. "But tell me, where is the necklace I gave you?"

With a meaningful cough, Rem strolled off.

Sammy waited until the minuet was under way before she answered. "I cannot wear your necklace, Stephen."

"Whyever not?"

"It's very extravagant, and I—"

"Nonsense! Nothing is too costly when it comes to you. I fully intend to spoil you shamelessly."

From an adjacent salon a clock chimed. Anders tensed, and momentarily distracted, he glanced at his timepiece.

"You don't understand." Once again Sammy was attempting to clarify her rejection of the viscount's necklace, and all that went with it. "I cannot allow you to think that what I feel for you is anything more than friendship. It isn't."

"I didn't expect it would be. We've known each other less than a fortnight. But in time—"

"No." Sammy shook her head adamantly. "Not in time. Not ever."

His eyes glinted with resentment. "Because of Gresham?"

"Yes."

"He's not the kind of man you should become involved with."

"That is for me to decide. Not you."

"You're making a mistake, Samantha. You're far too young and naive to see that Gresham's charm might be fatal, but his intentions are ruinous. Therefore, it is up to me to protect you, to help you see the error of your ways ... before any unalterable damage has been done."

Sammy had no time to respond to his patronizing sermon. The music ended and Anders's gaze darted swiftly back to his timepiece.

"Will you excuse me, my dear?" He hastily kissed Sammy's hand. "There's someone I must speak to."

Mutely, she nodded, hastily withdrawing her hand and fighting the urge to slap the viscount's pompous face. Not that Anders noticed her irritation. He had already left her and was easing his way across the ballroom.

Shrugging, Sammy dismissed him from her thoughts. She raised her chin, scanning the room for Rem.

He was nowhere to be found.

With a pang of unease, Sammy wondered if Rem's absence had been triggered by her dance with Stephen. If so, where would he have gone? He would never abandon her. Therefore, he must have stepped out, hoping the night air would cool his temper.

Inching toward the ballroom door, Sammy hastened down the hallway and slipped into the night.

Rem stood still as a statue, waiting to see where Anders would head. The fact that the lecherous viscount was up to something dishonest was unquestionable. Having carefully observed him over the past quarter hour, Rem recognized all the classic signs: Anders's subtle but distinct agitation, his repeated glances at his timepiece, his distracted behavior even during his coveted dance with Samantha. Every one of Rem's well-honed instincts screamed out that the bastard was up to no good.

Where the hell was he going?

Noiselessly, Rem fell back into stride, noting that Anders had reached the far section of Devonshire House, which bordered on Hyde Park. Dimly lit, quiet, it was the perfect place for a covert meeting.

"Pssst ..."

On the heels of Rem's thought came the sound of someone summoning Anders. The viscount evidently heard it, too, for he veered in the direction of the noise.

Following suit, Rem slid behind a profuse section of bushes and concealed himself.

"... couldn't meet you sooner ... portion of the money ... not for a week or two ... Bow Street ... examined the records ... nothing amiss ..."

Rem could barely make out the snatches of conversation, nor could he discern any physical details of Anders's companion other than his stocky build. The fog was too hindering, the men too far off. And Rem didn't dare jeopardize his identity by attempting to get closer.

A twig snapped in the distance.

"Rem?"

Sammy's voice rang out clearly, and Rem bit back a curse. He should have anticipated this. If Samantha hadn't been intimidated by the disreputable crowd at Boydry's, why would she be unnerved by strolling dark, deserted grounds alone at midnight? Dammit. Like a bloody fool, he'd assumed she'd wait for him in the ballroom.

"Rem ... is that you?"

Obviously, she'd heard Anders and his friend. Rem coiled, ready to grab her and drag her to safety.

An instant later she appeared, making her way closer—but not close enough—passing not twenty feet from where Rem crouched.

Anders and his companion froze.

"Who's there?" Sammy asked, evidently spotting the two men.

Rem's guts knotted and he had to forcibly restrain himself from going to her. *Wait,* he cautioned himself, appalled by his own impulsiveness. *There's no reason to suspect they'd hurt her. They might not even be armed. Or dangerous, for that matter.* But his instincts told him otherwise.

"Samantha? It's Stephen." Anders's reply followed a prolonged silence.

"Oh, Stephen ... forgive me. I thought—" An abrupt pause. "Mr. Summerson ... good evening." She sounded distressed.

"Lady Samantha."

Summerson? Arthur Summerson. The merchant. Rem stored that information for later, still battling with the compulsion to leap out and haul Samantha off.

"I didn't mean to interrupt ..." Samantha was backing away, once again nearing where Rem hid.

"It's all right," Anders called out, ostensibly trying to soothe her. Anyone listening would think his tone perfectly normal. But Rem's trained ear could make out the thin note of tension rippling through it.

"I'd b-best return to the ball," Sammy stammered. "Excuse me." She bolted.

Summerson made a move to go after her.

"Leave it." Anders's command cracked out, loud enough for Rem to hear.

"I don't trust that girl," Summerson shot back, his words equally as clear. "That's the second time she's mysteriously appeared during one of our meetings. And I have the nagging feeling I've seen her elsewhere."

"She's a child."

"Perhaps. But she's also Drake Barrett's sister. So, child or not, I plan to keep an eye on her."

"Let me worry about Samantha. You worry about Atlantis. Now, I'd best get back into that ballroom … before my absence is noted. We'll meet tomorrow at my office. Good night, Summerson."

Rem waited until both men had left before emerging from his hiding place, fists clenched with fury. To hell with objectivity, blast his ever-present cool and level head. Everything was changed now. For, whatever Atlantis was, whatever seedy dealings Anders was involved in, Samantha was at risk. And whether those dealings tied in with his mission or not, Rem thought, they had just become his top priority.

Let Anders or Summerson try to harm a hair on Samantha's head. Rem would kill them.

He had to think. But now was not the time. The most important thing now was to get Samantha away from Devonshire House and out of danger. Fast.

Scrutinizing the area, Rem determined the swiftest route back to the manor.

"Hello, sweetheart."

Stepping out of the shadows enveloping the manor's west wing, Rem ground out his cheroot and caught Sammy's elbow.

She started. "Where were you?"

Rem stared broodingly at the ground. His thoughts were in turmoil and, for the first time in years, so were his emotions. "You didn't expect me to stand by and watch you dancing with Anders, did you?"

Sammy recoiled from the harshness of his reply. "No, but …" She swallowed. "You're angry with me."

"Angry with you?" Rem drew a sharp breath, unable to dispel the dark sense of foreboding spawned by what he'd just overheard.

He couldn't explain the reasons for his somber mood to Samantha, nor did he even want to. All he wanted was to hold her soft, warm body in his arms, bury himself inside her and hold the world at bay.

As Rem stared soberly into Sammy's questioning eyes, something inside him snapped. He tugged her abruptly into the shadows, sliding his hand beneath her sable mane and drawing her against him. "Come here." He seized her mouth with a kind of rough, raw desperation. "Angry with you? No, I'm not angry with you, imp. You're all that is precious ... fire and silk in my arms." He parted her lips, delved inside, infusing himself with her beauty. "So sweet, so soft. Lord, I need you." He kissed her throat, the delicate line of her jaw. "Put your arms around me."

"Yes." Sammy twined her arms about Rem's neck, perceiving his urgency, her heart pounding with anticipation.

Whatever had instigated Rem's sudden breach of control mattered not. All that mattered was that her long wait was over.

"Samantha ..." Rem's hands roved restlessly up and down her back, seeking the deeper joining his body craved. "I have to be inside you."

Wordlessly, she nodded.

In one harsh motion, Rem drew back, flames erupting in his eyes. Valiantly, he battled the tempest pounding through his loins, commanding him to abandon his plan and take Samantha right here, right now, propriety be damned.

"Rem?" She lay her hand against his jaw. "What is it?"

The gentle question was Rem's undoing, feelings stronger than lust rushing through him with the impact of a tidal wave. He'd waited this long. He could withstand another hour to make it everything Samantha deserved. "Let's go."

He seized Sammy's hand, guiding her alongside the house until they'd reached the main entranceway, where some guests were departing, others arriving. Abruptly, Rem stopped, steadying his breathing, mastering his passion. When he was certain he'd regained control, he leaned forward, brushing Sammy's hair with his lips, murmuring quietly in the final seconds before they reached the others. "Remember what I said—trust me."

"I do," she whispered, totally at sea.

Her puzzlement was swiftly dispelled.

"An urgent business matter has arisen," Rem announced in a voice audible enough for those in the vicinity to overhear. "I must attend to it immediately."

As if on cue, the carriage bearing the Gresham family crest swung into the drive, slowing to a stop before them.

To Sammy's stunned surprise, the door opened and Boyd emerged.

"I've sent for Mr. Hayword, who has agreed to escort you home," Rem explained. "Please accept my apologies, Samantha. The situation cannot be helped."

Sammy blinked, so astounded by this turn of events that she couldn't speak.

"My lady." Boyd bowed, then extended his hand to assist Samantha into the carriage. "I'll see you safely to your Town house."

Baffled, Sammy turned to look at Rem. Their eyes met, and he gave an almost imperceptible nod.

It was enough.

"Very well." Gathering up her skirts, Sammy put her hand in Boyd's and climbed into the carriage.

"Thank you, Boyd." Rem moved to stand beside his friend, continuing to speak in the same normal tone. "I owe you a favor."

"You owe me more than that if I manage this one," Boyd muttered for Rem's ears alone. Aloud, all he said was, "It's my pleasure. Once I've seen Lady Samantha home, I'll go to your Town house and await you there." Signaling the driver, Boyd swung into the seat opposite Samantha and sent Rem a brief wave.

They rode a block in silence. After that, Sammy could no longer contain herself.

"What on earth is going on?" she demanded.

Boyd gave her a crooked smile. "What do you think is going on?"

"You're arranging for Rem and I to be together," Sammy replied with no trace of embarrassment. She leaned forward. "Are you really taking me home?"

"In a manner of speaking, yes."

"What does that mean?"

"It means I'm taking you to your home ... and to Rem's."

"What?" Sammy's eyes widened. "We're going to Remington's house?"

Boyd nodded. "Following our visit to yours. Now, I want you to listen carefully. When we arrive at Abingdon Street, we're going to approach your Town house slowly—slowly enough for passersby to see the Gresham crest nearing its destination. If need be, we'll wait until sufficient people have witnessed our approach. The carriage won't come to a stop ... if it does, there's always the chance your butler will hear us and come out, assuming you've arrived home." Another grin. "Which, despite appearances, you haven't. Now for the indelicate part. I hope you have no aversion to carriage floors. Because, when I say the word, I want you to drop down out of sight and stay there. Don't move or say a word until I tell you to. All right?"

Sammy could feel a sense of adventure surge through her. "Why, it's just like a Gothic mystery!" she exclaimed. "Complete with fog, clandestine activities, and a tangled plot. And, of course, a wondrous hero." She dimpled. "Two heroes, in fact."

Boyd chuckled, touched by her exuberance as well as her compliment. "Does that mean you'll do as I ask?"

"It does."

"Good girl." Shifting his weight, he peered out the window. "It'll be just a few moments now. We're lucky. Most of the *ton* is still reveling in evening festivities, so there aren't many carriages on the road."

He fell silent, the only sound that of their horses' hooves clomping down the street.

"Abingdon Street is just ahead," Boyd noted at last. "Are you ready?"

Sammy nodded.

"Excellent." He drew the curtains wider, allowing all curious eyes to see him escort Lady Samantha home.

A minute or two later the carriage slowed, crawling toward the Barrett Town house.

One carriage passed.

Then another.

"That was Lord and Lady Wilmington," Sammy murmured. "She is a voracious gossip."

Boyd beamed. "Wonderful."

Three more carriages passed.

"That should do it." Again Boyd leaned forward, looking intently out the window. The street was temporarily deserted. "Number fifteen … there. All right now, Samantha, duck."

Sammy curled forward and eased herself to the floor, crouching down and tucking her skirts around her.

The carriage came within a whisper of stopping. It paused for a long, drawn-out moment just outside Sammy's Town house door. Then it moved on.

Boyd said nothing, just stared straight ahead. They'd gone but fifty feet beyond the Barrett's home when the sound of horses' hooves reached their ears. Waiting for the precise instant, Boyd poked his head out the window and called loudly to his driver, "I've delivered Lady Samantha as promised. Now, we'll go to the Gresham Town house and await the earl. Then it's off to the gaming tables."

The carriage sprinted forward.

Joy sang in Sammy's heart. She was on her way to Rem. He'd made provisions for them to be together—painstaking, chivalrous provisions.

He was truly the most splendid of heroes.

Sammy rested her head on her knees and waited.

Her legs were just starting to cramp when the carriage came to a flourishing halt.

Boyd climbed down at once, knocking purposefully on Rem's front door. No answer. Just as they'd planned.

Striking a match, Boyd lit a cheroot and sauntered back to the street, smoking. Simultaneously, he assessed the vehicles on Rem's street. A few carriages. Enough people to spy him here, alone, but not so many as to cause him trouble. Good.

Leaning against the carriage, Boyd blew gray rings into the foggy skies, calling just enough attention to himself to be remembered. "Cover your head with your wrap," he instructed Sammy quietly without turning around. "And when I open the door, get out. Quickly and without a word. Go to the front door and knock." He ground the cheroot beneath his heel, waiting while the final carriage passed. Abruptly, he yanked open the door. "Now."

Her wrap cloaking her, Sammy alit, blinking as she accustomed her eyes to the foggy night. Following Boyd's instructions, she sprinted to the door and knocked.

The door opened.

Sammy entered.

The real evening had begun.

"Welcome, imp."

Rem's voice was a husky caress. "I trust you arrived here relatively unscathed."

"Relatively." Sammy lowered her wrap in time to see him lean past her and firmly shut the door.

They were alone. Sammy sensed it at once.

The lamps were turned down low, casting the hall in shadows. Pervaded by silence, the walls vibrated with heated anticipation, emanating excitement and longing and the wonderful, masculine scent of Rem. Sammy swallowed, feeling the palpable tension spring to life again, pulsing between them, inside them.

"Where are the servants?" she asked breathlessly.

"Gone." Rem braced his arms over either side of her, palms flattened against the heavy wooden door. "Does that frighten you?"

Sammy lifted her chin, met the smoky heat in his eyes and shook her head. "No." Reaching up, she traced his lips with trembling fingers. "I thought perhaps you'd truly sent me home."

"And left us aching? Never. I merely assured us long hours of privacy while protecting your reputation. If my strategy was successful, the entire *haute ton* believes you to be snug in your bed, blissfully asleep."

"Neither of which I intend to be … in my own bed, or blissfully asleep." She sighed. "I've waited forever for this."

"So have I." He kissed her fingertips, one by one, each kiss more intimate than the one preceding it. "And I swore to myself that when the time came to finally make you mine, I'd go slowly. Even if it killed me. But now"—he drew her fingers into his mouth, his breathing ragged—"I'm just not sure I can."

"Don't," she whispered. Her hands glided up his waistcoat, her arms twined about his neck. "Don't go slowly."

Rem's mouth came down on hers; hard, demanding, seeking all she had … and finding it. At the same time, he fused the distance between them, pressing her against the solid surface behind her, bringing her into absolute contact with the hardened contours of his body. "I want you," he said hoarsely. "I want to make love to you until every drop of passion is spent, until you shatter in my arms, until I pour my soul into yours. Samantha …" His arms dropped to her shoulders, slid down her back, effortlessly lifted her into the drowning hunger of his embrace.

Sammy returned his passion full measure, a sharing rather than a surrender, the events soon to follow predestined, since that stormy night in Boydry's. Loving Rem, making love with him, was as natural a step to her as breathing.

Rem's lips possessed her everywhere; her cheeks, her neck, her throat. He was keenly aware of Samantha returning his kisses, giving herself to him with an innocent abandon more devastating than the erotic acts of the most practiced courtesans. His body careened wildly out of control, hurtling him into a dark oblivion dominated by instinct and feeling. Gone was the expert lover and accomplished seducer, in their place a man as unprepared for the intensity of what was occurring between them as was the beautiful woman in his arms.

Somewhere in the dim outskirts of his mind, Rem secured a shred of sanity … enough to scoop Samantha off the floor, carry her up the stairs and into his bedchamber. He lowered her to the bed, following her down, capturing her mouth in another searing, blazing kiss, tugging the combs from her hair and letting the thick sable tresses cascade over his hands and down her back.

"I want you to feel things you never dreamed of," he breathed, capturing strands of black silk and bringing them to his lips. "I want this time—your first time—to be so perfect, so unbearably beautiful, you'll never forget it."

"I could never forget making love with you, Rem. Never." With breathtaking innocence, Sammy tugged at his cravat, slipping the knot free, only to begin unfastening his shirt.

Rem endured her untried attempts to disrobe him as long as he could. Then he caught her hands in his. "Let me."

A shadow of disappointment crossed her face.

Rem's heart constricted, and he brought her fingers to his lips, then back to his shirtfront. "Together," he whispered.

Moving Sammy's trembling hands under his, Rem unbuttoned his shirt and waistcoat, pulling the edges apart and pressing her palms to his naked flesh.

Sammy caressed his chest, leaned forward to nuzzle the mat of dark hair covering it. "You're so strong," she breathed, rubbing her cheek against the hard muscles and steely flesh. "I knew you would be."

A ragged groan erupted from Rem's chest, and he dragged her mouth back to his, kissing her savagely, nearly tearing her gown in his haste to remove it. He worshiped her bare shoulders with his lips and tongue, inhaling her scent, soothing her body's unconscious trembling, only to find he was shaking more violently than she. The thin material of her chemise gave beneath his onslaught, and, wordlessly, he lifted her against him, rubbing her naked breasts across his chest.

Samantha whimpered, drowning in heated sensation, clutching Rem's arms for support. Her nipples tightened painfully with each tingling brush of his hair-roughened flesh; her loins went liquid with longing. Gathering handfuls of wool, she tugged at his coat, wanting to rid him of every impediment to their joining.

Responding to her unspoken plea, Rem released her only long enough to drag off the offending coat, taking his open shirt and waistcoat with it. His torso bared, he gathered Sammy to him again, melding their naked flesh until she moaned, her head dropping helplessly to his shoulder. "So damned good," he ground out, absorbing her shudders. "Let me taste you, sweetheart."

Gently he eased her back, wrapping one arm about her waist and arching her up to his mouth. It had been mere days since their forbidden encounter at Vauxhall, but he was starved for the taste of her, the sweet, intoxicating flavor that was Samantha's alone.

He enveloped her nipple with a slow, teasing suction that taxed his control and made Sammy cry out, the sensation too overwhelming to endure. She begged him to stop, then begged him not to, shifting restlessly to deepen his velvety caress.

Rem moved to her other breast, tracing the nipple with his tongue, circling endlessly before giving in to her pleas and drawing the aching tip fully into his mouth. He began a tantalizing motion with his lips, alternately tugging and releasing the sensitized peak until Sammy's hips reflexively followed suit, rising and falling in conjunction with the rhythm of Rem's mouth.

The naturalness of her passion nearly pushed him over the edge. She was all innocence and fire, fierce in her wanting, breathtaking in her abandon. Like a new flower, she blossomed in his arms, reaching for the blinding light she knew he offered; uninhibited, untainted, unafraid.

Untouched.

Rem's heart swelled with that realization. Samantha was giving him her innocence. And he wanted to give her the world.

"Let me finish undressing you, love." His chest heaving, Rem lowered her to the bed. He cupped her breasts, traced the damp peaks with his thumbs, all the while watching her meadow-green eyes darken with passion, her breath come in harsh pants of need. "You are every fantasy I've ever dreamed," he told her huskily, gliding his palms to her waist, catching her gown and rended chemise, sliding them down over her hips.

A radiant glow suffused Samantha's skin, not a shred of doubt clouding her eyes, neither modesty nor shame diminishing the anticipation on her face. She lay, quiescent, while Rem peeled away her stockings, tossing them atop her discarded gown and chemise. Totally exposed to his scrutiny, she made no move to cover herself, remaining perfectly still beneath his consuming stare.

He made love to her with his eyes, drinking in her flawless beauty inch by inch, staking claim with every heated look. At last, with a rough, hungry sound, he allowed his hands free reign, stroking her hips and then her thighs, urging them to part for a more intimate caress.

The pulse in Sammy's body beat frantically, her insides melting with the same hunger she'd felt when Rem had caressed her in his carriage. How well she remembered the feeling of his knowing hands. How desperately she wanted to feel them again.

Blissfully, she shifted, her eyes drifting shut as she awaited his touch.

Rem lowered his head and buried his mouth in her sweetness.

Sammy cried out, instinctively reaching down, whether to push him away or pull him closer, she wasn't sure.

Capturing both her hands in one of his, Rem continued his exquisite assault, penetrating her ever so slowly with his tongue, simultaneously caressing the sensitive bud of her passion with his thumb. "God … your taste." He released her hands to cup her bottom, lift her into his seeking tongue. "This alone is enough to drive me over the edge. Tasting you. Claiming you." He raised his head. "Tell me you're mine."

How could she speak? The world was Rem's mouth, Rem's touch, Rem's words. Nothing mattered but the ecstasy he lavished on her senses, her soul. Answer him? Impossible.

Rem's ravenous gaze bored through her, seeing the declaration she couldn't utter. Wordlessly, he lifted her legs higher over his shoulders, opening her totally to his possession, sinking his tongue deep inside her, only to withdraw and repeat the caress again and again.

"Rem …." Sammy uttered his name on a shrill, heightened cry, everything inside her converging into a pinpoint of blinding sensation that intensified and grew, intensified and grew, until it splintered into a million blazing fragments, scattering her soul to the heavens, pouring her heart into Rem's. "Oh … Rem …"

Closing his eyes, Rem kissed Sammy's most intimate flesh, wringing another sobbing spasm out of her, sharing it, tasting it, unwilling to relinquish her even in the wake of her shattering release. He feathered his lips up the insides of her thighs and higher, knowing just where to stroke to prolong her wondrous sensations, where to linger to make it last. Even when she fell back, limp and exhausted against the pillows, he refused to stop, nuzzling her softly, pressing whisper-light caresses on her skin, gliding his fingers sensuously through the velvety wetness between her thighs. "So beautiful," he murmured. "So soft and warm and beautiful." He teased the opening of her body, entered her with his finger. "So excruciatingly tight." When she moaned his name, another current of sensation rippling from her body to his, his control splintered into nothingness. "Samantha …" He shuddered heavily, sweat sheening his body. "I …"

Inexperienced as she was, Sammy knew what to do. Guided by an age-old instinct, she came to her knees, her fingers finding the fastenings of his breeches and tugging at them. "Rem … please."

He wrenched off his shoes, kicking them aside and dragging down his breeches in one hard, violent motion.

"How magnificent you are," Sammy breathed, her reverent gaze fixed on his engorged manhood. "Powerful and strong … everywhere."

Rem came down over her, wedging her thighs apart with his knee. "I can't wait."

"And I don't want to." She smiled into his eyes, joyously opening herself to him. "I'm yours," she whispered, giving him the answer he'd sought moments ago. "I always will be." Her breath came faster as he settled himself in the cradle of her thighs, found the heated entrance to her body with his own. "Oh, Rem, I love you."

The reverent declaration was as right as their joining, the natural expression of what she'd known from the start. Sammy watched the spasm of pleasure contort Rem's face, but whether it was caused by her admission or the feel of her body taking his, Sammy wasn't certain. All she knew was that she loved him, loved him desperately, and she wanted to give him more pleasure than any woman ever had.

"Christ …" The word escaped Rem in a savage hiss, physical sensation such as he had never known gripping his loins as he pushed inexorably forward into her clinging resistance. Her internal muscles stretched gracefully to accept his intrusion, hugging him tightly, sending blinding surges of pleasure through his throbbing shaft. He fought the feeling, determined to stay sane long enough to breach her maidenhead as painlessly as possible. "Samantha ..." He reached the fragile barrier, braced himself on his elbows and looked down into her astonished face.

"I never imagined it would be so beautiful," she breathed.

Emotion clogged Rem's throat. "Neither did I." He guided Sammy's legs higher around his waist. "Samantha ... I've never wanted anything ... anyone ... more in my life than I want you now."

"I know." She wrapped her arms around his back, feeling his love, wishing with all her heart he would say the words.

Their gazes locked.

"Yes," he breathed, covering her mouth with his. "God, yes."

Sammy arched up as he pushed forward, and together they took her from girl to woman.

A hoarse shout erupted from Rem's chest, and he pressed deep inside her until he could go no farther. "Are you ... all right?" he managed, feeling her body's shock as it struggled to accept him.

She nodded against his shoulder, ignoring the shards of pain his entry had induced, thinking only of the pleasure of being one. "Rem?"

"Yes, love." It took all his discipline not to move. His body was screaming its need to withdraw, then plunge into her, over and over, until his clawing passion was spent.

"What happened to me before ..." She kissed his neck. "I want to feel it again ... only this time with you."

Rem groaned, succumbing to the fire burning through his loins. He pulled out gradually, almost completely, then sank slowly forward, testing to see how raw she was, how much penetration she could take.

He was rewarded with a melting sigh.

"Is the pain gone?"

In answer, Sammy rubbed her legs against his. "Don't hold back," she whispered. "I want to know everything."

Aroused beyond bearing, Rem responded wildly, burying himself inside her, his hips beginning a rhythm instinctively meant to caress her every inner muscle, her every tingling nerve. Despite the savagery of his own need, Rem moved with erotic precision, calling on every iota of his expertise to bring Samantha the most dazzling sensations any woman could know.

The frenzied spiraling began inside her again, coiling upward and inward, pulsing harder and harder with each thrust of Rem's powerful hips. Sammy dug her nails into his back, willing him to feel what was happening to her, and Rem crushed her closer still, dragging her up to meet each feverish thrust, impaling her on his fiery hardness.

He could hold back no longer.

When Samantha's hands found his buttocks, clutching him tightly, pulling him deeper into her sultry core, Rem lost the battle, succumbing to his scalding climax with a feral roar. He felt his seed explode from his body into hers, flooding her with his bottomless, unimaginable passion. "Come with me," he demanded, unwilling to touch heaven alone. "Now, love … come with me."

His plea, the frenzied motion of his hips, catapulted Sammy into her own mind-shattering release. She screamed this time, the pulsing surges of his climax intensifying her hard inner contractions beyond bearing. It seemed to go on forever, her body helplessly tossed on tides of sensation until at last she drifted, languorous and weak, back to earth.

Neither of them moved, their harsh breathing the only sound in the silence of the room.

Her eyes still closed, Sammy smiled, trailing her fingers along the hard plateaus of Rem's sweat-slick back.

Rem stirred, rolling to one side, Samantha clasped tightly in his arms. "Incredible," he muttered, barely able to speak. "Absolutely incredible."

Sammy kissed the hollow at the base of his throat. "More than that," she whispered.

Drawing back only far enough to look down at her. Rem caressed her flushed cheek with his knuckles. "The pain ... is it better now?"

"What pain?" Sammy turned her lips into his hand.

"Ah ... Samantha." He wrapped her closer, nuzzling her hair.

"Rem ... was I ... did I ... I mean you're so ..."

His lips were warm against the shell of her ear. "I never made love before tonight."

It was just what Sammy needed to hear, and too much for her to bear. Dizzy with joy, weak with fulfillment, she burst into tears, drenching Rem's shoulder, inhaling great gulps of air to calm her careening emotions.

The tantalizing scent of wildflowers accosted her.

Lifting her head in surprise, Sammy peered about for the first time since Rem had carried her to bed. And what she saw made the tears flow anew.

Flowers lined every surface of the room, were scattered along each window ledge. Their scent, subtle but sweet, filled the air with an intoxicating aroma she hadn't noticed in the wildness of the past hour.

Rising up on her elbow, Sammy encountered the rest of Rem's handiwork: a dozen glowing candles, their light as incandescent as that of the most radiant fire, a bottle of champagne, unopened and waiting on Rem's nightstand, and beside it, two stemmed glasses and a tray of fresh fruit.

"Oh, Rem ..." There were no other words to say. This overpower-ingly seductive man who'd had more women than she could count, to whom passion was a seasoned game played with casual ardor and culti-vated finesse, this same man had just made love to her as if she were the only woman on earth, and was now offering her not only the miracle of her first time, but all the romantic wonder her heart could hold.

Words were inadequate, tears interminable.

"Don't cry, sweetheart," Rem murmured, smoothing his thumbs over the damp tracks on her cheeks.

"It's all so beautiful."

"Not nearly as beautiful as you." He framed her face between his palms. "Just tell me this … does it make you happy?"

"I'll remember tonight for the rest of my life."

Tenderness, more vast than passion, constricted Rem's chest. "As will I," he replied soberly. Shifting slightly, he reached for the champagne. "And, given that tonight is what memories are made of, let's not waste a single moment of it."

Sammy stayed him with her hand, her eyes filled with heated promise. "No," she whispered. "Let's not."

SIXTEEN

"It's almost dawn, love." Gently, Rem stroked tangled strands of hair from Sammy's face.

"Let's ignore it," she murmured, blissfully lying in his arms.

He chuckled. "It would take very little convincing for me to do just that. However, I don't think Smithers would share my enthusiasm."

"After an evening of parties, Smitty won't expect to see me until noon. I won't be missed." Sammy traced the corded muscles of Rem's abdomen, dreamily wondering how many times they'd made love … how many more times lay ahead.

"You won't be missed; not even by Cynthia?"

"Cynthia … oh, Lord." Sammy's hand froze. "She'll have waited up for me. By now she's probably—"

"Just retiring for the night," Rem finished. "And totally unaware of your absence. But even the memories of Boyd's late-night visit will not be powerful enough to distract her by the first light of day. So I don't think she should find you missing from your bed."

That intrigued Sammy enough to stir. "Boyd called on Cynthia tonight?"

"Um-hum."

"After midnight? And she agreed to see him?"

"He's a tavern keeper, imp. His business doesn't shut down until then. Besides, his visit was a surprise."

"I can imagine." Sammy chewed her lip dubiously. "Are you certain she didn't turn him away?"

"Quite certain."

"How do you know?"

"Because if Boyd hadn't succeeded in diverting your diligent lady's maid, she would have paced the floors awaiting your arrival, and when you showed no signs of doing so, she would have long since broken down my door to find you."

Sammy's eyes twinkled. "True. Rem, do you honestly believe Boyd can win her over?"

"I do."

"She's endured a great deal."

"And, if I'm correct, Boyd intends to make sure she never again has to."

"I hope you're right. They're both wonderful people. I'd like nothing better than to see them happy … together."

"I hope I'm right, too." Rem's dimple flashed. "Then perhaps Cynthia will relinquish her role as your protector and cease attempting to rescue you from my sinful hands."

"They are sinful, my lord." Sammy smiled impishly, catching his fingers and smoothing them over the warm curve of her breast. "Sinful and wonderful."

"You, my love, could tempt the stars down from the sky." Rem took her mouth under his, molding her breast to his palm. Absorbing her delicate shudder, he savored her softness, wishing he could hold the world, and the new day, at bay. "I have to get you home," he murmured, his hands, of their own volition, moving hungrily over her body in a sensual exploration that made desire pound through his loins like cannon fire.

Sammy arched gracefully against him.

"Damn." Rem's breath erupted in a harsh growl. "I can't get enough of you." He parted her thighs to find her heated entrance, to caress the dewy wetness he'd claimed tonight as his, only his.

"Rem …" Sammy's response was immediate, absolute, her legs opening to offer him her soul.

"Another hour …" Rem managed, entering her with his fingers. Submerged in her essence, he was lost yet again to Samantha's fervent, honest passion, her total relinquishing of self. He inhaled the scent of their lovemaking, stroked the delicate softness of her flesh, and, with an indistinguishable groan of primal male need, he buried himself inside her.

"I'll have to dash up to my room." Sammy sighed, tucking the final pin in her hair and looking exasperatedly down at herself. "Because no matter how hard I try, I cannot smooth the wrinkles out of this gown."

Rem knotted his cravat and smiled. "Sweetheart," he said tenderly, walking toward her, "it wouldn't matter if your gown were intact. The glow in your eyes, the flush on your cheeks …" He brushed his lips across hers. "You look like a woman who's been well-loved … all night."

"You look rather disheveled yourself, my lord," she teased, buttoning his waistcoat.

Just outside, a songbird emitted its early morning melody.

Glancing toward the window, Rem noted the pale slivers of sunlight beginning to show themselves, proclaiming the new day. He framed Sammy's face between his palms. "Let's get you home. Before your servants arise."

Nodding, Sammy glanced back at the bed where she'd spent the past few incomparable hours. The pillows were rumpled, the bedcovers hopelessly tangled, and faint stains of her lost virginity streaked the stark whiteness of the sheets. *How symbolic,* she thought dreamily. *The tangible transition from child to woman.*

Lost in wondrous thought, Sammy feathered her fingers across the bedpost. She was leaving this room a different person than when she came, whole in ways she'd never known she was empty.

Yes, her innocence belonged to Rem now.

But the memories were hers forever.

"I'm ready," she said softly.

Watching the play of emotions on Sammy's face, Rem felt his chest constrict. He reached for her, drew her to him, his own insides raw, exposed. How could he comfort her? What words could he utter to alleviate the disenchantment that lay ahead?

He intended to offer her all he could, but his heart knew it wasn't enough—not for Samantha. Yet, hadn't he expected this? He, the experienced realist, had known from the start there would be an aftermath, a brittle shattering of Samantha's romantic bubble.

It was too late to berate himself. He'd gone into this with his eyes wide open, equipped with a foresight Samantha was too starry-eyed and naive to possess. But his emotions had eclipsed his reason, and now all he could pray was that he'd be able to fill Samantha's life with enough joy so she wouldn't ache from the lack of that which he could never give.

But one thing was a certainty. After tonight, Samantha Barrett was his.

A pounding at the door interrupted the intensity of Rem's thoughts.

Sammy started. "Rem? It's half after five in the morning …"

"It's probably Boyd," Rem soothed. "He expected me to deliver you home an hour ago."

Taking Sammy's hand, Rem led her down the stairs and through the hallway. He scooped up her discarded wrap and put it about her shoulders, then eased her behind the door and out of view. "Who is it?"

"Boyd."

Rem relaxed, yanking open the front door.

"Well! Good morning!" Boyd strode in as fresh and cheerful as if he'd had a full night's sleep. He saw Samantha and came to a screeching halt. "Oh ..." Hot color suffused his face. "I'm sorry, I didn't think—"

"It's all right, Boyd." It was Sammy who answered, walking toward him, hands extended. "I'm glad you're here. It gives me a chance to say thank you." Her eyes danced. "We didn't exactly have the opportunity to talk during our eventful carriage ride."

"No. We didn't."

To Boyd's amazement, Sammy bypassed his proffered hands, instead seizing his forearms and standing on tiptoe to kiss his cheek.

"Thank you," she whispered. "You helped make this the most wondrous night of my life." Undaunted by his embarrassment, Sammy added, "I hope your evening was fruitful, as well." She gazed up at him like a hopeful puppy.

Boyd glanced at Rem, then back at Sammy.

"You did visit Cynthia, did you not?" she persisted.

One corner of Boyd's mouth lifted. "Yes, I did."

"And, judging from your jubilant humor, I assume things went well. Cynthia likes you, you know. I can see it every time your name comes up. So don't be put off by her aloof manner. She's been badly hurt. Therefore, you must woo her slowly and gently ... but persistently. She needs a man who will not only care for her, but stand by her, regardless of how long it takes. A man like you. Once she believes—truly believes—that your feelings are genuine, unfaltering, she'll thaw. And I promise you, it will be worth it. Now," Sammy paused only to breathe, "tell me, were you really successful in keeping her from discovering my absence?"

Boyd looked totally dazed. "What? Oh ... yes."

"But our luck won't last indefinitely," Rem interjected. "Imp, we're leaving. Now. Neither dawn, nor your loving servants, will wait any longer."

"Very well." Sammy gave Boyd a grateful smile. "Again, thank you."

"It was my pleasure."

"Stay here," Rem instructed Boyd. "I'll be back shortly." Then he steered Sammy out the door.

The carriage ride was silent, fraught with emotional tension. "Boyd is a fine man," Sammy said at last. "You're lucky to have him as a friend."

"Yes. I am."

Sammy gazed candidly across at Rem, her heart in her eyes. "And you are even more wondrous a hero than I prayed you would be."

A hard knot of reality formed in Rem's stomach. "I'm just a man, Samantha. Oftentimes not a very nice one. I am no hero."

"You can say that after tonight?"

"Tonight was beautiful … a magical, extraordinary fantasy. But today is what's real."

"I won't believe that."

"You have to." Rem ached for the bewildered hurt he saw in her eyes. "Sweetheart, there are things about me you don't know."

"Then share them with me."

"It's not that easy. My life, my history—" He broke off. "You're precious and sheltered. Let it go."

"I can't. I want to know all of you." She leaned forward, lay her hand on Rem's jaw. "I love you."

Rem squeezed his eyes shut. He'd thought himself prepared for what lay ahead, for the hurt he would now have to cause her. He wasn't.

"I'll speak to your brother today," he said with quiet resolve, wanting to envelop her and free her all at once. "After that, I'll make arrangements for a special license. We can be married immediately."

Samantha's joy was extinguished by the resignation in Rem's tone. "You sound like a man condemned. Is the thought of wedding me so unpleasant?"

A rueful smile touched Rem's lips. "No, imp, never unpleasant. You're a rare and priceless treasure. I'll do everything in my power to make you happy."

"And you? Will you be happy?"

Until I see the sparkle fade from your eyes, he wanted to blurt out. "Yes, I'll be happy."

Sammy searched his face. "Why are you proposing? Is it because you took me to bed?"

"Absolutely not." This he could give her. "It was very much the other way around. I took you to bed only after I'd decided our future."

"How dispassionate. You decided our future. You made love to me. You proposed. Tell me, Rem, where do feelings factor into your plan?"

"I think you know how much I care for you."

"Care for me," Sammy repeated, chewing her lip. "What about love?"

This was the part Rem had dreaded most. "Love," he repeated woodenly.

"Yes. Love." She stared down at her clasped hands. "It would be foolish at this point for me to lie. I want to be your wife. I want that more than anything on this earth, and I have from the moment you walked into Boydry's. But I want you to wed me out of love, not duty." She raised her head. "Do you love me, Remington?"

"Samantha—"

"Do you love me?" she persisted.

"I care for you more than I've ever cared for anyone in my life, more than I ever dreamed possible. I want you with an insatiable intensity that astounds me. But love? The kind of love poets write about, men give their souls for, live for, die for ... the kind of love I know you want of me ... I'm just not capable of so vast and absolute an emotion."

"I won't accept that." Her lips quivered.

"Sweetheart ..." He reached for her.

The carriage came to a halt.

Pushing open the door, Sammy climbed down, battling desperately not to cry. "It's late, Rem. Or rather, early. We can't have this conversation now."

He caught her arm. "We can't turn back, Samantha. It's too late for that. And not only because of what happened tonight. Even if I hadn't made love to you, it wouldn't stop me from burning for you, from craving your sweetness, from killing any other man who touched you."

Sammy's anguished expression tore at his heart. "Imp ..." He cupped her chin. "I'll give you all I have to give; my devotion, my fidelity, my protection. You'll never want for anything—including an unlimited stream of novels from Hatchard's." Tenderly, he caressed her cheek with his forefinger. "And I'll bathe your senses in pleasures you've never even dreamed possible."

"Don't, Rem." Sammy shook her head to ward off the effect of his promise. "I need to think. And I can't do that when you seduce me with words."

"Don't think. Just consider us betrothed. Let me talk to your brother."

"No ... not yet." A lone tear slid down Sammy's cheek. "Under the circumstances, I'm not ready to deal with Drake."

From somewhere inside the Town house a door closed.

Sammy jerked around. "I have to go."

Rem couldn't remember the last time he'd felt so frustrated, so emotionally raw. "Meet me later today, then. We'll ride through Hyde Park." When she refused to answer, struggling instead to free herself, Rem's grip tightened. "Please, love," he added softly, "tonight was too beautiful to end like this. Please don't cry."

The tenderness in his voice was Sammy's undoing. She stopped struggling, staring up at him, a hard knot forming in her throat. She hadn't been wrong, her heart cried out. It was there; in his eyes, his tone, his touch. All his words, his professions of inability, were for naught, and she refused to accept them. Whatever in Rem's past had scarred him so deeply, tainted his ability to care, she would discover it. And, oppressive though it might be, she would combat it. Because she knew something Rem did not.

He might not think he loved her … but he did.

"I'll be ready at five." Gently, Sammy disengaged her arm, feeling even more a woman now than she had during those pivotal moments in Rem's arms. "Good night, Rem."

"So you actually heard Summerson say he planned to keep an eye on Samantha?" Boyd asked, leaning forward.

"Yes." Rem paced the length of his sitting room, brow furrowed in worry. "It was clear that her relationship to Drake made her a threat … to whatever illegal dealing Anders and Summerson are involved in."

"Atlantis." Boyd tapped his chin thoughtfully. "Sounds like the name of a ship."

"Yes, it does, doesn't it?" Rem came to a halt, exchanging a meaningful look with his friend.

"You're obviously thinking exactly what I am—that Anders and Summerson could be the culprits responsible for all the lost vessels."

"Responsible or merely working for those who are. I tend to favor the latter, at least in Anders's case. He hasn't the intelligence or the cunning to devise and carry out such a sophisticated scheme on his own. I don't know Summerson well enough to make the same judgment. But whether they're working alone or with others, the motive is there."

"Insurance money," Boyd put in.

"Exactly."

"But our Bow Street men examined Anders's and Summerson's records; in both cases they were impeccable."

"Anders muttered something of the kind to Summerson. Which tells us what we already know—that records can be tampered with."

"True." Boyd still looked troubled. "There's another hole in our theory," he continued with a frown. "The name Atlantis wasn't on the list Briggs gave you."

"All that says is that the Admiralty has no record of a ship by that name going down, or that the Atlantis hasn't sunk—or possibly even sailed—yet."

"How do you suggest we proceed? We have no proof."

"First, I'll contact Briggs, have him run a check on any ship by the name *Atlantis*. If such a vessel does exist, we'll find out who built it, who owns it, and what its current status is.

"In the interim, we need to more thoroughly investigate our friends Anders and Summerson: find out what they're up to, who their cohorts are, why they're conducting secret meetings at midnight." Rem gulped down a cup of black coffee. "Since they were clever enough not to leave clues in their business accounts, let's delve into their personal lives."

"Should I notify Templar and Harris?"

"Good idea. I'll need them to take over some of the covert work. I plan to spend most of my time keeping a close eye on Samantha. No one is going to hurt her."

Hearing the anxiety in Rem's tone, Boyd frowned. "Do you think Anders's relentless pursuit of Samantha relates to his illegal business dealings? That he wants to get close to her because of her connection to Barrett Shipping and that he's hoping to gain information from her without her realizing it?"

"I think Anders's interest in vying for Samantha's hand could very well have begun for those reasons. But no longer." Rem resumed his long strides. "I've seen the hungry look in his eyes when he watches her, and believe me, it has nothing to do with Barrett Shipping. I also saw his reaction tonight when Summerson attempted to go after her. Anders stopped him—quite insistently—ordering him to stay away. So, while I'm sure the viscount wants to learn all he can about whatever Barrett Shipping information Samantha might possess, I can safely say that his futile designs on her are quite personal."

Boyd cleared his throat. "How much do you want me to tell Templar and Harris?"

"Just tell them we'll all meet tonight at Annie's. By then I'll have mapped out our plan."

"Done." Boyd studied Rem's haggard expression. "Do you want to talk about it?" he asked at last.

"'It'? Which 'it' are you referring to?"

"The one that's tearing you apart. Other than worry. Is it guilt? Because if it is, I'd reconsider. That was one happy woman who left here a few hours ago." Boyd found himself chuckling. "She's quite a little whirlwind, your Samantha."

"She's like a dazzling watercolor, all vibrant and rare and beautiful. And fragile." Rem turned to stare moodily out the window. "I hate being the one destined to cause her pain."

"Why do you assume you will?"

"You, of all people, know that my capacity for deep feelings is long gone."

"Is it? It doesn't sound that way to me. It sounds to me like you're in love with Samantha Barrett."

"I am. God help her, but I am."

"Perhaps your capacity to love is greater than you think."

Rem shrugged. "Perhaps. But it can never be the all-encompassing love Samantha dreams of, the kind that dwarfs all else, that consumes one's life and one's being."

"I see. Quite a quandary. How do you plan to resolve it?"

"I plan to go to Allonshire and ask Drake Barrett for his sister's hand. And then I plan to do my damnedest to ensure that Samantha never regrets becoming my wife."

"But Rem—"

ANDREA KANE

"Enough. Let's talk about you." Rem poured himself another cup of coffee. "How did your evening with Cynthia go?"

"Much as Samantha portrayed in her one-sided discourse. Cynthia has rigid walls erected—walls that are not going to be easy to break down." He grinned. "Speaking of breaking down, I could barely get through her front door. It took me almost an hour to convince her to let me in."

"And when you did?"

"Smithers had no objection to our visiting in the sitting room, since Cynthia's mistress was out for the evening."

Rem snorted. "I wish he took as kindly to me. Most of the time he looks at me as if he'd like to toss me out with the rest of the rubbish. As does Cynthia. In fact, I'm firmly convinced that the only household member who doesn't find me distasteful is Lady Gertrude. Even Samantha's Maltese pup is cool toward me. He hasn't forgiven me for referring to him as a rodent."

Boyd chuckled. "Rejection will keep you humble, Rem. Besides, aren't you forgetting one very important Barrett? Someone who happens to think the sun rises and sets on you?"

"Samantha is too romantic for her own good."

"Then isn't it comforting to know that you can spend the rest of your days watching out for her?"

"I thought we were discussing Cynthia."

A grin. "We are."

"So you visited in the sitting room. You chatted. Did she warm up at all?"

"I never found her cold. But if you're asking if I'm making headway, I think so. It pains me deeply, Rem. Someone has hurt her, crushed her spirit so badly that she's afraid to trust anyone ... especially men."

"Why was she working at Annie's?"

"She'd only been there a week when Samantha rescued her. After she'd rescued Samantha, of course."

Rem started. "What are you talking about?"

"Didn't Samantha tell you how she and Cynthia met?"

"No. And I don't think I'm going to like this."

Boyd shifted uncomfortably. "Cynthia assumed you knew."

"Then tell me and I will."

"Evidently, the night you left Samantha at the opera you told her you were en route to a business meeting because you were short of funds."

"I did."

"She was worried about you and determined to see if she could help. She hid in your carriage and accompanied you to Annie's."

Rem groaned. "Now I *know* I'm not going to like this. The little fool! What did she think she was—"

"She loves you, Rem."

A muscle worked in Rem's jaw. "Go on."

"If you recall, that particular night you couldn't shake the feeling you were being followed. Well, you were right."

"I said, go on."

"Samantha stayed outside the brothel during our meeting. A group of ruffians accosted her. Cynthia bullied them off, threatening to tell Annie they were assailing one of her women. It worked. Samantha was grateful as hell. She hired Cynthia on the spot. End of story."

Dropping down into a chair, Rem swore softly. "She could have been killed."

"That's probably why she was reluctant to tell you about it."

"What the hell am I going to do with her?"

Boyd bit back a smile. "Probably a great deal of what you did with her last night."

"Probably. That's the only time I can be sure she's not in danger." Rem gave Boyd a measured look. "Samantha trusts Cynthia implicitly. I gather you do, too."

"I do. I'd also stake my life on the fact that she's never worked in a brothel before, and wouldn't have this time if the circumstances hadn't been dire."

"I could ask Samantha about Cynthia's history."

"You could. But I'd rather Cynthia tell me herself. I'm a patient man, Rem. Especially when I want something. And I want Cynthia. Badly. So I'll wait. Besides," Boyd added quietly, "many of us have pasts we'd prefer to forget. The present is all that matters … and the future."

"Did you make plans to see her again?"

Boyd's eyes sparkled. "Today is her day off. I'm going to close Boydry's early and take her to a coffeehouse for dinner."

"Good for you."

"What about Samantha? Are you seeing her tonight? Or are you going straight to Allonshire to talk to the duke?"

"I'm taking her for a carriage ride this evening. After that, we'll see. If I can't make it to Allonshire and back in time for tonight's meeting at Annie's, I'll visit Drake tomorrow. Either way, Samantha and I will be married within a week."

"A week? Why?"

"Why not?"

"Surely you realize a woman like Samantha will have dreamed of a church wedding, an elegant gown, lots of guests; not to mention what her brother will want for her."

"Surely *you* realize how impractical that is, given the circumstances."

"What circumstances? The fact that planning your wedding might detract from our bloody mission?"

"The fact that Samantha could be carrying my child."

"Not a likelihood after being together one night. And, even if she is, no one will be able to notice for several months. Which gives you more than enough time to give her the kind of wedding she deserves. In the meantime, just keep your hands off her for a month or so and your heirs will arrive without scandal."

"I can't."

The fervor of Rem's admission made Boyd start.

"You have no idea what happens when Samantha and I are together. Trust me, Boyd, abstinence is not an option; for either of us. The sooner I put a ring on her finger, the better. Moreover, I'll be in a better position to protect her when I'm her husband. No, the wedding must take place immediately."

Boyd gave a low whistle. "You're even worse off than I thought."

"I'm also exhausted." Rem rubbed his hand over the shadow of a beard that darkened his face. "So, if we're finished, I'd like to get some sleep."

With a knowing expression, Boyd rose. "See you at Annie's." He paused. "Oh … and Rem? Good luck with Samantha."

Samantha was praying for much the same.

Retying the velvet ribbon in her hair for the third time, she glanced at the clock and frowned. Unfashionably early, even without the benefit of Cynthia's able assistance. But that wasn't surprising. She'd had hours to select her gown and arrange her hair. In fact, aside from taking a bath and nibbling at her lunch, she had done naught but sit at her bedchamber window all day, gazing out at Abingdon Street and thinking of Rem.

'Twas just as well that it was Cynthia's day off, Sammy thought. Lord knew, she was not ready to face anyone, least of all her new friend, who would take one look at her and know exactly what had transpired. No, her emotions were still too chaotic, her transformation too new, too overwhelming to hide.

She'd awakened at noon, but remained abed until one, devoting a full hour to a tantalizing remembrance of last night. No dream could have been more perfect than the reality of becoming a woman in Rem's arms. She was his now, irrevocably so, and nothing the future held could change that.

The future.

That vast, unknown entity had dominated Sammy's thoughts for the duration of the day. She was not naive enough to believe the future awaited smooth and untainted … not with the deep trenches of Rem's past scarring its path. No, those trenches had to be mended, carefully and with an enveloping blanket of love.

It was up to her to do that. A formidable task indeed. But Sammy wasn't deterred. In fact, she was exhilarated. For at last her role as a heroine was defined.

Time after glorious time, Rem had proved himself to be her hero: rescuing her, protecting her, cherishing her as he introduced her to a world of dazzling sensations. Now it was her turn. She would be the most valiant of heroines, restore to her hero the peace he craved, and at the same time, heal the scars he abhorred and guide him to the emotional exultation he never knew he yearned for.

Rem was in love with her. Sammy knew it. And once she'd fulfilled her role as his heroine, he would belong to her as totally as she already belonged to him.

Smoothing her bodice, Sammy reminded herself that Rem wasn't aware of the depth of his own feelings. Nor could she thrust them at him. She had to patiently, steadfastly, chip away at the debris surrounding his heart, until it was free of its restrictive burden.

But first she had to find its cause.

It didn't involve a woman. Rem had told her so himself the night they'd attended the opera. He'd implied that his cynicism was precipitated by something far more devastating than a woman's deception.

But what?

Perhaps their upcoming ride through Hyde Park could provide her with some answers ... *if* she asked the right questions, carefully and without triggering Rem's self-protective mechanism.

Staring solemnly at her reflection, Sammy reminded herself that her goal was monumental, nearly impossible to attain. With the exception of Boyd, she was certain Rem had never confided his pain or his fears in anyone. Conversely, she could never imagine wedding a man who refused to share himself with her. It was an insurmountable impasse.

She could hardly wait to surmount it and become Rem's wife.

Voices drifted up from outside her window, and Sammy peeked through the curtains curiously. She had to smile at what she saw.

In the drive, Boyd was assisting Cynthia into a waiting phaeton, evidently escorting her out for the evening. But what a different Cynthia it was! Laughing, her face aglow, garbed in a feminine blue day dress rather than her primly starched uniform ... Cynthia looked positively radiant. Beaming ear to ear, Boyd climbed in beside her and urged the horses into a trot.

A momentous day off for Cynthia, Sammy thought with a fond grin.

Her grin faded and her heart began to slam against her ribs as, in the phaeton's wake, Rem's closed carriage rounded the drive. A liveried footman scurried about to open the carriage door for the earl, and Rem emerged, all elegant sophistication and unmistakable sexuality.

Sammy wet her lips with the tip of her tongue. The moment of reckoning was upon her.

Steeling herself, Sammy smoothed the folds of her white muslin carriage dress once, twice, trying to still her raw nerves. At last she gave up, opening her bedchamber door in time to collide with a young serving girl.

"Forgive me, m'lady." The girl regained her balance and curtsied, a mortified blush staining her cheeks.

"The fault was mine," Sammy answered gently. "Did you come to tell me that the Earl of Gresham was here?"

"Yes, m'lady. I did."

"Then you've done your job ... and survived a collision with a clumsy and jittery dolt. Thank you."

The girl looked astounded. "Thank *you*, my lady." Eyes wide, she backed away, then turned and scooted off.

Sammy took a deep breath and started down the hall. Turning the corner, she nearly fell over a sprinting ball of fur that whizzed by her like a streak of white lightning.

"Rascal! For goodness sake!" Sammy clutched the wall for support.

Rascal slowed down only to bark triumphantly, then raced off with the coveted stocking he'd apparently pilfered from Cynthia's room.

Rolling her eyes, Sammy set off for the stairs again, determined to reach them without further mishap. Evidently it was not meant to be.

Rounding the second floor landing, she smacked into Aunt Gertrude, nearly catapulting the elderly woman down the entire flight.

"Oh, Aunt Gertie, I'm so sorry!" Sammy steadied her aunt, wondering if all these casualties heralding her way to Rem were a prelude to the obstacles she would soon face.

"No harm done," Gertrude assured her, blinking a bit. Then she gave Sammy a conspiratorial smile. "Besides, I know why you're in such a hurry! I just saw that handsome Earl of Gresham awaiting you in the sitting room."

"Yes, we're en route to Hyde Park." Guilt pricked at Sammy's conscience as she realized that she was on the verge, yet again, of going out without a proper chaperon. "Please join us, Aunt Gertie." The invitation nearly stuck in her throat. "I'm certain Remington would be delighted to have you as his guest."

"You're right. I do need a rest." Aunt Gertrude yawned. "Have a lovely time, dear." She patted Sammy's arm.

"But Cynthia is off today," Sammy felt compelled to add. "And I'm aware that—"

"A hat?" Gertrude paused, her eyes narrowed assessingly. "Yes, you should wear a hat; that dress cries out for one. Now, let me think. A hat … a hat …" She snapped her fingers. "I have just the thing. Wait here." She tottered off, excitement crackling about her. A moment or two later she returned, clutching a wide-brimmed straw hat boasting five rows of red satin ribbon, three huge lavender flowers in the front and a bevy of billowing yellow ostrich plumes around the rim.

Sammy didn't know whether to laugh or cry.

"Here, dear." Gertrude pressed the monstrosity into Sammy's hands. "I insist that you wear it to impress that splendid escort of yours."

"But—"

"No buts. Be off with you!" Aunt Gertrude shooed Sammy toward the stairs.

Still dazed, Sammy complied. What more could she do? She'd tried, several times in fact, to do the proper thing. She had no intention of giving Fate another opportunity to change her mind.

Hat in hand, Sammy descended the steps and entered the sitting room.

"Hello, Rem."

He turned instantly, that devastating smile curving his lips, revealing his dimple. "You look beautiful, imp." He absorbed her slowly, possessively, his gaze openly intimate and caressing. Suddenly, his brow furrowed. "What is *that?*"

Biting back laughter, Sammy tucked the hat beneath her arm. "I'll explain later. Can we go now?"

"Alone?" His question emanated heated longing.

Sammy nodded.

"Come." He asked no further questions.

The moment the carriage left the drive, Rem pulled the curtains closed and swung across to sit beside Sammy.

"How much time do we have?" she asked softly, staring at her clenched hands.

"I told my driver to keep circling the park until I tell him otherwise."

"Good. We have much to discuss."

"No, imp, we don't." He raised her chin with a gentle forefinger. "You're going to be my wife. That's all there is to discuss." His gaze fell to her mouth. "Frankly, I'd hoped to put these hours to better use."

"Rem, I'm not a plaything. I'm a woman."

"I know." He brushed his lips over hers.

"Oh, Rem." Sammy wasn't certain why, but she had a sudden, desperate need for him to hold her. She pressed closer, laying her head on his shoulder, seeking some level of comfort that only he could give.

Rem seemed to understand, perhaps better than she. His arms closed around her, enveloping her in his strength, his warmth. "Don't be afraid, sweetheart," he whispered, his breath ruffling her hair. "Everything is going to be all right."

"I am afraid. And I don't even know why."

"Last night nearly brought me to my knees." Rem's voice was a husky caress. "What happened between us was beyond anything I've ever encountered, even remotely, in the past. So, isn't it natural that you, who came to my bed a complete and total innocent, would be a bit shattered by its intensity? I know I was … I still am."

"I want more." Sammy gripped the lapels of his coat.

"I know you do." Rem didn't pretend to misunderstand. "And I'll give you everything I have to give."

She raised her head. "I shall never ask for more than that."

He kissed her; a slow, melting exploration of her mouth. "Would it help if I told you I never even believed myself capable of this much?"

Sammy smiled against his lips. "I don't believe you, my lord. I imagine scores of women have told you how devastating your kisses are."

Rem chuckled. "I wasn't speaking of my kisses."

"I know." Sammy twined her arms about his neck, feeling his muscles tighten in response. She was strangely touched by the effect she had on him, moved by the knowledge that, despite the vast number of women who had preceded her, she alone had captured Rem's invincible heart … whether or not he knew it. "I love you, Rem," she whispered.

He lifted her onto his lap, tugging the velvet ribbon from her hair and tangling his fingers in the cascading tresses that tumbled over her shoulders. "I want to drown in you," he muttered, dragging her mouth back to his.

Welcoming all the unspoken love in Rem's kiss, Sammy was utterly, entirely lost. Everything faded into obscurity; her plans, her thoughts, her very breath. All she knew was Rem. Rem and how much she loved him.

His mouth ravaged hers, taking, giving, drawing her tongue forward to mate with his. She gasped when his lips left hers, but her breath lodged in her throat as his mouth found the pulse point in her neck, the curve of her shoulder, the arch of her breast. Her bodice was down … how, when, she had no idea. All she knew was that his lips were surrounding her nipple, circling it, scraping it, drawing its aching peak into the heated cavern of his mouth. Sammy clutched Rem's shoulders, throwing her head back, all of last night's urgency crashing through her as if it had never gone, hot, violent need throbbing in her loins, pooling between her thighs.

"Rem …" She sobbed his name, moving helplessly against him in a wild, undulating motion.

"Christ." It was a harsh growl, a reverent prayer, uttered from deep within Rem's soul. He couldn't think, didn't care about anything on earth but Samantha and losing himself in her melting warmth. He lifted her, unbuttoning his breeches and raising her skirts all at once.

"Rem?"

He met her gaze from beneath passion-heavy lids, wildly battling the pounding urge beating inside him, the heedless voice that commanded him to take her, all of her, now, and damn everything else to hell.

Seeing the confusion in her eyes, he paused. "Is this what you want?" he demanded, his voice rough with unquenched desire.

"Yes."

"Then tell me."

"I want you, Rem." Her voice was reckless with passion. "Just tell me how."

Her innocence was the most powerful aphrodisiac Rem had ever known. He groaned, feeling himself harden nearly beyond bearing. "Put your knees on either side of me," he managed through clenched teeth. "Do it now, Samantha, before I lose my mind."

She complied instantly, draping her skirts about them, encasing their bodies in an intoxicating, erotic cocoon.

Rem watched her eyes as he entered her, driven nearly crazy by the sexual awakening he saw there. "Deeper," he commanded, seizing her hips and pulling her down to envelop him. "So deep that we're one."

"Oh …" Sammy quivered as she caught the motion, rising up only to sink down again, taking him as far inside her as she could.

"Samantha …" Rem slid his hand around her nape, tugging her mouth down to his. "Kiss me." He arched up and into her. "Now move with me."

It was heaven and hell combined, a heightening of the senses that was beyond bearing. Their lips moved feverishly in conjunction with their bodies, each frenzied thrust taking them deeper inside each other, bringing them closer to the shattering brink. Sammy's thighs clenched convulsively around Rem's, her untutored body desperate, pulsing with its need for release.

"Please, Rem … I can't bear it."

"I know. God … I know."

The carriage hit a bump, driving Sammy forward, burying Rem still deeper inside her.

"Rem!" It was a sob, a plea, a celebration.

He worked his hand beneath her enveloping skirts, between their straining bodies, and found her. Ardently he stroked her swollen flesh, his opposite palm digging into the small of her back. He pulled her into him, hard, simultaneously raising up to bury himself to the hilt. His mouth ate at hers, his fingers burned into her aching depths, and Sammy catapulted over the edge, her blind cry of release silenced only by Rem's devouring mouth.

Rem followed her into the blistering pleasure, unable to stop himself even if he willed it. Samantha's inner muscles contracted around him, possessing him sweetly, totally, rendering him mindless, hurling him into his own excruciating release. He poured himself into her, burning explosions of sensation that hammered through him like gunfire, heaving his body into hers again and again, flooding her with the endless flow of his seed.

Sammy tore her mouth from his, unable to remain silent, sobbing his name with each exquisite spasm of her body. Instinctively she arched, taking all of Rem's scalding climax, watching his face as he gave it to her.

They floated, suspended as one, for a few magnificent moments. Then they drifted back to earth.

Sanity returned slowly.

Rem's head fell back against the seat cushion, his arms tightening reflexively around Samantha. She was shaking uncontrollably, her face buried in his shoulder, and he absorbed her hard shudders, dragging great gulps of air into his lungs.

The carriage rounded a curve, jostling its dazed occupants back into reality.

Sammy lifted her head.

A tender smile touched Rem's lips, his expression one of weary amazement. "You're unbelievable." He wrapped a wave of sable hair around his hand. "Utterly, astonishingly unbelievable."

"*We're* unbelievable," she corrected breathlessly, tracing his lips with her fingertip. "Utterly, astonishingly unbelievable." She brushed his mouth in a kiss of infinitely poignant beauty.

"When will you marry me?"

"Rem ..." Indecision warred on her face.

"Don't even think of saying no," he warned, ominous clouds erupting in his eyes, darkening them to near-black. "Not after what just happened in this carriage. Not with my body still buried in yours. Not when my child could be growing inside you. I mean it, Samantha. 'No' is not an option."

"Rem, I love you so much," she said in a broken whisper.

The darkness dissipated as quickly as it had come. "Marry me, then." He tugged her head back to his chest, his hand shaking as he stroked her hair. "Let me talk to your brother tomorrow ... please."

Sammy could feel Rem's anguish as tangibly as if it were her own. It was deep and devastating, involving far more than his plea for her to become his wife, far more than the unwilling love he had yet to admit. And she knew what her answer must be; the only one that would permit her to grapple with his pain and help him heal.

The only answer for either of them.

"Yes, Rem. I'll marry you."

SEVENTEEN

"Do you want a big church wedding?" Rem murmured, working the tangles from Sammy's hair with his fingers.

The window curtains remained drawn, but Sammy's gown was rearranged, Rem's breeches refastened as the carriage made its seventh trip around Hyde Park.

"Would you mind terribly?" She twisted around to see his face, simultaneously scooping Aunt Gertrude's hat off the carriage floor.

A corner of Rem's mouth lifted. "You never did explain that unusual headpiece."

"It's Aunt Gertie's. She generously offered to lend it to me.

"I see. Did you select this particular one?" Eyes twinkling, Rem stroked one of the garish plumes.

"Not exactly. Actually, I didn't request any hat at all. I merely asked Aunt Gertie if she wished to chaperon us on our carriage ride through Hyde Park, given that today is Cynthia's day off. She misunderstood."

"I see." Rem lifted Sammy's disheveled tresses and pressed his lips to her nape. "In that case I'm terribly grateful. I would have found a chaperon very inconvenient on this particular ride."

Sammy shivered. "Rem, I don't think we can risk another seven trips around Hyde Park. Besides, we were discussing our wedding."

"So we were." Reluctantly, Rem resumed his task, threading sable strands free of each other. "I asked if you wanted a grand church ceremony."

"And I said yes, unless, of course, you object."

Rem chuckled. "Would it matter?"

"Of course! If it makes you unhappy, we won't do it."

"How very biddable you are, imp ... just like the night we attended the opera when you ignored my instructions to go home and instead hid in my phaeton and rode with me to Shadwell."

Sammy went white. "How did you find out?"

"A better question is, when were you going to tell me?"

"I wasn't. I would never lie to you, Rem," Sammy added hastily, seeing his jaw tighten. "I just didn't want to upset you."

"Why would I be upset? Just because those ruffians might have killed you?"

"You're angry."

"I'm protective. I want you safe." He cupped her face between his palms. "Don't endanger yourself again."

"I won't." She gazed up at him and sighed. "You're going to be a terribly domineering husband, aren't you?"

"I think you'll manage to keep me in my place. Samantha ..." Rem's tone turned sober. "You have a loving heart and a vibrant spirit. I never want to squelch either. But remember what I said about disenchantment being inevitable?"

"I remember."

"Not everyone in the world is a fine, decent human being. You'll meet very few worthwhile sorts in that particular section of Shadwell."

"I met Cynthia."

Rem groaned, rolling his eyes to the heavens. "I give up. I'll just have to follow my first impulse and keep you in bed throughout your waking hours."

"You'll get no argument from me there, my lord." Sammy's smile was beatific. "So you see? I really am quite biddable when your demands are sound." Her loving taunt triggered a thought in her own mind. "Speaking of which, I had a messenger take Stephen's necklace to him at Anders Shipping this afternoon. So that makes two of your demands I obeyed."

"Samantha." Rem's jaw went taut, his expression dark. "I don't want you anywhere near Viscount Anders, is that clear?"

"Rem," Sammy sighed, "I've told you I feel absolutely nothing for Stephen—"

"I don't trust the man. He's scum. Stay away from him."

Taken aback by Rem's lethal tone, Sammy nodded. "All right."

"I'm sorry, imp." Rem softened, tenderly tracing the smooth curve of her cheek with his knuckles. "I just want to take care of you, to keep you from getting hurt." He raised her chin, forcing her to meet his gaze. "I want you to promise me something."

"Anything."

"Promise me that no matter what events might occur, you'll tell me about them. Even if you don't want to alarm me." He swallowed. "Even if they're dangerous."

"Like when those ruffians followed me in Shadwell?"

"Precisely. Or any other situation that might cause you harm or pain. Promise me. It's the only way I can keep you safe."

"I promise." Sammy kept her gaze fixed on his. "But I want you to make the same vow."

"What?"

"I'm pledging myself to you, Rem, as your soon-to-be wife. Now I want the same pledge from you."

Rem's lips twitched. "Do you anticipate rescuing me from danger?"

"Perhaps."

"Very well." Seeing how serious she was, Rem sobered. "I offer you the same vow."

"You'll tell me of anything that threatens you with harm or pain?"

"I will."

"Good." Sammy readied herself for the battle that would momentarily ensue. "Tell me about your past."

Rem started. "My past?"

"Yes, the years before I met you."

"Women, you mean?" Rem kissed the tip of her earnest nose. "I told you, imp, you have no competition. My feelings for you are unique. I have no intention of going to any other woman's bed—"

"Not the women."

A cautious light dawned in Rem's eyes. "What is it you want to know, then?"

"About your years at sea. About your career in the Royal Navy. About whatever pain has caused you to be afraid to care."

Shutters descended. "That part of my life is over. I'd rather not discuss it."

"You gave me your word."

"Why is it so important to you?" Rem held up his hand to ward off her reply. "Never mind. I know the answer. You want to know everything about me. Well, sweetheart, it's just not that simple. There are things you wouldn't—couldn't—understand."

"Try me."

"You're too sheltered to understand and too beautiful to be tainted with that kind of ugliness."

"I'm already being tainted by it. It's keeping me away from you. As far as sheltered …" Sammy inhaled slowly. "I'm not nearly as sheltered as you suspect."

Rem inclined his head. "What does that mean?"

"This last war with America … did you spend most of it at sea?"

"Only a small portion of it." Rem had long since memorized this particular reply. "I wasn't as experienced in American waters as some of our other captains. So I served sporadically, whenever I was needed. The rest of the time I helped train new officers so England's navy would remain strong."

"You were a hero," Sammy stated emphatically. "I remember reading about you."

A smile touched Rem's lips. "What does my service during the recent war have to do with your sheltered existence?"

"Scandal reaches everyone, whether at home or at sea. I merely wondered how much of the Barrett horror story you heard firsthand and how much you learned later."

"I know bits and pieces," Rem answered vaguely.

"You needn't protect me. I know every last horrid detail, including some I doubt you know." Sammy lowered her eyes. "My brother Sebastian is an immoral criminal who has spent the past three years in Newgate for murder."

Rem wrapped his arms about her. "I wasn't certain how much Drake allowed you to learn."

"Drake would have preferred I be exposed to as little as possible. Unfortunately, it was hardly his decision to make; not with all of England buzzing with the ugly scandal. I was fifteen … hardly an oblivious infant. It was horrible; worse than that.

"In any case, you know all those sordid details already. Here's something you don't know; something Drake did manage to keep quiet." Sammy drew a slow inward breath. "Sebastian also tried to kill Drake. He was involved in a plot to sink Drake's ship and annihilate not only Drake, but his entire crew. All to possess the coveted title of the Duke of Allonshire."

"Damn," Rem swore softly. His reaction wasn't grounded in the shock Samantha assumed it was, for none of what she'd just disclosed was a revelation to him. He'd been privy to Drake's brush with death, just as he'd been privy to every sea-related incident that had taken place in British or American waters during the War of 1812. But never in his wildest dreams had he imagined Samantha knew the extent of Sebastian's cold-blooded depravity.

"Thank heavens Drake survived ... although his ship did not," Sammy continued, her voice quivering. "But no one knew Drake was alive ... not for weeks. The missive that reached Allonshire proclaimed him and his entire crew to be missing at sea and presumed dead."

"I remember. The *Times* carried the story."

"Perhaps it carried the story, but it couldn't express the torment I experienced. No newspaper could convey my sense of desolation, the sheer terror of realizing I was utterly alone. My mother had died when I was a child, my father was ailing, near death, and my brother—the only brother I ever loved and who loved me—was gone forever. Sebastian didn't give a damn for me, or for anyone else, for that matter. My sense of loss, my pain, were unendurable. How I wished I'd gone down with Drake and his ship." Sammy raised damp eyes to Rem. "Now does that sound to you like a sheltered young girl who has never known anguish?"

Rem felt a rush of protectiveness so powerful it hurt. "I wish I'd been there."

"I know." Sammy brushed aside her tears, taking Rem's hand in hers. "But it's all behind me now, and I didn't resurrect it to elicit your sympathy. I had a reason. Two reasons, in fact. First, so you'd see my life has not been merely a gilded fairy tale. And second, so you could gain the same all-important insight I did and apply it to your past as I did to mine."

"And what is this insight, my magnificent dreamer?"

"That out of grief comes joy. That you can never lose faith in love or life." Sammy smiled through her tears. "From the vestiges of my suffering came my life's richest blessings. Not only did Drake return to me, but he brought his bride with him. Alex is both mother and sister combined, as well as the most loving and nurturing of friends. And do you know what else? She and Drake had unknowingly conceived Gray during their fateful trip. Seven months later, he was born. They named him in honor of our father, Grayson." A twinkle. "Actually, Drake couldn't dispel his customary arrogance completely. Gray's entire name is Drake Grayson Barrett. But we've always called him Gray. And now we have Bonnie, too. So you see, joy can be born of tragedy. For me ... and for you."

"You're too beautiful for this world," Rem murmured, a tremor in his voice.

"Share yourself with me," Sammy whispered. "Please. Give me a chance to heal the pain."

"Some pain cannot be healed, imp. No matter how much you will it." Taking in Sammy's earnest expression, Rem sighed. "I have no momentous secret to reveal. Reality is just a cold and ugly thing."

He was relenting. Sammy could feel it. Eagerly, she seized this rare opportunity she was being offered.

"You spent most of your youth at sea. Why?"

"The army was too stationary for my tastes."

"No, what I meant was, what made you choose any type of military career? Why were you so anxious to leave England?"

"I had nothing monstrous to escape, if that's what you're asking. My parents died before I reached my teens, and I had more than enough money to indulge myself."

"Have you sisters or brothers?"

"No. I'm an only child—one who grew up to be a terribly restless man."

"You wanted something that was truly yours, a mark you could leave on the world. Being the Earl of Gresham wasn't enough. You needed more than to oversee your estate, gamble at White's, and drink each Season away." Seeing the startled lift of Rem's brows, Sammy grinned. "I've just given you Drake's reasons for taking to the sea, albeit as the captain of a merchant brig. You and my brother are more alike than you realize."

"Evidently."

"You're a titled nobleman. You could easily have bought yourself a commission. But you didn't."

"No. For once I wanted to earn something, not have it handed to me because of who I was. I didn't keep my background a secret; I merely insisted that it not be used to benefit me."

"When did you become a lieutenant?"

"The regulations required me to be nineteen before I could take my exams." Rem's dimple flashed. "I was seventeen."

"How did you manage that?"

"I had a flair—for navigation and for making situations work to my advantage. The three captains under whom I'd served were impressed with my seamanship. They all submitted certificates of service, which the examining board weighed heavily in their decision. In light of the glowing recommendations, they then decided to glance only briefly at the slightly modified birth certificate I produced. Thus, my appointment."

"You're a rogue, my lord."

"Indeed. But a determined one."

"And you were a captain before you were twenty—the youngest captain in the Royal Navy." Sammy's voice rang with pride.

"That I owe to Admiral Nelson's brilliant command at the Battle of Copenhagen. My heroism was merely the result of his."

"You admired Lord Nelson a great deal, didn't you?"

A muscle worked in Rem's jaw. "I was fortunate enough to serve under him for five years. He taught me the meaning of leadership. His instincts were flawless, his commitment to his ship and country absolute … even if risks had to be taken. He was a genius."

Sammy watched the emotion that ravaged Rem's face when he spoke of his mentor. "So you followed your dream. Did you capture it, Rem? Did the navy fulfill that gnawing void inside you?"

"'Twas a double-edged sword, Samantha. The navy assuaged my restlessness, gave me the opportunity to learn from the finest commander in all of England, and introduced me to the best friend I've ever had." A pause. "It also tore out my soul, obliterated my ideals, and hardened my heart."

Swallowing past the lump in her throat, Sammy chose to address one of Rem's positive references. "I'm glad Boyd was there for you. When did the two of you meet?"

"Boyd came aboard the *Ares* as a midshipman just after the Battle of Copenhagen."

"The *Ares*?" Sammy's eyes lit up. "Was that the name of the ship you captained?"

"The ship I eventually captained, yes. When I met Boyd, I was a mere lieutenant. We covered many miles together, Boyd and I: the West Indies, Portugal, Gibraltar, the Mediterranean. We also witnessed countless deaths together."

"In battle?"

"Not only in battle, Samantha." Rem stared ahead, seeing shadows of memories long buried, never forgotten. "I can't begin to describe to you what it was like, how tenuous life was. We never knew who would survive and who would not. When we traveled to the West Indies, the heat was blistering, the filth rampant. Every day men succumbed to yellow fever. Elsewhere we were plagued by scurvy, spoiled foods, and diseased women. In the winter, typhus struck—fatally. And, of course, there were the bouts with nature.

"I remember one particularly fierce storm in the Mediterranean. I had just turned eighteen. My captain asked me to shimmy up the mainmast and fix the rigging that had been torn to shreds by the slicing winds. The rain was so cold, my fingers instantly numbed … but I forced myself to ignore the stinging pain. I had no choice—no one else was skilled enough to repair the badly tattered jibs and topsails. The sole other crewman adept enough to assist me was a youngster named Haber—he couldn't have been more than fourteen. He was a skinny, freckled lad who had a hell of a talent with rigging, and a gentle, amenable nature; always grinning, always helpful. Without a single complaint, he maneuvered his way up and climbed out to work beside me. I remember tying that last bloody section of rigging, hearing Haber's jubilant whistle over the crashing of the waves. I made my way back to the mast just as a blast of wind struck, pitching the ship—and us—violently. I grabbed onto the mainmast, held on with every fiber of my being … and reached for Haber with my free arm. I can still see the look of terror on his face. He couldn't reach me—nor I him—and he was just too bloody frail to hold on. He fell to his death right before my eyes … and there wasn't a damned thing I could do to stop it. To this day, I can still hear his scream, see the waves drag him under."

Rem stared down at his shaking hands. "And, yes, there were the battles. Sick, needless bloodshed that I loathed but could do nothing to prevent. And then at Trafalgar …" Having unlocked his carefully sealed chasm of pain, Rem couldn't seem to stop talking. "Do you have any idea what it was like for me to watch him dying? Not a quick, painless death, but a slow, agonizing one?"

"Admiral Nelson?" Sammy managed. "Was the *Ares* that close to the *Victory*? You actually saw him struck?"

"Our ships were directly beside each other," Rem replied woodenly. "The battle commenced just before noon. The *Victory* was one of the first two ships to cross over the enemy line … despite all the warnings Admiral Nelson received that, as the fleet's commanding officer, he should not expose himself to the grave danger evoked by leading the way into battle. Nelson scoffed, entertaining no thought for his own personal safety, concerned only with annihilating the enemy.

"An hour later the *Victory* had been crippled; the wheel shattered, the sails demolished, the bow torn by cannon fire. She continued to be under direct siege. The *Ares* came to her aid. It was just shy of half after one when I saw Admiral Nelson go down on the *Victory's* quarterdeck. It was bad; I knew it the moment the surgeon examined him and ordered his men to take Nelson below. They complied. That was the last time I saw the admiral alive." Rem swallowed. "Later, I learned that a musket ball had pierced his chest, shattered his lung and lodged in his back. By half after four he was gone."

"Oh, Rem ..."

Rem continued as if Sammy hadn't spoken. "The triumph was his, everything he'd ever hoped to accomplish. But instead of standing proudly at the head of his fleet, celebrating the downfall of Napoleon's navy, he was lying beneath the *Victory's* gun deck bleeding to death. He'd given so much to England, had so much more yet to give. And to what end? Where is the justice, Samantha? Tell me that— where is the goodness you seem always to find?"

"There is no justice." Sammy lay a trembling hand on Rem's jaw. "Not in this case. But there is goodness. Admiral Nelson was a hero in the truest sense of the word ... and not only because he gave his life *for* his country, but because he dedicated his life *to* it. You said it yourself, he'd accomplished all he intended, and more.

"Tell me this, Rem: would Lord Nelson be proud of Trafalgar's outcome? Would he applaud the victory he'd ensured and his fleet had achieved?"

Slowly, Rem nodded. "Yes. That was my sole consolation. We attained precisely what Admiral Nelson sought: the total obliteration of Napoleon's navy. We took nineteen French and Spanish ships as prizes, yet gave up none of our own. Yes, Nelson would have reveled in our triumph."

"Then he's at peace, Rem. Moreover, he will never truly die, for no one will ever forget him; not his countrymen, and certainly not those who were lucky enough to serve by his side. Is that not goodness?"

"I suppose it is. It is also the only reality that has granted me some measure of my own peace."

"But it's not enough comfort for you to allow yourself the risk of caring."

Rem blinked, seeming to return from some faraway place. "I do care, Samantha. Just not with the same full and untainted heart as you do."

"Given your feelings, why didn't you resign from the navy immediately after Trafalgar?"

Was it her imagination, or did Rem stiffen?

"I considered it. To some extent, I did. As I told you, my consistent, active duty ceased after Trafalgar. With an occasional commission during our latest war with America, I've been landed for nearly a decade now, training our future officers for whatever fate holds in store for them. Sadly, there are certain things I cannot simulate, no matter how vast my experience. Each man must confront those things on his own … and grapple with them in his own mind and heart."

"I love you now even more than I did before."

A tender smile touched Rem's lips and he pressed Sammy's head to his chest. "Do you, imp? I'm glad."

Laying her palm over his heart, Sammy asked softly, "There's still something more, isn't there?"

This time it was *not* her imagination: she felt Rem's muscles contract like a bowstring, shock rippling through them in harsh waves.

"No."

"Is it that you don't trust me?"

"Dammit, Samantha!" Rem jerked away, alarmed by her unexpected show of insight. This was one territory he dared not let her tread, one truth he could not permit her to uncover. "Of course I trust you. I've shared more with you this past hour than I've shared with another soul in over a decade." His jaw set. "But I've stripped away as many layers of myself as I intend to. No matter how close we've become, there's something you must understand. I've lived one and thirty years on my own, unconstrained and independent. I can't—won't—change. So do not, in that stubbornly romantic mind of yours, assume that I will suddenly begin to report my every action and confide my every thought."

"Not even to me?"

"No. Not even to you." Samantha's pain gripped Rem as fiercely as if it were his own, but he fought it, knowing that in this case he had no choice. In order to protect his cause, and her safety, he had to keep the portion of his life that belonged to the Admiralty and to England carefully concealed. "Samantha, you're going to be my wife, and I'm going to do my damnedest to make you happy. But as I've continually told you, your idea of love and marriage is infinitely more all-encompassing than mine. I'll compromise where I can, but don't expect me to bare my soul as you do; it's an impossibility. Accept it—for both our sakes."

"I can't."

"You must." He turned to face her. "I'll indulge you in all ways I can—all but this. I am as I am, imp."

Sammy's eyes grew suspiciously bright. "Would you please take me home now? You've given me a great deal to ponder."

"Samantha—"

"No more, Rem." She shook her head. "You've explained yourself quite thoroughly. Now I need to be alone."

Gripping her shoulders, Rem's eyes bore deep into hers. He started to say something, then broke off. "Dammit," he swore softly. "Dammit to hell."

Leaning past Samantha, he yanked apart the curtains, opened the carriage window and ordered his driver to return to Abingdon Street.

Silence punctuated the final moments of their ride. When the carriage halted at number fifteen, Sammy pushed open the door and climbed down unassisted. "Good night, Remington."

"I'll be traveling to Allonshire to speak with your brother first thing in the morning," he informed her in a steely tone that forbade defiance.

Sammy turned, scooping Aunt Gertie's hat off the seat and tilting her head back to gaze up at Rem. "Thank you for confiding that fact in me. For an autonomous man like you, it must have been quite a sacrifice."

The words were as close to a barb as Samantha could muster, and Rem was aware of their sting. But what really clawed at his gut were the tears glistening on Samantha's long dark lashes.

Instinctively, he started to go after her, then checked himself. Watching her disappear into the Town house, he slammed his fist against his knee, knowing there wasn't a damned thing he could do to ease her pain.

Nor to preserve the purity of her faith.

In Allonshire's gilded sitting room, the duke clasped Lord Hartley's hand.

"I appreciate your riding all this way to congratulate me on Bonnie's birth."

"She's a beautiful infant, Drake. Your father would be proud."

"Yes, I rather suspect he would." Drake smiled fondly. "He always had a special place in his heart for Sammy. I think he would be pleased for me to have at least one daughter of my own to spoil." Chuckling, Drake headed toward his sideboard. "What can I offer you for refreshment? Brandy?"

"Actually …" Hartley shifted uncomfortably. "Now that you've brought up Samantha … I did have one other reason for visiting Allonshire."

Drake came to a dead halt. "What about Samantha?"

"Probably nothing. Certainly none of my business. Still, I do feel some sense of responsibility toward the child—she is Grayson's daughter."

"You're alarming me, Hartley. What's wrong with Samantha?"

"Nothing is actually wrong. And I don't mean to question your judgment. If you believe Remington Worth is the sensible person to look out for Samantha's well-being, I suppose you know what you're doing. But I wonder if you've considered his reputation ..."

"What the hell are you talking about? What has Gresham got to do with my sister?"

Hartley blinked. "He's doing what you asked of him: escorting Samantha about Town in order to keep her from falling prey to various disreputable blackguards. What concerns me is—"

"I asked no such thing!" Drake thundered. "I'm working with Gresham, building a ship for him. But that's as far as our association goes. I'd have to be out of my mind to entrust my sister to a womanizer like him—hell, he's been in every bed in London!"

"Oh dear." Hartley ran his fingers through his hair. "Then why would he say ...?" A relieved thought suddenly illuminated the elderly marquis's face. "Perhaps Gresham's intentions are truly honorable. Perhaps he invented that story in order to discourage Anders from pressing such a determined suit."

"*Anders?*" Drake's eyes flashed emerald fire. "That accomplished blackguard is pursuing Samantha, too? Dammit!"

"I didn't mean to upset you—"

"You didn't." Drake was already halfway across the room. "If you'll excuse me, Hartley, I have some business to attend to. Urgent business."

Leaving Hartley gaping in his wake, Drake took the steps two at a time, exploding into Alex's bedchamber, his powerful body quaking with rage.

Alex put down the novel she'd been reading, curiously assessing her husband's rigid stance.

"I'm going to London," he bit out.

"What's happened?" With the innate understanding of Drake that only Alex possessed, she confronted his violent outburst, perceiving instantly that his tirade was rooted in distress as well as anger.

"I'll kill him—*them.*"

"Who? Why?" Climbing out of bed, Alex marched up to face her husband. "Drake, tell me."

He frowned. "You shouldn't be out of bed."

"I feel fine. Now who is it you plan to kill?"

"Anders. Gresham. Both."

"Does this involve Barrett Shipping?"

"Worse than that. It involves Samantha."

"Samantha!" Alex sucked in her breath. "You'd better explain."

"I can't. All I know is that Hartley was just here, questioning my decision to place Gresham in charge of Sammy's welfare and adding that Anders was avidly pursuing her."

"But you didn't place Gresham—"

"I know that. Evidently, Gresham doesn't." Drake shoved his fingers through his hair. "When I think of how that man stood here not three days past, proclaiming that he'd only seen Sammy under the most casual of happenstance, never even flinching when I vowed I'd kill any man who touched her." Striving for control, Drake cupped Alex's face. "Will you be all right if I leave you alone for a day or two, princess?"

"I'm hardly alone, Drake. We have scores of servants, Molly is constantly by my side, Gray pops in and out all day, and Humphreys spends so much time in the nursery with Bonnie and me, he doesn't even bother to listen for arriving guests. Eventually, they give up knocking and go home." Alex caressed the taut lines of worry on Drake's face. "Go to Samantha."

As always, Alex was the only one capable of easing his anguish. "Thank you, princess."

"Just promise me one thing. Promise me you'll listen to Samantha. All you've heard thus far are rumors and speculation, all of which could be totally false. And even if Samantha has been receiving the viscount or the earl, give her a chance to explain *before* you explode."

Drake scowled. "I'll try."

"She's growing up, Drake," Alex added softly. "We must let her do so."

"I know. All right ... I'll control myself." Thunderclouds darkened Drake's face. "*Then* I'll kill Gresham and Anders."

EIGHTEEN

"Where the hell is Harris?"

Rem's mood was blacker than black. None of his men ever kept him waiting, and Harris had picked one hell of a time to begin.

"He should be here by now, Gresham." Nervously, Templar rose, wiping sweat from his face and scanning Annie's for a sign of his colleague.

"Yes, he should." Rem set his mug of ale down on the table with a loud thud. "And he'd better have one bloody good reason for being late."

"Rem, did you hear from Briggs?" Boyd asked quietly, attempting to calm Rem's unusually harassed state.

"Yes. The Admiralty found no record of any English ship by the name of the *Atlantis;* not currently sailing, not under commission to be built, not even recently retired. None."

"Another dead end." Boyd took a deep swallow of ale. "Then what was Anders talking about? What's 'Atlantis'?"

"Templar, who checked out Anders Shipping?" Rem demanded abruptly. "You or Harris?"

"I did." Templar shifted uneasily, then dropped back into his chair, rubbing his palms together. "Why? Did I miss something?"

"No. How did Anders behave while you were reading through his records?"

"Calm as death. Never even flinched."

"Interesting." Rem leaned forward, a coiled assailant ready to strike. "I want you to find something on that bastard. I don't care what it is, just find it."

"But I scrutinized every damn page of—"

"Not at his office. At home. Anders is involved in something illegal. I'd stake my life on it. Do you understand what I'm saying, Templar? Get into his bloody house and find something to implicate that son of a bitch."

"What about Summerson?" Boyd interjected.

"I'm willing to bet that whatever Templar finds on Anders will incriminate our friend Summerson as well. If I'm wrong, Templar can check Summerson's house next. But if I'm right, there's no need to put Templar at risk twice."

Boyd nodded, then gestured toward the front of the brothel. "Harris just got here." A long silence followed. Suddenly Boyd's eyes narrowed. "He's not alone, Rem."

On the heels of Boyd's announcement, Harris made his way over to their table, a ruddy-faced man with thinning gray hair by his side. "Sorry I'm late," Harris began, guiding the older man forward. "But under the circumstances, it was unavoidable."

"So I see." Rem kept his expression carefully unreadable. But the piercing look he shot Harris clearly stated that the Bow Street man had best know what he was doing.

"Are you with Bow Street as well?" the stranger blurted out to Rem, his voice and hands shaking.

"No." In one unblinking second, Rem assessed the obviously terrified newcomer. Ruddy complexion, work-roughened hands, rope and wind burns. "My name's Gresham. This is Hayword and Templar. Templar works with Harris at Bow Street. My friend Hayword and I are ex-navy men. We help Bow Street out when we can."

A spasm of relief crossed the other man's face. "So you're working with Harris on this case?"

Rem had guessed right. This man was a sailor running from danger. "We are." He indicated a chair. "Have a seat, sir. I'll have Annie bring you a mug of ale. You look like you need one."

With a terse nod, the stranger sat, rubbing the back of his neck fitfully until his ale arrived. He tossed it down in two swallows. "I could be killed for what I'm about to tell you." He gave a harsh laugh. "Unfortunately, I was almost killed anyway. So I have little to lose."

"You've been aboard a ship for … let's see … a fortnight, possibly more. For whatever reasons, you've returned. Why?" Rem finished his ale and lit a cheroot.

The sailor's mouth fell open. "How on earth did you know that?"

Rem shrugged. "By your color. You've been exposed to sun. And wind—your face is raw from its force. Also I recognize the signs of a man who's recently handled rigging. I assure you, it takes neither a mind reader nor a genius to notice obvious clues such as those. Now, are you prepared to tell me your name?"

"My name's Towers." As he spoke, Towers inclined his head in Harris's direction. "No wonder Bow Street calls on your friend Gresham. I would, too."

"Lucas Towers," Rem realized aloud, visualizing Briggs's list in his mind's eye. "Captain of the merchant ship the *Bountiful*, reported missing from the English Channel, together with its cargo and crew, three weeks ago."

"That vessel, as I recall, was en route to the West Indies," Boyd added.

"It was also part of Anders's fleet." Rem exhaled wisps of smoke. "Good to have you back, Towers."

First amazement, then panic, flashed on Towers' face. Anxiously, he scrutinized the crowd milling about Annie's brothel, as if to ascertain that he was not being overheard. At last he leaned forward and lowered his voice. "You're astoundingly accurate, gentlemen. I am—was—the captain of the *Bountiful*. My ship did vanish and she did belong to Anders Shipping."

"Now, the next question is, did Arthur Summerson have cargo aboard that vessel?"

"No." Rather than pondering the question, Towers shook his head immediately. "He didn't."

"How can you be so certain so quickly?" Rem demanded.

"Because there was no real cargo aboard my ship."

"What?" Harris's eyes widened.

"The records indicated that there were valuable goods being carried: furniture and jewelry. But as I later learned, the boxes in my hull were filled with stones and rags."

"And whoever the alleged cargo belonged to collected an enormous amount of money for goods he never sent," Rem concluded, grounding out his cheroot. "Now all we need to know is, which merchant's name was on those records?"

"I have no doubt it was Summerson's," Towers replied, again without hesitation.

Rem started. "No doubt? Why?"

"Because Summerson visited the *Bountiful* every day for a week before we sailed, and stayed for hours. Because he met with Anders three or four times behind closed doors. Because every time they emerged, they were discussing the cargo he'd be transporting aboard my ship." Towers drew a slow breath. "And because Summerson just exchanged a fortune of money with the bastard who sold my crew."

"Sold your ..." Suddenly it all clicked in Rem's mind. "You're telling me that Summerson paid a privateer not only to dispose of your ship and its fictitious cargo, but to sell your crew?"

"I am."

"And are you also saying Anders is involved?"

"That I don't know. I never actually saw Anders do anything illegal, and I can't prove he knew the cargo was phony. Summerson was alone when he and the privateer met at the dock."

"When was that?"

"An hour ago. Just before I saw Harris and realized from his uniform that he was with Bow Street. Summerson and his pirate friend didn't notice me … not that they were looking. They assumed I was long since on my way to wherever I was being sold to. My escape was pure luck … and thank God for it."

"Damn … there's got to be something to implicate Anders," Rem muttered, his brain going a mile a minute. "Keep talking, Towers. Tell me about the attack on your ship; where it happened, how it was done, where you and your men were taken and how you got away."

"It was just south of the Goodwin Sands, sometime between midnight and one A.M. The privateer ship was shielded by the Dover cliffs; we never even saw them coming. They just rowed alongside the *Bountiful* in their longboats, bound and gagged us, and dragged us back to their vessel. From there we were blindfolded, taken to a deserted island in the middle of nowhere, and informed that we were about to be sold as slaves. I preferred drowning. When I saw my chance, I slipped into the water. I managed to unbind my ropes and stay afloat long enough to signal a passing English ship. Here I am."

"What did you tell the captain who rescued you?"

"Only that I'd been thrown from my ship during a storm. I didn't have to explain further. My uniform had been seized. I wore only these." Towers indicated his faded shirt and pants. "The captain had no reason to believe I was anything other than what I claimed to be. He transported me back to England."

"You arrived tonight?"

"Yes."

"And when you docked and left the ship, you saw Summerson?"

"Summerson and his privateer."

"You actually saw them exchange money?"

"I did."

"That's enough evidence to hang Summerson," Boyd proclaimed, triumph lighting his eyes.

Rem nodded, still deep in thought. "What about the privateer?"

"I could identify him in a minute."

"I'm sure you could. But tell me, did he say anything during the time he held you captive? Anything specific or memorable?"

"He didn't do much talking. All he did was taunt us."

"What did he say?"

Towers shrugged. "That we were going to vanish without a trace, that no one would ever see us again, that we'd be swallowed up, forgotten, like the lost isle of Atlantis. He muttered the same thing to Summerson just now on the dock—something about Atlantis being a success. It must be his sick idea of humor."

Rem's eyes met Boyd's. "That's it," he said quietly. Turning back to Towers, he added, "Captain, just one more thing. During the week prior to your sailing, did you overhear any conversations between Summerson and Anders?"

"Nothing unusual." Towers' brow furrowed. "Just snatches here and there. All the usual prattle: the number of boxes in the cargo, the weather, that sort of thing."

"Anything else? Think, Towers. It could be important."

"They boarded the ship the morning we sailed, said they wanted to check it out together," Towers recounted slowly, thinking aloud. "Anders was concerned about something, because Summerson kept telling him to stop worrying, that he'd calm their nervous partner down. Then they left."

"Partner?" Rem gripped his mug with both hands. "Summerson used that word?"

"They both did. That didn't strike me as odd; businessmen often deal with more than one partner, don't they?"

"Anders referred to a partner, too? You're sure?"

"Of course I'm sure! Anders was the one who said their partner made him uneasy because he was so skittish about his investment. Is that significant?"

"There's someone else working with them," Rem said aloud.

"But who?" Boyd rubbed his chin.

"I intend to find out." Rem rose. "Harris, why don't you take Captain Towers home with you? It will give him a safe, comfortable place to stay while we're gathering our facts."

An unspoken message passed between Rem and Harris. Towers' life hung in the balance; it was up to them to keep him alive.

"No problem." Harris stood. "Come, Captain. You must be exhausted."

Towers cleared his throat. "I owe you all a great debt of thanks, which I'm unsure how to repay."

"No thanks are necessary." Rem's stance stiffened, his gaze locked with Towers'. "But you never saw Hayword and me before in your life, so you certainly wouldn't recognize us if you saw us again. Isn't that correct?"

"Absolutely."

"Good." The tension eased from Rem's body as quickly as it had come. "Thank you for talking to us. You're in good hands."

"Obviously, so is England," Towers murmured in an awed tone. Rem glanced at Harris. "Nice work." With that, he was gone.

"Your Grace?" Hatterly, the Barrett's Town house butler, rubbed his eyes and tightened the belt of his robe. "Forgive me, sir, I had no idea you'd be arriving."

"Nor did I." Drake swung off his greatcoat. "I apologize for disrupting your sleep. I assume my sister is abed?"

"Why, I assume so, sir."

"Good. I want to see her." Drake was already halfway to the steps.

"Your Grace?" Smitty made his way down the hall, not only awake, but fully dressed and alert at half after four in the morning. Serving by Drake's side, Smitty had grown accustomed to arising before dawn, both at home and at sea. "We had no idea you'd be visiting … what a wonderful surprise!"

"I doubt you'll feel that way in a few minutes, Smitty," Drake muttered for his valet's ears alone. "May I see you in the sitting room?" he said aloud.

"Of course." With a cordial nod, Smitty followed.

Drake closed the doors behind them. "We're alone now. Let's dispense with the pretense and the formalities. What the hell is going on here?"

A corner of Smitty's mouth lifted. "Why I do believe you've missed me."

"Very funny." Drake didn't smile. "As a matter of fact, I find getting along without you extremely difficult. After all these years, I rely upon your friendship, your insight, and your skill. In fact, there are very few situations that could convince me to part with you, even for a short while." Drake folded his arms across his chest. "One of those situations, however, happens to be my sister's coming out. So, I'm asking you again—what the hell is going on here?"

"I heard you the first time, Your Grace. What specific aspect of Lady Samantha's Season are you referring to?"

"The Viscount Anders. The Earl of Gresham. Am I being specific enough for you?"

Smitty paled a bit. Loyalty to Drake warred with loyalty to Samantha. "I do recall informing you that Lord Gresham came to our rescue when that horrendous storm suspended our trip to London."

"And I recall informing you that I'd thanked Lord Gresham in person when he came to Allonshire. What about since then? Have either Gresham or Anders been pursuing Sammy?"

"Lady Samantha has attended so very many balls ..." Smitty hedged. "It's hard to recall all the gentlemen who have made a favorable impression on her."

"Try."

"Have I mentioned how highly Lady Gertrude regards both Viscount Anders and the Earl of Gresham?"

"Lady Gertrude?" Drake sputtered. "Smitty, my aunt wouldn't know a rake from a clergyman. So that's hardly consolation, is it? Now, cease this cat and mouse game and answer my question."

"Please don't put me in this position, sir," Smitty requested with quiet dignity. "I care very much for both you and Lady Samantha."

"Not to mention that Lady Samantha can speak for herself." Sammy shut the door firmly and crossed the room. "Honestly, Drake, I can hear your bellowing all the way in my bedchamber." She stood on tiptoe and kissed her brother's cheek, ignoring his furious expression. "You're going to awaken the whole household."

"Evidently, that doesn't include you—you're already awake and dressed. Why is that?" Drake demanded. "It's not even dawn."

Sammy dimpled. "I wanted to see the sun rise. It's like watching an artist create a dazzling painting. Not to mention that I fully intended to reread my favorite sections of *Mansfield Park* ... until I heard your thunderous arrival." She inclined her head quizzically. "What have Smitty and I done to make you so angry?"

"Is it true that you've been cavorting with the Viscount Anders and the Earl of Gresham?"

Sucking in her breath, Sammy looked quickly at Smitty, who answered her unspoken question with a brief shake of his head. "I ... I ..."

"Bloody hell." Drake raked his fingers through his hair. "Which one? Or is it both of them?"

"Stephen merely visited once or twice and danced with me at several balls," Sammy blurted out. "I have no feelings for the man and certainly have done nothing to encourage him." Frowning, she considered her statement. "Of course, he did give me that expensive necklace, but I sent it back right after I told him it was far too extravagant to give to a woman who wanted only to be his friend. I realize he has some foolish misconception that I shall change my mind and welcome his advances ... but that's not about to happen. I wish he and Remington weren't always fighting, because it makes it terribly awkward and uncomfortable when we run into him. But Rem cannot seem to control his compulsion to protect me. I suppose, if I were to be honest, I'd have to admit that I enjoy his possessiveness. Still, I can't imagine he'd even suspect I'd be interested in another man under the circumstances."

"Circumstances?" Drake echoed. Clenching his fists, he battled for the control he promised Alex he'd exert. "Samantha, are you telling me you're involved with Remington Worth?"

"I'm going to marry him." Sammy sighed. "If that quick temper of yours had permitted you to wait a few hours longer, you could have saved yourself a trip. Rem is riding to Allonshire this morning to ask for my hand."

That did it. "No."

Sammy recoiled as though Drake had struck her. "What?"

"You heard me—no. No, I will not see Remington Worth; no, you will not convince me otherwise; and *no*, you will not marry him."

"But why?" Sammy whispered. "Why?"

"Because I forbid it." Drake turned his blazing stare on Smitty. "Pack your things and Samantha's at once. You're coming home to Allonshire with me. Tonight."

"Consider what you're doing, Your Grace," Smitty tried, his troubled gaze traveling from Samantha to Drake and back.

"More importantly, what have *you* been doing? I sent you to London to look after Sammy, not to deliver her into the hands of a disreputable rake!"

"Don't blame Smitty!" Tears glistened on Sammy's cheeks. "He tried to keep me from seeing Rem. But like my brother, I have a mind of my own. I love him, Drake," she added in a small, shaky voice.

"No, Samantha, you don't love him."

"Yes ... I do."

"We'll discuss it later, at home."

"I won't go."

Drake started. "What?"

"You're being completely unreasonable." Sammy backed away until she felt the door handle behind her. "And I will not obey like some small, docile child. I'm a grown woman, Drake. When will you accept that?" In one sharp movement she yanked open the door and fled from the room.

For a long silent moment Drake merely stared after Sammy's retreating back, pain and shock alternately reflected on his face. In all of her eighteen years, Sammy had never turned her back on him, never fled from his presence. Never ... until now.

Recovering, Drake moved toward the hall. "I've got to go after her."

"No, Your Grace." Smitty stepped in his path. "Give Lady Samantha some time alone. You'll only make matters worse by confronting her now."

Drake swallowed. "Exactly how far has this relationship gone?"

"I'm not Lady Samantha's confidant, sir. But I would suspect she does have very strong feelings for the earl."

Slowly, Drake averted his head until his gaze locked with Smitty's. "I don't think I like what you're telling me."

"I'm not telling you anything, Your Grace."

"If that bastard has touched my sister—"

"Agonizing will get you nowhere. Neither will threatening the earl or coming to blows."

"Then what the hell do you suggest I do, Smitty?"

"I suggest you accept that you're not able to deal with this situation rationally."

"I already accept that. But I'm Samantha's brother—I feel like her father, dammit. And there's no one who loves her as much as I do and who could better handle her—"

"Yes, there is," Smitty interrupted. "Your wife. Let the duchess talk to Lady Samantha. She will do an excellent job of listening"—

Smitty let the word hang purposefully between them—"as well as guiding."

Drake blinked. "Alex … yes. Sammy always does confide in her, maybe she'll do so this time as well. Of course, nothing of this magnitude has ever happened before, so I'm not sure how Alex will react. An innocent child like Sammy, barely of age, getting involved with a rogue like Gresham, who uses women for only one thing. Hell!" Drake slammed his hand against the wall. "I don't know if even Alex is equipped to combat this dilemma."

Smitty's eyes twinkled, his memory clearly recalling an identical dilemma in the not-so-distant past. "Oh, I think she can, Your Grace. Rest assured, I think the duchess will manage just fine."

Boydry's was dark.

Any passerby would assume the pub had closed for the night.

"Now what?" Boyd tossed off a glass of gin, watching Rem pace the silent room.

"Now we find out the identity of Anders's other partner. Fast." Rem paused, scowling at his drink. "We're not discussing ships alone anymore, Boyd. We're discussing men; men who are being sold like chattel. It sickens me."

"It appears that your instincts about Anders were right."

"No." Rem shook his head. "I never would have thought he'd go this far. Money, yes. Lives, no. The bastard has surprised even me." Rem's lips thinned into a grim line. "This sheds a whole new light on that conversation I overheard between Anders and Summerson at Devonshire House. Samantha could be in grave danger."

"Yes, she could."

"I've got to work fast."

"Towers' statement is all the evidence we need. Anders's association with Summerson, his reference to Atlantis, Summerson's connection to the privateer—that's more than enough to put them away for a long, long time."

"That would be fine, *if* putting them away was all we wanted. But it isn't. We want their partner." Rem clenched his fist. "We've got to find out who he is. Then we'll close in on the three of them."

"And in the meantime?"

"In the meantime it's up to me to protect Samantha."

"Lady Samantha, did you say?" Rem's butler sniffed. "My lady ... I'm sorry. The earl is just not at home."

"But he *must* be home—it's nearly dawn!" Sammy felt close to hysteria. She'd run all the way to Rem's Town house, unconcerned about her reputation, unconcerned about anything but getting to Rem before Drake did.

"I assure you, he is not."

"Where is he?"

"Pardon me?" The butler blanched.

Sammy inhaled sharply and tried again. "What is your name, sir?"

"Peldon, my lady."

"Peldon, do you know who I am?"

He shifted a bit uncomfortably.

"I thought not. Well, I am not one of the earl's paramours. I am Lady Samantha Barrett, the Duke of Allonshire's sister, and"—she paused for effect—"the Earl of Gresham's betrothed. Remington and I are to be married in less than a month." Even as she said the words, she prayed they were true. "Now, I don't want to have to tell Lord Gresham that you were uncooperative. But I do need to see him at once. It is urgent, or I would not be here unchaperoned. So, I'd appreciate if you—"

"Forgive me, my lady." Peldon had turned a curious shade of green. "But the truth is, I'm not precisely certain where the earl is. I do know that he's with Mr. Hayword."

Boyd. Of course. "Thank you, Peldon." Sammy gave him as brilliant a smile as she could muster, although she suspected he knew more than he cared to admit. "You've been a great help. I'll be sure to speak highly of you to the earl. Now, I need just one more favor … a carriage."

"A carriage, my lady?"

"Yes. I wal—rode here with friends. They assumed the earl was at home. Now I'm without a vehicle."

"Oh, I see. Well, the earl took his phaeton, so I'll have the carriage brought around at once."

"Oh, would you?" Sammy's relief was instant and genuine. "You are a saint, Peldon. Thank you with all my heart." She began to wrack her brain. Where would Rem and Boyd be? At Annie's? At Boyd's house … wherever that was? Where?

Sammy had endured all she could. Her lips began to tremble in frustration.

"Of course, you understand this is just speculation"—Peldon's brow furrowed in concentration as he brushed an imaginary speck from his uniform—"but I believe I would try Mr. Hayword's establishment, my lady … if your reasons for seeking out Lord Gresham are as urgent as you say. It seems to me I recall—"

"Boydry's! Of course! Oh, Peldon, you're wonderful!" This time Sammy cast protocol to the wind and hugged the startled servant. "Thank you!"

Fortunately, Rem's carriage driver knew the quickest route to Boydry's, as Sammy could scarcely recall its exact location. A half hour later the tavern stood before her.

Hastily, Sammy gathered her skirts and made her way to the bolted door. Her hand poised to knock, she hesitated, for the first time pondering what she would say, how Rem would respond to what she told him. Not with fear, that was for certain. The man was afraid of nothing, not even her formidable brother.

Footsteps sounded from within, and instinctively Sammy stepped back and hid behind the door as it creaked open.

"Incidentally, Rem, I assume you recall it was Hartley's company that built the *Bountiful*." Boyd's muffled words reached Sammy's ears.

"Yes, I remember that from Briggs's list." Rem paused in the doorway, rubbing his temples. "I have no reason to distrust Hartley. Still, I'm grateful as hell that Barrett Shipping didn't construct Towers' ship, if that's what you're getting at."

"That's exactly what I'm getting at. You're in a precarious enough situation with Samantha. You don't need to worsen it by having to question her again."

"No. Thankfully, we can get our answers elsewhere. At this point I don't think I could live with myself if I had to use Samantha to garner facts on—" Abruptly, Rem broke off, as if sensing that he and Boyd were no longer alone. Slowly, like a tiger assessing its prey, he averted his head, searching the dimly lit walk leading to Boydry's. Then, without warning, he grabbed the door handle and pulled, simultaneously whipping out his pistol.

His piercing stare met Sammy's horrified one.

"Samantha ..." Rem lowered the pistol, visibly shaken, and took a step toward her.

Sammy's face drained of color, but she didn't retreat. "Tell me what I'm thinking isn't true," she demanded in a fierce whisper. "Tell me."

The agony in her voice tore at Rem's heart. "What you're thinking isn't true."

"You weren't using me all this time? Last night ... tonight in your carriage ... everything you said, did ..."

"No ... dammit no!" Rem shook his head violently as he reached for her. "If you believe nothing else, believe that."

"Rem? Who the hell ... Christ!" Boyd went white when he poked his head out and saw Samantha.

"Go home, Boyd. Get some sleep. I need to talk to Samantha. Alone." Rem drew Sammy against him.

The door closed quietly.

Dazed and unmoving, Sammy tried to grasp all she had just overheard. "Who are you, Remington Worth?" Her eyes fell on Rem's pistol as he tucked it away. "Or should I say *Worthless?* Who are you really?"

Despite the drama of the situation, Rem felt himself smile. "I'm not the villain in a real-life Gothic, if that's what you're thinking. Listen to your heart, not your fanciful mind." Softly, he kissed her hair. "Sweetheart, I know you're confused. I can't do a thing to abate that. But as far as what's happening between us—it was, *is,* real. I am not using you."

"All your questions about Barrett Shipping—the brig you commissioned Drake to construct—and now, what I just heard you say … you're investigating those missing ships, aren't you?"

"I can't answer that."

"You're not really in any financial difficulty, are you?"

"No."

Sammy leaned back, solemnly studying him. "I don't know you at all."

"You know me, Samantha." Rem framed her face between his palms. "Better than I know myself, perhaps."

Her eyes closed against the bittersweet pain. "You warned me, didn't you? That there was a part of your life—as well as your heart—you could never share? But I didn't listen."

"Imp … look at me." He waited until she complied. "You're going to have to forget everything you overheard here tonight."

Sammy met his penetrating silver stare and saw the gravity and magnitude of his command. "Just answer one question. Whatever you're doing, whoever you're working for, do you intend to harm my brother?"

He didn't hesitate. "No."

"All right." Shakily, Sammy inhaled. "Then I've forgotten everything I heard since I alit from the carriage."

A muscle worked in Rem's jaw. "You humble me."

"What can I do to help?"

"You can stay out of peril." Rem glanced around, suddenly reminded of where they were. "What are you doing at Boydry's? Before dawn, no less."

"I needed to see you." Sammy gripped Rem's arms, reassailed by the emotional impact of her quandary. "Drake is in London. He knows about us." Her eyes misted. "He's forbidden me to marry you."

"Damn ..." Rem scowled, evaluating this unexpected development. "When you say he 'knows about us,' what exactly do you mean?"

"If you're asking, does he know we've *been* together, I'm not sure. The argument didn't get that far. I told him I loved you, that you were going to visit Allonshire today to ask for my hand."

"And?"

"And he blew up. He told me he wouldn't see you, nor discuss the idea of my wedding you. He ordered me back to Allonshire, immediately."

"Under the circumstances, that doesn't surprise me," Rem muttered, his mind racing. He knew what had to be done. The question was, could he convince Samantha to comply without shattering her faith entirely?

"Imp," he began, praying her belief in him was strong enough to withstand this inopportune test. "I have no right to ask this of you, especially after all that's happened. But I'm asking nonetheless: do you trust me?"

"And I'm answering as I always have: I trust you with my life."

A knot of emotion clogged Rem's throat. "I'm honored as well as humbled." Gently, he smoothed Sammy's hair from her face. "Do as your brother says."

She started. "What?"

"Go home with Drake. Spend some time with Alexandria and your new niece. Tell them you need time to think, to make plans. Tell them anything you want. Just stay at Allonshire until I come for you. And Samantha ..." His hold on her tightened. "I will come for you."

The doubt and betrayal he expected to see never appeared. Instead, insight, stark and absolute, illuminated Sammy's eyes like a blaze of fireworks. "Whatever you're involved in ... it's dangerous."

It was Rem's turn to be startled. "I've been told by hundreds of people that I am impossible to read; a true enigma."

"Those people obviously weren't in love with you."

He stared deep into her eyes, and something painful and profound moved within his chest, blanketing the past in a dark and distant memory, spawning a soul-stirring emotion that terrified him with its intensity. "I love you, Samantha Barrett." The words escaped before he realized he'd said them.

"I know you do," Sammy whispered, twining her arms about his neck. "But I so needed to hear you say the words." Joyful tears filled her eyes. "Thank you, Rem."

With a low groan, Rem dragged her closer, capturing her mouth under his. "What did I ever do to deserve you?"

"So many things. You're tender and caring, but at the same time fearless and protective. And loyal. A true hero ... *my* hero."

"Keep believing in me," Rem breathed fiercely, pressing her head to his chest. "No matter how difficult it becomes, keep believing in me."

Fear clutched Sammy's heart. "I know you're walking into danger." She gripped his coat. "Please ... be careful."

"A hero would never refuse his heroine's request," Rem murmured, his voice hoarse with feeling. "Rest assured, my lady, I'll soon be riding to Allonshire to claim you. Now go and await my arrival."

NINETEEN

"I thought I might find you here."

Alexandria crossed the library and sank down on the settee beside Samantha. "What are you reading?"

"I have no idea," Sammy answered honestly, closing the book. "I've read the same paragraph seven times."

With an understanding nod, Alex folded her hands in her lap. "Are you ready to talk?" she asked frankly. "Or is it too soon?"

A tiny smile touched Sammy's lips. "I wondered what was taking you so long. I've been home for two days."

"I thought you needed some time. Besides," Alex sighed, shaking her head, "it's taken me every bit of the two days to calm your brother down."

"I'm sorry, Alex. This is the last thing you needed. You've barely regained your strength since Bonnie's birth."

"Despite Drake's incessant worrying, I feel wonderful and have been up and about for days. As for your twinges of guilt"—Alex took Sammy's hand in hers—"anything that troubles you, troubles me as well. In all ways but blood, we're sisters."

"I know. I …" Sammy's eyes filled with tears and she launched herself into Alex's arms. "I don't know what to do," she sobbed. "I'm home … and yet I'm not. I've only been away a fortnight, and yet it was a lifetime. I'm the same, and yet I've changed." She drew back, wiping her cheeks self-consciously. "I never used to cry, and lately it seems that's all I do. You must think I'm quite mad."

"No, Sammy." Alex stroked Samantha's hair tenderly. "I don't think you're mad. In fact, I've felt very much the way you're feeling right now."

Sammy stared at her beautiful, self-assured sister-in-law. "When?"

"When I fell in love with your brother."

Silence.

"You're in love with Remington Worth, aren't you?" Alex pressed gently.

"So much that it hurts. But every time I try to say it, Drake flies into a rage. I don't want to anger him, but I can't stop loving Rem."

"Drake worries about you, Sammy. And so do I. But it's different for me; I'm a woman, and I remember what it feels like to fall in love with an overpowering, disreputable man. Unfortunately," Alex grinned, "Drake remembers what it's like to *be* that overpowering, disreputable man. And he's terrified that Lord Gresham will hurt you."

"I understand. Drake wants to protect me. But why won't he give Rem a chance? Why does he refuse to even see him? I'm not so naive that I don't know what Rem's life was like before we met; how many women there were. But all that's changed now, Alex. He loves me; I know he does. His intentions are entirely honorable. Why won't Drake believe that?"

"He will … in time. But Drake still thinks of you as a child. You recall how vehemently he opposed the idea of your being brought out even one day before your eighteenth birthday."

"Well, I'm eighteen and two months now. And he hasn't improved."

"My point exactly. He's brooded since you left for London; over Smitty's competence as a guardian, over your inexperience at rebuffing the immoral blackguards of the *ton*. And now, in Drake's mind, his worst nightmare has been realized. One of those immoral black-guards has won your heart."

"So what do I do?"

"Try to call on just a small amount of the patience that you and I are so severely lacking. Drake will soften; I promise."

"If you say so."

"Tell me about him."

Sammy's head came up. "Rem?" Her eyes glowed. "Oh, Alex, he's so wonderful."

"I've met him several times. He's very handsome."

"Yes ... he is." Sammy grinned impishly. "I fell in love with him the moment I saw him, even before we spoke. Was it that way for you and Drake, too?"

Alex's lips twitched. "Actually, I think Drake and I would have killed each other if we could."

"Yes, I know, but underneath it all, you were drawn to each other from that first instant. You probably fell in love right then and there but never realized it."

"I won't argue with you—our feelings for each other were certainly intense. But then, Drake is a very volatile man. Is Remington?"

"Yes ... and no. Like Drake, Rem is a force to be reckoned with. But unlike Drake, Rem keeps his power carefully restrained. Outwardly, he's so charismatic he makes women melt. Yet there's something almost dangerously controlled about him, as if there's a volcano inside threatening to erupt. At the same time, I know he'd never hurt me. Does that make sense?"

"He sounds much like your long-awaited hero."

"He is."

Silently, Alex contemplated Sammy's radiant face, her own worry unappeased. After three inseparable years, she, better than anybody, understood Sammy's innocent, fanciful mind. She also knew that if Sammy's loving heart went astray, the results could be disastrous.

Taking a deep breath, Alex plunged right in. "Sammy, you say Remington is in love with you. How do you know?"

"He's told me so ... in words and in actions."

"Then why didn't he declare his intentions to Drake the day he was at Allonshire?"

"He was shielding me; he wanted to wait for the right time."

"He told you this?"

"Yes."

"But if he loves you, why has he made no attempt to reclaim you?" Alex raised her hand to stave off Sammy's protest. "I know Drake ordered you back to Allonshire. But the way you described the earl, he doesn't sound like the kind of man who could be deterred, even by Drake, *if he* wanted you—loved you—enough."

Sammy had opened her mouth to reply, when Rem's words resounded clearly in her head. Imp ... you're going to have to forget everything you overheard here tonight. ...Tell them anything you want. Just stay at Allonshire until I come for you. And Samantha ... I will come for you.

Slowly, Sammy exhaled. "Rem hasn't come for me because I asked him not to ... at least not right away."

Alex looked puzzled. "When did you speak with him?"

"I ran straight to his Town house after my argument with Drake."

"Samantha, it was the middle of the night!"

"I barely noticed. Not that it would have made any difference. I could never have left London without seeing Rem." She raised her chin. "Were you in my position, you would have done exactly the same thing."

"You're right. I would have." Alex gave her a wry smile. "Or perhaps worse."

"The decision to comply with Drake's command was mine. Rem agreed to give me some time to talk to Drake and, hopefully, to change his mind. But he won't wait forever. Any day I expect him to explode into Allonshire and come to blows with my brother."

"Not a pleasant thought," Alex commented dryly. "Speaking of waiting forever—" She broke off, unsure of how far she dared trespass.

"Rem has had scores of women," Sammy responded to the unasked question. "But all that ended the day we met. He's told me so himself … and I know it's true every time I'm in his arms. Oh, Alex, I see the wonder of discovery in his eyes; as if he never knew he could feel these things, as if we're both experiencing them for the first time—together."

Alex cleared her throat. "Sammy, no matter how I phrase this next question, there's no way to alter the fact that I'm prying. My only excuse is that I love you. So forgive my boldness. And if you choose not to answer, I'll understand."

"All right."

"How far has this relationship progressed … physically?"

Sammy rubbed her skirt between her fingers.

"Pretend I never asked."

"No, Alex, I want to answer you." Sammy looked up, her expression tender, open. "You're the one who explained to me what happens between a man and a woman, and how beautiful it can be when love is involved. Watching you and Drake—the way you look at each other—I could only imagine what you meant. Well, now I know."

"I see." Alex chewed her lip. "Did he seduce you?" she blurted out.

A grin. "Actually, I'm afraid I seduced him." Seeing Alex's stunned expression, Sammy explained, "Rem was being entirely too noble, worrying about my reputation and my inexperience. He did everything he could to discourage me. But to no avail. Finally, he just surrendered to the inevitable." She leaned forward. "Alex, he arranged things so no one would suspect we were together, including the servants. He filled the room with flowers and wine. He was so incredibly tender, so loving … as if we were the only two people on earth. Seduction is born in the mind; making love in the heart. This was making love in its truest form."

Alex's eyes were damp. "You really have grown up, haven't you?"

"I want to be Rem's wife more than I've ever wanted anything in my life. Please, Alex, help me."

Rising, Alex squared her shoulders and squeezed Sammy's hand. "I'll talk to Drake again. Between us, you and I will make him see reason. And then, Lord help us, we'll both have our heroes."

* * *

"No. Definitively, unequivocally no. Samantha will not marry the Earl of Gresham."

Drake tossed one Hessian boot to the floor, sending the other crashing after it.

"You're being completely irrational." Alex propped her chin on her knees, regarding her husband calmly from the center of her bed,

"I don't give a damn. Sammy is a child. She knows nothing about falling in love and less about unprincipled rakes."

"That description sounds remarkably familiar." Alex frowned as she allegedly pondered that thought. "I know! Three years ago. You remember—the innocent girl who collided with the impenetrable rogue? The rogue who tried to seduce her the first night on his ship?"

"All right, princess. You made your point." Drake shot Alex a dark look.

"You can't change Samantha's feelings. Nor can you undo what's been done."

Drake's fingers paused on the buttons of his shirt. "What's been done? What the hell does that mean?"

"It means she loves him, Drake."

Swearing softly, Drake sent his shirt sailing to the floor beside his boots and sank down wearily on the edge of the bed. "I don't want to hear any more." He dropped his head into his hands, vulnerable in a way only Alex was permitted to see. "I'm at a loss, princess."

Alex lay her cheek against his bare back. "Do we have the right to deny Sammy the same joy we share? She told me today that everything she's learned about love, she's learned from us."

With a groan, Drake turned, tugging Alex against him. "You really believe this is right, don't you?"

"Yes."

A prolonged silence hovered as Drake grappled with his doubts. "What do you want me to do?"

Smiling softly, Alex kissed the taut muscles of her husband's chest. She knew how much this concession cost him, and she loved him all the more for it. "For now, nothing. Except perhaps to cease stomping around like a wounded bear. But whenever the earl does descend on Allonshire, I want you to listen to what he has to say. It's going to be difficult ... for both you and Lord Gresham. But you owe it to Sammy to listen with your heart as well as your mind. Do it for her"—Alex raised her face to gaze up at him—"and for me."

Conflicting emotions warred on Drake's face before he relented, tangling his hands in his wife's tawny hair. "You know I'd take on the devil himself for you, princess."

Alex caressed his nape, drawing his mouth down to hers. "It's too late, Your Grace. I've already tamed him."

"Templar turned up nothing." Rem crumpled the note Boyd had handed him and flung it across his sitting room. "Anders's house is as void of clues as his office, dammit."

Boyd rubbed his unshaven chin. "So we're right back where we started two days ago."

"You look like hell. You and Harris have spent forty-eight bloody hours at the docks. Neither of you has spotted that privateer yet?"

"No. But we knew this tactic was a gamble, Rem. For all we know, he could have taken to sea by now. He could also have disguised himself in any number of ways. It wouldn't take much to become unrecognizable to us; I've never laid eyes on the bastard, and Harris only caught one fleeting glimpse of him that night he met Towers."

"What about Towers' description?"

"Despite the captain's belief that he'd committed the culprit's face to memory, his actual description was weak. Average height, heavyset, black hair, beard."

"That sounds like every bloody sailor in London."

"Exactly."

"Perhaps I should talk to Towers myself."

"I think that's wise," Boyd agreed. "You have a way of helping people remember information they never knew they possessed."

"Fine. I'll visit Towers tonight." Crossing the room, Rem retrieved the discarded note only long enough to tear it to shreds and toss the remains into the fire.

Boyd's glass paused halfway to his lips. "You're going to Harris's place? Wouldn't it be safer to follow our usual procedure and meet at Annie's? Harris could bring Towers with him."

"No. I can't risk Captain Towers showing himself in public. If Summerson or his privateer were to spot him, his life wouldn't be worth a damn."

"Neither will your position with the Admiralty if you start visiting the Bow Street men at their homes. Meeting them for a drink is one thing, calling on them socially is another. If anyone sees you—"

"Maybe it doesn't matter anymore," Rem replied softly.

His vital proclamation hung in the air like the charged aftermath of gunfire.

Boyd's sober gaze met Rem's, astute but unsurprised. "No, maybe it doesn't," he agreed.

Silence permeated the room as the significance of what was occurring sank in.

At last Rem gave an ironic laugh. "I never would have believed this if it weren't happening. An eighteen-year-old romantic innocent … and I can barely get through each day without her. Me; the skeptic, the impervious rake. Inconceivable, wouldn't you say?"

"No. Miraculous, I would say. You're a lucky man, Rem."

"I won't dispute that fact." Rem didn't smile. "It's as if Samantha is pouring all the good back inside me."

Boyd nodded his understanding. "Based upon your inference that protecting your identity is no longer important, I presume you've been giving thought to the future … to what you intend once you and Samantha are wed."

"I think of little else. I can't put her at risk, Boyd, and you know she would be if she were privy to my full involvement with the Admiralty. Nor can I stash her away at Gresham, keep her separate from what I do, as I once thought I would."

"Because she's suspicious of your activities?"

"Because she's Samantha." Rem savored each word as he uttered it; a decision he'd come to days ago but was only first giving voice to. "Because I love her too much to place her second in my life. Hell, because I want her with me all the time, every day, everywhere. Because I want to give her everything she needs, everything *I* need: my heart, my future, my children." Rem broke off, wonder in his eyes.

"It's time, isn't it?" Boyd pronounced gently. "Finally, my friend, it's time. For both of us," he added.

The implication of Boyd's final phrase struck home.

"Cynthia?" Rem questioned.

"Cynthia." Boyd grinned. "Of course, she doesn't know it yet, although I'm arrogant enough to believe she cares. And as I've said, I'm a patient man. A few months is a small price to pay for a lifetime."

Peace, unimaginable but absolute, pervaded Rem's soul. "Fate works in strange ways, doesn't it?"

Boyd nodded. "It's time to rebuild our lives."

"I agree. And not only because of Samantha and Cynthia, although, Lord knows, they're the finest of incentives." Seeing Boyd's quizzical look, Rem clarified, "Instinct tells me we've beaten the odds too many times, my friend, and that discovery is no longer eventual but imminent. Ten years is a long time to flirt with danger in our own backyard."

"You're saying we should quit while we're ahead … or, in this case, alive?"

"That's exactly what I'm saying. We've trained Harris and Templar well. With occasional guidance from us, Briggs will scarcely notice we're gone." Rem's lips set in a grim line. "But first we're going to uncover the plot behind those missing ships and put Anders and Summerson in Newgate where they belong. Them, their privateer friend, and whoever else they're working with. I'm half tempted to seize Anders and beat the truth out of him. But enticing as that prospect might be, it's too risky. If assaulting Anders doesn't scare him into giving us the names we need, we'll have alerted his anonymous partner, who will then escape unpunished. If only we could find a way to make them surface on their own—" Abruptly, Rem stopped, a steely light dawning in his eyes.

"I know that look. You've thought of something."

"As a matter of fact, I have. Of course, my plan hinges on what I learn from Captain Towers. If I can get what I need from him tonight, I'll be riding directly to Allonshire. There, I'll elicit Drake Barrett's cooperation."

"Does that mean you intend to tell Drake Barrett of your work for the Crown? Prior to our fulfilling our mission?"

"Yes. I trust the man. His actions both at sea and at home have shown him to be irrefutably loyal to England. Moreover, for what I have in mind, his assistance will be not only invaluable, but necessary."

"I see." Boyd coughed tactfully. "May I ask, is your newly conceived plan the only reason you're riding to Allonshire to speak with the duke?"

"I think you already know the answer to that question. No. I have another, all-important purpose for my trip. I intend to leave Allonshire with Drake Barrett's blessing to marry Samantha." A muscle flexed in Rem's jaw. "Not that His Grace—or anyone—could prevent me from making Samantha my wife. But Drake means the world to Samantha, and without his approval, our wedding cannot be the magical fantasy I intend for my starry-eyed bride. So, for Samantha's sake, I'll swallow my pride and make a proper request. But if he fights me ..." A poignant pause. "Who am I kidding?" Rem amended softly. "I'll grovel if that's what it takes to ensure Samantha's happiness." Roughly, he cleared his throat. "In any case, with Drake's assistance and a modicum of luck, my plan should work nicely. Then, you and I will have our culprits and Briggs will have our resignations." The shutters of the past lifted as Rem spoke. "At which point, Boyd, the war will finally be over."

Two hours later the final battle plan commenced.

"Gresham ... come in." Harris looked totally stunned to see Rem standing in his doorway ... and thoroughly exhausted from his forty-eight-hour vigil with Boyd.

"Sorry to barge in like this," Rem apologized, shrugging out of his coat. "But I'd like to try speaking with Towers."

"I don't know how much good it'll do. Between all my questions and his unfounded dread that the privateer who captured the *Bountiful* will somehow discover his whereabouts, I'd say Towers is at the end of his rope."

"Evidently." Glancing past Harris, Rem watched Towers pace anxiously about the sitting room. "It's a damp night, Harris. Coffee would be just the thing to warm the chill from my bones. Would you mind making some?"

Rem's off hand request needed no further explanation.

"Right away." Harris disappeared into the kitchen.

Draping his coat over his arm, Rem strolled into the sitting room and lowered himself into an armchair. "Good evening, Captain."

"If you've come to ask me about the privateer, I've already described him to Harris," Towers replied abruptly. "I can't remember anything more specific." Haggard and drawn, Towers continued pacing, running a shaking hand through his hair. "I wish to God I could—the bastard took my ship, my crew—but I can't even give you a decent enough description to ferret him out." With a guilty look, Towers paused. "In truth, I'm sure I'd recognize him if I saw him again. But, Lord forgive me, I'm too terrified to find out."

"You'd recognize him ... and he'd recognize you," Rem submitted quietly. "No, Towers, involving you in our search is not an option."

Relief flooded Towers' features. "I'm a coward, Gresham."

"That's not cowardice, it's caution. Stop berating yourself. It's undeserved. Your ordeal was harrowing. You're lucky to be alive." Casually, Rem lit a cheroot. "My suggestion is to stop trying to refine the description of your captor. Instead tell me about the island he took you to."

"The island?"

Towers looked surprised, and distracted, exactly as Rem had hoped. Experience had long ago taught him that people remembered far more when they spoke spontaneously and without pressure.

"There isn't much to say." Towers straddled a chair, rubbing his forearm across his sweating forehead. "The island was small, grassy, with a few scattered trees and narrow stretches of sand and rock. As I told you, I have no idea where it was; we were blindfolded, our hands and feet bound."

"They uncovered your eyes when you reached the island?"

"Yes. The sunlight was bright, though. It took me a while to recover enough to see."

"I'm sure. Could you hear talking?"

"Yes ... that's when that scum started taunting us about Atlantis. The rest of the time he was muttering to his crew."

"Were there many of them?"

"I saw twenty, maybe more. They did whatever he told them to."

"They feared him."

"We all did. There was something menacing about him."

"I'm sure he handled his crew as brutally as he did you."

"He was never actually violent." Towers' brows drew together as he tried to explain. "Our fear was based on what we knew he was capable of doing; that frigid, emotionless voice grating out his orders … like he didn't give a damn who lived and who died. Which, of course, he didn't."

"How long were you on the island?"

"One night. I escaped the next morning."

"Did he allow you food? Water?"

"We were given a few berries and some sips of water, only so we wouldn't die before reaching our destination. They fed us when they uncovered our eyes. That was the first time the pirate captain spoke directly to me. He yanked off the cloth binding over my eyes, gripped my shirt with one of his enormous fists, and shoved some berries at me. I ate them—I was too hungry to be proud—but I wanted to spit them in his filthy, scarred face. Not long after, we were given water, then our eyes were covered again, until daybreak. I've already told you the rest." Towers slumped in his chair. "Dammit, Gresham, I wish I could remember more."

"You have." Rem ground out his cheroot and rose. "You've told me enough to pick out the privateer who's working with Summerson."

Towers blinked. "But you said you needed a more thorough—"

"And you provided it." Rem scooped up his coat. "Originally all you said was that he was of average height, heavyset, with black hair and a beard. Now you've added that he has a raspy voice, large hands, and scars on that portion of his face that is exposed. An excellent description." Rem crossed the sitting room. "Tell Harris I couldn't stay. Thank you, Captain Towers."

The ride to Allonshire took the better part of an hour, and Rem used every precious moment of it to finalize his plan. Ironic that everything was coming to a head at once; his mission, his confrontation with Drake, his future. And it all depended on this one, all-important meeting.

The meeting Drake Barrett knew nothing about.

The iron gates of Allonshire loomed ahead, and Rem's gut clenched. He was unused to feeling off balance, and the reality of it was disconcerting, though unsurprising. Until now he'd been fighting for England, and defeat was inconceivable. But tonight he was fighting not only for his country, but for his future.

The carriage slowed, stopped, and Rem alit, more determined than he'd ever been in his life … and more vulnerable.

"Hello, Humphreys." Soberly, he greeted the butler. "I'd like to see the duke."

"Is he expecting you, Lord Gresham?"

"He most certainly is, Humphreys. We both are."

Alexandria Barrett's clear voice interrupted whatever Rem had been about to say. Walking forward gracefully, she nodded her permission at Humphreys. "By all means, ask the earl to come in."

"Very good, Your Grace." Humphreys stepped aside at once.

"Thank you, Your Grace." Rem bowed, a puzzled look in his eyes. "I appreciate your cordial welcome."

Alex assessed him silently for a moment. "Humphreys, wait a quarter hour before telling the duke that Lord Gresham is here," she instructed. "I want to meet with the earl myself. We'll be in the yellow salon."

"But Your Grace—"

"That will be all, Humphreys."

Alex gestured for Rem to follow her down the hall to the cozy yellow salon in Allonshire's southern wing. "We'll have some privacy here. Come in, Lord Gresham." Swiftly, she closed the doors behind her.

"May I offer my congratulations on the birth of your daughter?" Rem opened gallantly.

"Thank you." Alex paused when she reached the sideboard. "Now, may *I* offer you something?"

"An explanation, perhaps." Rem's dimple flashed. "Forgive my abruptness, Your Grace, but I have to wonder—"

"Alexandria. My given name, as I'm sure you recall." Alex poured two glasses of claret. "And there's no need to apologize ... at least not for your understandable curiosity. For your intimacy with Samantha, now that is indeed another thing." Inclining her head, Alex offered Rem his drink.

Rem stared, automatically taking the proffered glass.

"Some of Sammy's candor is derived from her brother, my lord. The rest she acquired from her close relationship with me. To your health." Alex raised her glass.

"And to yours." Rem chuckled. "I have the feeling this is going to be a most interesting chat."

Alex placed her half-filled glass on the table, leaning forward to face Rem directly. "I won't waste time. Humphreys is very loyal to the duke and will wait not an instant beyond the quarter hour I requested to announce your arrival. As a result, in precisely twelve minutes my outraged husband will be exploding into the yellow salon to demand an explanation for our chat. Therefore, may I begin with the facts, my lord?"

"Remington. And, yes, please do."

"I love Sammy as if she were my own. She is one of life's rarest treasures, beautiful inside as well as out, with a heart of gold and a spirit to match. And it appears you are the fortunate man on whom she's bestowed that heart ... among other things." Alex paused. "Now my position. If you love Samantha as much as she loves you; if you are everything she swears you are, her knight-in-shining-armor, her once-in-a-lifetime hero, then I'll march into Drake's study with you this instant, stand right beside you and face my husband head-on, arguing away any objections he still harbors with every emotional weapon I possess. But if you're not in love with Sammy, if you've merely seduced her, acquired her as one of your numerous female possessions, and are toying with her affections and her tender heart, you'd best tell me now, or instead of merely having you thrown out, I'll make certain you wish you were never born. Is that clear enough, Remington?"

A corner of Rem's mouth lifted, his expression one of undisguised admiration. "You're everything Samantha said you were and more. Yes, Alexandria, that's perfectly clear." Rem finished the last of his claret, facing Alex with the same straightforward candor she'd just shown him.

"I never believed in love, certainly not for me. I had my reasons, none of which matter any longer—because Samantha exploded into my life like a burst of dazzling fireworks, blasting all my cynicism, my lack of faith, into nothingness. She turned my world, my heart, upside down, fragmented all the walls I'd erected, and filled me in ways I never knew I was empty. To answer your question, I love Samantha with an intensity that staggers me. She is more to me than my own life, more essential than the air I breathe, more impelling than my past and all the scars it wrought. I'm going to make her my wife, fill her life with joy and children of our own. And, with all due respect, Your Grace, I'll destroy anyone who tries to stand in my way."

A radiant smile lit Alex's face. "That's all I wanted to hear." Her glance darted to the clock on the mantel. "Our time is almost up. I suggest we find Drake before he finds us."

They were halfway through the hall, rounding the foot of the marble staircase, when a white streak shot by them, followed by a cry of outrage and a shout of laughter.

"I'll recover your stocking, Cynthia. Fear not." Sammy darted down the steps, her skirts lifted indecently high so as not to impede her progress. "Alex!" she called, spotting her sister-in-law. "Grab

Rascal! He's taken Cynthia's stocking again—" Abruptly, she halted, her eyes widening as she saw the man who stood beside Alex.

Valiantly, Sammy strove for control, ordering herself to display the proper decorum, to temper the exuberant reception that threatened to erupt from within her.

Rem showed no such restraint. "Samantha." Unthinking, uncaring, he reached for her.

That was all it took.

With a half laugh, half sob, Sammy launched herself into his waiting arms. "Oh, Rem." She kissed his jaw, buried her face against his chest. "You're here."

Rem's hands shook as he stroked her hair. "God, I've missed you, imp," he breathed, his voice thick with emotion.

"When did you arrive at Allonshire?"

"Moments ago. I'm on my way to see your brother."

That made Sammy draw back, search his face anxiously, then look past him to Alex. "Please don't let Drake say no."

Alex glanced from Sammy to Rem, visibly moved by the emotion hovering between them. "If I had any intention of allowing your brother to stand in your way, that possibility has been thoroughly dashed by seeing the two of you together." She raised her chin. "Sammy, you wait here. I'll show Remington to Drake's study. The two of them have a betrothal to arrange."

"Thank you, Alex," Sammy whispered. Reluctantly, she detached herself from Rem's embrace. "I'll be in my room … pacing and fretting."

Rem brought Sammy's hand to his lips. "Neither is necessary. Our betrothal is as good as sealed." He laced his fingers through hers. "Trust me, love."

Standing on tiptoe, Sammy kissed his chin. "You have yet to disappoint me, my lord," she murmured. Turning, she sprinted up the stairs.

Rem watched Sammy's retreating back, making no attempt to hide the love in his eyes.

"Shall we?" Alex prodded gently.

"By all means." Rem's dimple flashed. "Lead the way to the lion's den."

Outside the study door, Humphreys was waiting, squinting at his timepiece. With a dignified nod, he snapped it shut and raised his hand to knock.

"I'll announce the earl, Humphreys," Alex interrupted hastily.

The butler paused, then lowered his arm. "Very good, Your Grace." A sudden thought diverted his attention and, abruptly, he brightened. "I should check on Lady Bonnie. She was a bit fretful this evening." Bowing, he headed off to the nursery.

Alex squared her shoulders and faced the closed study door. "Try not to come to blows," she murmured to Rem as she knocked.

"I'll do my best."

"Yes?" Drake's deep voice called out.

"May we come in?" Alex poked her head around the side of the door.

"Of course, princess. We?" Drake asked, suddenly realizing Alex's use of the plural.

"Yes … we. Lord Gresham and myself."

Drake came to his feet in one slow, fluid motion. "I didn't know Lord Gresham had arrived," he returned icily.

"I informed Humphreys that I would announce the earl … *after* we had a pleasant chat." Alex opened the door more fully, gesturing for Rem to enter. "Now that we've finished, I've brought him to you. To talk. And to listen." The plea in Alex's voice was as plain as the beseeching look in her eyes.

Her husband was immune to neither.

"Gresham." With enormous effort, Drake strove to be cordial. Briefly, his frosty gaze flickered to Alex. "Leave us, princess."

"But—"

"Alexandria, I want to talk to the earl alone."

Alex sighed resignedly, knowing better than to argue with that particular tone of voice. "I'll be with Samantha in her bedchamber." She gave Drake an engaging smile. "Have a nice chat, gentlemen."

The door closed behind her.

Despite the oppressive silence, Rem couldn't help but chuckle. "I'm captivated by your duchess ... a most charming, forthright young woman."

"As is my sister."

Rem's humor vanished. "Yes, she is."

"Sit down, Gresham. You have a great deal of explaining to do."

"More than you could possibly imagine," Rem agreed, lowering himself into the designated chair. "I have a wealth of information to impart. I won't insult you by procrastinating or speaking in riddles. I'll merely begin at the beginning and relay the whole situation to you. But first I must ask for your word that nothing we discuss will leave this room."

"What the hell are you talking about?" Drake demanded. "What has all this got to do with Samantha?"

"Nothing. And everything."

"Sammy swears she's in love with you ... and you with her. She tells me you've proposed marriage. Have you?"

"Yes."

"Before or after you seduced her?"

Rem gritted his teeth and fell silent.

"You son of a bitch." Drake slammed his fist onto the desk. "You're not only a cad, but a liar as well. You sat in this very room, discussed the building of your bloody ship, and looked me straight in the eye when you told me you'd only run into Samantha at an occasional ball. And all that time you'd already taken her to your bed? What kind of scoundrel are you?"

"I hadn't taken her to my bed, dammit!" It was Rem's turn to bolt to his feet. "And I have no intention of demeaning what Samantha and I share by reviewing the details of our relationship. I wouldn't even be asking for your blessing if it didn't mean so much to her. But it does."

"Don't sound so bloody noble. Wedding Samantha would be impossible without my consent. She's not of age."

"Don't underestimate my capabilities, Allonshire. I'd whisk Samantha off to Gretna Green if I had to. Your dissension wouldn't thwart me for an instant."

Drake inhaled sharply, his hands balling into fists. "Then why the hell come to me at all?"

"Because I love Samantha. And she happens to adore you. She'd be devastated if she couldn't have your approval. So I'm asking for it. The choice of whether or not I receive it is yours. Either way, Samantha will become my wife."

For the first time, a flash of uncertainty flickered in Drake's eyes. "If you love Sammy as much as you profess, why didn't you approach me before things got out of hand?"

An ironic smile touched Rem's lips. "Because things got out of hand the moment I laid eyes on your sister. I didn't realize it, of course. And once I did, I fought like hell. But some battles are destined to be over before they've begun."

"I don't know what to think." Drake dropped wearily into his chair.

A stab of understanding struck, triggering a wave of compassion. "I'll make her happy, Drake," Rem pledged quietly. "As my countess, Samantha will want for nothing. She'll have security, position, all the luxuries money can buy … not to mention countless new Gothic romances to read, and a fireside specifically for her regal pet to warm himself." Abruptly, Rem's light tone vanished, superseded by an emotion too vast to contain. "She'll also have a husband who will protect her tender heart, indulge her untainted spirit, and keep only unto her for the rest of his life. In short, not a day will go by that Samantha doesn't know she is loved. You have my word on it."

Drake raised his head, studied Rem for a long moment. "You know my sister remarkably well." He swallowed. "And you love her a great deal."

"So much that it terrifies me."

A reminiscent light dawned in Drake's eyes. "I've encountered that particular terror myself." Slowly, purposefully, he extended his hand. "You'd best keep your promises, Gresham, or you'll have me to answer to." His expression softened. "Make Sammy happy."

"I intend to." Rem clasped Drake's hand, then reseated himself. "And now I'd like to tell you the rest of what I came to say, at which point I think you'll understand the complexities of my courtship with Samantha and why I was so reluctant to succumb to my feelings … as well as why I was less than honest with you."

"Go on."

"I must stress what I said earlier: you cannot disclose this conversation to anyone. The security of our country may be at stake."

With a perplexed look, Drake nodded. "Very well. You have my word. What we discuss stays in this room."

Rem leaned forward. "As you know, numerous British vessels have disappeared mysteriously these past months."

"We pursued this subject last time you were here, Gresham. I hope you're not again implying that—"

"The Admiralty has asked me to investigate the matter. I'm in the process of doing so. That's the real reason I met with you last week about my brig."

Drake's jaw dropped. "The Admiralty selected you? Why?"

"Because I've been working with them for over a decade now—since the Battle of Trafalgar. And, at the risk of sounding pompous, my success rate has been quite good. The Crown is pleased."

"Christ." Comprehension struck Drake, hard. "You're telling me you've been secretly—"

"Exactly. Now can you understand why I didn't want to get involved with Samantha? I was determined not to expose her to danger ... something I was constantly immersed in."

"*Was?* Has your situation changed?"

"Everything's changed. *I've* changed." Rem's jaw set. "I'm going to explain the national dilemma to you, at which point I plan to ask for your help. Once this mission is successfully completed, I intend to submit my resignation to the First Lord of the Admiralty. The rest of my life belongs to Samantha and our children."

Drake was still reeling. "Your revelation doesn't ring true. How could you be an agent of the Crown when, during our recent war with America, you spent so much time at sea captaining a flagship?"

"That was a fallacy, fabricated by the Admiralty to protect my true role during the war. I did go to sea, but not as a naval captain. In fact, I wasn't even assigned to one vessel, but traveled from ship to ship gathering information for the Crown. I observed our fleet in battle, assessed the American strategy and provided the Admiralty with my analysis of our strengths and our enemy's weaknesses. It was my job to know everything that occurred in national or foreign waters ... and to use that information to aid our country."

"Even if I choose to believe you, I'd be a fool if I didn't ask for proof."

"Yes, you would," Rem agreed. "Obviously, I carry no documents to link me with the Admiralty." Rem scrutinized Drake's reaction. "Would it suffice if I provided you with details no customary naval captain is privy to? Specifics about the annihilation of your ship *La Belle Illusion* and the part your brother Sebastian played in it? Would you like me to recite from memory the report on the incident that the Admiralty has on file, including my determination of what *should* have been the outcome of the battle had it not been for your brother's interference?"

"Stop." Grimly, Drake held up his hand. "That's all the proof I require." Leaning forward, he added, "I've protected Samantha as best I could by not dwelling on the horrid details of our brother's crimes, Remington."

"As have I. And now that you're satisfied with my explanation, we need never speak of it again."

"Agreed. Now get to the current crisis."

Carefully, thoroughly, Rem outlined the situation and the suspects to Drake.

"So that's why you came to Allonshire last week." Drake nodded thoughtfully. "You were delving into what I might know about the missing ships."

"It's also why I initially began pursuing Samantha," Rem added, bent on obliterating all misconceptions. "I hoped, since she was your sister, that she might inadvertently possess revealing information. Or at least that's what I told myself. The truth is, it was easier to believe I was courting Samantha for the sake of my mission than to admit I was falling in love with her. I'm not sure that's something you can understand."

"I can. Better than you think. And I respect your honesty." Drake rubbed a quill between his fingers. "You're convinced that Anders and Summerson are working with someone else?"

"With at least one other person, yes. It's up to me to find a way to expose them … or to encourage them to expose themselves."

"How are you going to do that?"

Rem gripped his knees. "That's where I need your help. I have an excellent description of the privateer. The problem is, I have no idea when he'll show his face. My guess is, he won't risk discovery by appearing during daylight hours. But eventually he'll have to meet with Summerson, to get his next sum of money. And I intend to be there when he does."

"But if you confront him and Summerson then, you'll still lose any chance of apprehending their unknown partner."

"Exactly. So I plan to have a private talk with our pirate friend … after Summerson takes his leave. As a privateer, he's bound by neither document nor friendship, and his interests are entirely his own. So I needn't worry about him alerting the others. With the proper amount of persuasion, perhaps I can convince him to convene a meeting of all the parties involved."

"That makes sense. But how do you intend to survey the docks each night without being noticed?"

"Barrett Shipping overlooks a large section of the Thames, as well as the entire area surrounding Anders Shipping."

"So it does." A glint of understanding lit Drake's eyes.

"No one would question your watchman for making his nightly rounds, would they?"

"Certainly not." Drake rose, intrigued and decisive. "Consider yourself hired, Gresham. As of tomorrow night, you work for Barrett Shipping."

TWENTY

"I still can't believe it! By the Season's end, I'm going to be the Countess of Gresham!" Sammy danced around the room, swinging Rascal in the air.

"Why can't you believe it? You've been plotting this for weeks now," Cynthia muttered, her brusque tone belied by the twinkle in her eyes.

"You can't fool me, Cynthia. You're thrilled for my happiness. So stop pretending." Sammy hugged Rascal tightly. "You shall become a Worth, as well," she informed him. "And we'll all live happily ever after."

"An original thought."

Sammy turned to give her friend a knowing look. "Perhaps not original, but also not unique. When are you going to admit to me that you care for Boyd Hayword?"

Cynthia flushed, hastily turning down Sammy's bed.

"You didn't answer me."

"There's nothing to say."

"I know you've been seeing him. And I know he cares for you. He all but told me so."

"Did he?"

"Yes." Sammy stroked Rascal's fur absently. "Boyd won't hurt you."

"Perhaps not intentionally." Cynthia stared down at the bare white sheets. "But what about when he learns who … what I am."

"He already knows who and what you are. What you *were* was a victim. Tell him the truth; give him a chance to understand … and to help you understand yourself. Then put the past where it belongs. Behind you." Sammy reached across the bed to take Cynthia's hand. "You're a wonderful friend; a fine, decent human being. You deserve to be happy."

"But what if I can't make Boyd happy?"

"That's nonsense. Why wouldn't you be able to—" Sammy broke off as a flash of insight occurred. "You mean in bed, don't you? You're worried that you'll disappoint him when you make love."

Cynthia turned away. "I can't discuss this, Samantha."

"You *must* discuss this." Sammy placed Rascal on the bed and turned to face her friend. "Cynthia, what that blackguard did to you, what happened at Annie's, that bears no resemblance to what it will be like with Boyd."

"How do you know?"

"Because when you and Boyd are finally together, it will be rooted in love, and you'll feel what I feel when I'm in Rem's arms: tenderness, excitement, wonder. It's a closeness beyond comprehension; as if we're one. Believe me."

"Boyd's been an absolute gentleman. I know he's waiting patiently, but I'm just not ready. It's too soon."

"Talk to him, Cynthia. I promise you won't frighten him away. Then let time and nature take over."

Cynthia smiled faintly. "When did you become so wise?"

"When I fell in love."

Silence. "The thought of caring scares me to death," Cynthia whispered at last.

"You're far from alone," Sammy returned cheerfully. "Just look at the two reformed rakes under this roof. My brother, who thought of women as worthless chattel and now cherishes his wife with all his heart, and Remington, who was transformed from a faithless womanizer to the most splendid of heroes. Without Alex and me to open their eyes, both men would have remained paralyzed by their pasts, unable to love. Let Boyd do the same for you."

"All right, Samantha. I'll try."

"And you'll succeed. Now, on to tonight's arrangements." Sammy glanced at the bed, tapping her forefinger thoughtfully to her lips. Her gaze fell on Rascal, who was rolling merrily amid the fluffy pillows, and her whole face lit up. "Perfect!"

"What's perfect? What arrangements?" Cynthia demanded. "I'll never get used to your wild vaulting from one subject to the next."

Sammy was barely listening. "Rascal, if we tuck you into the bed amid three pillows and give you two of your favorite stockings to chew on—Cynthia, you'll have to provide those—it might just keep you still enough for my plan to work. Cynthia, will you spend the night in my bedchamber? Just as a precaution, really. In case Alex should visit. No one else comes to my room after dark. Also, Rascal detests sleeping without company. This way you can be his companion and my sentry all at once!"

"Samantha." Cynthia gripped her shoulders. "What are you talking about? Why are you hiding Rascal in your bed and why would he be alone if I went to my own chambers? Where will you be?"

Sammy arched her brows in exasperation. "With Remington, of course."

"With ... Remington." Cynthia repeated the words slowly, as if she were unsure she had heard them correctly. "Are you totally mad?" she hissed. "You're going to spend the night with the earl under your brother's roof?"

"Of course. Rem will only be at Allonshire this one night. At daybreak, he'll be returning to London. After that, who knows when we'll have another opportunity to be together."

"I have a novel idea: why not wait for your wedding night?"

A grin. "My, you've become quite a prig. The wedding isn't for two months. I've barely survived two days! No, Cynthia." Sammy began enthusiastically stuffing pillows beneath the bedcovers. "I refuse to lie awake all night knowing the man I love is doing the same right down the hall." She straightened, her cheeks glowing. "Will you help me … please?"

"I must be totally insane," Cynthia muttered, rolling her eyes to the heavens. "Very well; what would you have me do?"

"Thank you!" Sammy hugged her. "No more than what I just said: furnish Rascal with two stockings, post yourself near my door to ward off guests, and spend the night in my bedchamber. Oh! And one more thing." Sammy dimpled. "Help me don my new peach night rail."

"Remington Worth had best prepare himself. Nothing in his experience has prepared him for Samantha Barrett."

Another impish grin. "I know. Glorious, isn't it?"

Rem was every bit as restless as Samantha.

Tossing off his second glass of brandy, he stood at the bedchamber window, staring off into the night, planning his procedure for tomorrow. He'd map out a walking route of the docks for himself during his carriage ride back to London. The scrutiny would begin tomorrow night at dusk and continue every night thereafter until the culprits were apprehended. At which point Rem could pursue his future.

Smiling, he recalled the expression on Samantha's face when Drake had called her down, given her his blessing. Joy, love, gratitude, excitement; her beautiful, expressive features had revealed them all. She'd hugged her brother, Alex, Smitty, Humphreys … and four or five footmen who happened to be in the vicinity. Then she'd gazed up at Rem with such love that even the footmen beamed their approval.

Rem had stared down into those incredible jade-green eyes, his own chest tight with emotion, and lightly kissed her cheek.

ANDREA KANE

What he really wanted was to take her to bed.

Slamming down his brandy glass, Rem shrugged out of his shirt and tossed it to the chair.

Two months, he reminded himself, scowling. Two endless, bloody months.

He'd never last.

He was in the midst of plotting lengthy closed-carriage rides around Hyde Park when his door creaked open.

Instinctively, Rem seized his pistol, aiming it at the widening doorway.

"That's the second time you've pointed a pistol at me, my lord." Sammy shut the door firmly behind her. "I assure you, there are better ways to ensure my cooperation."

"Samantha?" Rem lowered his arm, staring at her incredulously. "What are you doing here?"

"If you need to ask me that, it's been far longer than I realized." With a firm click, Sammy turned the key in the lock. Brushing wisps of hair from her shoulders, she began walking slowly toward Rem. "I wanted to ask your opinion of my new night rail. Do you like it?" She stopped a mere foot in front of him, tilting her head back to watch his face.

Rem could scarcely speak, much less think. The pale silk of her gown was nearly transparent, its layers clinging to Samantha's lush curves, its bodice so low that the entire upper slope of her breasts was exposed.

His breathing harsh, shallow, Rem clenched his fists, strove for a semblance of reason. "Sweetheart, we're at Allonshire. I don't think …" He had no idea what he was going to say. Whatever it was, the words were never uttered.

Samantha pressed her palms to his bare chest, gliding them through the tufts of hair, up over the taut muscles and warm flesh to his massive shoulders. "I've missed you so much," she breathed, pressing her lips to where his heart pounded furiously. "And I want to celebrate … truly celebrate … our betrothal." She stepped back, met his burning gaze, and, in one brisk motion, tugged her night rail over her head and dropped it to the floor. "Can we, Rem?"

"Christ." The word was both capitulation and prayer, as Rem dragged her into his arms, crushed her body to his. "I don't think I can make it to the bed," he growled, his hands possessing her everywhere at once.

Whimpering with pleasure, Sammy reached down to unfasten Rem's breeches, tugging at them with impatient hands.

Rem tore them off himself, kicked them away, lifting Samantha from the floor until her breasts brushed his chest.

Their eyes met.

"Here?" Sammy whispered, offering him her soul.

"No," Rem replied, passion suddenly dwarfed by tenderness. "Not here." Wrapping his arms securely around her, he walked to the bed and lowered her to it, following her down. "Here," he murmured reverently, framing her face between his hands. "In bed, where I can touch every inch of you, feel your heart beating against mine, hold you after you've shuddered in my arms. Here, where I can truly show you how much I love you."

"Oh, Rem." She tugged his mouth down to hers, kissing him with all the skill he'd taught her and all the love that filled her heart. "Am I really going to be your wife?"

"Really. Irrevocably. Eternally." He punctuated each promise with a bone-melting kiss.

"I want a houseful of children with silver-gray eyes and devastating dimples." She stroked her hands down his back.

"And pure, trusting hearts and romantic dreams," he agreed, trailing his lips down the hollow between her breasts.

Sammy's breath caught in her throat when Rem turned his head, nuzzled the warm curve of her breast, and simultaneously caressed her thighs with slow, tingling strokes of his hand. He shifted again, drew her achingly taut nipple into his mouth, and Sammy had to bite her lip to stifle her cry of pleasure.

"So sweet," he breathed. "So extraordinarily beautiful." He moved to her other breast, his own breathing ragged, tugging lightly at the crest until he felt Sammy shift restlessly beneath him. "Yes, darling," he replied as if she'd spoken. Ardently, he enveloped her nipple, bathed it with his tongue, while his hands urged her thighs to part, opened her to his touch.

He shuddered when he found her, so satiny wet he had to grit his teeth against the climax threatening to erupt in his loins. He entered her with his fingers, feeling her inner muscles clench around him, then expand in wondrous welcome.

A soft cry escaped Sammy's mouth, and Rem lifted his head, covered her lips with his, and drank the muted cry into himself. "Move against my fingers," he breathed. "I want to feel you."

Sammy arched, her nails digging into Rem's back at the burst of pleasure his deeper penetration brought. He withdrew, then glided forward again, beginning a motion Sammy's body understood. Of its own accord, her hips began to move in conjunction with his fingers, her thighs parting to his possession. With each motion of his hand, she became more abandoned, undulating, tightening, desperate to hold him longer, deeper inside her.

"God," Rem rasped, withdrawing his fingers and rising to his knees. "I want you every way there is ... all at once." He cupped her bottom, lifting her to his seeking mouth. "I need to know your taste again."

Writhing in his arms, Sammy pressed her fist to her mouth, frantically trying to silence a scream. Her entire body was on fire, and Rem's tongue was stoking the flames so high she wondered if she'd survive. He took her to the tantalizing brink of sensation, her muscles taut, poised, frantic for release.

Then he stopped.

"No!" Wildly, she reached for him. "Rem ... don't."

"I won't. Never." He came down over her, wrapped her legs around his waist with shaking hands. "Open your eyes, love. I want to watch you." With one erotic motion of his hips, he penetrated her softness. "Now." Even as he spoke, she began convulsing in his arms. "Go ahead and scream," he whispered, covering her mouth with his. "Samantha ..." The last was a harsh groan into her open mouth, his powerful body shuddering with unbearable pleasure. "God, Samantha."

He matched each spasm of her body with his own, pouring into her with more emotion than he ever knew he possessed, drinking in her cries of pleasure and giving her his.

So this was peace.

"I love you so much, Rem." Sammy's breathing, her words, were uneven, her body still quivering with magical aftershocks.

"You make me whole," he murmured, his face buried in her hair, his body buried inside hers. "And I love you more than all your dreams combined."

"Do you think anyone heard us?"

Rem grinned, happiness suddenly inundating every dark corner of his newly awakened soul. Rolling to one side, he clasped Sammy tightly to him. "I'm sure no one heard us, imp. I myself drank in all your exquisite little cries of passion."

Sammy smiled against his chest. "Does that mean I pleased you, my lord rake?"

"You nearly killed me, my lady."

Leaning back, Sammy chewed her lip in mock dismay. "Are you implying you're already spent?" She sighed. "'Tis a pity. I had exhilarating plans for the remainder of the night." Seductively, she reached down to caress his length, feeling him harden instantly at her touch. "You see, I have yet to explore you, my lord. You've given me such intriguing possibilities to contemplate; ways that I might learn your body as you learned mine ... with my hands, my mouth." Her fingers paused, hovered. "But if you're too tired, I'll understand ..."

Sammy laughed softly as Rem seized her wrist, dragging her hand back to his throbbing body and showing her without words that he was, in fact, quite revived.

"I was going to find you in the morning, before I left Allonshire," Rem murmured, absently stroking the sable waterfall of Sammy's hair, which cascaded across his chest.

"Well, now you don't have to. I'm right here." Sammy closed her eyes, curled closer against Rem's powerful body. "Moreover, the morning would have been infinitely unsatisfactory. Why, all we could do was talk … and probably not even in private. Whereas tonight …" She sighed contentedly.

A deep chuckle rumbled in Rem's chest. "Once wed, am I to expect my poor body to be repeatedly ravished by my innocent bride, then?"

"I'm afraid so, my lord. I find myself becoming quite addicted to your extraordinary skill and stamina. Do you mind very much?"

"I'll adapt." He caressed the smooth slope of her back. "With astounding ease, in fact." Abruptly, he rose onto his elbow and twisted around to gaze soberly down into Sammy's face. "I love you, imp. You've given me joy and laughter and enough love to heal wounds I always believed fatal. I want to give you the world, with all the magic you believe it holds … to be every bit your hero." Rem stroked his knuckles across her cheek. "Dawn will be here in an hour. We need to talk."

Sammy regarded him with solemn understanding. "You're going to share all of yourself with me, aren't you? To tell me whatever it is you've been keeping from me?"

"This information has been undisclosed to anyone prior to tonight. To divulge who I am, what I do, could endanger countries, lives." Rem shook his head, negating the frightened widening of Sammy's eyes. "I'm not saying this to frighten you, imp. I'm just explaining why I've kept myself from you and why it's crucial that you understand the highly confidential nature of what I'm about to disclose."

"All right," Sammy whispered. "I won't tell a soul."

"I know you won't." A tender smile touched his lips. "I trust you with my life," he added, intentionally repeating the very words she'd used to him. "I work, not only for the Admiralty, but for the Crown. Since they approached me a decade ago, I've taken on numerous inflammatory missions, some on English soil, some abroad, all of which, if not successfully completed, could have meant disaster for our country."

"Oh my God." Reflexively, Sammy clutched Rem's arms. "You're telling me you're a spy."

"I'm telling you I've had the opportunity to preserve England's strength and to right some very ugly inequities, during both war and peacetime."

Sammy's mind was racing. "During our recent war with America …?"

"I moved among our fleet, assessing strengths, recommending tactics. On other occasions I performed a similar role in Europe."

"Europe? I don't understand. Napoleon's navy is no longer a threat."

"But Napoleon himself is." Rem's jaw set. "Was," he amended. "I've alerted Wellington to Napoleon's strategy for his recent insurrection. In short time, Bonaparte's reign will end … this time for good."

"My head is spinning," Sammy whispered.

Gently, Rem ruffled her hair, trying to soften the impact. "Do I surpass even your Gothic novels?"

"Rem." Sammy pushed herself to a sitting position. "My novels are inventions of the mind. This is real … and dangerous." She swallowed. "I'm afraid."

"Don't be." He gathered her against him. "I'm completing my final mission. Once it has been resolved, I plan to resign."

"Because of me?" Sammy blinked back tears.

"Until now, my life didn't matter. Now it does."

"I should be noble, insist that you continue to serve England as brilliantly as you obviously have been." Sammy's voice quivered. "I can't. I love you too much. I can't lose you."

"You'll never lose me, imp. Never." He raised her chin, kissed her damp cheeks. "Don't cry." His dimple flashed. "Not unless your tears are spawned by passion or pleasure."

"Oh Rem." She flung her arms around his neck. "I'll fill your life with so much love … I swear you'll never regret your decision."

Fiercely, he held her warm, soft body in his arms. "Ah, imp, from the moment you smiled up at me from that seedy counter in Boydry's, there was no decision to make. I was yours, body and soul … even if I was too dull-witted to recognize it. The past is over, and I'm more than ready to let it go."

Sammy drew back, drying her eyes. "You said something about a final mission. It involves the missing ships, doesn't it?"

"Your novels have stood you in good stead," he teased softly. "Yes."

"And that's why you began visiting me, taking me to Hatchard's, dancing with me at Almack's—you thought I might know something. Why? Because of Barrett Shipping; because I'm Drake's sister?"

"Yes. But you made quick work of that plan. Once I tasted your sweet, beautiful mouth, I was lost."

Sammy sat back on her heels. "I asked you this the other night at Boydry's. I'm asking again. Does your investigation include Drake?"

"It didn't then. It does now." He silenced her protest, placing a forefinger across her lips. "I've elicited your brother's help in exposing the culprits."

"You've …" Sammy's eyes widened. "Does that mean you told Drake who you are?"

"Yes. I didn't give him all the details I just gave you, but I did tell him I'm an agent of the Crown. I also disclosed the specifics of this particular mission. He is being tremendously helpful."

"Do you know who's responsible for the sinkings, and why?"

"We know several of the offenders and their motives."

"Is Viscount Goddfrey one of them?"

Rem gave her a quizzical look. "That's the second time you've brought Goddfrey's name up. Are your suspicions based solely on the conversation you overheard at Almack's regarding Goddfrey's disappearance?"

Sammy fingered the bedcovers uneasily.

"What aren't you telling me, imp?"

"Well, 'tis true I overheard Stephen and Lord Keefe discussing Viscount Goddfrey's disappearance, expressing their concern over the viscount's vast number of lost vessels and depleted fortune ... plus the increased dangers of sailing in British waters. But I was privy to another conversation which I haven't had occasion to mention to you."

"In other words, I'm going to throttle you when I hear these details. Go ahead."

"Well, I couldn't clear my mind of what Stephen and Lord Keefe had said. I kept worrying about the effect these perils could have on Drake. So ..." Sammy chewed her lip, stalling as she pondered Rem's reaction.

"Samantha ..."

"I did a little investigating of my own," she blurted out at last. "The morning after the Almack's ball I slipped away at dawn and made my way to the docks, where I waited and listened."

"You visited the docks at dawn ... alone." Rem inhaled sharply. "Surely someone must have recognized you as Drake's sister and demanded that you return home?"

"I'm sure I was spotted, but I don't believe I was recognized." Sammy steeled herself for the explosion. "I was garbed in one of our gardener's clothes."

"Hell and damnation," Rem ground out, his teeth clenched to stifle the outburst that would doubtlessly awaken the whole household. "Am I going to have to tie you up in Gresham's sitting room once we're wed, to prevent you from darting about on these impulsive excursions of yours? The London docks, Shadwell … what next?"

"I was terrified for Drake. What if he'd been captaining one of those missing ships? I went to the docks to protect him, just as I went to Shadwell to protect you."

"Samantha." Rem framed her face. "Are there any other little jaunts you've taken that I should know about?"

"No."

"Then in the future, would you mind sharing your worries with me and allowing me to take the risks?"

"Unless they threaten you, my lord. Then I'll do whatever I must to shield you."

All Rem's fury dissipated at the earnest honesty of her reply. "I suppose I cannot argue with that," he murmured tenderly. "I'll have to instead make certain that I'm never again in danger."

Sammy smiled. "That would be ideal."

"So … in your travels along the Thames, you overheard a conversation about Goddfrey that prompted your suspicions?"

"Yes." Sammy relayed the conversation of the two dock workers. "So I thought, having never met the viscount, that his personal circumstances might have been enough to provoke the crimes. His family relationships were strained, he'd run off without a word. It further occurred to me that, even if Goddfrey weren't responsible, perhaps he was the target of the sinkings, and that all the other attacks were merely being done to cast aspersion elsewhere." She frowned. "Now that I say it aloud, I realize how utterly ludicrous it sounds. Perhaps I have read too many novels."

"Your reasoning is not ludicrous." Rem smoothed the pucker from between her brows. "And there is truth to it—Goddfrey was in trouble. He was being blackmailed by an unscrupulous scoundrel who, at one point, I suspected was involved in the sinkings. He wasn't. He also won't be extorting money from anyone again."

The triumphant gleam in Rem's eye struck Sammy instantly. "You apprehended him yourself, didn't you?" she guessed.

"With some help." Rem grinned. "Remember that meeting at Annie's you accompanied me to, uninvited? That's what we were discussing. 'Tis also why I had to feign financial difficulties … even to you. Although I must admit I found your compassion more moving than I can say."

"You were setting the stage for this scoundrel's downfall!"

"Precisely."

Rem's earlier revelation precipitated another question. "With some help," Sammy repeated. "Is Boyd working with you as well?"

"Boyd will be offering his resignation along with mine. And, despite our long-term friendship, I suspect I have little to do with his decision."

"Cynthia." Sammy's eyes twinkled.

"Indeed."

"They'll be wonderful together. I know it." A pause. "Rem, if Lord Goddfrey isn't involved, then who is?"

Rem's features hardened to granite. "We haven't yet discovered all the conspirators. The identity of at least one is still an enigma to us. We do know that his two other partners have employed a privateer to attack the vessels … and we have a thorough description of that pirate."

"Two other partners? Do you know who they are?"

"We do." Rem's probing gaze met Sammy's. "They are Arthur Summerson the merchant and the Viscount Anders."

A harsh gasp escaped Sammy's lips. "Stephen?"

"Stephen."

"Dear Lord." Sammy pressed her palms to her cheeks. "You're certain?"

"Very certain. Why do you think I didn't want you anywhere near the bastard?"

"I assumed it was purely jealousy, because Stephen wanted me." Sammy's eyes widened, not with dismay, but with realization. "Was his interest in me all a sham?"

"Unfortunately, no. The scum really does want you. Which makes me want to kill him all the more. I nearly did so that night at Devonshire House when you interrupted his little tête-à-tête with Summerson."

"You were there?"

"A mere fifteen feet away, imp, in the bushes to your right. I followed Anders from Devonshire House. I'd been observing him all night—all week, in fact—trying to fathom his inexplicable and sudden affluence. For a man my sources claimed was nearly destitute, he seemed to be affording some rather extravagant diversions: a high-stake game of whist at which he cheerfully lost thousands of pounds, and an enormously expensive necklace."

"The one he gave me."

"Yes. So, when I saw how jumpy he was at the Devonshire ball, I became curious. I followed him across the grounds and hid in the bushes while he met with Summerson … which is where I was when you came looking for me. As for Summerson, that was a revelation. Until that moment I had no idea he was involved. Speaking of Summerson"— Rem took Sammy's hands in his—"upon your intrusion, he behaved rather oddly. He watched you scurry off and threatened to go after you, muttering something about this being the second meeting of theirs you'd interrupted and about your looking familiar—and I don't mean as Drake Barrett's sister. Think, imp, do you know what he meant?"

Sammy lowered her eyes. "I know exactly what he meant … and it will explain to you why I 'scurried off,' as you put it. The morning I visited Stephen's office—do you recall; it was the day you and Boyd came upon Cynthia and me at the docks …?"

"I remember. The morning after Anders's ship went down."

She nodded. "When I first entered Stephen's office, another man was there talking with him. I had the distinct feeling I'd interrupted a heated discussion."

"Arthur Summerson."

"Yes. Even then Mr. Summerson was uncomfortable around me, staring at me as if we'd met before. I convinced him it was because I was a Barrett."

"But it wasn't?"

"No. The dawn I snooped around the wharf in my gardener's clothes, I accidently stumbled upon Lord Hartley deeply immersed in conversation with another gentleman. I knew the marquis would recognize me, boy's clothes or not; he's known me since birth. So I darted between the warehouses and made my escape. I eluded Lord Hartley's detection … but not his companion's. At the time, I had no idea who that other gentleman was … until Stephen formally introduced us in his office. It was Arthur Summerson. Evidently, although he'd only spied me beside that warehouse for an instant, he remembered my face."

"What you're telling me makes me twice as grateful that I got you away from London when I did—before Summerson could hurt you."

"Do you really believe he would?"

"He's a murderer, Samantha. A murderer, a thief, and an immoral animal. If he had the slightest glimmer of a notion that you were suspicious of him, he wouldn't hesitate to silence you, permanently. But that's never going to happen." Rem's brows darted together. "Why would Summerson be meeting Hartley at dawn?"

"Oh, Rem, no." Following Rem's line of thought, Sammy shook her head emphatically. "Lord Hartley is the kindest, most gentle man I've ever known. He and my father fox-hunted together, made their fortunes together, spent holidays together. He would never commit the kind of crimes you're suggesting."

"Every man is capable of committing crimes if pushed far enough, imp. True, some motives are uglier than others. But the fact remains that, until I seize every man involved in this conspiracy, no one is above suspicion."

Sammy stared at Rem for a long moment. "I can see now why the Admiralty depends upon you. You do battle with a clear head and a brilliant, logical mind."

"If you're implying that I'm brutally unfeeling, you're right," Rem replied grimly. "But remember, imp, until you came into my life, emotions were unneeded. I'm firmly convinced I was heartless."

"You're so wrong." Sammy stroked his jaw. "That's not what I meant at all. To the contrary, I'm impressed by your ability to remain unbiased. As for being heartless, your heart is—has always been—extraordinary. The problem was, it belonged to the world, leaving no part of it for yourself. Now, it belongs to me. But fear not, my lord, I intend to take excellent care of it … forever."

Reverently, Rem pressed Sammy's palms to his lips, first one, then the other. "I'm relieved to learn that my heart is in the finest, most loving of hands."

Sammy swallowed past the lump in her throat. "Now … tell me everything. We must resolve this case in record time so I can begin ministering to your poor, neglected heart."

"*We* are not going to resolve anything, imp. *I* am."

"I was just speaking figuratively," Sammy amended at once. "What is the reason for Stephen's and Mr. Summerson's hateful scheme? Who is the mysterious privateer, and how do you plan to expose him? How many others do you suspect are involved, and what is Drake doing to assist you in your search?"

"Another bevy of questions. I should be accustomed to them by now, shouldn't I?" Rem teased tenderly. Wrapping Sammy's hands tightly in his, he told her everything: beginning with the insurance money Anders and Summerson would procure from their fictional losses, progressing to Captain Towers and the conversation he'd overheard about the conspirators' mysterious partner, and culminating with the odious fact that, not only was Towers' ship annihilated, but his men sold as slaves, earning additional profits for Summerson and his accomplices.

"You and Boyd have no idea who this horrid pirate is?" Sammy asked, white-faced.

"I have a detailed description of him. Now he must be unearthed … which is where your brother comes in." Seeing Sammy's puzzled look, Rem continued. "Drake is giving me the access I need to the docks. As of tomorrow night, I'll be assuming the role of Barrett Shipping's night watchman, strolling the docks from Barrett to Anders Shipping and back. The moment that privateer shows his face, I'll grab him. At which point I'll convince the bastard to summon his cohorts. *All* of them. That should nicely resolve the question of how many men are involved, *and* force them all to surface. The rest should be easy."

"Easy? To confront a roomful of dangerous—probably armed— men? Rem …"

"I won't be alone. Boyd will be there to back me up, along with several other reliable men—men I've worked with for years. I'll be safe, imp." He smiled. "And then I'll be yours."

"All these years I've been a child and you've been putting your life on the line for England," Sammy whispered incredulously, the full impact of Rem's position hitting home. "No wonder you found me so foolishly amusing."

"You, my darling, are my savior, my heart and my future … all of which are far from foolish. If you had any idea how much I need you, you would understand how desperate I am to keep you safe." Rem framed her face between his palms. "Promise me you'll do as I asked. Let me take the risks. I'll have Boyd bring you word of my progress each time he visits Cynthia. And the moment I've apprehended the culprits, I'll return to Allonshire … and you. Promise me."

Sammy nodded. "I promise. I'll do just what I vowed." Silently, she recalled that vow: to share her worries with Rem and allow him to take the risks.

Unless the danger threatened him.

At which point, she would act.

TWENTY-ONE

The watchman's stance was infinitely relaxed.

His gaze, however, was that of a tiger stalking its prey.

Wary, acute, it enveloped the entire wharf, end to end, absorbing all that was visible, plus a good deal of that which was concealed.

Three days into his vigil, Rem had witnessed more two-bit crimes than he cared to recall: wharf rats passing stolen goods from hand to hand, pickpockets slithering up and down the docks counting their night's spoils, smugglers carrying bags of tobacco from anchored ships. More than once Rem had found himself lunging forward to seize them, and had to forcibly exert self-restraint, reminding himself that he was a mere night watchman, not a Bow Street runner.

And still there was no sign of the privateer.

Where the hell was the bastard? True, he might already have returned to sea, but Rem's instincts said not. He knew the minds of these sea wolves. Having just returned, jubilant, from his capture of the *Bountiful,* and with no notion that Captain Towers was alive and restored to England, the pirate would doubtlessly be enjoying the funds Summerson had already paid him, while plotting to collect more before leaving English soil on his next pillage.

No, Rem was willing to bet the culprit was still in London.

And damn him to hell, he'd be found.

Flexing his muscles, Rem began the return trek to Barrett Shipping, scrutinizing all the shrouded corners of the docks that, as experience had taught him, were meeting points for scum.

He was just rounding Anders Shipping, when a shadowy figure slipped through the narrow alley leading to the warehouse. Quickly scrutinizing the area, Rem ascertained that he was undetected, then walked soundlessly in pursuit. Flattening himself against the warehouse wall, he inched along, praying he wasn't wasting his time stalking a street urchin whose intentions were merely to steal a shilling for food.

"That's the last payment for now. You'll get more after you've completed your next task."

The muffled words obliterated Rem's doubts. The voice belonged to Arthur Summerson.

Heart pounding in anticipation, Rem waited.

"A pleasure t' do business with ye." The answer was uttered in a low, harsh rasp: Towers' exact description of the privateer's voice.

"I'll say farewell now, Fuller. You'll be taking to sea by week's end."

Fuller.

Rem slid his hand into his pocket until it closed around his pistol's cool handle. Gripping it tightly, he silently maneuvered back to his original path, nonchalantly resuming his watchman's rounds.

A moment later Summerson emerged from the path beside the warehouse, walking right by Rem and disappearing into the night. In the aftermath of his fading footsteps, a husky form followed suit, striding into the open and moving directly past the innocuous-looking watchman.

In the blink of an eye Rem's arm was around the privateer's throat.

"What the—"

"Listen to me, Fuller," Rem instructed in a cold-blooded whisper. "You have two choices. You can either come quietly with me to a private place where we can talk, or I can break your neck here and now and throw your body into the Thames as food for the gulls. It's up to you."

"I'll … come …" Fuller wheezed.

"Good." Rem extracted his pistol, shoving it in Fuller's ribs. "Now turn around and start walking. If any passerby should spot us, let's just pretend we're having the friendliest of strolls together. If you choose to elaborate on that explanation, I'll have no compunction about putting a bullet in your back. Is that also clear?"

"Who th' hell are ye?"

"I asked if that was clear, Fuller?" Rem dug the pistol deeper into the pirate's back.

"Damn." Fuller winced. "All right. Ye win."

"Fine. Let's go."

Ten minutes later Rem thrust Fuller into Barrett Shipping's darkened warehouse and locked the door behind them.

"We have a great deal to discuss." Rem's fingers tightened on his pistol. "Sit down … where I can see you."

"Ye can't see anything in 'ere."

"You'd be surprised. For example, I can see your hand creeping toward your boot. Continue," Rem ordered, when Fuller halted. "Then toss your knife onto the floor … along with any other weapons you have." Rem lowered his gun a tad. "Let me give you some advice, Fuller. Even if I were unarmed, you'd be dead less than a minute after coming at me. Therefore, why not spare your life and my energy? Forego any idea you have of slitting my throat. It's not going to happen. And maybe, just maybe, if you tell me what I want to know, I might let you live."

Hearing the chilling resolve in Rem's tone, Fuller swallowed audibly and complied, sending two ugly knives clattering to the warehouse floor. He didn't sit, but stood warily against the wall.

"Good." Rem scooped up the weapons, tucking them, and his pistol, into his pocket, keeping his hand securely beside them. "Now,

ANDREA KANE

I want to know everything about the assignments you've been receiving from Mr. Summerson."

Fuller blanched. "Who are ye?" he whispered again. "What do ye want?"

"Fortunately for you, you're a very small part of what I want, else I would have shot you down days ago. Now, tell me about Summerson, his partners, and your role in sinking their ships."

"I don't know what yer talkin' about."

"I'm not certain you understand me, Fuller." Rem drew out one of the pirate's knives, fingering the blade thoughtfully. "I'm not a patient man. In fact, my patience is rapidly ebbing. If you continue to avoid my question, I'll cease being a gentleman and resort to other methods of persuasion." The blade glinted ominously.

"All right! I do work fer Summerson now and again. And I do 'elp myself to a bit of 'is cargo."

"His cargo? Don't you mean his men?"

"I don't 'urt his bloody men."

"You just sell them." Rem advanced menacingly at the pirate. "Who do you work for?"

"Ye said it yerself. Summerson."

"Who else?"

"I don't know."

In an instant the knife was a hair's breadth from Fuller's throat. "Don't insult me, Fuller. I get angry when I'm insulted."

"I'm not lyin' t' ye. I've 'eard 'im mention 'is partners ... but never by name."

"You're trying to tell me the only one you've ever seen, the only one you get your money from, is Summerson?"

"That's right." Fuller nodded, wincing as the blade nicked his skin. "I meet 'im at the same spot each time. 'E pays me. That's all."

"The same spot? Funny, you met him in the open a few days ago to collect your money after capturing the *Bountiful*."

Sweat trickled down Fuller's cheek, soaked into his beard. "I 'ad no choice. I needed my money and I was late gettin' back. We were supposed t' meet the night before. I couldn't make it."

"Why not?"

"Th-The weather …"

"The skies were fair all week long."

"We were f-farther out than I expected …"

"More likely you were searching the waters for the crewman who escaped before you could sell him—Captain Towers. Tell me, were you relieved not to find him? Did you assume he'd perished in the Channel?"

Fuller's eyes were wide with fear. "I didn't 'urt 'im. 'E disappeared. If 'e drowned, it's not my fault."

"Then you'll be pleased to know he didn't drown. He's alive, well, and restored to England. Isn't that splendid news, Fuller?"

"Ye're lyin'," the privateer whispered.

"I must say, Captain Towers' description of you was remarkably accurate. Good enough to hang you the moment I turn you in to Bow Street."

"Is that what ye're gonna do t' me?"

"As I said, if I wanted you dead, you'd be buried by now. No, what I want from you, Fuller, is a favor."

"A favor?"

"Yes. Send a message to Summerson. Make it sound like you're running completely amok, frenzied with worry. Tell him you've all been found out—you, him, and his partners. Tell him you received an ominous missive, threatening to expose all of you and send you to Newgate. Convince Summerson that an immediate, urgent meeting must be called for tomorrow night. Make sure you tell him it's crucial for everyone involved to be present, that one of you is actually an informant. Demand to see all his partners face-to-face. Make your writing as unstable as possible, so that even if Summerson is unconvinced he's been found out, he'll do as you ask simply to calm you down and keep you from doing something foolish."

"Where do ye want us t' meet?"

"At Anders Shipping, half after four tomorrow … in the wee hours just before dawn."

"I guess ye plan t' be there."

"Another word of advice, Fuller." Rem lifted the knife, flattening his palms against the wall on either side of Fuller's head. "Don't even consider alerting anyone or fleeing prior to the meeting. In either case, I'll hunt you down within the day and kill you where you stand. My men are everywhere; they know what you eat, where you sleep, who you talk to. There's no escaping me. So don't try." Rem leaned closer, his eyes boring into Fuller's scarred face. "I assume I've made myself clear."

A shaky nod.

"Good."

"What about after the meetin'? Then what are ye gonna do with me?"

"I repeat, you're insignificant in this matter. If you do as you're told, I'll throw you back to sea to rejoin the slime from whence you came. However," Rem gripped Fuller's shirt, "I'd better never hear about you pilfering another ship. Understood?"

"I don't 'ave a choice, do I?"

"No. You don't." Rem straightened. "Now, I'll produce a quill and paper and we can begin composing that letter. It's been a pleasure chatting with you, Fuller."

"Did you have a good time? Or need I ask?" Sammy placed her current novel face down on the bed, grinning at the telltale flush staining Cynthia's cheeks.

"Yes. Thank you for allowing me the day off. Boyd and I really needed to talk. We rode for hours." Cynthia hovered in the doorway. "I told him, Samantha."

"And?"

"And he believed me—truly believed me. He was enraged ... murderous, in fact. Not at me, as I'd feared, but at the nobleman who'd forced himself on me. Had I not begged Boyd to let it go, I believe he would have ridden to Surrey and killed the man himself. To defend my honor. Me, Samantha. Boyd actually feels I'm worthy of defending." There was wonder in Cynthia's eyes.

"Now why doesn't that surprise me?"

A genuine laugh erupted from Cynthia's chest. "You may gloat as much as you wish. You were right—and thank God for it."

"Did you discuss the aftermath of your horrid experience?"

"If you mean, did I tell Boyd about my fear of intimacy, yes. Do you know what he said?"

"No. What?"

Cynthia sank down on the bed beside Samantha, clutching her friend's hands. "He said that it was natural for me to be afraid since, after all, it would be my first time. I reminded him that it was far from my first encounter, and he disagreed adamantly, saying that I'd been violated and used ... but never made love to. So, in all ways that mattered, I was a virgin. Samantha, he looked into my eyes and told me he was determined to be the first, the only man, who would ever make love to me. He told me he loved me and that he would wait as long as it took—forever, if need be—for me to return his love. And that once I did, he intended to marry me and spend the rest of his life showing me how special I was."

"Oh, Cynthia, I'm so happy for you." Sammy flung her arms around her friend's neck.

"He wants to invest in a coffeehouse, to close Boydry's," Cynthia murmured in a dazed tone. "He said that Boydry's is tied to a past he no longer needs, whatever that means."

Sammy blinked back tears, knowing precisely what Boyd meant. "What a marvelous idea. The two of you can create the most splendid coffeehouse in all of London ... Hayword's, in honor of the new Mr. and Mrs. Hayword."

"Samantha ..." Cynthia drew back. "I haven't said—"

"But you will." Sammy dashed away her tears. "I shall miss you, of course. You are quite splendid at arranging hair. Ah, well. I'll just have to wear my unruly tresses in a simple style until a new lady's maid can be engaged. As for helping me dress, I'm certain Remington will be more than willing to take on my gowns' troublesome buttons ... permanently, in fact. So you can feel free to marry the man you love. My only condition is that you accompany Boyd to Gresham on all his visits ... which, from what I understand, number two or three times a week. Then, on alternate days, we shall visit you. You see, I have no qualms about relinquishing you as my lady's maid, but I could never bear losing you as my friend." Sammy's voice quavered. "I love you, Cynthia. And so does Boyd. He's going to make you ecstatically happy."

Abruptly, Cynthia stood, averting her head and dabbing discreetly at her eyes. "I believe our friendship has taken an unexpected turn. Rather than hardening you to the realities of life, I fear I've become as sentimental and softhearted as you. I weep, I glow like an innocent schoolgirl, I allow myself to fall in love." She turned to meet Sammy's gaze. "Thank you."

Sammy didn't trust herself to speak. She merely nodded, her heart in her eyes.

"Oh, before I succumb to an entirely inappropriate emotional display ..." Cynthia reached into her pocket and extracted a folded slip of paper. "Boyd asked me to give you this. It's from Lord Gresham."

"Oh, thank you!" Sammy bolted to her feet and snatched the note.

"I have some tasks to tend to," Cynthia added tactfully. "Summon me when you need me."

Already immersed in her reading, Sammy didn't reply. Nor, knowing her friend, did Cynthia expect that she would. Smiling, Cynthia closed the door behind her.

Sammy dropped back onto the bed, frowning. This note was different from its two predecessors. Rem's other letters had spoken of his love, of the ache he felt being apart from her, and of the frustration he was encountering as a result of his unsuccessful endeavor, which Sammy understood was a cryptic way of stating that his disguise at Barrett Shipping had, as of yet, yielded no results.

This missive, however, was terse, stark, impersonal—it was Remington Worth, special agent to the Crown:

The moment of reckoning is upon us. I'll come for you tomorrow night. Until then, remain securely at Allonshire with your family.

Thoughtfully, Sammy read between the lines. Then, refolding the note, she began to pack.

Anders Shipping was deserted.

The lone figure unlocked the door and entered, lighting an oil lamp in preparation.

He'd scarcely completed his task when the door hinge squeaked, and another silhouette stepped inside. "Anders? Is that you?"

"Of course it's me!" the viscount snapped, turning down the lamp as low as he could without casting the room in total darkness. "Who the hell were you expecting?"

The Marquis of Hartley rubbed the back of his neck with a shaking hand. "Summerson, perhaps."

"Summerson will be here any minute. I came early to unlock the door."

"Do you know what this is about?"

"I only know what you do: Summerson got a frantic note from his privateer friend. As a result, he ordered us to meet here at half after four to find out if Fuller is really being threatened by someone who can expose the whole lot of us, or if it's just his way of bleeding us for more money."

"What if someone really has discovered our plan?" Hartley began to pace. "God, I wish I'd never agreed to this. I should have lost my company rather than keep it alive with stolen funds."

"It's a little late for regrets, isn't it, Hartley?" Summerson strode into the room. "Now stop this nonsense. We have enough to contend with—we certainly don't need one of your attacks of conscience."

Hartley had no chance to reply. The door banged open and Fuller entered, leaving the door ajar. "Are ye all 'ere?"

"Yes. We're all here," Summerson snapped. "Now, what's this about? Who wrote you that letter?"

"That's what I want t' know." Fuller scratched his beard. "It could be one of ye, now couldn't it?"

"That's preposterous!" Hartley burst out. "Why would we thwart our own scheme? If one of us is imprisoned for theft, we'd all be close behind!"

"Maybe ye was gettin' cold feet."

"Or maybe you were getting greedy." Anders whipped out a pistol. "Isn't that truly the case, Fuller?"

Fuller's eyes bulged. "I thought ye said they were all soft but ye, Summerson. Ye told me they'd never even 'eld a weapon in their 'ands!"

"Shut up, Fuller," Summerson ordered.

"How interesting." Anders tossed Summerson a look. "Pray continue, Fuller." He cocked his pistol. "What else did Mr. Summerson tell you?"

"Nothin'."

"Why don't I believe you? Why do I suddenly get the distinct feeling something is transpiring that I know nothing about? Tell me, Fuller," Anders advanced toward the pirate, "do you and Summerson speak of us often?"

"I didn't even know 'ow many of ye there was until now."

"Well, now you not only know how many of us there are, but you've seen our faces. Convenient, wouldn't you say? Now the truth, Fuller—there is no letter, right? There's only your greedy little mind ... and perhaps a special arrangement with Mr. Summerson here?"

"Cease this absurdity, Anders!" Summerson fired out. "I assure you, there is no conspiracy between me and this privateer."

"Fine. Then why don't I correct his false impression of our ineptness by blowing off his head?"

In a flash Fuller's knife was out, whizzing through the air and striking Anders in the arm. The pistol thudded to the floor.

"I've 'ad enough of this, Summerson!" Fuller rasped over Anders's cry of pain. "Keep yer bloody money—I don't want it! Ye'll have to find someone else to peddle yer men in the West Indies. I'm through workin' with ye—ye're all crazy!"

"Shut up, Fuller!" Summerson thundered.

"Peddle our men?" Hartley managed, wrapping his handkerchief around Anders's bloody wound. "What men? What does he mean, Summerson?"

"I mean yer friend 'ere 'as been cheatin' ye," Fuller taunted, his eyes blazing. "Ye really think 'e's been satisfied with the meager sums ye've been collectin' on the cargo that ain't there? Ye believe 'e 'ad me attack the ships that wasn't yers just to throw everyone off-track? Think again, ye fools! The bastard's been paying me extra to sell the sailors from those ships … made a pretty penny, too. Enough fer me t' take more than my 'alf without 'is knowing it. 'Ow's that, Summerson? Ye're being cheated, too!"

Summerson's pistol emerged in a glint of steel. A shot rang out. Fuller gasped and fell to the floor, dead.

"Dear God!" Hartley had gone white. "Are you mad? You just murdered a man!"

"Obviously human life isn't a priority of our *partner's*." Anders spat out the word, blood seeping slowly through his handkerchief. "Nor is loyalty." A vein throbbed at his temple. "You swindled us, you filthy son of a bitch."

"Anders, do you realize this means we're implicated as well?" Hartley interrupted, his breathing irregular. "Condemning those

sailors to lives of bondage is now our crime as well. We could hang—
" He broke off, unsteadily loosening his cravat.

"Neither of you would have had the backbone to do what I
did. You were both content believing Atlantis was some two-bit
insurance fraud." Summerson stepped unconcernedly over Fuller's
lifeless body. "Look at you." He gestured toward Hartley. "You're a
quivering nervous wreck, old man; more trouble than you're worth.
And you," he pivoted toward Anders. "You're the lowest form of
hypocrite. You want it all—but you don't want to dirty your aristocratic hands. So I did it." Summerson threw Anders a contemptuous look. "I did the work. I took the risk. All that Atlantis truly
signified was through my doing, my plan. So why the hell shouldn't
I keep the money for myself? Besides, you'd only squander it away
on your weaknesses—gambling and women. You're of little more
use than Hartley."

With a low oath, Anders bent, his uninjured arm reaching for
his pistol.

"Don't touch it," Summerson commanded, leveling his gun on
Anders. "I've killed once. There's nothing to stop me from doing it
agai—"

A shot exploded through the room, striking Summerson's weapon and sending it crashing to the floor.

"You're wrong, Summerson. There *is* something to stop you
from doing it again. Me."

Rem loomed in the doorway, a rigid, uncompromising pred-
ator, his own flintlock cocked and ready. "You heartless bastard—
you're going to experience, firsthand, exactly what those enslaved
sailors did. As of now, you're imprisoned for the rest of your life."
Rem stalked Summerson, his expression lethal. "Unless of course the
magistrate elects to hang you by the neck. Which would befit another of your crimes—the one you just committed here." Rem gestured
toward Fuller's inert body. "Right before my eyes."

"Gresham ..." It was Anders who uttered Rem's name, belatedly reacting to Rem's unexpected intrusion.

"You, Anders, are scum." Rem cast the viscount a venomous look. "For reasons of my own, I'd like to shoot you where you stand. Unfortunately, Summerson just obliterated my grounds for doing so with his admission. If only you'd assisted him and Fuller in peddling those men, I'd have no qualms about ending your wretched life here and now."

"Who do you work for? Who are you really?" the viscount managed, clutching his wound.

"I'm the man who's going to ensure you never steal another penny. You sicken me."

"This wasn't about Samantha then, was it?" Anders realized aloud. "All this time—"

"Don't ever speak Samantha's name again. In fact, don't even think it. If you do, I'll make certain you hang right alongside your conniving merchant partner."

A sharp intake of breath from the Marquis of Hartley made Rem avert his head, raking Hartley with contemptuous eyes. "You are my gravest disappointment. Why, Hartley? Was the money that important?"

"I was losing my company, Gresham," Hartley choked out. "It was all I had—a legacy to pass on to my heirs. How could I face myself if I threw it away? How could I face the *ton*?"

"You're going to have to do both. Only now you not only have a floundering company to explain, but your own reprehensible behavior. You've disgraced your family name far more unforgivably than mere poverty ever could."

A lightning-quick motion caught Rem's eye, but he merely glanced up, unruffled, as Summerson lunged past him en route to the door, desperate to make his escape.

"Where are you headed, Summerson?" Boyd inquired, stepping into the merchant's path and grabbing him, locking an iron forearm around his neck. Holding him securely, Boyd stood patiently while Harris bound Summerson's arms securely with a thick piece of rope.

That task completed, Boyd strode toward Anders.

"I'm wounded," the viscount whimpered pleadingly, pointing to the blood seeping through his makeshift bandage.

"A pity." Rem seized Anders's uninjured arm and shoved him at Boyd. "Get him the hell out of here, before I reconsider and kill him. Once for me. And once for Samantha."

"So," Anders muttered with a speculative look over his shoulder, "this does concern your feelings for—"

"Speak her name and you're a dead man." Rem turned his back on Hartley and stalked the viscount, pistol raised.

"Don't bother, Rem." Boyd dragged Anders toward the door. "He isn't worth a bullet."

Rem halted, lowering his arm. "You're right. Take Summerson and Anders to Bow Street. I'll finish up here, then follow with Hartley. Tell Templar to come down and dispose of Fuller's body."

"Done." Boyd propelled Anders out into the night, simultaneously calling instructions to Harris.

Rem watched them go. "As for you, Hartley—" he began.

"Don't move, Gresham." The cold barrel of Hartley's pistol jabbed Rem in the back. "And drop your gun."

Concealing his astonishment, Rem complied. Silently, he chastised himself for underestimating Hartley's precarious state of mind. "Do you plan to shoot me?" he inquired calmly.

"Only if I must." Hartley's voice and hand shook. "I'm an old man, Gresham. I'd never survive Newgate. I don't want to kill you, but I have little to lose at this point." He gave an hysterical laugh. "This is all a horrid dream. I keep waiting to awaken."

"Hartley ..." Rem started to turn.

"Don't!" The hysteria dissipated; the weapon prodded harder, making Rem wince. "You're going to accompany me in my escape,

Gresham. Once I'm free, I'll release you. But if you try to stop me, I'll shoot you."

"No, Lord Hartley, you won't."

Both men's heads snapped around at the sound of the soft feminine voice.

"Samantha!" Rem's pupils dilated in shock. "Lord ... no! What the hell are you doing here? Get out!"

"I'm sorry, Rem. That is something I cannot do." Yanking off her gardener's cap, Sammy walked toward them, weaponless but for her wits.

"Samantha?" Hartley wiped a sleeve across his face. "This doesn't concern you, my dear. You'd best—"

"But it does concern me, my lord. You see, the man you're holding a gun on is the man I love. And I cannot allow you to hurt him. Which, knowing you as long and as well as I do, I cannot believe you would." She paused, inclining her head. "I remember when I was small, my father used to tell me that should I ever require help while he and my brothers were away, I could always summon you, that you were a fine decent man ... a man to be trusted. Do you feel any of those traits apply to you right now, my lord?"

Tears trickled down Hartley's cheeks. "You're a child, Samantha. You don't understand—"

"Yes. I do understand. I followed Stephen here, and I overheard everything. I understand you built ships for Anders Shipping, then, together with Stephen and Mr. Summerson, stocked those vessels with worthless cargo so you could collect the insurance money when the ships were seized. I understand that, in your case, thievery is the sole extent of your crime ... not that I expected otherwise. Most of all, I understand that you must have had an excellent reason for becoming involved in so gruesome a plot."

A sob escaped Hartley's lips. "Hartley Shipping was nearly bankrupt. I forged the records so no one would suspect. I didn't know where to turn ..."

"'Tis often easier to be a child than an adult," Sammy murmured. "In childhood we are told to whom we can turn; as adults we are expected to resolve things on our own. In truth, my lord, that is a dreadful fallacy, for none of us ever stops needing the support of those we love. I'm sorry you had to bear your anguish alone. I'm sorry the terror was so acute that it forced you to take steps you would never otherwise have taken. I don't condone your actions. But I still believe that my father was right. You are, inherently, a fine, decent man. Please don't prove Father and me wrong."

Rem tensed, prepared to make a move, but Sammy shook her head.

"The marquis needs no coercion. He will face his actions willingly, and with the knowledge that it's the only way he'll ever be able to forgive himself. I, in turn, will talk to Drake. Between the two of us, I feel confident that we can offer enough evidence of Lord Hartley's fine character to convince the court to reduce his punishment significantly—enough to effect the necessary retribution while eliminating a term in Newgate. My father would want it that way." A soft smile touched Sammy's lips. "So you see, Lord Hartley, you do have somewhere to turn."

A spasm of emotion crossed Hartley's face. "You were a precious child, Samantha ... a brilliant ray of sunshine and a blessing in your father's life." His voice broke. "You haven't changed. Grayson would be extraordinarily proud." Slowly, the marquis retracted his weapon, extending it, handle first, to Rem.

"Father would be proud of you as well, my lord," Sammy told Hartley as Rem relieved him of his pistol. "The decision you just made was a remarkably courageous one." She lay her hand on the elderly man's arm. "Thank you," she whispered, pained by the lost look on his face. "I'll go home at once and speak with Drake. You should know, however, that my reasons are somewhat self-serving. Remington and I are being married in two months' time. Since my father can be present only in spirit, it would mean a great deal to me if you would attend in Father's stead, see me walk down the aisle on Drake's arm and join with the man I love. Would you do that for me, my lord?"

Hartley straightened his stooped shoulders. "I'd be honored," he replied with as much dignity as he could muster. He inhaled sharply, then headed toward the door. "I'm ready, Gresham."

Rem was still reeling from what he'd just witnessed. "Him? Oh, yes. Bow Street." He glanced dazedly at the gun in his hand, then slowly assessed Sammy in her gardener's apparel. "Is that the customary attire donned by Gothic heroines when unraveling a mystery?"

Sammy's grin was impish. "No, my lord. In that way, I am unique."

"In many ways," Rem muttered, shaking his head. "Tell me, when did you take it upon yourself to come to London?"

"The moment I received your last missive. I realized at once that you needed me."

"I don't recall saying—"

"You didn't have to. My heart simply knew. Just as it knew Lord Hartley wouldn't disappoint me." Sammy caressed Rem's jaw. "I didn't get here a moment too soon."

Rem turned his lips into her palm. "That faith of yours … it's going to be the death of me, imp." His gaze fell to her mouth and his dimple flashed. "I don't know whether to kiss you or throttle you. In fact, I'm not even certain exactly what just happened here."

Sammy gave him a dazzling smile. "I'd much prefer the kiss. As for what happened, that's easy enough to recount. I rescued you, my lord. Just as I promised I would."

EPILOGUE

"Drake, I truly think you're worrying needlessly." The Countess of Gresham handed her brother a brandy and, shifting her current novel off to the side, sank down on the tufted sofa in Gresham's green salon.

"I'm not worrying, Sammy," Drake returned, scowling. "I'm reconsidering. What the hell ever possessed me to involve Barrett Shipping in a business venture?"

"It was a brilliant decision. Lord Hartley could no longer maintain a failing company, so you relieved him of that responsibility. The price he received for the sale of Hartley Shipping was more than enough to both repay his debts and to finance the first of his West Indies excursions. He's determined to recover those poor sailors, and I don't doubt that he will. Now, he is fully pardoned and can put the pieces of his life back together, while you can make Hartley Shipping prosper. It was an ideal purchase."

"Except that I didn't purchase it."

"What difference does that make? Barrett Shipping and Hartley Shipping have now merged and will become the most successful and exceptional shipbuilding firm in all of England."

"With a new name and two men at the helm."

"Drake," Sammy sighed. "I know you detest sharing control of anything with anyone. But you've managed to adapt to marriage. Surely you can adapt to having a business partner? Especially one who is as brilliant and strong-willed as you. Why, you'll be an incomparable team!" Sammy's eyes twinkled. "After all, I doubt anyone could challenge your authority more than Alex does."

"Very amusing," Drake commented dryly. "As far as your description of my partner's brilliance, wouldn't you say you're just the least bit biased?"

"You're right. I am. About both of you. I happen to think you're the two finest, most wonderful men in the world."

The sound of horses' hooves signified an oncoming carriage.

"It appears that the *other* finest man in the world has arrived." Drake tossed off his drink.

With a grin, Sammy rose. "You really like him, don't you? And you respect him, too."

Drake scowled. "I wouldn't have entrusted one of my most valuable assets to him if I didn't."

"Your company?"

"My sister." Drake leaned forward to ruffle Sammy's hair. "Now I'd like to hasten the signing of those final papers. Alex is expecting us all at Allonshire for a celebration dinner, and from what I understand, Gray has completed his latest creative effort: painting a new warehouse sign that reads 'Barrett-Worth Shipping.'"

The salon door swung open, and Sammy was across the room in a flash.

"Hello, imp." Rem caught his wife in his arms and held her to him, still overcome, after three months of marriage, by the exuberant inner beauty of his magnificent bride.

"I missed you." Despite Drake's presence, Sammy twined her arms around her husband's neck, gazing up at him with glowing eyes.

"And I you, sweetheart." Tenderly, Rem kissed her. "I couldn't wait to get back."

"You've been gone three hours," Drake reminded them, going to refill his glass.

Chuckling, Rem lowered Sammy's feet to the floor, taking her hand in his as he crossed the room. "Indulge us. We're newly married."

"I'll try." Drake couldn't stifle a grin. "Were the papers to your liking?"

"To *both* our likings," Rem amended. "They contain all the terms we agreed to. Once we apply our signatures, Barrett-Worth can begin operation." Rem brandished a quill. "Who shall go first?"

Silence.

Rolling her eyes to the heavens, Sammy walked over to the desk and extracted another pen. "Here. Sign simultaneously. Then there can be no argument as to who was the initial owner of the newly formed company. And I shall be your witness, as I am committed to both halves of the partnership."

"An excellent idea," Drake concurred.

Together, the two men dipped their quills and put their signatures on the official document that declared them equal partners.

"At last!" Sammy hugged both men. "Let's rush right to Allonshire and share the news with Alex, Gray, and Bonnie."

Purposefully, Drake extended his hand. "To a long and fruitful partnership, Rem."

Rem's dimple flashed as he clasped Drake's hand. "With minimal violence and bloodshed."

Sammy gazed from one man to the other, her heart so full she thought it might burst. She cared not that life didn't emulate novels, for she could imagine no happier ending than the one taking place here right now. With a joyful smile, she watched her two greatest heroes merging their futures.

The brother she adored.

And the man of her dreams.

ACKNOWLEDGMENTS

As always, a never-ending profusion of love and thanks goes to my lifeline of a family, Brad and Wendi—my one-of-a-kind hero and heroine. And an extra-special hug to my own little Rascal, who wreaks havoc in our house and brings unconditional love into our lives. In Wendi's words, you're immortalized, Rascie!

We hope you enjoyed this book from Bonnie Meadow Publishing.

Connect with us on BonnieMeadowPublishing.com for more information on our new releases!

Other ways to keep in touch with Andrea Kane:

andreakane.com

facebook.com/AuthorAndreaKane/

@andrea_kane

goodreads.com/AKane